AFTER MELANIE

A Selection of Recent Titles by Gloria Goldreich

Novels

WALKING HOME
DINNER WITH ANNA KARENINA
OPEN DOORS
THE GUESTS OF AUGUST
THE BRIDAL CHAIR
AFTER MELANIE *

* *available from Severn House*

AFTER MELANIE

Gloria Goldreich

This first world edition published 2019
in Great Britain and the USA by
SEVERN HOUSE PUBLISHERS LTD of
Eardley House, 4 Uxbridge Street, London W8 7SY.
Trade paperback edition first published
in Great Britain and the USA 2019 by
SEVERN HOUSE PUBLISHERS LTD.

British Library Cataloguing in Publication Data
A CIP catalogue record for this title is available from the British Library.

ISBN-13: 978-0-7278-8871-6 (cased)
ISBN-13: 978-1-84751-996-2 (trade paper)
ISBN-13: 978-1-4483-0209-3 (e-book)

All Severn House titles are printed on acid-free paper.

Severn House Publishers support the Forest Stewardship Council™ [FSC™],
the leading international forest certification organisation.
All our titles that are printed on FSC certified paper carry the FSC logo.

Typeset by Palimpsest Book Production Ltd.,
Falkirk, Stirlingshire, Scotland.
Printed and bound in Great Britain by
TJ International, Padstow, Cornwall.

For Clive Sheldon, Brian Amkraut, Allison Freedman

ACKNOWLEDGMENTS

My dear friend, Norma Hurwitz, a long-time dedicated volunteer at the Back Door Thrift Shop of The Hebrew Institute of White Plains, inspired me to focus on the thrift shop by relating tales of her own experiences with her usual verve, humor and compassion. My son, Harry Horowitz, rescued the work in progress numerous times with his unsurpassed technical skill. Jennifer Weltz, my persistent and creative agent of the Jean V. Naggar Literary Agency, provided insightful suggestions. My thanks to all of them.

ONE

They sat opposite each other at the dinner table, tears of melting vanilla sorbet weeping their way down the clear crystal dessert goblets. Their eyes were averted from the empty chair between them. Still wearing his office uniform, his well-tailored gray suit and the white shirt that had not lost its starch, it occurred to Judith that David looked like a guest at his own table. She herself wore the same pale-blue tracksuit she had worn the previous day: a streak of tomato sauce hardened on the left sleeve, the pocket slightly ripped. She had meant to change but then, as with so many things she meant to do these days, she had simply not bothered. She regretted that now, knowing how proud David had always been of her appearance. It was unfair, especially now, to deprive him of the simple pleasure of looking at her approvingly. She moistened her napkin, dabbed at the stain and gave up. It made no difference and, besides, he was not looking at her. His attention was focused on the bills that she had left at his place.

In a monotone he told her that there was a charge on the credit card bill for a meal at La Belle Place, an error that he would rectify. It was a restaurant they liked, but they had not eaten there . . . since. He did not complete the sentence. There was no need. *Since.* It was his code word for all that he could not, would not say.

She glanced at her watch. It was only seven, the minutes inching by, the meal ending and the evening emptiness beginning. Conversation was exhausted. They had already commented on the vagaries of the weather, the laxness of their gardener. She told him that a shutter on the window in her den had to be replaced. He nodded and they fell silent because silence was less dangerous than the intrusive words they might speak. By tacit consent, they retained the privacy of separate and secret sorrow. They did not want to break each other's hearts.

'Coffee?' Judith asked.

'No,' he replied, too sharply.

She nodded, rose and drew the drapes, unwilling to witness the slow dying of the light. He watched her as she moved from the dining room to the living room, straightening a window shade, moving an earth-colored ceramic bowl in which she had arranged an assortment of pale shells and scarlet bittersweet. Judith's grace, even at the simplest of tasks, still moved him. She had studied ballet when she was younger, and her posture, her every gesture, reflected the discipline of dance. He had always thought of himself as clumsy and it had always surprised him that she had never found his awkwardness a deficit. It had, in fact, amused her. He remembered how she had laughed – a lilting, rippling laughter – if he stepped on her toes when they danced or allowed a package to slip from his grasp. But he sensed that his ineptness now evoked her irritation. He had, during these last terrible months, grown clumsier than ever, dropping cutlery, fumbling with his keys, spilling coffee. At the office he knocked over files, misdirected emails. Amanda, his personal assistant, had spent a precious half hour that very afternoon reorganizing papers he had thrust off his desk as he reached for his phone.

'It's all right. Of course you're distracted,' Amanda had said in her faux maternal voice. 'I understand.'

He had nodded, resenting her kindness, indignant at her words. How could she understand his grief, his loss? She was childless. By choice, she had told him. Neither she nor her husband had ever wanted children. It was a confidence offered in the aftermath of an office Christmas party, probably to counter his uncharacteristic and perhaps boring boasts of his children's achievements – Brad's engagement and admission to law school, Melanie's induction into the middle-school honor society.

But, of course, that party, those foolish exchanges with Amanda, had been *before*. His life now was reduced to those two disparate eras – *before* and *after* with an occasional *since*.

He sighed, unbuttoned the top button of his white shirt and removed his tie, twisting it through his fingers. It was of a soft gray weave, a long-ago gift from Judith, chosen, she had said, because it matched his eyes. A birthday present, an anniversary gift? The question nagged stupidly, irrelevantly. Judith would remember, of course. Her gifts to him were always selected with great care and given with shy pride. Now and again she would hand him a wrapped package containing a shirt of a particular softness or a sweater of a gray-blue color, purchased, she might explain, for no reason at all, but simply because she loved him. Perhaps the tie had been one of those impulse gifts, but he would not ask her. He had to be very careful. He would speak only the words he had rehearsed so carefully.

She began to clear the table and he coughed softly.

'I think it might be time to think about doing something about her bedroom,' he said and folded and unfolded his napkin, staring straight ahead.

'*Her* bedroom?' Judith asked. '*Her* bedroom,' she repeated, her voice flat.

She looked down at the plate in her hands that held half the lamb chop she had struggled to eat. The fat was clumped into a pale bubble; shreds of meat adhered raggedly to the bone. She waited, willing him to say their daughter's name aloud and knowing that he would not. He refrained from uttering it, she supposed, fearful that the syllables would congeal in his throat and choke him until he could no longer breathe. His emotional cowardice angered her.

Melanie's room. Say Melanie. That mental command, unuttered, unheard, was her silent unshared mantra. *Melanie. Melanie. She had a name. Our daughter had a name. Say it.*

He moved his water glass, shook the napkin out and placed it on the table.

'If we cleared the room out, we could use it as a den. Maybe a guest room,' he continued. 'I could use it as a home office.'

'We have a den. We have a guest room.'

She carried the plate into the kitchen and scraped it, taking a dull satisfaction in the soft thud the bone made when it fell into the newly installed garbage bag.

'A home office, actually. I'll need room for my files, my computer if I'm going to work more hours from home,' he called after her as he played with the cutlery, arranging and rearranging his knife, fork and spoon in odd sequences: a stainless-steel triangle, a stainless-steel square, the utensils gleaming against the red table cloth. It was a boyish habit which

she had once found endearing but now unnerved her. The clink
of metal against metal grated, and she moved too swiftly from
the kitchen to the dining room. She swept the offending silver-
ware away, thrust it into the dishwasher and returned to sit
beside him.

'And are you going to work more hours from home?' she
asked.

'That was what we talked about. That was what we agreed
on,' he reminded her. 'You remember. Brian suggested it and we
both thought it was a good idea.'

'Yes. I remember. But that was before.'

Her voice drifted off. She wondered if either she or he would
ever again complete a sentence. They said *since, before* . . .
Why could she not simply say, *That was before Melanie died*?
They did not say, *Since Melanie died.* She allowed the two
words, so fragile, so dangerous, to tumble through her mind.
Melanie died. Melanie died. She scraped crumbs from the table-
cloth and thought to risk speaking them aloud.

'And this is now. Not before. We still have our own lives to
live,' he retorted.

His harsh words, echoing her own usage, each monosyllable
saturated with contained irritation, silenced her. She recognized
his anger, but he was not a man who shouted. He pushed his
chair back and left the dining room, carefully closing the heavy
oak door. He was not a man who slammed doors.

'Before what? Say it, damn it. Say it,' she called after him,
although she knew he could not hear her, knew that he had
already retreated into the sanctuary of the living room and
settled into the deep armchair that faced the fireplace. The radio,
always tuned to WQXR, played too loudly, keeping him safe
from her voice, safe from the fierceness of her grief.

'Say it,' she commanded. 'Before. Before she died. Before
Melanie died. Say it aloud. Melanie is dead.'

She repeated the words to his absent presence, tears
streaking her cheeks, clutching a crumpled napkin, as she
willed herself to accept the unacceptable, terrible truth. Yes,
Melanie – laughing, lovely Melanie – their surprise child,
born after ten years of implacable infertility, was gone from
their lives, her death sudden, unfathomable and inexplicable.

They were alone, she and David, alone and bereft in a house with too many rooms, awkward and uncertain with each other.

Such awkwardness and uncertainty had ambushed them. So young when they first met, so immediately at ease with each other, they had, in the halcyon days of their togetherness, talked with unrehearsed fluidity, walked hand in hand with matching step, whispered loving secrets, laughed in unison.

They had marveled, during those early days, at the miracle of their finding each other in the bewildering labyrinth of their large and unwelcoming university. They had reveled in the discovery of shared delights. Their love and laughter sustained them throughout their undergraduate years and they had married a week after graduation, plunging into their lives with unguarded optimism, their fellowships in place, their future unmarred by shadows of doubt. Everything was planned. Everything was programmed. She would get a doctorate in literature, concentrating on women writers. David was a star in the MBA program. They had rushed through their courses, juggled part-time jobs, their lives a whirlwind of achievements, a trajectory leading to security and success. And all had gone according to plan.

The years had passed. Their dreams were realized, their careers in place, David a partner in an arbitration firm, she a tenured professor of literature with a concentration on women writers. Their home was established, their suburban life pleasant. They had thought to have at least two children. They wanted two children. Their son, Brian, conceived with ease, born without difficulty, was a source of delight as he grew into boisterous and self-sufficient boyhood. They waited. But despite their yearning, a yearning compounded by increasing anxiety, Judith failed to become pregnant again.

Reluctantly, they searched for solutions, wandering through the maze of fertility clinics, invasive examinations, tense and futile visits to doctors that drained their marriage of vitality and caused them to retreat into an uneasy silence. She saw the sadness in David's eyes, felt her own heaviness of heart and spirit, but she dared not share her thoughts with him. The silence that grew between them offered protection of a kind.

Words might invoke a treacherous reality and perhaps force them into a decision they were not prepared to make. Their unhappiness was surely temporary; unacknowledged and undiscussed, it remained amorphous, unreal. They resigned themselves to waiting patiently, hopefully, for the sad season of their marriage to end.

They knew that the new uncertainty and melancholy they felt was not unique. The marriages of many of their friends and acquaintances had not weathered the winter of midlife ennui. Each report of divorce or separation frightened them. Lorraine, Judith's long-time friend and colleague, submitted her resignation. She was leaving her job, leaving her husband, leaving her life.

'My marriage is over,' she told Judith. 'Seth and I have nothing to say to each other. Why should I spend the rest of my life living with a man I can't talk to? I'm treating this as a bad chapter in my life and moving on.'

'Lorraine is leaving Seth, leaving the university,' Judith told David that night.

'Why?' He struggled to subdue his shock.

'She said that there was too much silence between them, that their marriage was a bad chapter in her life. I thought to tell her that there were lots of chapters in a marriage. Maybe if she waited and turned the page, a new and happier chapter might begin. But I knew it would be of no use. Her mind was made up.'

'What sort of a chapter are we in?' he asked, an uncharacteristic question. He had surprised himself by asking it.

She saw the fear in his eyes, felt her own fear ferment into a bilious sourness.

'I wasn't thinking about our marriage,' she said too swiftly. 'I'm not like Lorraine. I would not let that happen to us.'

It was on that night, in the wake of that conversation, that they had held each other close, their bodies entangled in a swift and convulsive passion ignited by a terror they feared to acknowledge. She had always been certain that it was on that night that Melanie was conceived and the new chapter in their marriage began, all melancholy, all unease, vanquished. They were wondrously restored to each other. With Melanie's birth, excitement filled their home. Brian shouted with delight, babbled happily about his baby sister, hovered over her crib, her playpen, offered her toys of his own design. Judith had thought he might display jealousy. His joy took her by surprise. What a son she had, what a wonderful son. She and David hugged him, held their daughter close, smiled at each other, smiled at their good fortune.

Melanie, from the earliest days of her enchanted infancy, invigorated their lives, provided them with new focus, new hope. They spoke her name each day with loving enthusiasm. *Melanie said. Melanie did.* She was their mutual marvel, her presence filling their home, her future filling their dreams. Brian, given a camera as a bar mitzvah gift, took endless photographs of his little sister. Portraits sprouted on their mantelpiece; her smiling face looked down from bookcases in their offices, dangled from magnets on the refrigerator.

Melanie at play. Melanie reading. Melanie at one birthday party and then another. Melanie and Brian holding hands. Melanie on the first day of middle school, tumbling into adolescence. Melanie laughing up at David and Judith, beaming at Brian, holding hands with Denise, Brian's wild-haired fiancée whom she called her 'sister-in-love'. Clever Melanie. Marvelous Melanie.

And then, with heart-stopping suddenness, she was gone. Her death so swift, so sudden, so without the slightest warning, left them reeling with disbelief, numb with denial. It had not happened; it could not have happened. But, of course, it had. Aneurysms, they learned belatedly, give no warning, allow for no preparation.

They were plunged into a despair they could not articulate. They mourned her with unabated, uncomprehending grief. Their life was refrozen into a tundra of unspoken words, unshared feelings. David slept fitfully and awakened trembling, frightened by phantasmagoric dreams he could not recall. Brian wept in Denise's arms. Melanie's photos were swept from the mantle and replaced with a single formal studio portrait. The refrigerator door was barren.

Yet another chapter, Judith thought bitterly.

Unable to sustain the solitude of sorrow, she sought out a therapist: wise, gray-haired Evelyn who listened intently and spoke very slowly, very softly.

'Allow yourself to mourn. Let it out,' Evelyn said, as though the grief was held captive in the secret dungeon of Judith's heart. 'Talk about it.'

How patiently Evelyn explained what she called the fivefold acknowledged stages of grief. *Denial. Anger. Bargaining. Depression. Acceptance.*

Acknowledged by whom? Judith wondered. Mentally, she canceled out that learned formula stage by stage. She had not denied the reality of Melanie's death. For anger she substituted agony. She had made no bargains, recognizing that she had no chips with which to gamble.

Depression? She rejected that cold, clinical word. She preferred the simplicity of 'sorrow', the majesty of 'lamentation'. She thought to quote Emily Dickinson to Evelyn. *Tis not that dying hurts us so . . . Tis living hurts us more . . .* But she would not challenge the therapist whose insights were too expensive to dispute. As for that final stage, *acceptance*, of course she accepted her daughter's death – how could she not? – but never would she be able to make her peace with it – if that was what acceptance meant. But she would take relief wherever she could find it. Not acceptance but relief.

Evelyn would be proud of her, Judith thought now, standing in the kitchen and thinking about David's words. She had not argued with him. She had not disagreed. But sorrow had overcome her and, dutifully, she'd submitted to it. She was letting it out.

Tears were coming. She wiped the counter clean and allowed them to fall. It was her nightly ration of grief, her earned release after a day of silent endurance. She wept as she restored the spices to the rack and hung the copper pots on their clever hooks. She wept as she swept the floor and wiped the counter yet again. Only when the kitchen was returned to pristine order did she reach for the crumpled Kleenex in her pocket and wipe her eyes. She was, she told herself, learning to take control of the days of her life, her new life. She was, after all, moving on.

She roused herself from bed each morning, forced herself to eat breakfast, then vomited, rinsed her mouth and went to her therapy appointment. She sat at her computer and typed out research ideas which she deleted by late afternoon. She prepared careful meals, often forgetting that there would be only two for dinner. She shopped with a false intensity of purpose, consulting lists she did not remember composing. Slowly, very slowly, she was relinquishing the odd rituals of misery. And perhaps David, with his reference to Melanie's room, was doing the same. The thought gave her pause, soothed her.

She washed her face at the kitchen sink, dried it with a paper towel and stared at herself in the small ceramic-framed mirror that Melanie had placed on the windowsill between two small pots of African violets.

'I like to see myself when I wash the dishes,' Melanie had explained, and Judith had asked no questions. It was, she knew, a harmless pre-adolescent conceit. The rush of steam from the hot water turned her daughter's fair skin a tender pink and curled the fringes of the dark bangs that hung unevenly across her high forehead. Melanie, standing on tiptoe, had looked at herself in the mirror as she rinsed glasses, now winking flirtatiously, now wrinkling her nose cunningly, now smiling, now frowning. She was a child rehearsing for what Jane Austen had called her 'coming out', her emergence into the complicated world of defined femininity. Judith, who had written extensively on Jane Austen, was amused to see Melanie behaving like a Bennet daughter – the mirror, of course, always an appropriate Austen prop.

David, oddly faithful to Jewish ritual, had removed that small kitchen mirror during the shiva week, but Judith had set it back in place when the official mourning period ended. She had stared at it on that first day of an arduously resumed normalcy, as though Melanie's moist and rosy face might look back at her. Magical thinking, she knew. It was her own stricken, uncomprehending visage that was captured in that steam-streaked mirror that she wiped clean each evening. It would, she thought, with an irrationality that she both recognized and condoned, be disloyal to Melanie to remove the mirror.

Staring at her own reflection, she saw that the frozen mask of sorrow that had, for so many weeks, held her face rigid had melted. Her hazel eyes had lost the glaze of bewilderment peculiar to the newly bereft. Her skin was burnished by the harsh sunlight of new spring, a result of the very long walks she obediently took each day on the recommendation of wise and expensive Evelyn. Her dark hair, newly styled and attractively layered – yet another of Evelyn's suggestions – framed her oval face.

She toyed with a wayward strand and remembered a friend of her mother's, Bertha Lefkowitz, a plump woman whose thick hair had once been coiled into a jet-colored bun. It was said that when Bertha Lefkowitz received a telegram informing her that her son, Milton, had been killed in Vietnam, her black hair had turned snow-white, even as she stood in her doorway, clutching the yellow slip of paper that changed her life forever.

Remembering Bertha Lefkowitz, Judith marveled that her own dark hair had not lost all color when the very young doctor told them, with sorrow in his eyes and death on his lips, that their daughter was lost to them. That she had been spared. Only a very few strands of silver shimmered in her night-dark hair. Was her grief, she wondered, less profound than that of Bertha Lefkowitz? Had she loved her daughter less than Bertha Lefkowitz had loved her son? Stupid, foolish thought, she knew, and she grimaced at herself punishingly.

She dimmed the kitchen light and wandered into the living room where David, pale and sad-eyed, sat with the *Times* unopened on his lap as Mahler's Fourth filled the room with symphonic sorrow. Her heart turned to see how tired he looked. He was a tall man, but his shoulders were rounded now as though weighted by the burden of unremitting sadness. His narrow face was ashen. His eyes were closed as though he did not have the energy required to lift his pale lids, or perhaps because he did not think there was anything in his silent and tasteful living room that was worth looking at.

His fatigue did not surprise her. Except for the week of mourning, he had taken no time off, plunging into a difficult arbitration. She supposed that the complex arguments of his profession absorbed him and provided a barrier against his grief. That, at least, was Brian's explanation. But she knew that David's work and the long commute into the city had always been a strain. He had complained of it for years, had even spoken of perhaps buying a studio in Manhattan.

It was, in fact, Brian, all those months ago, in the distant era of *before*, who had suggested an alternative. Why shouldn't his father work from home now and again?

'Dad can't deal with the traffic,' he had said. 'He should work more days at home. Less stress. It would give him more time with you, more time with Melanie. Denise thinks so, and so do I.'

Newly engaged, Brian rushed to introduce his fiancée's name into every family discussion. *Denise thinks. Denise says.* Judith reproved herself for resenting Denise's new presence in the life of their insular family and simply nodded her agreement.

A doable idea that David should work from home, she had thought then, more convenient and less expensive than an urban *pied-à-terre*. They had a den or they could build an extension for a home office. She had imagined David interrupting his work to help Melanie with her math homework. Perhaps they would take a late-afternoon bike ride, father and daughter pedaling down sun-streaked roads. In the evening the three of them would gather around the table for an early dinner, and they would listen with amusement as Melanie bubbled over with anecdotes of her day, imitating her teachers, complaining about her friends.

That idea had coalesced with the approach of Judith's long-awaited, hard-earned sabbatical. There would be no need to review lecture notes, to grade papers. Their evenings could be leisurely. It would be good for David, good for Melanie, good for her, good for all of them to spend time together. David working at home, she free of all academic obligations, both of them focused on Melanie. But, of course, all those plans had been formulated *before*.

Before Melanie's death . . . Before that last morning when she had raced out to catch the school bus, clutching her half-eaten Pop Tart and waving a peremptory goodbye. Her face was flushed, her ponytail swinging, one blue knee sock sliding dangerously down her chubby calf. It had been an ordinary morning. They could not have known, they would not have believed, that she would be dead before the end of the day.

Unbelievable. Judith clung to the word. Even now, all these months since Melanie's death, and despite the agonizingly slow passage of time, it was beyond belief, although the events of that last day were frozen in memory.

Judith had been thinking about dinner that afternoon, the very first day of her long-awaited sabbatical, when the phone rang. She had lifted the receiver as she stood beside the open freezer touching the packaged meat, pondering whether to defrost veal or lamb, chicken or steak: thoughts that were never completed, decisions that were never made for a dinner that was never prepared.

'Am I speaking to Judith Mandell, the mother of Melanie Mandell?' A telemarketer, Judith had thought, but she did not hang up. Her fingers stuck to the icy parcels as she listened to words that she could not assimilate. The caller, a woman, identified herself. She was a volunteer, a hospital volunteer, she explained and, in a gentle voice, laced with practiced sympathy, she added that it was important, very important, that Judith come to the local hospital at once.

'It's about your daughter, Mrs Mandell. Your husband is already on his way.'

'My daughter? My husband? But why? But what?'

Her heart plummeted. Her hands trembled. She did not know what questions to ask, and there were, of course, no answers. The phone had gone silent. She hung up, slammed the freezer shut. Dizzied, she clung to the metal handle for support and the phone rang again.

David's voice was tight, his tone harsh. 'Don't drive. Take a cab to the hospital. I'll see you there. I'm already on the highway.'

'Why a cab?' she asked, but he had hung up.

She called a cab, grabbed her purse and sat at the edge of the cracked leather seat next to the driver, urging him to drive faster, faster, tossing a handful of bills at him as she hurtled out the door when they reached the hospital. She did not hear him call after her. She raced up the steps into the reception area where David, his face beaded with sweat, his car keys jangling in his trembling hand, waited for her. Someone led them to an elevator. Voices murmured. They heard words they could not understand. Chairs were offered and declined. A nurse motioned them toward a waiting room, but they shook their heads and stood huddled together in the sterile hospital corridor. A doctor, a very young bespectacled man, too thin for his oversized white jacket, too young perhaps to be a father himself, joined them. He answered their agonized questions in a steady, calm voice. His account was succinct. He had perhaps attended a training session on how to inform parents of the death of a child.

He told them that Melanie had been rushed to the hospital from her school where she had collapsed so suddenly that an ambulance had been summoned even before a stunned administrator could call them. She was dead on arrival in the emergency room. An aneurysm had exploded in her heart.

'She did not suffer, not for a moment,' the young doctor assured them. 'It was a gentle death.'

He spoke softly as though offering comfort of a kind, but David would not be comforted. Judith swayed, held her hands to her ears, blocking out the words he spoke with such calm finality. She refused to hear those words. She refused to believe them.

'Thirteen-year-old girls do not die!' David's voice, shrill and furious, had reverberated, drowning out the hospital sounds, the supposedly soothing muzak, the hum of lifesaving machines, the rhythm of slow-moving rubber-wheeled gurneys. The nurses, in their gay pastel jackets, paused and stood stock-still; the parents of other patients moved away, as though his grief might be contagious and place their own children at risk. Judith had clutched his arm and together they had followed the doctor into the room where their daughter lay on a white-sheeted bed, her ponytail unloosened, her dark hair falling about her face, now cold and white as alabaster, drained of all expression. Both her blue knee socks curled about her ankles. Judith, crazily, pulled the socks up, straightened them, and even thought to comb her daughter's hair because the ponytail had become undone. Instead, she had pressed her face to Melanie's, had kissed each smooth cheek, already death-frosted, and lightly touched the rosebud lips with fingers that would not stop trembling.

David had wept as they drove home, but he had not wept again, not at the funeral – a blessedly brief service, the rabbi at a loss as to how to eulogize a child. He had not wept during the prescribed days of mourning, and even now, months later, his angular face was expressionless, his narrow gray eyes dry.

Evelyn had suggested that he was perhaps unwilling to dilute his grief with tears. It was, Judith thought, a probable explanation.

She herself had learned how to portion out her sorrow, how to weep alone in her very clean kitchen. She pitied David even as he angered her. She needed words, she needed comfort; he offered only silence and the darkness of denial. His struggle was solitary, his stresses unshared. It was not his fault. It was not her fault.

His deficits were not unfamiliar to her, as hers were not unfamiliar to him. It was perhaps, she thought disloyally, those very deficits that had drawn them together and locked them into a magnetic coupling, her strength his weakness, his strength her weakness, their love for each other nullifying any emotional inequities. It was a pattern set in place from their earliest days together. They had been so young when they met, so young when they married.

Too young perhaps.

The thought came unbidden, and its disloyalty startled her, filled her with guilt. This was no time to regret their marriage. They had Brian. They had had Melanie. They had each other. His love for Melanie had been equal to hers. His grief, too closely held, was weighted on the same scale as her own. This was yet another sad chapter but one that they would overcome. How unfair she was to David, how miserly her compassion. Standing in the living room, staring at her husband, she was overcome with regret.

The last movement of the Mahler drifted into silence. David's eyes were closed, but she knew he was not sleeping. She sat beside him, pressed her cheek to his, felt his hand soft upon her head, the tenderness of his touch a wordless forgiveness.

'I'm sorry,' she said softly. 'You're right. I'll start clearing out her room tomorrow.'

He nodded. 'Wait for the weekend. I'll help you. Or call Denise. She wants to help.' His suggestion was quietly offered.

'No. It's all right. I'd rather do it alone. I have the time.'

It was an understatement, she thought bitterly. She had nothing but time now – endless empty hours.

The leisure of her sabbatical, a time she had thought to devote to Melanie, had morphed into a curse. Bitterly, she remembered her golden fantasies. She had imagined shared mother-and-daughter lunches, shopping trips, stolen weekends, family vacations; she and Melanie at the theater, walking through museums, cooking together. Their year together would be a gentle initiation, an adventure in bonding, calculated deposits in the memory bank.

Now that expanse of empty time would be devoted to recuperation (Evelyn's carefully chosen word) and perhaps, hopefully, reconciliation (the rabbi's stuttered suggestion during his one brief and painful pastoral visit). She did not ask him if any mother he had encountered during his years of pastoral counseling had ever been reconciled to the death of a child.

She had no compass to guide her through the daylight hours, no agenda that demanded her attention. For the very first time in her life she awakened each morning with nothing to do, no place to go. She did not want to read. She did not want to write. She forgave herself for the disinclination.

Sabbaticals, after all, were meant to provide time, to offer respite and renewal. She claimed the respite, but as yet there had been no renewal, and she had found no use for the time. But now a usage had presented itself. She would work on clearing Melanie's room and then converting it into a home office for David. There would be meetings with carpenters, painters. It was a project, and she had always been very good at projects.

'Brian said that Denise wants to be helpful, wants to feel part of the family.' David was oddly persistent.

'I'll manage alone,' she said.

Denise tried too hard, gifting Judith with carefully wrapped copies of *Tuesdays with Morrie*, *Songs and Sonnets* and *Blue Nights*, books that remained unopened and unread. Judith, knowing herself to be unkind, thought Denise to be well meaning but intrusive. She did not want her in Melanie's room, touching Melanie's things. That was a task she wanted to accomplish alone.

'All right,' David agreed. 'As you wish.'

'I don't wish.'

She went to the window, drawing the drapes back so that she could see the wind gently stir the branches of the trees; their tender unfurled leaves glistened in the half darkness. The winter of their discontent, the long gray days of loss and longing, were nearing an end. Warmth hovered close. A new season was beginning.

She felt David's eyes follow her as she turned and left the room.

TWO

D avid awakened very early the next morning, relieved that Judith was still asleep. He dressed and moved stealthily through the silent house, pausing outside the closed door of the room that had been Melanie's without going in. He ate a swift breakfast and drove to the station, looking forward, as always, to the soothing quiet of the half-empty commuter train and then his solitary walk from Grand Central. He found the quiet streets, not yet throbbing with the frenetic pace of urban life, calming after the tensions of the previous evening. He understood Judith's need for comfort, but he despaired of assuaging her grief when he could not cope with his own.

He arrived at his office before the rest of the staff drifted in and welcomed the quiet that enabled him to reply to his emails without distraction. Swiftly, he composed one memo after another, pressed the 'send' button and sat back.

He switched his computer off and submitted to the recurring wave of sadness that washed over him each morning at that very hour. He was safe then, in the security and silence of his professional cave, before the thundering arrival of his co-workers, before phones began to ring and fax machines buzzed with staccato insistence. In this impersonal room, where his academic degrees and professional certificates hung on walls painted a neutral off-white, it was safe to submit to his sorrow. Here, he was at a remove from Judith's uneasy concern, her impatience with his muteness, his inability to follow her lead and organize a retreat from grief.

He sat very still in his deep leather desk chair, in front of his blank computer screen. In that odd stillness he allowed himself to remember Melanie's trilling laughter and the flecks of gold in her hazel eyes. He closed his eyes and imagined his daughter running toward him, her cheeks flushed, her arms outstretched, her ponytail bobbing. He remembered her as a toddler and then as a schoolgirl, a twirling ballerina dancing into adolescence. Briefly, so briefly, in reverie and memory, she came alive for him. He sat immobile, his hands clutching the arms of his chair, fearful that if he moved, she would disappear from memory. He wondered why he did not weep. He would have welcomed tears. Their saline heat might melt the sorrow and anger that had frozen its way across his heart when that thin, bespectacled young doctor spoke of her death. It had been gentle, painless, he had said.

David had wanted to break the man's steel-rimmed glasses, to seize him by the throat, to force him to admit that there was no gentleness in death, certainly not in the death of a child. *My child. Melanie.* He had, of course, done nothing, launched as he was, then and thereafter, on the frigid floe of his sorrow.

He envied Judith, who wept so quietly each night as he lay beside her, but she did not invite him to share her grief and he dared not intrude upon it. He had only this quiet hour in his silent wide-windowed office cave, shielded by the blank screen of his computer, his whiteboard gleaming. The wood-framed portraits of Brian and Judith stared down at him from their perch on a filing cabinet. He had blanketed Melanie's portrait in bubble wrap and placed it carefully in the bottom drawer of his desk.

'Melanie.'

He struggled to say her name aloud, but it emerged as the slightest of whispers. He could not bear to give it voice. 'My baby,' he said instead. 'My little girl.'

A light knock on his office door, unusual at such an hour, startled him.

'Yes, what is it?' he called, his voice harsh with annoyance.

The door opened and a slender silver-haired woman, wearing a pale-blue dress, a blush rising to her pale cheeks, stood in the doorway. He recognized her. Nancy – her last name escaped him – a senior administrator with whom he had worked on several projects. She had been out of the office for some months. Compassionate leave, he recalled, although he could not remember why she had been granted that corporate compassion. An ill parent, most likely. The discussion of her leave, occurring when he was overwhelmed by his own loss, had not interested him.

'Nancy,' he said, apologetically now. 'You surprised me. It's so early.'

'Yes, I know. I arranged to come in early for a few weeks, a kind of flex time, so that I can be home when my daughter gets out of school,' she said.

'Yes. Of course. Your daughter.' The words were dry as dust on his tongue.

She approached his desk, stood very close. He inhaled the scent of her perfume. Lilac. Melanie had loved lilacs. He remembered suddenly a spring morning when she had plucked a blossom from the bush in their garden and tucked it playfully behind her ear. Its fragrance had drifted toward him as he pressed his lips to her cheek. He stared at Nancy, irrationally annoyed at her for invoking the memory.

'I've been away,' she said, her voice hesitant as though she feared that her words might offend. 'Out of touch. I only heard yesterday about . . .' She hesitated, searching for appropriate words. 'Your loss,' she continued, softly, hesitantly. 'I wanted to offer you my condolences.'

'Yes. That's very kind of you,' he said coldly.

He plucked up a document, signaling his need to return to work. He wanted her gone, but she lingered.

'I'm so sorry. So very sorry. I know how terrible it must be for you. I understand. I've been there.'

'Where?' he asked harshly. 'Where have you been?'

His voice was hoarse. His hand trembled. The paper he held fluttered to the floor.

She did not answer but reached for his hand and covered it with her own, stroking it gently until the tremor was calmed. The softness of her skin, the tenderness of her touch, ambushed him. He wept then, releasing a reservoir of unshed tears that streamed down his cheeks, vagrant drops falling on her hands. She did not stir, this soft-voiced woman whose last name he could not remember, but waited patiently until the torrent of his grief subsided. Only then, as he reached for his handkerchief, did she bend to retrieve the paper he had dropped. She placed it on his desk and left, closing the door very softly behind her.

He sat back in his chair, stared at his damp handkerchief, then went to the window and opened it. He felt the cool breeze upon his face and stared down at the sun-swept street so far below him, suffused with an unfamiliar calm.

He waited until later that morning to ask Amanda, his assistant, about her.

'Nancy. Yes, Nancy Cummings. Poor Nancy.'

Amanda, a queen bee in the hive of office gossip, knew everything and could be counted on to reveal her knowledge.

'Why *poor* Nancy?' he asked.

He kept his eyes fixed on his computer screen, his tone even and slightly bored.

'She's a widow. Her husband was killed in a car accident when she was six months pregnant. So she's a single mother with a ten-year-old daughter. And just a few weeks ago her mother, who had been helping her, passed away.'

'Yes, things must be difficult for her,' he murmured noncommittally.

Her mother's death, then, was the reason for her compassionate leave, he realized, but he understood, instinctively, that it was her husband's death that had impelled the swiftness of her compassion, her understanding of his tears. Yes, she had 'been there'. She too had endured the bleak surreal terrain of a loss so sudden and unexpected that it defied either comprehension or acceptance.

'Poor Nancy Cummings,' Amanda repeated.

'Yes. Poor Nancy Cummings,' he agreed.

He searched for her extension in the company directory, called her and invited her to lunch.

She had accepted without hesitation and they sat together in a small, dimly lit bistro, mutually agreed upon because it was at a reasonable distance from their office.

'I want to apologize,' he said, when they had both ordered, surprising each other and their shy little waitress by the sameness of their selections – onion soup and Greek salads.

'No need,' she said. 'Perhaps I presumed. But when I heard about your daughter's death, I thought of how I had felt when my husband died. It was so sudden. So without warning. Steven left for work that morning and kissed me on the cheek. An hour later a policeman was at the door telling me that he had been killed. A head-on collision, a car going the wrong way. The policeman was very kind, very young, and as he talked, I put my hand to my cheek and thought, "No, Steven can't be dead. I still feel his lips against my skin." And I stood frozen in the doorway as the poor policeman went on talking. "Killed instantly," he said. "No pain."'

David nodded. 'The doctor who told us about Melanie said that she died a gentle death. No pain, he said. Every word he uttered was unbearable.'

'It wasn't their fault. They didn't know what to say – your doctor, my policeman,' she murmured. 'And we did not know how to hear them.'

'I know. I heard the words, the unbearable words. *Dead. Gentle.* But I couldn't process them. Not until I saw Melanie.'

He closed his eyes against the memory of his daughter, her face as white as the coarse hospital sheet on which her lifeless body rested, laughter gone from her lips, light gone from her eyes. Judith had bent forward to kiss her cold cheek, to pull her sock up so that it lay straight against her calf. As though that mattered. As though anything mattered.

Remembering, all these months later, he thought that he might weep yet again but he did not. Nancy was speaking and he leaned forward to hear her.

'Those words. *Killed. Dead. No pain.* Unbearable,' she murmured. 'I know. I did not think I could bear it. I thought that I would not be able to go on living without Steven.'

'But you did.'

'Ah, I had no choice. I was six months pregnant. I had to bear it for the child that was coming. For my Lauren.'

'A daughter.' He spoke the words in a whisper.

'A daughter,' she repeated. 'She's ten years old now. So I did bear it. I managed. What I could not manage was the fact that no one seemed to understand the impact of a death that comes without warning. The death of someone so young, so full of life. No one knew what to say to me, and no matter what they did say, I felt only numbness and anger. I wanted to shout at those well-meaning comforters and tell them that they could not understand. He was alive and then, minutes later, he was dead. It was so sudden. So without warning.'

Her voice broke. She reached for her water glass, stared across the table at him and then closed her eyes.

'So it was with Melanie,' he said. 'Sudden. Without warning.'

He paused and wondered if his grief might have been lessened if he had been prepared, if Melanie had been ill or there had been some sort of congenital defect. Perhaps. But even then the knowledge that she was gone from his life, from their lives, his and Judith's, would be a weight upon his heart, a heavy stone of sorrow that could neither be lightened nor shifted. At least not yet. He smiled sadly at Nancy. Her sorrow, even after a decade, had not ended, yet she had taken control of her life. He felt the barest glimmer of hope.

'Yes. You managed,' he said.

'I coped. As I had to. There was no choice. And I had my parents, who were wonderful. They're gone now, but they helped me until I could help myself. I was fortunate to have them, to have my work. And now I'm fortunate to have a wonderful child, my Lauren. We just moved into a new apartment where she'll have her own room. No furniture yet, but she's just excited to have her own space. She'd be a happy child if only she could understand the new math.'

She smiled, relieved to have left mention of death behind, relieved to be talking about something as inconsequential as her daughter's homework problems.

'Melanie had problems with that damn math also,' David said, marveling that he spoke his daughter's name with such ease. 'I spent hours trying to help her grasp it.'

'I'm afraid that I can't do as much for Lauren. Math was never my strong suit.' She smiled regretfully.

Their food arrived and, for the first time in months, he ate with appetite, aware of the taste and texture of the soup, the crispness of the vegetables.

'I was sorry to hear about your mother,' he said, remembering Amanda's revelation, so eagerly offered.

'Yes. But she had been ill for months. Cancer. We – my brother and I – had known she was dying. She had been ill before and she was not a young woman. So we were prepared. It was a slow death. And not gentle.'

She repeated the words he had spoken, but there was no irony in her voice. She spoke a truth they both recognized.

'A riddle: what is better – a swift and painless death that leaves the survivors in shock or a lingering illness with an anticipated ending?' he asked.

He knew it to be an intrusive question, but even as he spoke, he felt an odd relief at his ability to share the thought.

'That is a riddle for those who have not endured what we have endured,' she replied quietly, sadly. 'They were too young – my Steven, your Melanie. Too young for any death at all.'

And then it was she who began to weep. He reached across the table, took both her hands in his own and held them until her tears were exhausted and the shy little waitress removed their empty plates and returned, without asking, with a carafe of coffee.

'She thinks we're lovers,' Nancy said. 'She doesn't know that we're a support group of two developing a twelve-step program.' She smiled, her fleeting sorrow banished.

'Perhaps we should tell her that we're secret sharers.'

'Yes. Secret sharers,' she agreed.

There was no need to speak of what they shared. They had each been struck by sudden lightning, death bolts as swift and mercurial as quicksilver. There was a mutuality to their sorrow and comfort in the gentle, honest relief they offered each other, all judgment withheld, all fear suspended.

Such comfort, he realized with regret, was what he was afraid to solicit from Judith. Her own sorrow was too profound; he feared to add his sadness to the grief that silvered her cheeks with tears in the darkness of the night. Nancy had mingled his sorrow with her own.

He paid the bill, leaving their shy little waitress an exorbitant tip. It was understood between them that they would meet again. They had their work in common and he knew her to be an excellent researcher. He mentioned a project he was working on and she offered suggestions. He asked for her home address and her cell phone number and wrote them carefully in his address book.

'I should like to meet your daughter,' he said. 'Perhaps I could help her with her math.'

'Perhaps.' She smiled.

They left the restaurant separately, aware of the need for corporate propriety, although there had been no impropriety. Nor would there be, he assured himself. He called Judith when he returned to the office, but she was not at home and he did not leave a message.

THREE

Judith sat in Evelyn's book-lined consulting room and tonelessly recounted her conversation with David.

'He's right, of course,' she said. 'We should do something about the room. Melanie's room. I'm going to start. I told him I would. It's just hard. Very hard.'

'Why are you so reluctant to . . .' The therapist struggled to find a word that would not wound, would not offend. She breathed deeply and continued, her tone neutral. 'Dismantle her room?'

'It's all I have left of her. Her things. Her space.' Judith spoke softly, hesitated and then added, with defiant resonance, '*Melanie's* things, *Melanie's* space.' How strange it was, she thought, not for the first time, the comfort that came with the simple utterance of her daughter's name. 'It's all I have left of her,' she repeated.

Evelyn nodded. 'I understand that feeling, but you know you have more than that. A great deal more. Things are only things. Space is only space. You have your memories. You have your love. Melanie will always be part of you, but you have your life to live. You know that. It's time to move on, Judith.'

'Time to dismantle?' Judith asked bitterly, thrusting the word back at her, but Evelyn caught it unflinchingly.

'Exactly,' she said. 'You have a lot of dismantling to do. Actual and symbolic.'

She glanced at her watch and Judith nodded and rose from her seat, her hour of expensive wisdom concluded.

David is right, Evelyn is right, she told herself as she drove home. It was time to accept, time to move on, time to dismantle. She shuddered at the word, but then it was only a word. She would get on with it. She was skilled at getting on with things.

At home she ate a swift lunch, ignored the ringing telephone without even glancing at the caller ID. It was David making a conscience call of regret and apology, she knew. Regretful and apologetic herself, she lifted the receiver on the fourth ring, feigning breathlessness, when he called again a little later.

'I just got in,' she lied.

'I was worried. I know I upset you last night.'

'David, I'm fine. Really. And you were right. I'm going upstairs now to begin . . .' She hesitated and settled reluctantly on Evelyn's word. 'Dismantling Melanie's room,' she continued, oddly proud of her new courage.

She spoke reassuringly. David needed reassurance, she knew. She pitied him for the solitude of his grief.

'Don't work too hard,' he said, and she was grateful for the caring gentleness of his tone.

'I'll be fine,' she assured him and hung up.

With grim determination, she carried two large black trash bags upstairs. The door to the room that had been Melanie's was closed and a *Do Not Disturb* sign, purloined from a hotel during a half-remembered family vacation, dangled on the door-knob. Melanie had added *THIS MEANS YOU!* in magenta Magic Marker.

Her hand trembling, her heart beating too rapidly, Judith turned the knob and paused on the threshold, to shield her eyes against the sudden brightness. She had not entered the room since Melanie's death. The cleaning service had probably dusted the surfaces, but no one had thought to draw the candy-striped drapes and lower the blinds. The rose paint of the walls, the color that Melanie had so stubbornly insisted upon, had faded to an anemic pink. The window was tightly closed and the scent of Melanie's lilac body gel and talc lingered in the stale air. The cleaners had barely tidied the room, leaving it in the wild disorder of a careless and carefree young life interrupted without warning.

Rhomboids of sunlight danced across tangles of tights and a scattering of brightly colored sweaters strewn across the red-carpeted floor. One sneaker peered out of a faded backpack, its mate tossed across an open geometry text book. Amid the clutter of papers and folders on the windowsill there was a hairbrush with tendrils of dark hair still clinging to the bristles.

Judith surveyed the all too familiar mess, choking on the pointless and ridiculous mental reprimand that sprang to mind.

When would Melanie learn to be more careful of her things? The question came unbidden; the answer boomeranged and pierced her heart. *Never, of course. Never. Never* was a word she would have to learn to accept.

She lifted a pink cashmere cardigan, remembering that she had not wanted to buy it. It had been very expensive and Melanie was so careless, but she had agreed in the end, because she wanted to see Melanie smile and earn her daughter's swift and impulsive hug. And there had been a hug, she remembered, and a kiss, deliciously damp upon her cheek.

She held the cardigan close, stroked the soft wool and inhaled the lingering scent of lilac. She folded it carefully, buttoned each pearl button and placed it on the unmade bed.

She picked up the hairbrush and one by one she plucked out the dark strands of Melanie's hair, winding them about her finger in a silken ring. She went to the window and opened it wide, grateful for the sudden breeze that breathed its way sweetly into the room. And then she began to work in earnest.

Swiftly, she consigned still useful garments into a bag to be donated to the synagogue thrift shop. Her efficiency served as a protective shield against the invasive thoughts that intruded with each item she handled. She steeled herself against the memory of when Melanie had worn a cute plaid skirt, an apple-green woolen dress, a magenta fleece – magenta, always bright, gay magenta, Melanie's favorite color since nursery school. The magenta crayon in the giant box of Crayolas had, inevitably, been worn down to a stub.

She pulled the price tags from a white tennis dress bought on sale in anticipation of the spring season and the onset of tennis lessons. She tossed it into the bag. They had been too optimistic. There had been no tennis lessons. Melanie had never known another spring. She had died before the season of warmth.

Tears came without warning. Judith wiped her eyes, bit her lip and went back to work.

The ring she had fashioned from the strands of her daughter's hair slipped from her finger.

The floor was swiftly cleared, the closet emptied. She did not pause. One bag was filled and then another. She cinched them shut and heaved them down the stairs. She would have coffee. Coffee would restore her. She made herself a cup, drank only half of it and carried an entire box of trash bags up to the room.

She filled one of them with shoes, sandals and boots, barely worn ballet slippers, party pumps and sneakers, Bass oxfords, still new because Melanie had hated them, magenta flip-flops, worn thin because Melanie had loved them. She filled the next bag with underwear. She tossed in training bras for the budding breasts that would never mature into a full bosom and nylon panties, the colors of the rainbow, embroidered with the days of the week. There were pajamas, socks and a clutter of headbands and neckerchiefs, scrunchies and barrettes. Judith barely looked at them, intent only on emptying the bureau drawers, before turning to the desk.

They had bought the small white desk at Ikea when Melanie entered middle school.

'It will help her get organized,' David had said with the certainty of a man who had fought a natural propensity for disorganization and distraction all his life.

'We live in hope,' Judith had laughed.

But Melanie, of course, after the first paroxysm of delight, had abandoned the desk to chaos. Scraps of paper poked out of the small cubbies. Half-filled notebooks were scattered across the surface, scarred by neon Magic Markers, hardened scabs of pink nail polish, and pale-blue doodles – happy faces and sad faces, musical notes and flowers. There was a box of personalized stationery, Melanie's name printed, inevitably, in magenta, a gift from Denise, Brian's fiancée, who often gave whimsical, thoughtful gifts in her attempt to become part of the family. Denise had wanted to be Melanie's big sister and now she wanted to be Judith's daughter, occasionally and hesitantly calling her 'Mom'. It was an intimacy that Judith resented but which she allowed. She would not be unkind to the pleasant, caring girl whom Brian loved.

She threw the box of stationery into the wastepaper basket and opened a drawer that contained a jumble of rubber bands and paper clips, pencil stubs and dried-out Bic pens. A small pile of carefully folded notes on rainbow-colored Post-its was crammed into an envelope. She read one, then another.

Do you want to come to my house this afternoon? Don't tell Angela. Claire.

Do you want to sit next to me at the pep rally? Harvey.

Judith smiled. Melanie had had friends. Claire had liked her. Harvey had liked her. She felt grateful to these children, whom she knew only by sight. All Melanie's classmates had come to her funeral; pale and bewildered, they had trailed after Miss Fein, their young teacher, who had also been pale and bewildered. They had all sent carefully composed letters of condolence, a class exercise, she supposed. Judith had tied them together with a magenta ribbon and hidden them in a corner of her closet.

She turned to the largest cubby where a bright pink diary nestled. It was her own gift to Melanie on her last birthday, chosen because it had a small gold lock and she wanted her daughter to know that she had gifted her with privacy. Judith herself had kept a diary as a girl, obsessively filling the blue lined pages of a standard black-and-white speckled notebook with her thoughts and feelings and hiding it each evening at the bottom of her underwear drawer. She had been, she knew, inspired by Anne Frank. She, an only child, born to hardworking parents late in their lives, had, foolishly, dramatically, imagined herself to be as unhappy and isolated as the martyred Dutch girl. A latchkey child, returning from school to an empty apartment, she had consigned her secrets to her diary, writing of her loneliness and misery, her desperate yearnings, her irrational fears. Those entries, read and reread, vested her with clarity of a kind, offering her relief and comfort.

She had thought that Melanie might derive the same comfort from confiding in the pink leather diary. But Melanie had not locked it, and Judith opened it and began to read.

Melanie's handwriting was cramped, each brief entry punctuated with exclamation points, hearts and stars. She had experimented with pink ink and then with purple. She favored single sentences.

I don't want to go to tennis camp!!!

I love Denise but I like our family just as it is – the four of us. I wish we could stay that way forever. Still, the wedding will be so much fun. Oh, why am I so confused?

I hate Mr DeAngelo. He picks on me!!! But I love Miss Fein.

She's so pretty, so sweet. She gave me an A on my essay about snow.

I wish Mommy would stop nagging me about my room. It's my room.

I don't think Angela wants to be my friend any more. She sits with Lena at lunch. But I don't care. Claire wants to be my best friend.

I think I like Harvey – I mean really like him. I love my pink cardigan. It makes me feel really pretty. I'm going to wear it to the pep rally***. Harvey is going to sit next to me. I guess he thinks I'm pretty. I hope he does!!!

Judith smiled. Her daughter's words comforted her. She thought to tell David that they had buried a happy child, a girl who had hated her math teacher but loved her English teacher, who treasured her brother, tolerated her parents' loving interventions and knew herself to be pretty, or, at least, pretty enough. She was glad that the pink cardigan, so grudgingly purchased, had made Melanie feel pretty. The boy named Harvey had wanted to sit beside her at the pep rally. The girl named Claire had invited her to her house. Melanie. She closed the pink diary, pressed it to her heart and set it aside.

In another cubby of the desk she found a sheath of clippings from bridal magazines, photos and illustrations of teenaged girls in wide-skirted pastel gowns. She fingered the swatches of magenta velvet and magenta silk to be considered for the gown Melanie dreamed of wearing when she glided down the aisle as a junior bridesmaid at her brother's wedding.

Judith carried the diary and the swatches of fabric into her own room and placed them beneath her silk scarves in the bottom drawer of her bureau. A senseless salvage of her daughter's brief life, she knew, but it was oddly important to her.

'Enough,' she told herself sternly and went downstairs to put the water on for spaghetti.

'I made a good start on the room,' she told David at dinner that night. 'I'll work on it again tomorrow.'

'It's not too much for you?' he asked.

'I'm managing,' she said.

She did not ask about his day. He did not mention Nancy Cummings.

It took her two days to box up the contents of Melanie's crowded bookcases. Melanie had tenaciously retained books from every stage of her brief life. The oversized picture books of her childhood with their brilliant illustrations on glossy paper shared a shelf with the chapter series of her girlhood. *Babar* and *Goodnight Moon* nestled against *Anne of Green Gables* and *Little Women*.

Judith sat cross-legged on the floor, wearing jeans and a sweatshirt, the dark helmet of her hair covered by a red bandanna. She opened and closed one book after another, wiping the spines, sneezing at the clouds of dust that floated free as she turned pages.

She stared at the etchings in a book of fairy tales and tried to remember the endings. What had happened to Rapunzel after she let down her hair? Did the sleeping beauty and the prince live happily ever after? A foolish question. Everyone lived happily ever after. In the land of fairy tales, thirteen-year-old girls did not die. If they fell asleep, even into the most profound and ominous sleep, the kiss of a prince awakened them. She sighed, put the oversized book into the carton and reached for the copy of *Little Women* that she had given Melanie on her tenth birthday.

They had read it aloud, alternating chapters. Judith confided that Jo had always been her favorite. It fell to Melanie to read the chapter on Beth's death. Her voice had faltered and she had wept.

'It's so sad.'

Judith too had cried. They offered each other scraps of Kleenex, then laughed in embarrassment at the luxurious catharsis of their own foolish sorrow.

She set the book aside and decided that she had filled enough bags and cartons for the day.

The next morning she leafed through the tattered copy of *Make Way for Ducklings*, Melanie's favorite book during her toddler days. Her grape-jelly-stained fingerprint purpled the picture of the parade of ducklings headed toward the safety of the pond. Judith hesitated and then consigned it to the carton. She read an entire chapter of *A Wrinkle in Time* before adding it to the bag of chapter books. She decided to keep the beautifully bound volume of Andersen's fairy tales that David had bought at a book stall in Copenhagen. She placed *Goodnight Moon* and two volumes of *Curious George* and the Harry Potter books on a separate pile. She would keep them. Brian and Denise would have a family. These books would be Melanie's tender legacy to her brother's children.

The thought, irrational and whimsical as she knew it to be, comforted. She held tight to it as she left the room and repeated it to Evelyn at her morning therapy session.

The wise bird-faced woman perched on the edge of her leather chair and chirped approvingly.

'A good thought. Progress. You are moving toward the future.'

'Am I?' Judith wondered.

Her hand flew to her head. She, always so careful of her appearance, had forgotten to remove the red bandanna. She smiled and Evelyn smiled. That too, she supposed, was progress, a relaxation of control. A dismantling of useless grief. A moving on.

She returned to Melanie's room with renewed determination the next morning. She removed the candy-striped curtains, stripped the bed of the matching candy-striped comforter and the gaily patterned sheets and pillow cases, and carried them down to the washing machine. She pulled the poster of Taylor Swift from one wall and the one of Justin Bieber from the other, ripped them up and tossed them into the wastepaper basket. She opened the battered wooden jewelry box in which Melanie had kept the few pieces she seldom wore – a heart-shaped gold locket, a slap watch that no longer kept time, two narrow silver bracelets. She slipped both of the bracelets on to her own wrist, pleased by their musical jangle, and placed the box on a shelf in her own closet.

She managed to roll up the red area rug and drag it out to the hallway and, with a spurt of energy, she vacuumed, dusted and washed the windows, furiously scouring each pane, looking out now and again at the apple tree across the way, wondering when it would burst into blossom. By late afternoon the room smelled of Windex and shadows danced across the barren mattress, the cleared and empty surfaces of the white desk and bureau and the empty white shelves of the bookcases. The new sterility reminded her of a hospital room. She stared at the cartons and the black bags, filled to overflowing with the sad residue of Melanie's brief life, and a wave of nausea swept over her.

Thrusting Melanie's bracelets into her pocket, she left the room and hurried downstairs. There was a meatloaf to be heated, an apple cake to be baked, salad to be cut up. Brian and Denise were coming for dinner and staying over, as they did every few weeks.

She knew that Brian and Denise saw their visits as an obligation, assuming their presence to be a comfort. Which it was. Judith was grateful. David was grateful. The young couple's discussions, their confidences about Brian's courses and Denise's community fieldwork, shattered the silence of their sorrow. Glancing at each other, listening with as much interest as they could muster, she and David were reminded of their own lives as graduate students, when their hours of intimacy were furtively scavenged from the deadlines for papers and the demands of their part-time jobs. Like Brian and Denise, they had anticipated a bright future. Death had not been part of that long-ago scenario. She wondered now if they had ever uttered the word.

She thrust the dark thought aside and concentrated on her preparations for the evening, darting from the kitchen into the dining room, hurrying upstairs to place clean towels in the bedrooms.

She reminded herself to be grateful for Brian's concern, for Denise's cheerful and patience acquiescence. She would teach herself to like Denise. David was already fond of her, despite his mild hesitation when Brian announced his engagement.

'They're too young to be getting married. Brian has two more years of law school.'

'Actually, they're older than we were,' Judith had reminded him. 'And we both had years of grad school ahead of us.'

She and David had married one week after graduation, their

wedding small and full of joy. She had carried a bouquet of wild flowers, the sun had shone golden upon the gossamer fabric of their wedding canopy and a string quartet had played softly.

Everyone had marveled at how well and economically Judith had managed the service and the reception.

'But that's my Judith,' David had said proudly. 'She can organize anything.'

Was that still a source of pride for him, after all these years? She dismissed the thought. Hastily, she added hearts of palm to the salad because they were his favorite.

Denise brought flowers – daffodils, the first blossoms of the season. Brian brought wine. They smiled proudly at each other as they held their gifts out to Judith and she kissed them both. Her handsome son was tall and grave-eyed like his father. His petite freckled bride, her auburn hair caping her shoulders, her green eyes glinting behind her oversized red-framed glasses, kissed David on the cheek, took Judith's hands in her own.

Judith told them, over dinner, that the room was now empty except for the furnishings.

'The room?' Brian asked. 'Oh, yes. Melanie's room.'

He blushed as though he had uttered a forbidden word; his hand trembled as he reached for his water glass.

'I put everything in bags and cartons. Books, clothing, other stuff. The synagogue thrift shop will take most of it. They insist that all donations be gently used, so we're OK on that score. Whatever I saved is in good enough shape. Very gently used. There's only the furniture to deal with,' Judith said.

'I think Nancy will want it for her daughter's room,' David said.

'Nancy. Who is Nancy?' It was not a name she had heard before.

'She's one of our senior administrators. A nice woman. A widow with a young daughter. She happened to tell me that she just moved into a new apartment and has very little furniture. Her little girl is sleeping on a futon.'

He poured himself a cup of coffee without looking up.

'If it's all right, I'll ask her if she wants what we have and if she can arrange to have it moved to her apartment.'

'That's fine,' Judith said, flinching at the thought that another child would sleep in Melanie's bed, sit at Melanie's desk, hide her secret treasures in its clever cubbies.

'I can take the bags and cartons over to the thrift shop with you tomorrow,' Denise offered. 'I don't have a class until late in the afternoon.'

'That would be helpful,' Judith agreed.

They ate the apple cake in the den and watched the news, before going upstairs. They were all tired, they agreed.

'Let's have an early night for once,' Brian said, and Denise nodded.

Judith did not tell them that all their nights were early. Evening after evening, she and David carried their books up to their room and trained their bed lamps on the unread pages. Now and again they struggled for conversation.

Was the room too hot, too chilly?

Had he remembered his dental appointment?

Did she want to renew their subscription to the Philharmonic?

Judith tried to remember what they had talked about before Melanie's death. Everything, she supposed. Everything and nothing, weekend plans, household trivia and, of course, Melanie. She was ever central to their lives. Their home rang with her laughter, was dominated by her moods – now up, now down, tantrums and exuberance exploding in inexplicable sequence. With Melanie in their lives, there had been no vacuum of silence to fill. With Melanie gone, they drowned in the solemn silence of her absence.

They trooped upstairs, Denise and Brian hand in hand, she looking up at him and tripping on a step.

'Clumsy,' Brian teased as he caught her and turned her toward him and kissed her on each cheek. She laughed, blushed, looked back at Judith and David who trailed behind them and immediately turned away. Judith thought to tell her that their brief gaiety was not an affront but she said nothing.

They paused beside the closed door of Melanie's room where the hallway was blocked by the rolled-up red rug.

'It has to be cleaned,' Judith said. 'I'll send it out tomorrow.'

'It's in good shape. I'm sure Nancy will want it. Is that OK?' David asked.

Judith nodded. 'Fine,' she agreed. 'Ask her when she can arrange to have it picked up.'

She was anxious suddenly for the room to be totally emptied, stripped of furniture, the black trash bags and cartons gone, the walls painted, the floors scraped and polished. The wide window that overlooked the apple tree in the front garden washed and fitted with new shades. Within weeks tender white apple blossoms would burst into full bloom amid shining dark leaves. There would soon be a new season, a new beginning. How she yearned for a new season, a new beginning.

She felt in her pocket for Melanie's bracelets and slipped them on to her wrist. The metal was cold against her skin.

FOUR

The synagogue to which they had belonged for many years was located in a neighborhood that had once been residential but was now populated by big-box stores, small businesses, mid-sized corporations and the county's largest hospital. On its lower level a thrift shop had flourished for many years. There had been talk in the congregation of relocating to a new site. Committees had been formed, surveys taken, but long-standing members, including Judith and David, had an affection for the brick building with its intricate network of arches and gables. It was repeatedly argued that the thrift shop was an excellent source of income, easily accessible to the budget-conscious employees of the local businesses and the hospital. The shop, which offered donated clothing and household items, was called Gently Used, a name proudly invoked by the staff of volunteers who managed the sales, sorted through the contributions and priced and tagged each item.

Judith herself had never volunteered. It was not, she told herself, her sort of thing. Besides, she could never manage, given her schedule at the university. To compensate for her failure to participate in the communal effort, she had periodically brought her family's discarded clothing, dutifully dry cleaned and neatly bagged, to the shop. It amused her that her donations, like all others, were always carefully examined before being accepted.

'We want only gently used items,' Suzanne Brody, the volunteer manager, repeated each time Judith appeared.

'"Gently used" is Suzanne's mantra,' Judith murmured to Denise as they carried the first of the huge black bags up to the shop.

Denise laughed, even as Judith frowned.

They pushed the door open and a confluence of odors wafted toward them. They inhaled the lingering scents of detergent and perfumes, deodorant and perspiration, the sad commingled pungencies of other people's lives. A few weary women clutching worn, oversized purses inched their way around the shop, pausing at the trestle tables, fingering first one garment, then discarding it for another.

Judith noted, with relief, that Suzanne Brody was not there. The counter was manned by Libby Goldsmith, a sweet young mother of twins. Judith remembered that Libby Goldsmith had brought a fruit platter to her home during the week of shiva, and she hoped that she had written her a note of thanks. It appeared that she had because Libby smiled at her and hurried to relieve them of the huge black plastic bags they carried.

'Oh, Judith, I'm so relieved to see you,' she said breathlessly. 'I'm here on my own – Lois was supposed to partner with me but she had car trouble and Suzanne has a doctor's appointment. I just got a call from my Mitchell's school. He has a fever and they want me to come and get him. I wonder if I could ask you to do us an enormous favor. Could you man the counter at least until Lois or Suzanne gets here? There are customers here already and I just don't know what to do. I can't leave the shop alone, but I'm desperate to get Mitchell to the doctor.'

Judith hesitated and tried to think of a reason to refuse, but she read the worry in Libby Goldsmith's eyes. She knew what it was like to be summoned to care for a sick child. She herself had, after all, bolted out of a lecture she was giving on Edith Wharton when the department secretary handed her a note telling her that Brian's school had called because he had fallen in the playground and sprained his wrist. She had abandoned the presentation of a paper at an MLA conference in Philadelphia because Melanie was running a fever.

She trained a regretful smile on the distraught young mother. 'I'd love to help you but I've never worked here. I haven't the slightest idea of what to do. I'd be a disaster, Libby,' she protested weakly.

'Oh, the prices are all marked. Children's things on these shelves. Women's clothing at the other end. Boys' and men's stuff over there. A sort of dressing room behind that shower curtain, although hardly anyone uses it. Household stuff all over the place. The cash register is open. There's a pile of plastic bags under the counter. It's really simple. I'd be so grateful, so grateful.'

Libby glanced nervously at her watch, fumbled in her bag for her car keys.

It was Denise who responded. 'Don't worry. We'll figure it out,' she said, her voice calm and comforting. 'You get to your son. We'll manage, won't we, Judith?'

She smiled brightly and Judith managed a reluctant nod.

'I suppose so,' she agreed, annoyed with Denise for volunteering, annoyed with herself for hesitating.

'Oh, thanks. Thanks so much.'

Libby, pale with worry, nodded her appreciation and fled just as a weary, dough-faced woman, her fleshy arms weighed down by a pile of infant clothing, approached the counter.

Judith looked helplessly at Denise and then went to the cash register, relieved to see a small calculator in the open drawer. She smiled at the woman, looked at the tag on each small garment and tallied up the amount due. Denise carefully folded onesies and sleepers, pausing to hold up a bright green snowsuit and pronouncing it the cutest thing ever.

'It's for my grandson. For next year,' the woman said, her face brightening.

'I bet he'll look adorable,' Denise said, and she put it into a separate plastic bag.

Judith glanced at the calculator. 'Sixteen dollars for everything,' she said. 'You got some great bargains.'

'I know. I know. I always do good here.'

The woman opened her worn black leather bag, fished out a change purse and slowly removed one dollar after another, her pudgy fingers fumbling with the creased bills. She counted them, then counted them again, her lips moving soundlessly. She fumbled for change, studied the coins. Her face collapsed in disappointment.

'I got only fifteen bucks,' she said. 'I thought I had more. OK. Maybe take out one of the undershirts. Or two. I think they were fifty cents each.'

'Don't be silly.' Judith shook her head. 'Fifteen dollars is fine.'

'Thanks, Mrs. Thanks so much.'

She heaved a sigh of relief, hoisted the plastic bags and hurried out as though fearful that Judith might change her mind and force her to surrender the two tiny undershirts.

'That was so nice of you,' Denise said admiringly. 'I didn't know what to do.'

'It made me feel good, actually,' Judith admitted. 'But I hope Suzanne Brody doesn't find out. Rumor is she runs this place with an iron hand.'

It was strange, she thought, to feel such gratification from such a small action, strange also to be so pleased by Denise's words. She busied herself counting the bills in the cash register as Denise turned to a pale girl, who approached her hesitantly.

A waitress on her morning break, Judith assumed, glancing at her striped, grease-streaked uniform and the flimsy net snood that covered her hair. She watched as Denise led her to a far corner of the store and pulled a teal-blue silk formal dress from the hanger. The girl smiled, held it up to her body, fingered the fabric. Color rose to her cheeks. She pulled off the snood and her dark hair tumbled to her shoulders. Denise led her to the improvised dressing room, pulling the shower curtain closed. Minutes later, the young woman emerged, wearing the blue silk gown, the shimmering fabric draped with subtle graceful folds over her slender form, her eyes newly bright.

Judith watched them, moved by Denise's instinctive kindness. She was still staring at them when Suzanne Brody swept in, her arms laden with winter coats, all of which seemed to be of the same navy-blue wool and lined with the same red fleece. She trained a thin smile of recognition and surprise on Judith and dropped the coats on to the counter.

'Judith, how nice of you to be here. I'm late because I had to pick these coats up. A donation from Ed Weinstein. Winter stock he couldn't sell. We'll store them until the fall. But where are Libby and Lois?' she asked. 'They're on the roster for this morning.'

She pointed to the calendar pinned to the wall, names penciled in on each date.

Judith shrugged, recalling that she had never liked Suzanne, whom she had known casually through the years because her son and Brian had been classmates. Suzanne had been the chair for numerous school fundraisers, always efficient, always officious.

'Libby's little boy got sick at school and Lois had car trouble,' she replied. 'We were dropping some donations off and Libby asked if we would help.'

'We?'

'I am with my son Brian's fiancée,' Judith replied coldly and pointed across the room to where Denise was rummaging through a box of loose fabric. 'She's helping a customer just now,' she added, watching as Denise pulled out a white stole and draped it over the young woman's shoulders.

'She's being overly helpful,' Suzanne said curtly. 'This isn't Lord and Taylor.'

'She's being nice,' Judith retorted.

She stared Suzanne down and decided that she was very like Eva, the judgmental secretary of the English department at the university, a woman much admired for her efficiency and much disliked for her authoritative manner. Assumed to have either an independent income or a wealthy lover, she was always impeccably dressed, her tweed skirts and cashmere sweaters a startling contrast to the loose shirts and worn jeans favored by harried, hard-pressed graduate students. Her clothes defined her even as Suzanne's outfit – her well-pressed gray slacks, and the elegant patterned silk scarf that draped her black jacket – proclaimed her status. Eva would never be mistaken for a struggling teaching assistant and Suzanne would never be mistaken for a Gently Used customer.

'Perhaps if we had more help, we could afford the luxury of being nice,' Suzanne said.

Judith frowned. Suzanne's retort was well aimed.

They turned away from each other as Denise and her beaming customer approached, chatting companionably.

'You look terrific in it,' Denise said. 'And the stole is just perfect.'

'I just love it. And you were so great to help me out. I was really nervous about what to wear to this wedding. My boyfriend's whole family's going to be there.'

'I had fun doing it.' Denise smiled happily, and Judith knew she spoke the truth.

It pleased and reassured her that Denise, kind-hearted and wildly disorganized, would be Brian's wife. It was her concern for others that had spurred her toward a social work degree,

Brian had explained proudly. He had, from their first meeting, delighted in Denise's cheerful optimism, her talent for joy. Melanie had also recognized it.

'I love Denise,' Melanie had once said. 'She's so much fun.'

Judith remembered feeling a foolish pang of jealousy. She had wanted her daughter to think that she too was 'so much fun'. She shivered at the memory as she watched Denise fold the blue gown and place it in a box.

'I'll just ring it up for you. The gown is eleven dollars and the stole didn't have a price on it. Let's say two dollars. Thirteen dollars. Is that OK?' Denise asked.

'More than OK.'

She reached into the pocket of her uniform and counted out the thirteen dollars – two fives and three singles. Tip money, Judith knew.

'Have a good time at the wedding,' Denise said.

'Sure. Gotta rush. My shift's beginning.'

The door slammed behind her and immediately swung open. Four chattering women, all wearing the standard blue smocks of nurses' aides, rushed in.

'Damn! It's lunch hour. And pay day at the hospital. Our busiest time. And I'll be all alone unless Lois shows up, which doesn't seem likely. I don't know what I'll do,' Suzanne said. 'Could you possibly stay?'

She turned to Judith who recognized the reality and sincerity of her distress. More and more customers were pushing their way in, some in groups, some alone, men and women both. They headed for the racks, rummaged through the piles of garments arranged on shelves, delved into gaping bins of shoes, each pair tied together with rough cords.

Judith hesitated. 'I guess so,' she said reluctantly.

She turned to Denise who nodded her agreement. 'I have hours until my seminar. I'll catch an express train.'

They worked rapidly then, the three of them, alternating at the cash register, darting from children's clothing to women's dresses, to men's shirts. Wire hangers fell to the floor, creating a dissonant metallic chorus. They dashed about, picking up fallen garments, bagging purchases and making change. And then suddenly the rush ended. Watches were consulted, anxious confirmations of time exchanged. The lunch hour was over. Clutching their plastic bags, the Gently Used customers hurried back to work, and Suzanne, Judith and Denise exchanged collegial smiles of relief.

'Is it like this every day?' Judith asked.

'Mostly on pay days. But we usually have more volunteers helping. We'll be getting the municipal workers later in the week and then we're swamped when welfare checks arrive. Everything is fairly predictable and our volunteers are usually very reliable.'

Suzanne turned to the cash register and began to count the bills, smoothing them out and arranging them in piles. Ones, fives, tens, three lone twenties. The calculator clicked.

'Not a bad day at all,' she said and smiled proudly. 'We took in four hundred and thirty dollars. That'll pay the synagogue electric bill.'

'That's terrific,' Judith said.

She glanced at her own watch. If they left now, she would be able to take Denise out for coffee before dropping her off at the train station.

'Judith, I wonder if you could arrange to give us a couple of hours a week. I know you teach, but if you could squeeze us in, it would really be helpful. I don't want to play the guilt card, but most members manage to do their share,' Suzanne said, her face averted.

Judith smiled, aware that they both knew that she was, in fact, playing the guilt card.

'Actually, I'm not teaching this year. I'm on sabbatical,' she said.

'Oh, yes. I should have realized. *Because* . . .'

'No. It was arranged *before* . . .'

The same evasive shorthand, the unfinished sentence because death could not be mentioned. Suzanne Brody's refusal to give voice and word to the grim reality of her loss suffused Judith with an irrational anger.

'Before my daughter – before Melanie died,' she added with a sudden surge of courage and watched as Suzanne Brody turned away, either in shame or in sympathy.

It was Denise who broke the uneasy silence. 'I wish I had

the time to volunteer,' she said. 'It's sort of interesting. And you were really good at it today, Judith. You might actually enjoy doing it.'

Her voice was calm and controlled – perhaps her social-worker-in-training, or her don't-piss-off-your-future-mother-in-law voice, Judith thought bitterly.

She chastised herself at once. It was simply Denise being nice, wanting to help, and perhaps speaking the truth. It was just possible that she might, in fact, enjoy working in the shop. It would at least give her somewhere to go, something to do. She would give it a try. Why not? Certainly Evelyn would approve. Her therapist would see it as progress, a tentative step out of the enclosure of her grief, a dismantling of her self-imposed isolation. Evelyn loved the word 'dismantling'.

She turned to Suzanne. 'All right,' she said, 'I'll give it a try.'

'Wonderful.' Suzanne's smile was self-congratulatory. She had taken a risk and prevailed. She took up the calendar, her fountain pen at hand. Judith was amused. Of course Suzanne would not use a ballpoint pen. Eva, the department secretary, also preferred a fountain pen.

'Afternoons. Let's say twelve to three. Lunch hours are so busy. That all right?'

'Fine,' Judith agreed. 'But maybe only three or four days a week.'

She would have one day a week for research or writing, and the mornings and the late afternoons to concentrate on decorating David's home office. Not that there would be that much to do. A reconfiguration. A computer table, bookcases, a sleep-sofa. Pickle pine walls. Real wood or laminate? She would work it out. She wondered when David's co-worker Nancy would pick up the furniture. She would ask David to find out.

Denise touched her arm and they left together. There was, after all, time for a quick snack. Bloomingdales, she decided, seized by a sudden desire to buy Denise a gift, a foolish extravagant gift, perhaps soaps and sachets, fragrances that celebrated the new and tender season of spring. *Progress*, she thought. *Yes, indeed. Progress.*

FIVE

David arranged for Nancy to pick up the furniture on the Sunday. Judith thought to leave the house, reluctant as she was to see the remnants of Melanie's life disappear into the maw of a rented U-Haul truck. In the end she stayed, hoping that Nancy Cummings might arrive with her small daughter. She wanted to meet the child who would sleep in Melanie's bed, sit at Melanie's desk.

She packed the newly laundered bed linens, the candy-striped comforter, curtains and chair pillow into oversized plastic bags. She would tell Nancy that they had to be washed on the gentle cycle and that only cold water should be used for the comforter. She rehearsed the words she might say to Nancy's daughter. She would perhaps tell her that Melanie had chosen the pattern herself, but immediately dismissed the thought. It would be unkind to tell a child that she slept on the counterpane of a girl who had died.

But Nancy was accompanied only by a tall, thin, bespectacled young man, her nephew who had rather grudgingly agreed to help. Her daughter, she explained, was at a birthday party.

'How nice,' Judith said, battling her envy of Nancy because her daughter was alive and invited to birthday parties.

Nancy, like her nephew, was tall, thin and bespectacled. She wore very white sneakers, jeans and a loose white shirt. Her long silver hair framed her angular face and brushed her shoulders. Judith thought of her mother's friend, Mrs Lefkowitz, whose hair had been blanched by sorrow for her fallen son. Perhaps Nancy's hair had also been silvered by the shock of sudden grief. She dismissed the thought. It was more probable that Nancy was one of those rare women whose hair turned silver prematurely and she had been smart enough to refrain from dying it.

'This is Jimmy, my sister's son,' Nancy said, looking up at her nephew and holding her hand out to Judith. 'Isn't it sweet of him to give up a Sunday to help me?'

'Hey,' Jimmy said, and the color rose to his cheeks. Clearly he did not want to be thought of as 'sweet'.

Strike one for Nancy, Judith thought and realized that she wanted to dislike the woman whom David had praised for her niceness and her ability to rise above adversity. A single mother, a widow, always uncomplaining, always competent, he had said, as though to justify his reasons for offering her Melanie's furniture. He had not spoken of Nancy's quiet, fragile beauty, which he had surely noticed. A surprising omission, Judith thought – but then perhaps not so surprising.

They stood uneasily on the porch until David came out. He shook hands with Jimmy, smiled at Nancy. An awkward word-less greeting, but appropriate, Judith thought. The removal of the furniture was awkward and painful for all of them.

'Coffee?' she suggested, seeking to ease the tension. 'I have some great pastries. Jimmy?'

'Actually, we stopped at a Dunkin' Donuts on the way up,' Nancy said. 'We only have the truck until three so we'd better get started.'

'Sure. Of course.'

Stupid of her to feel rebuffed. Even stupider to have gone out so early to buy Danish. This was not a social occasion. Nancy was not a friend.

David led them upstairs and Judith sat on the porch and watched as they trekked in and out of the house. The furniture was light and Jimmy easily managed the desk with Nancy trailing behind him, carrying the chair. He and David together carried the bed out and then returned with the mattress balanced between them. Such a small bed, such a small mattress. Judith thought she saw a small indentation on the mattress as it was carried past her and imagined it to be the imprint of Melanie's body. She felt a stab of pain and squeezed her eyes shut as though to blind herself against the memory of Melanie curled up in her bed, nestled in the circlet of soft light cast by the bed lamp. Biting her lip, she sat back and waited as the screen door opened and shut, and Jimmy and Nancy went up and down the stairs.

'You all right?'

David sat beside her, placed a cup of coffee in her hand.

'Fine,' she lied. 'I'm fine. Are you helping them?'

'They don't really need me,' he said.

'Yes. They seem to be managing.'

'Nancy is . . .'

'Yes. I know. Very competent.'

She marveled that he did not hear the bitterness in her voice.

'Judith. Please. I understand.'

He drew her close but she remained rigid in his uneasy embrace.

Jimmy came out carrying the bureau and Nancy followed him, holding a drawer. In her outstretched arms, it resembled a small white coffin. Judith turned away and took a sip of coffee, strangely pleased when the scalding liquid burned her tongue, pain canceling out pain.

She did not look up as Jimmy hoisted the newly cleaned rug, mummified in brown paper, and she did not turn as Nancy, in sequential trips, had carried all the drawers into the truck. She rose then and gave her the oversized plastic bag that contained the newly laundered bed linens, the candy-striped comforter and the matching curtains. She offered no suggestions for laundering them.

Nancy grasped the heavy bag and smiled her gratitude.

'I think that's everything,' she said. 'I really want to thank you for being so generous. My daughter will be delighted. Right, Jimmy?'

'Yeah. I guess.' Again he blushed, gangly and uncertain, his duty to his aunt done, clearly wishing himself away from this house where a sad-eyed couple sat on matching pine rocking chairs that remained immobile.

'I'm glad you could use it all,' David said, holding his hand out to Nancy.

'Yes. Glad,' Judith repeated after him, the words heavy on her tongue.

She set her coffee cup down and watched them walk down the path to the truck. She stood suddenly.

'Nancy!' she called, surprised by the urgency in her voice.

Nancy turned, her silver hair sweeping across her shoulders.

'Her name. What's your daughter's name?'

'Lauren,' Nancy replied and smiled, her chiseled features

newly relaxed, her face radiant. 'Lauren Rose,' she added, and the name floated toward Judith through the sweet spring air.

Judith nodded, strangely comforted by the knowledge that a small girl named Lauren Rose would sleep in Melanie's bed beneath Melanie's candy-striped comforter.

She waved and Nancy waved back. Together, seated side by side on the porch, she and David watched the truck drive away.

'Lauren Rose. A pretty name,' she said.

'She's a nice child,' he said.

'You've met her?' she asked in surprise.

'Yes. Nancy's brought her to the office once or twice,' he replied.

He remained on the porch as she went upstairs. She entered the empty room, divested now of every remnant of Melanie's presence. Nancy or Jimmy – most probably Nancy – had thought to sweep the floor. The broom and the dust pan rested in a corner. The window was open and a soft breeze brushed her cheeks. She looked out and saw that the tiniest of white buds lay furled amid the shining leaves of the apple tree. Melanie would have noticed that, would have summoned them to her window to peer out at the nascent blossoms. Tears seared Judith's eyes and she turned and left the barren room, closing the door very softly behind her.

SIX

David, burdened with two major projects, asked if Nancy Cummings could be assigned to him. Considerable research was required, and he knew her to be familiar with the statistics. He did not deceive himself. There were other researchers who were equally and perhaps more familiar with his work, but he wanted Nancy. He admitted to himself that he needed Nancy.

And, as it turned out, they worked well together. She, seated opposite him, dealt with the spreadsheets, making corrections, underlining inconsistencies, while he planned his approach, referring to her work, asking questions, relying without hesitation on her answers. He found her presence comforting, her consistent calm reassuring. The project was complicated but uninteresting. At the end of the day, when Amanda came in to announce that she was leaving, David realized that he had not yet completed his presentation. He sighed and turned to Nancy.

'I need another hour, maybe two hours,' he said. 'Can you stay?'

'If the babysitter can.'

She reached for the phone and he heard her speak with the sitter (a promise of double her hourly fee, instructions on heating up the casserole in the fridge). She spoke softly to her daughter, her tone laced with love. 'I won't be too late, darling. Edie will give you dinner.'

A pause. He imagined the child's protest. Annoyance. Anger. Or perhaps not. She might be more accepting than Melanie had been when she was disappointed or thwarted. Melanie had been a passionate child, accustomed to being the center of her parents' universe, fierce in asserting what she believed to be her rights, her eyes flashing, her cheeks burning. Nancy's daughter was, he supposed, more acquiescent. She had had to be.

He did not turn from his computer screen as Nancy continued to speak soothingly to her daughter. 'When I come home,

I'll help you. The math can't be that hard. Don't worry. It's just a quiz, not a really big test, and you're my smart, hardworking girl. Love you, baby.'

She hung up, shrugged and turned back to her notes.

'Was she upset?' David asked.

'Only because she has a math test tomorrow. I'll try to help her when I get home – if I can. That stupid new math.'

'If you want, if she wants, I could probably help her make sense of it. I used to tutor Melanie.'

He fell silent, recalling the evenings he had sat beside Melanie at her little white desk, helping her to solve mysterious problems, watching her grip the pencil too tightly as she formed uneven columns of numbers, hearing her chirp of delight when at last she understood what was required.

'That would be great if you're sure you have the time,' Nancy agreed, and suddenly the pace of their work accelerated.

They were finished in less than an hour. Nancy returned to her cubicle to check her messages and get her coat. David called Judith to tell her he would be late coming home.

'Still at the office,' he said. 'A complicated project.'

He was glad that Nancy was not in the room as he spoke. He did not want her to hear him lie to his wife. He did not know why he had dissimulated, but then it was not really a lie, he told himself. He was, at the moment, still at the office, they had been working late and it was a complicated project.

They stopped to pick up sandwiches and he insisted on buying a cupcake with pink icing for Lauren.

'It earns forgiveness from small girls,' he said, and she did not ask him how he knew that.

Nancy's apartment was in Chelsea, a swift taxi ride from their office. Lauren, elfin-faced, her braces gleaming, her auburn hair twisted into a loosening braid, bounded to the door to embrace her mother. How relieved he was to see that she did not resemble Melanie, yet how pleased he was to feel the warmth of her small hand in his own. Nancy introduced him as 'the nice man I work with' and reminded Lauren that the furniture in her room had been his gift.

'Oh, I love it all,' she said. 'Everything looks so nice. Come and see.'

He followed her into the room and stood in his daughter's world. Melanie's candy-striped curtains were on the windows, fluttering in the soft breeze. The matching comforter covered the small familiar bed, beside which he had knelt so often, to kiss her good morning, to kiss her goodnight, to feel her small hand upon his head. A pair of fuzzy green slippers lay on the red rug and unfamiliar books were arranged on the white shelves of the bookcase. The cubbies of the desk, once crammed with the minutiae of Melanie's happily disordered life, were now neatly arranged. One contained a small notebook, another a pin cushion, another a magnet to which a chain of pastel-colored metal paperclips adhered. Clearly, Lauren was a child who craved order and created it for herself.

She munched her cupcake as he and Nancy ate their sandwiches and then, as Nancy prepared tea, he sat beside Lauren at the small desk and slowly, patiently, explained the problems in her notebook. Unlike Melanie, Lauren held her pencil loosely and, unlike Melanie, she grasped the concept without difficulty. She smiled with relief. She did not chirp with delight.

'I got it,' she called to her mother. 'I understand.'

She beamed her gratitude at David and he smiled at her and joined Nancy in the living room where they sat side by side on the gray sofa and sipped their tea.

They did not speak. They did not touch. Suddenly, without warning, David's eyes overflowed. He wept, quietly, abundantly. Nancy watched him in silence and, when at last the tears ceased and he fumbled for his handkerchief, she took his empty cup and refilled it.

'It's all right,' she said softly. 'It takes you by surprise. The grief. Those waves of sadness. I know.'

'And you? Does it still surprise you?' he asked.

'Not as often. Not as intense. But it never goes away. All these years later, I still feel the shock. Probably because it was so sudden. Steven was alive, laughing, hugging me, and then, minutes later, the policeman was at the door, telling me he was dead. I felt as though I had been struck by lightning. Hit by a thunderbolt. I remember that I touched my cheek. It was still damp where he had kissed me.'

'Yes, lightning,' he repeated. 'Exactly.'

He wondered that he had not realized before that the young doctor's words had been just that – a bolt of verbal lightning that seared his consciousness, scorched his heart.

'So, yes. I still start crying, sometimes bawling if I'm alone and no one can hear. I never know what will trigger it. A sunset. A scrap of music. A couple passing me, walking hand in hand. Or nothing at all. And then the tears come. Sometimes I'm glad of them. It would be sad if everything was gone, all the love, all the memories, and the only thing that remained of Steven was a hole in my heart. It helps to cry, to feel the loss, to weep my way through it.'

She did not look at him as she spoke.

He sat back against the soft gray cushions, grateful for her words, her gentle reassurance, grateful that his sorrow was understood and shared, relieved that he had wept.

He rose to leave and she walked him to the door.

'You have a very lovely daughter,' he said.

She nodded. 'You were so good with her. So helpful. So at ease.'

He had been at ease with Lauren, he knew, perhaps because their brief tutoring session had been so familiar to him. He had recognized the circlet of lamplight on her workbook, the touch of her small fingers against his own as she reached for a pencil, the gentle sway of the drapes against the window. All visual and tactile recreations of precious hours he had almost forgotten.

'Daddy, the drapes are dancing,' Melanie had said one night as he knelt beside her bed. Her words, whispered in that childish lisp, had delighted him, and he had delighted in remembering them as Lauren's gaze had rested briefly on the window where those same drapes had swayed in a slight breeze. He had thought that he might repeat Melanie's whimsical words to her but he had remained silent. He would not speak of the daughter he had lost to a child who had never known her father.

'You're sure she understands that stupid math?' Nancy asked.

'If she doesn't, I'll come again,' he promised.

He smiled, said goodnight and stepped out into the soft darkness of a starless night.

Judith was asleep when he arrived home and he wondered if he should wake her and tell her that the knot of his grief was loosening, that he had wept, spoken his daughter's name and sat beside Nancy's daughter at the desk that had been Melanie's. Instead, he straightened her blanket and placed his hand briefly and lightly upon her head.

He was gone before Judith wakened the next morning, but he left her a note on the kitchen table telling her that it was possible that he might not be home for dinner. He anticipated a conference call that might extend into the evening. He would call. 'Have a good day,' he scrawled, and it was only when he reached the station that he remembered that he should have added 'Love'.

Judith read the note, crumpled it, then straightened it and saw that the word 'good' had been scrawled over an erasure of 'great'. Of course he would not wish her a great day. That word had vanished from their lives. She noted too the omission of the word 'Love'. She shrugged and moved with a new purposefulness. She had something to do that day, somewhere to go. The thought pleased her.

She stood before her closet, uncertain about what to wear for her first official stint at the thrift shop. Certainly not the casual suits that had been her university wardrobe and definitely not the worn sweatpants and tracksuits, the indifferent uniform of her home-bound mourning. She settled at last on a pair of khaki slacks and a loose white shirt, adding a tie-dyed silk scarf that Melanie had crafted in an after-school program and proudly presented to her on her birthday. It had been Melanie's last gift to her. She draped it around her neck, touched it lightly and hurried downstairs. She had a lot to do, she reminded herself sternly.

Seated in the breakfast nook, sipping coffee and nibbling at a slice of dry toast, she made lists. There were measurements to be taken in the room soon to be David's office, which she forbade herself to think of as 'Melanie's room'. Evelyn would be pleased to hear that.

Judith anticipated the therapist's cool approval, her standard utterance. *Progress.* What was she supposed to be progressing toward? Judith wondered, as she concentrated on the pad in front of her.

The floor of the room would have to be scraped, the windows

double-glazed and fitted with new shutters. *Referrals, Estimates*, she wrote.

Propelled by a burst of energy, she rummaged in a drawer for a tape measure.

Two hours later, with the measurements of the room neatly recorded in a small notebook, messages left with neighbors who had recently completed renovations, and an actual appointment scheduled with a carpenter, she drove to the synagogue thrift shop.

She was relieved to find Libby behind the cash register and Lois, her car trouble obviously resolved, going through a rack of men's business suits with a middle-aged African American man. He wore ill-fitting jeans and a very worn plaid flannel shirt.

'Mrs Mandell. I mean, Doctor Mandell. It's so nice of you to volunteer,' Libby said.

'Judith. Please call me Judith. How is Mitchell?' she asked, pleased that she remembered the child's name.

'He's fine. In school today, thank heavens. It was nothing serious. It was so great of you to help out. And we're so glad you decided to volunteer. Let me show you where to put your bag.'

Judith followed her to a small room in the rear. Two purses were on a table beside a pile of empty Whole Foods shopping bags. An Eileen Fisher poncho, clearly not a donated item, hung on a wooden hanger.

'Our stuff – Lois's and mine. Lois is working with me today. Do you know her?'

Judith nodded and placed her purse next to the others.

'Suzanne wants all our personal stuff in here because the door can be locked,' Libby explained.

'She's afraid that there may be thieves among our customers?' Judith asked wryly.

Libby did not return her smile. 'Suzanne's actually afraid of a lot of things,' she said cryptically, as they went back into the shop. 'Things haven't been easy for her.'

Judith said nothing more. Suzanne's life did not interest her.

Lois was at the cash register in earnest conversation with her customer. She nodded at Judith and turned to Libby.

'We have a bit of a problem,' she said softly. 'This is Mr Jameson. He lives in the new housing project on Prospect Avenue and he's found this suit that fits him perfectly.'

'Terrific. It's sometimes hard to find that good a fit,' Libby murmured. 'Then what seems to be the problem? Is it priced too high?'

Judith leaned forward. The handwritten price tag read fifteen dollars.

'No. The price is fair. Very fair. But the thing is I don't have any cash. They broke into my apartment last night. Kids. I think they were kids. The cops don't know and they don't care. Anyway, they got all the cash I had – a hundred bucks hidden in my fridge. Smart little bastards. They knew just where to look. But worse than that, they took my two suits – the only ones I got. I've been out of work for two months now, but I got an interview this afternoon and I gotta go to it in a suit. I thought maybe you could let me have this one on credit and I'll pay you back from my first paycheck. I don't like to ask but I got no choice. I'll understand if you can't do it, but I'd sure appreciate it if you could.'

He stared down at the floor as though afraid to meet their eyes, afraid to hear their refusal.

There was no refusal.

'Of course we can give it to you on credit,' Libby said without hesitating. 'But do you have a shirt, Mr Jameson? And a tie?'

'My neighbor's gonna lend me a shirt and tie. And they left my church shoes. That's why I figure they were kids. I got really big feet and the shoes wouldn't fit them.'

He laughed and Libby and Lois smiled. Judith stared in admiration, startled by his good humor, by their kindness and gentle generosity.

'I'll give you gals an IOU,' Mr Jameson said. 'Just give me a pad and a pen.'

'No need,' Lois objected.

'Yeah. I got a need to do it. I ain't no beggar,' he replied.

Libby nodded and slid a pad and pen across the counter. Laboriously, he wrote out an IOU for fifteen dollars and signed his name.

'Enjoy the suit, Mr Jameson,' Libby said. 'And good luck on the interview.'

'Fingers crossed,' he muttered. 'Gotta go through this life with fingers crossed. Thanks, ladies. Thanks a lot.'

He left and Libby opened the cash register and slipped the IOU beneath a pile of single dollar bills.

'Best if Suzanne doesn't see it,' she said. 'We kind of broke the rules here.'

She turned to Judith who nodded, oddly pleased to be included in their benevolent complicity.

'Fingers crossed,' she repeated to herself. 'Gotta go through life with fingers crossed.'

Suzanne Brody breezed in minutes later, impeccable in a pale-blue sweater and sharply pleated beige linen slacks, her arms laden with empty plastic bags which she tossed on to the counter.

'We were running low,' she said, flashing a proprietorial smile and disappearing to deposit her oversized handbag in the locked room.

Back at the counter, she set out pads and pencils, two calculators and a neat pile of smaller shopping bags. Judith recalled that Suzanne had been a successful investment banker before marrying the very prominent Dr Brody and becoming a professional volunteer, chairing fundraisers for the synagogue, community charities and the PTA. Her son, Eric, had been Brian's classmate, but the boys had not been friends. There had been some unpleasant gossip about Eric Brody, but she could not recall what had been said. It had been unimportant to her then and it was unimportant to her now.

'Get ready for the onslaught,' Suzanne said. 'Welfare checks arrive today.'

It was not an onslaught that began but rather a slow parade of weary men and women. Exhausted young mothers, their lank hair framing narrow faces crenelated with worry lines, clutched their children's hands as they rummaged through stacks of clothing. African American women drifted in, some too thin, some morbidly obese, all of them so soft-spoken that Judith strained to hear them as they asked their hesitant questions.

'Where are skirts for girls?'

'I'm looking for sleepers. You had a bunch last week.'

A Latino woman, her narrow form weighted by the

protuberance of a pregnancy she seemed barely able to support, whispered her question. 'You got any boys' shoes, miss? Size nine?'

Judith moved quickly. She found one item, then another, held them out for inspection. A plaid skirt was tossed aside but an almost new pale-blue sleeper was snapped up. She found a bin marked *Boys' Shoes*. She bent over it, repelled by the acrid odor of sweat mingled with powder, although Suzanne had been careful to explain that all shoes were cleaned and, like everything else in the shop, 'gently used'. There were no size nines. The pregnant woman sighed, knelt beside her and plucked out a pair of laced shoes, size ten.

'He'll grow into them,' Judith said, feigning optimism.

'Maybe yes. Maybe no. But at least he won't be barefoot,' she replied and looked down at her own feet where a toe poked its way through a very worn brown oxford.

'We have lots of women's shoes,' Judith said.

'Maybe next week. Today I'm worried about my boy.'

Judith turned away and helped a pale young woman, who held an even paler whimpering infant, search for a stroller. They found a battered Maclaren. The relieved mother settled the baby in it and smiled gratefully.

Waves after wave of shoppers came and went in a steady flow. The cash register rang open, rang shut, cheerful tintinnabulations that sounded over the voices of complaining children and crying babies, soothing voices and angry exchanges.

'Hush now, don't cry, baby.'

'Hey, lady, I had my hands on that sweater. Give it over.'

'I'm looking for a blanket. A summer blanket. They used to be on that table. Why do you keep shifting stuff around?'

'Sorry,' Judith said. 'Blankets and linens are over there.'

The topography of the shop was easily managed. Judith supposed that Suzanne shared her proclivity for order; perhaps she, like Judith herself, saw it as a defense against the inevitable and irrational chaos of life itself. It shamed her to think of how often she herself sought comfort by cleaning out a closet or alphabetizing her spices.

Even now, experiencing a sudden unease, she wandered over to an untidy shelf of women's sleepwear and, with gratifying mindlessness, soothed herself by folding the scattered garments. A soft voice interrupted her.

'Excuse me, miss. I'm trying to find a nightgown. The kind that's open at the front? You know what I mean.'

Judith turned and smiled at the sweet-faced young Asian woman who held her baby very close. Her high-necked blouse of turquoise silk was tightly buttoned, but breast milk had seeped through the fabric and formed damp aureoles which the infant licked, her tiny tongue whipping about the stains.

Judith nodded. 'You need a nursing nightgown,' she said.

She rummaged through a pile of sleepwear, triumphantly pulling out a pink gown that buttoned down the front, similar to the delicate batiste negligees she had worn when she nursed Brian and then Melanie. She had consigned two of them to the bottom drawer of her bureau, placing them beneath the long white gloves worn on her wedding day, the lace mantilla David had bought her in a Spanish market, the scarf that had draped her doctorate gown – her private archive of tender souvenirs.

The young mother smiled gratefully and brushed her child's cheek with the soft fabric of the nightgown. The infant's satin-smooth hair was jet black and her skin was the color of sunlight. She was, Judith thought, perhaps three or four months old, that sweet postnatal age when a baby's body gathered weight and smiles formed on tiny lips.

She closed her mind against the memory of the infant Melanie's weight upon her body, of the thrust of the rosebud mouth as it sucked at her breast. Melanie had always nursed with her eyes closed, dark lashes brushing cheeks as soft as the petals of wild flowers.

'What is your baby's name?' she asked.

'Jane. And I am called Emily.'

She smiled. 'Can you come again tomorrow? I have two other nightgowns at home and I'll bring them in. I think you'll find them helpful.'

A grateful nod, a shy smile. The baby cried. Three single dollar bills were pressed into Judith's hand.

'Enough?' The question was shyly asked.

'More than enough. Come back tomorrow.'

'Tomorrow.'

Judith watched as she hurried out, holding the baby close, the plastic bag that contained the nightgown dangling from her slender wrist.

Smiling, she helped one customer and then another. She straightened counters, folded sweaters, placing the brightest colors atop the soft pyramids that would soon be destroyed by grasping hands. The tide of customers did not abate. Plastic bags were exhausted and Suzanne replaced them with the pile of Whole Foods carriers.

Lois left, apologizing. 'My daughter. A three o'clock dentist appointment,' she explained and hurried out.

New volunteers arrived, worked for an hour and left. Fewer and fewer customers entered. By four o'clock the small shop was empty and Suzanne Brody hung the 'Closed' sign on the door and opened the cash register, carefully sorting the bills into piles and counting them.

'What's this?' she asked and held up a slip of paper, tucked between two dollar bills.

Libby looked up. 'I let a Mr Jameson take a suit without paying. He'll give up the money when he gets his paycheck,' she said.

'That is not our policy,' Suzanne said icily. 'You can be sure you'll never see your Mr Jameson again.'

'And I'm sure that we will,' Libby replied, her color rising.

'Who makes policy?' Judith asked daringly.

Suzanne did not answer. She tucked the bills and change into a large manila envelope.

'I have to get to the bank,' she said, ignoring both of them.

The envelope disappeared into the maw of her handbag and she left, closing the door very softly.

Judith looked at Libby, who shook her head and sighed.

'She's tough,' Libby said forgivingly. 'But she's very dedicated. I come in only two days a week, but she's here every day. She totally reorganized the shop and made it really profitable. She works very hard. And things aren't easy for her.'

'You don't have to apologize for her,' Judith replied. 'Things aren't easy for any of us.'

Libby blushed. 'Yes. I know. I didn't mean – I know . . .'

Her voice trailed off and her face was flushed. She could not say what she did not mean, nor could she speak of what she knew.

Judith understood her sudden confusion. She put her hand on the younger woman's arm. 'It was very sweet of you to bring that fruit platter when my daughter – when Melanie died,' she said softly.

Driving home, she realized that she had spoken with astonishing ease. *When Melanie died*, she had said very calmly. She wondered whether Evelyn would approve. Would she congratulate her? She smiled at the thought and stopped at a roadside stall to buy the small red potatoes that David especially liked. They could have dinner on the screened porch and talk quietly. Yes, tonight she could battle the silence between them. She had ammunition. She could tell him about her afternoon, about Mr Jameson and the sweet-faced Asian mother. She would confide that she thought Suzanne Brody was a real bitch. A Jewish American princess playing Lady Bountiful. David had always been amused by her caustic assessments of casual acquaintances. He might smile. That would be good. That would be restorative.

She let herself into the house, set down the bag of potatoes and listened to the messages on her answering machine. The carpenter had changed the hour of his appointment. Denise wondered if she and Brian could come for the weekend. A neighbor had left the names of painters, glazers. And David had called to say that he would definitely be delayed. A conference call scheduled for the morning that would require research and preparation. No need for her to worry about dinner. Disappointed, she dialed his cell phone. It rang four times before he picked up.

She heard music, murmuring voices, a woman speaking very softly, David's hissed shush.

'I left a message, Judith,' he said. His office voice, cool, controlled. The music stopped, the voices were stilled. 'I have to prepare for this conference call.'

'I know. I just wanted to know how late you would be. I can hold dinner.'

'I'll grab something in the city, maybe order in,' he said.

'All right, then.'

She waited for his reply, perhaps for a regretful apology.

'Don't wait up for me,' he added.

She heard a child's high-pitched voice in the background and then the sharp click as he snapped his phone shut.

She stared at the silent receiver. It was the voice of a small girl, she knew, a child clamoring to be heard.

'Lauren. Of course, it was Lauren,' she said aloud.

Lauren Rose, silver-haired Nancy's small daughter, who slept in Melanie's bed and studied at her small white desk.

She willed herself to calm. There was no reason why David should not be at Nancy's apartment. She was perhaps helping him prepare a presentation and they were working at her apartment because she could not get a sitter. Perhaps there was material stored on Nancy's home computer which David did not want entered into the office system. A variety of explanations occurred to her, all soothing rationalizations which failed to soothe.

It was ludicrous, she knew, to suspect David – her quiet, quiescent David – of infidelity. He abhorred the very concept, spoke with fury and contempt of men who betrayed their wives. His own parents' marriage had been poisoned by his father's brief and never-forgiven affair. She was certain, then, that his presence in Nancy's apartment was work-related. She decided that she would ask him, when they next spoke, how Melanie's furniture looked in Lauren's room and whether the candy-striped curtains fit across her windows.

She recalled suddenly how he had hung those same curtains in Melanie's room, obediently following her sweetly uttered imperious instructions. 'Too high, Daddy. Too close together.' Melanie had clapped when they were properly hung and flung herself into his arms.

Did David remember that when he stood in Lauren's room? She closed her mind against her wild imaginings. Instead, she called Denise to tell her that of course she and Brian could come for the weekend.

'How is the thrift shop working out?' Denise asked hesitantly.

'I think it's going well,' Judith replied. 'It's actually interesting and I am kind of enjoying it.'

She smiled and realized that it was indeed interesting and she was, in fact, enjoying it.

'Good,' Denise said, a congratulatory, almost maternal note in her voice.

Denise would make a wonderful mother, Judith thought, the sort of mother who exulted over a child's drawing and admired small initiatives. She herself had tried to be that kind of mother – generous with praise, lavish with concern, her maternal exuberance tainted by the guilt she felt for the long hours she spent at the university. Still, she had tried. That was what women like herself did. They tried.

'Give Brian my love,' she told Denise and hung up.

She made herself a cup of soup, went up to her room, opened her bureau drawer and found the maternity negligees. She shook them free of their fraying tissue paper cocoons. A moon-shaped milk stain on the pale-blue fabric had resisted laundering. She lifted the nightgown to her mouth and foolishly, crazily, licked the stain. It did not taste of milk; it did not taste of Melanie.

She carried it into the bathroom, washed it with great care, succeeded at last in rubbing it clean. She hung it on the towel rack. She would iron it in the morning.

She went to bed, overcome by a fatigue so weighty that she could barely lift her hand to turn off her bed lamp.

SEVEN

She feigned sleep when David arrived home late that night and yet again when he left the next morning. She dressed quickly for her early-morning appointment with Mike Andrews, a much sought-after carpenter. She greeted him, holding her half-empty coffee cup, and led him upstairs. He was a pleasant-faced, burly man who strode through the newly empty bedroom and pressed his very large hands against the bare walls.

'Well built,' he said. 'They'll sustain built-ins if that's what you have in mind.'

'Yes. I thought built-in bookshelves. Maybe a cabinet of the same wood. It's going to be a home office for my husband.'

He looked around. 'A nice-sized room,' he said. 'I guess it was your daughter's. Your husband's not going to want pink walls.' He laughed conspiratorially and scraped away a fleck of paint. 'It's great when the kids move out and you get to fix the house up for yourselves,' he continued. 'My wife turned our Lucy's room into a sewing room when she got married. She and her husband live in Pittsburgh. Costs us an arm and a leg to fly out there. Is your daughter close by?'

'Yes. Yes, she is,' Judith said.

She turned away. She had not lied. The small cemetery where Melanie was buried, her grave marked by a simple pink marble gravestone (pink, always pink – in death as in life), was only a few miles north of their home. It would not cost them an arm and leg to visit her. Unlike Mike Andrews and his wife, she and David did not visit their daughter together.

She knew when David had been to the grave because he left small, smooth pebbles on the pink marble to mark his visitation. She had found one there on the day she planted a small rose bush which the nursery had assured her would bear pink blossoms in high summer. There had been yet another smooth stone there a week later and she had placed a minute splinter of heart-shaped black slag beside it. There was, as yet, no blossom on the rose bush.

'Well, I bet your husband will be glad of the space,' Mike Andrews went on, indifferent to her silence. He whipped out his metal tape measure. 'Shelves along this wall. You don't want them near the window. And how big a cabinet?'

'I'm not sure. I'll have to ask my husband.'

'What kind of wood?'

'Dark. Walnut maybe?'

'I'll bring you some samples. I guess your husband will want to see them.'

'Yes. Good.'

They arranged a time when he would return. He stared at the room again before he left. 'A great space,' he said approvingly. 'My daughter's room was this color – a kind of pink. The wife kept it that way. Reminds her of Edie, she says, and pink is OK for a sewing room. But not for a man's office. You going to paint the walls or panel them?'

'I haven't decided,' she replied tersely.

She wanted him gone, this pleasant man whose married daughter had moved to Pittsburgh. She wanted him out of the barren room so that she might press her face against the cold pink walls and weep herself into calm.

He left, but she did not weep. Instead, she hurried to her car, remembered the nightgowns, returned to the house, thrust them into a bag and drove to the thrift shop.

It was less crowded than on the previous day.

'No pay day. No welfare checks,' Suzanne explained. 'It'll give us a chance to sort through the new donations. They come in heavily at this time of year. Spring cleaning, you know.'

She led Judith into a storage room where cartons and shopping bags overflowed with clothing and household items. Mountains of books tied together with cord were shoved against a wall. An entire *Encyclopedia Britannica* formed an uneasy tower, oddly topped by a huge sad-eyed panda, its seams leaking discolored stuffing.

'We toss the toys and give most of the donated books away,'

Suzanne said. 'No one wants them. There's no market for used books.'

'So I've heard,' Judith said drily. 'What about the encyclopedia?'

'They're obsolete. Everything's on the internet. You must know that. You've got kids . . .' Her voice trailed off. Her cheeks blazed. She had remembered too late that Judith no longer had kids. Only a dead daughter and a grown son.

Judith stared at her. 'No,' she said coldly. 'I don't know that. Our children loved our encyclopedias. Brian loved the maps in our *Britannica*. He traced them for school reports and he sometimes studied them even when it wasn't a school project. Melanie was addicted to "The Book of Stories" in our very old *Book of Knowledge*. Twenty volumes. My mother bought them with coupons she cut out of the newspaper. The internet can't replicate that.'

She marveled that her voice did not tremble, that she could speak of Melanie, in a room cluttered with the detritus of other people's lives. She turned away from Suzanne and lifted the first volume of the *Britannica*. The vellum binding was unmarked and soft to her touch, the pages intact.

'It's in very good condition,' she said. 'I think it might sell.'

'All right. If you can find a place for it.'

Suzanne, recovered from her brief embarrassment, had moved on and stood beside a plastic bin. 'This is full of Judaica. You'll be shocked at what people give away.' She held up a silver Seder plate, a yellowing embroidered challah cloth, a kiddush cup dark with grime which she dropped on to the Seder plate. The metallic clang jarred. Judith thought of the woman who had embroidered the challah cloth, the man who had lifted the kiddush cup each Sabbath eve, of the family who had celebrated the Seder.

Emily Dickinson's lines sprang to mind: *If I should die, And you should live, And time should gurgle on.*

Of course, time would always gurgle on. Lives ended, the treasures of the dead were discarded, once-precious items were sent to charity shops, to be picked up and set down by indifferent browsers. And time, always and ineluctably, gurgled on. She was glad now that the furnishings of Melanie's room were not lost to an anonymous gurgle but were in the room of silver-haired Nancy's daughter, Lauren.

Suzanne's voice intruded. 'Customers are coming in. You see to them and I'll start sorting through this stuff,' she said as she lifted the challah cloth and tossed it aside. 'Stained. I wish people wouldn't give us things that aren't in good condition. When donations come in, make sure you accept only things that are saleable – you know, gently used. You may have to be firm when you refuse. Tactful but firm.'

'I'll try,' Judith said, amused by Suzanne's officiousness.

A slow but steady parade of donors wandered in throughout the morning. Young women in tennis dresses, carrying shopping bags of clothing, smiled up at her and glanced down at their watches. They were all in a hurry, eager to get to the courts and manage a few sets before their children returned from school. They did not have the time for Judith to examine the contents of their bags and they smiled brightly when she asked the mandatory question. 'Everything in good condition? Everything gently used?'

'Of course.'

They explained that they were giving away their children's outgrown clothing, shirts their husbands no longer wore, clothing they themselves had tired of. One young mother plucked a white tutu, the price tag still dangling, from her overflowing Bloomingdales bag.

'See. Brand new,' she told Judith. 'Who knew she would give up ballet before I even removed the price tag?'

'Yes,' Judith murmured. She thought of Melanie's pink tutu and her never-worn white tennis dress, that price tag also still in place.

Who knew she would die before I even removed the price tag? she thought bitterly, even as she smiled at the woman whose daughter had refused ballet.

'Some little girl will be glad to have it,' she said and turned to the next donor.

Every donation was gently used and laundered, the scent of detergent wafting out of the shopping bags. Others were shrouded in the clear plastic of dry cleaners. Judith asked the estimated value, wrote out receipts, nodded her thanks.

There were cartons of crockery, offerings of pots and pans, carried in by middle-aged women whose faces were still masks of grief.

'From my mother's house. She died a few weeks ago.'

'From my mother-in-law's kitchen. We had to place her in a home. Dementia. She can't even remember my husband's name.'

'Sad.'

The mother-in-law with dementia had had wonderful taste in ceramics. Judith fingered a set of cream-colored egg cups, a collection of rainbow-colored ramekins, all selected with a discerning eye by a once-sophisticated woman who no longer knew her son's name. The danger of living too long, Judith thought. The scales of life were unevenly balanced, weighted down by those who lived too long and those who died too young.

She looked up from writing the receipt, handed it to the woman who had delivered the ceramics, and was relieved to notice that only one donor remained. She smiled at a man who looked very familiar. Her memory jolted into gear and she realized he was Jeffrey Kahn, a former neighbor whom she had not seen for many years. A pleasant man, she recalled, with a pleasant wife, Sylvia, a cultivated woman who spoke English with a charming accent. Jeffrey was a doctor – an ophthalmologist, she thought.

She and David, in years long past, had occasionally socialized with the Kahns – a casual situational friendship that had withered when Jeffrey and Sylvia moved to a northern exurb. She noted that he had aged but was not much changed. He was still thin, his features sharp, laugh lines rimming his closely set gray eyes. His thick hair was dark and only lightly tinged with silver.

'Jeffrey, how good to see you,' she said.

'Good to see you too, Judith,' he replied. 'I hadn't expected to find a familiar face here.'

'How is Sylvia?' she asked.

He averted his gaze and was silent for the briefest of moments. He clasped and unclasped his hands over the small carton he had placed on the counter.

'I don't suppose you heard. Sylvia died two months ago.

Cancer. Uterine cancer,' he added, his voice dropping to a whisper.

'Oh, I'm so sorry. I didn't know.'

She stammered, hesitated and wondered what more she might say. She herself had not found words of condolence to be comforting, but she was aware that he was waiting, perhaps paralyzed by her awkward silence, or perhaps by his own awkward sorrow.

'She was so lovely, such a charming woman,' she offered now, aware of the uselessness of her words. She remembered the futile sentences spoken by visitors who had paid condolence calls during Melanie's shiva.

Melanie was such a pretty girl. So bright. So lively.

She was such a smart child.

So outgoing.

Such sentiments, meant to comfort, had pierced her heart, compounded her sorrow. She had repeated them to Evelyn, clutching the therapist's box of Kleenex. 'Does it matter if she was pretty, bright, lively? Why do they say that? Dead is dead.'

She would not blame Jeffrey Kahn if he railed against the words she had chosen. *Lovely. Charming.* Accurate adjectives. Sylvia had been lovely and she had been charming, but that was of no importance. *Dead is dead.* Sylvia's charm and loveliness were no longer.

But Jeffrey nodded and smiled. 'Yes. Yes, she was,' he said. 'Charming and lovely. Thank you for saying that, for remembering her that way.'

She was moved by the graciousness of his response. She should have said as much to those visitors when they spoke to her of Melanie. She should have thanked them for remembering her daughter as they did. Melanie, in their memories, would forever be pretty, bright, lively, just as Sylvia Kahn was remembered as a lovely and charming woman.

'Actually, it's because of Sylvia that I'm here,' he said. 'Because of her things.' He pointed to the small carton. 'You probably don't remember, but she had a passion for jewelry. Some of it is quite nice and the girls and I thought you might want to sell it here.'

'The girls?'

'Yes. Beth and Amy. Our daughters. You remember them?'

'Of course. They were small girls when I last saw them. It's been years.'

'No longer small girls. Busy young women. They both live in California now – Amy's married with a baby, and Beth is in her last year of med school. They stayed on after the funeral and the shiva and tried to help me get organized. They wanted to go through Sylvia's things. They did what they could but they hardly made a dent. There is so much in her closets, her drawers. Sylvia took care of her things, never discarded anything. At least I've sorted through some of the jewelry. That's what I have here.'

He flipped open the lid of the small carton and Judith stared down at a tangle of intertwined beads, glittering rhinestone pins, tarnished silver bracelets and chains. She reached in and lifted a green enamel brooch in the shape of a butterfly.

'Pretty,' she murmured, and placed it on the counter.

Intrigued, she rummaged through the carton, plucked out a ring rimmed with blood-red gemstones, a trio of silver bracelets, a mother-of-pearl cameo.

'Some of this may be valuable,' she said.

He shrugged. 'It doesn't matter. The girls didn't want them. I don't want them. At least if you sell them here, the money will help the synagogue.'

'Yes. That's true.'

She toyed with a malachite necklace, wound it about her wrist and set it down. 'Jeffrey, do you mind if I don't give you a receipt today? I have no idea what all this is worth. I'd want someone with a little more experience to estimate it.'

Suzanne Brody – cool, calculating Suzanne – would know what to do. She would judge each piece, perhaps bring them to a jeweler for appraisal.

'Of course I don't mind. But I wonder if I could ask a favor of you. Sylvia's clothes.'

'Sylvia's clothes?' she repeated and looked at him in puzzlement.

'Her clothes. I hoped that someone from the thrift shop could help me sort through them. She had a huge dressing room, built-in closets full of suits, coats, dresses. Shoes. Boxes and boxes of shoes, some of them barely worn. Handbags. Drawers and drawers of stuff. Too much for me to cart down here. It would be so helpful if you or someone else could go through her things, pick out what you think you can sell and arrange to get everything over here. It's just an idea, but I don't know what else to do. It's a lot to ask, I know, but I'd be grateful for the assistance and it could bring the shop some revenue. Actually, lots of revenue. Sylvia only bought the best and, as I said, she took wonderful care of everything. If you could help . . .' His voice trailed off and he averted his eyes as though embarrassed by his request. He was not a man at ease with asking favors.

'I understand,' she said. 'And I'd be glad to do it. It's just that I'm a little overextended right now.'

'Yes. Of course. Your teaching schedule. I should have realized.' He stepped back as though retreating from his request.

'Actually, I'm on sabbatical but . . . well, there are other things.'

She thought to tell him about Melanie, to trade a death for a death, but she remained silent. The Kahns had moved before Melanie was born. He had probably not known of her birth. What, then, would be the point of telling him of her death?

'Look, let me talk to someone here and I'll figure out my own schedule. Give me your phone number and I'll call you and see what I can arrange,' she said.

'Great.'

He handed her his card. She had not been wrong. He was an ophthalmologist.

'You're still practicing?' she asked.

'Three days a week. Since.'

'Since,' she repeated, strangely gratified to note that he too spoke in the abbreviated cryptography of the newly bereaved. *Since. Before. After.* He scrawled his home phone number on another card.

'We'll talk,' he said. 'Regards to David. And to Brian. He was in Beth's class, you know.'

'Yes. I remember.'

She watched him leave the shop, glancing at his watch as he stood in the doorway, wondering perhaps how to fill the empty hours, reluctant to return to a silent house shrouded in cobwebs of memory. Even as she stared at him, a soft voice interrupted her thoughts.

'Lady, please, lady. You said to come back today.'

Emily, the young mother with skin the color of buttercups, smiled shyly at her. She wore a simple white blouse and a dark skirt. Her baby, wrapped in a makeshift gingham sling, rested against her breast. A wreath of woven white flowers crowned the infant's shining black hair.

'Perhaps you did not remember,' she said. 'The nightgowns.'

'But of course I remembered,' Judith assured her. She reached under the counter and handed the bag of flimsy garments to her.

'Oh, this is so very good of you. I thank you.'

She opened her purse but Judith brushed the bills she held out away. 'My gift to you,' she said. 'No money.'

Emily smiled. Her dark, almond shaped eyes glinted with gratitude. 'How good of you. How kind of you,' she said softly.

'My pleasure,' Judith replied and realized that she spoke the truth. She was pleased. 'My name is Judith,' she added. 'I hope you'll come again. We get some very lovely things for babies. Beautiful babies like your Jane.'

Emily bowed her head. A blush brushed her cheeks, turning them rose-gold. 'Yes. Thank you, Mrs Judith. I will see you again. Soon.'

'Soon,' Judith replied.

She remembered seeing a beautiful little smocked dress with matching tights amid the infant clothing and she hurried across the store to retrieve it. It was, she thought, perfect for a child who wore a garland woven of white flowers on her jet-colored silken hair.

Suzanne Brody took over the counter and busily made an entry in an account book.

'How did you manage with Doctor Kahn?' she asked, barely looking at Judith. 'I saw him come in. Poor man. I suppose he's going through Sylvia's things now.'

'He left these pieces. I think some of them might be valuable.'

She showed Suzanne Brody the carton of jewelry.

Suzanne fingered a brooch, held a string of beads up to

the light. 'You're right. Some of it could be worth something. We'll get it all appraised,' she said. 'Anything else?'

'He wants someone to go to the house – there are all his wife's clothes, shoes, handbags, scarves, he said. Probably designer scarves.'

'We've had requests like that before. We've done it. Sometimes it was worthwhile. Sometimes it turns out to be tons of shmattes.' Suzanne frowned.

'Sylvia Kahn's things will not be shmattes,' Judith replied.

'Could you find the time to do it? Maybe one of the other volunteers could help you.'

'I'll think about it and let you know.'

'All right. Thanks.'

Suzanne emptied the register and opened her ledger. She did not look up when Judith left.

Judith drove home suffused with an earned fatigue. She had always enjoyed the deserved exhaustion that followed a satisfying day of work. How strange that the thrift shop, at such a remove from her reference books and computer, her colleagues and her students, was affording her that familiar satisfaction. She would shower before David got home and she would prepare the dinner she had planned for the previous evening. A veal roast. The small red potatoes roasted with rosemary and thyme.

She would tell him about Jeffrey Kahn and ask him whether she should accede to his request. They would talk about it. It would, at the very least, give them something to talk about. That and the plans for his home office. The carpenter's questions lingered. Did David want the room painted or paneled? She looked forward to such a conversation. Drinks before dinner perhaps, their voices rising and falling in easy exchange, the pattern of their earlier years recreated at the sunset hour. Normalcy restored. She accelerated, chose a shortcut. She wanted to be home before David arrived.

EIGHT

As they sipped their after-dinner coffee, Judith told David about Jeffrey Kahn's visit. He was sorry to hear that Sylvia Kahn had died and he thought it would be kind of Judith to help Jeffrey. But only if she had the time. Only if it would not be too much of a strain.

'I worry about you, you know,' he said.

He did not look at her as he spoke. He feared that she would not believe him, would not welcome his concern. He knew how proud she had always been of her independence, and he, in turn, had been proud of how easily and happily she had maneuvered her way through both her professional and personal landscapes.

With Brian's birth, she had curtailed her teaching schedule, canceling an entire semester so that she could nurse him, urging David to witness how avidly their son sucked at her breast, how strongly his tiny fingers tightened about their own. He had laughed, she had laughed. They were bonded in joy. In time, she had found an au pair and returned to the university, rushing home each day to cuddle Brian, to prepare the odd treats he favored – slices of banana swathed in peanut butter, bits of frankfurter sandwiched between Ritz crackers. She had delighted in his toddlerhood, waved goodbye as he rushed from her on his first day of school and sped away to attend a conference on George Eliot.

She had managed Melanie's birth with similar ease, although Melanie had not been as pliable a child.

'Girls are more vulnerable,' Judith had said, always fiercely protective of Melanie.

She had, in fact, scheduled her sabbatical year to occur at what she called a crucial juncture, at a time before Melanie was overtaken by the perils of adolescence.

'I want to organize things to do with her, experiences that will always mean something to her,' Judith had said, and he had understood that she wanted to create an archive of happy memories for their daughter.

An inveterate list-maker, she made a list of such 'meaningful experiences' in one of her ubiquitous moleskin notebooks. *Fun things*, Melanie had labeled the plans which they discussed with shared enthusiasm, shared anticipation.

It would be *fun* to spend a weekend in the city with Melanie, *fun* to take her skiing in Vermont, *fun* to organize Denise's bridal shower with her. It would be *fun* for the whole family to go on a cruise together.

'Please, Daddy. It will be such fun. Denise and Brian want to do it.' Melanie had been complicit. The word *fun* came easily to their golden girl.

She had pulled David's ear, grasped his hands and danced him around the room.

'Please, Daddy.'

'I'll think about it.'

His laughter had matched hers, that shared merriment a kind of acquiescence. He had called a travel agent, asked for cruise brochures. They had arrived the day of Melanie's death.

A month later he had found Judith's moleskin notebook in the wastepaper basket, the pages covered with lighthearted *fun* plans shredded. He had not spoken of it to Judith. He was careful not to violate the privacy of her grief.

Even now he regretted telling her that he worried about her and braced himself for her reaction.

'Why would you worry about me?' she asked, slapping down a fork, arranging the plates in a pile. 'I'm managing. I get excellent advice. Evelyn says that I am making progress. She tells me that I must be strong, take on new challenges, new diversions. She says I must make my way through the stages of grief until I get to acceptance.' She laughed bitterly. 'A stupid idea. Will I ever accept her death? Will I ever reach acceptance? Will you?'

He shook his head. *Acceptance.* The very word repelled him.

She began to clear the table, her face averted, unwilling to look at him as he struggled to answer her unanswerable question. He abandoned any effort to do so.

'I'm worried because I know how difficult it was for you to

deal with . . .' He hesitated. 'Her room. Her things,' he continued, the words so softly intoned that she strained to hear them.

'Melanie's things. Melanie's room,' she said daringly. 'I hardly think I'll have a problem sorting through Sylvia's clothing. A very different experience. No emotional involvement there.'

'Yes. Of course. I understand,' he agreed. 'It's different. Very different.'

He turned away, but not before she saw the glint of unfallen tears in his eyes. She moved toward him, but too swiftly he rose from the table and left the room. Within minutes she heard the strains of Mozart's *Requiem* and knew that he sat alone in his deep chair, surrounded by the music of sorrow, his refuge as poetry was her own.

She remained alone at the dining-room table, staring down at her empty coffee cup, In this, their shared home, they were each isolated on separate islets of sorrow. She heard his cell phone ring, heard him talking very softly. He did not tell her who had called and she did not ask him.

'I won't be home for dinner tomorrow night,' he said when she came into the living room.

No excuse was offered, no explanation. She nodded. She needed no excuse, no explanation. She understood that he would be having dinner with silver-haired Nancy, probably to discuss a project they were working on. But why, then, did he not tell her as much? It puzzled her that she felt no sense of betrayal. What would Jane Austen or white-gowned Emily Dickinson, the literary heroines of her academic discipline, have said to that? A foolish question. Childless and unmarried, they had never experienced the loss of a child, the loss of loving ease. They would have no wisdom to offer her.

As always, she went up to their bedroom earlier than David. As always, she undressed in the darkened room and lay awake, her eyes closed, listening for his step upon the stairs.

She kept Jeffrey Kahn's card in her wallet and glanced at it now and again as the days passed. She would call him – of course she would – either to agree to his request or to decline it, but she had not yet arrived at a decision. She was, she acknowledged, reluctant to disrupt the new and soothing rhythm of her days at the thrift shop.

'It's a relief to wake up knowing what I'm going to do, where I'm going,' she told Evelyn.

The therapist nodded. 'A routine is one way to practice avoidance,' she said drily.

'And what am I avoiding?' Judith retorted angrily, although she knew the answer.

She was avoiding her own despair, David's silences, his withdrawal, his absences. She was avoiding sharing her mourning with him. They were drifting away from each other, she and David, and she wondered if they could ever return to the mooring that had secured their marriage for so many good years.

She stared angrily at Evelyn, who glanced at her watch and smiled, her gentle indication that their session was over. She walked to her car, thinking, not for the first time, that it was time to terminate a therapy that no longer seemed therapeutic. Her fault, perhaps, for remaining silent. Evelyn's fault, perhaps, for being so confrontational. She did not want confrontation. She wanted the avoidance provided by her new daily routine.

Each morning she greeted the workmen who invaded her home, smiling at the electrician and his assistant, the carpenter and his two agreeable red-faced sons, who trudged heavily upstairs to the room that she no longer called Melanie's bedroom but did not yet think of as David's office. She took phone calls from the floor scraper who canceled one appointment after another. It had been decided that the room would be reconfigured, although the window would still face the apple tree on which Melanie had charted the changing seasons.

Mommy, there are green leaves. Mommy, there are white flowers. Mommy, look, tiny apples! Her daughter's voice, trembling with excitement and delight, echoed in memory.

The window would, in fact, be widened.

'More light,' the contractor had said, and she had nodded her agreement.

By ten o'clock on most mornings she was on her way to the thrift shop. Suzanne Brody had given her a key.

'There are mornings when I may be late,' she had said, 'and I'm sure I can rely on you. The other volunteers have so many obligations – you know, kids, family stuff. You and I are empty nesters.'

'I understand.'

There was no discussion, although she wondered about Suzanne Brody's son, Eric. Obviously, he was gone from her home. Clearly, Suzanne's nest was as empty as her own.

On mornings when Suzanne was late, Judith turned the key in the lock, grateful for that brief respite of silence. She flicked the light on and inhaled the commingled odors of clothing and various objects offered for sale, each one redolent of a vanished past. Unpolished candlesticks nestled against chipped candy bowls; teacups, bereft of their saucers, littered scratched end tables.

The volunteers, like children playing house, enjoyed arranging the orphaned curios in attractive displays. Walnut bookends, carved in the shape of birds, supported brightly jacketed best-sellers, the titles changed from one week to the next. Now and again a small table was set with a discarded luncheon service and golden-hued wine glasses. Dessert forks of silver plate, polished by Lois in off hours, were placed beside each setting. The table itself and its settings were from different homes, each item the once-precious possession of a house-proud woman. Judith speculated that they might have been wedding presents, treasured legacies, perhaps an anniversary gift, now sadly rejected and unwanted.

In the quiet of those early-morning hours, she wandered through the shop, straightening the piles of clothing, rearranging the dresses and suits on the racks, organizing coats and jackets according to size. This was what she loved to do, what David had once called her special talent, her gift for organizing time and objects, arranging her family's life and her own.

Evelyn would probably call such obsessive organizing avoidance, she supposed as she moved on, arranging sweaters and shirts into neat piles that she knew would soon be in disarray. Avoidance, she decided, was not always to be avoided.

The pace of the mornings was often slow. Purposeless wanderers drifted in and out, the unemployed clutching cell

phones that did not ring, young mothers pushing strollers
grateful for a place to go, elderly men and women inventing
errands to fill empty hours.

One Monday morning, the first customer arrived only minutes
after Judith opened the door. She was an old woman, her hair
very white, her cheeks very pink, her hands threaded with
erupting blue veins, standing tall and erect.

'I'm looking for a black handbag, dearie. Not a shoulder
strap. And nothing that's too worn,' she said imperiously.

Judith found a black handbag. It contained a wallet and the
wallet, when the old woman opened it, contained a dollar bill.
She handed it to Judith.

'Some people,' she said angrily, furious with the unknown
woman who had been careless enough to give away a bag
without checking it. She did not buy the bag.

An old man was in search of a cane, and Judith walked him
over to a corner where three pronged canes and walking sticks
with ivory and bronze handles leaned against the wall. She
pointed to one topped with a carved wooden bird's beak, but
the old man chose another of heavy wood because it had a
brand-new rubber tip. He bargained valiantly to pay less than
the five dollars marked on its tag. Judith entered into the game,
resisted his first offer, countered it and settled at last for three
dollars. They smiled at each other and he lumbered out, each
step accompanied with a triumphant thump.

Students from the neighboring high school, on a break
between classes, barreled through, the girls pausing at bins that
contained still-sealed tubes of lipstick and bottles of cologne,
the boys rummaging through the very small supply of baseballs
and mitts, tossing a cap with a faded logo to each other. They
laughed and called to each other and dashed out without buying
anything.

A shift of volunteers arrived – Lois bubbling with tales of
the exploits of her clever twins, Libby depressed because of a
quarrel with her demanding mother-in-law. Judith smiled at a
new volunteer, a middle-aged woman who wore latex gloves,
because, she said, she feared that the donated merchandise might
be full of germs. Perfectly coiffed, her hair sprayed into place,
impeccably dressed, she stayed only for an hour; when she

removed her gloves, Judith saw that her very long fingernails were painted the same blue as her eyeshadow.

'We'll never see her again,' Lois said wryly.

Judith filed each incident away. Amusing stories to share with David. She would try. Try to share, to wend her way back to where they had been. *Before.* The fortress of silence had to be penetrated. There was too much at stake, too many years of happiness and sorrows shared, hopes realized, hopes denied.

One slow afternoon Lois and Libby tried on donated gowns, preening themselves before the cracked mirror. Briefly masquerading as prom queens, the young mothers laughed as they modeled bouffant dresses. They persuaded Judith to model a nurse's uniform. She agreed reluctantly, grinned at herself and adjusted the starched white cap to a becoming angle on her shining dark hair. Libby insisted on dotting her cheeks with a touch of blush. She laughed aloud, her first spontaneous burst of pleasure, she realized, *since* . . . since Melanie died. She congratulated herself on completing the thought.

'You don't look a day over thirty,' Lois crowed.

'If only,' she retorted.

At thirty she had been the busy mother of an active small boy, chasing after Brian on weekends, capturing him in a fierce embrace, brushing his cheeks with kisses and smoothing his hair. At thirty she had been an untenured instructor focused on becoming an assistant professor, her life ribboning happily out before her. She would get tenure and have another child. She and David had wanted at least two children, perhaps three. At thirty she had not realized that she could be ambushed by sorrow, defeated by death.

Too swiftly, she peeled off the uniform. 'Thirty was a long time ago,' she said, and they all laughed uneasily.

Suzanne Brody arrived, carrying extra shopping bags, extra hangers and an armload of new donations. She haunted neighborhood dry cleaners who gave her unclaimed items. She cajoled boutique owners to donate outdated, unsold merchandise.

'You have to know where to go, how to get them to donate,' she advised the others, displaying her gains, smiling proudly. She clearly knew how to do both. Hurriedly, then, they hung up the new acquisitions.

Everyone was needed when the lunchtime crowd invaded. The stacks of clothing Judith had folded so carefully were tossed about, racks were stripped, rejected suits and dresses discarded or carelessly rehung. Weary women, hospital aides still in their pale-blue uniforms, cafeteria workers, their hair still gathered in snoods, ferreted out clothing for themselves and their families. Men rummaged through suits.

A very young pale man needed a jacket. 'For church. For my son's christening,' he explained. 'He was premature, too small, but now he's fine.'

A portly older man in grease-stained overalls wanted a suit. 'A funeral. The wife's uncle. A pretty old guy. But a nice guy.'

Birth and death, weddings and funerals, were all part of the thrift shop experience. The inventory was routinely exhausted and replenished.

Emily and her baby appeared once or twice a week, and always Judith offered them the choice items she had plucked from new donations. Almost new onesies, apple-green and lemon-yellow. A white sweater with colored wooden buttons shaped like balloons. One button had been loose and Judith herself had tightened it. Emily smiled, thanked her and offered her scraps of news. The baby was sleeping through the night. She no longer disturbed her husband when he studied. Yes, her James was a student. A medical student. Oh, he was a smart man, her husband. Her eyes sparkled when she spoke of him. Judith smiled, remembering how the very mention of David's name during their early years together had filled her with the warmth of love and desire.

Late one afternoon, when she and Libby were at the counter, the man whose IOU remained in the register came in.

'Mr Jameson,' she said, proud that she remembered his name. 'How nice to see you again.'

Libby looked up and held her hand out. She too had not forgotten the dignified man who had needed a suit so desperately.

'Can we help you find something Mr Jameson?' she asked.

He smiled in return. 'Yeah. You can find my IOU. I got the job and, like I said, I'm paying you with my first paycheck.'

'But—'

Judith's protest was cut short. Libby held up a cautionary hand as she searched through the register. Within seconds she found the flimsy IOU.

'Here we go, Mr Jameson,' she said, and he counted out one ten-dollar bill and five singles.

'And now,' he said, 'I'm going to buy myself a sweater.'

'Important to take his money,' Libby murmured. 'He's not a man who would want charity.'

'I can't wait to tell Suzanne he came back,' Judith said maliciously. 'She doesn't trust anyone.'

'She has her reasons,' Libby said quietly. 'Trust is hard for her after what she's been through.'

'What does that mean?' Judith asked.

'Her husband. He left her. Walked out one morning and never came back. Left all his clothes hanging in the closet, his books on the shelves, even his underwear in the drawers. I guess Suzanne figures if she couldn't trust her husband, how can she trust anyone? It's a tough attitude, but I sort of understand where she's coming from.'

'But why?' she asked. 'Why did he leave her?'

Marriages that came undone had always intrigued her. They were grist for the novelist's mill. She had written a well-received paper on literary marriages mired in unhappiness, concentrating on *Madame Bovary* and *Anna Karenina*.

'I'm just curious,' she said apologetically to Libby. 'I knew them slightly years ago, when our sons were in the same class. They seemed happy enough.'

'That's what everyone says when a couple gets divorced,' Libby said.

Judith remembered Stanley Brody, a florid-faced man who had occasionally accompanied Suzanne to parent meetings. He kept his laptop open and checked his email during presentations, now and again glancing impatiently at his very expensive watch. Asked to serve on a committee, he always declined. Asked to make a contribution to a class project, he always wrote a very large check.

'He never seemed like a man who would walk away from his life,' she said.

Libby shrugged. 'Midlife crisis, I guess. Or maybe another

woman or maybe both. And there were problems with their son. Big problems. Suzanne, of course, never talks about it, although in this community everyone sort of knows what happened, and if they don't really know, they have theories. It was bad. Drugs, probably. But after the divorce Suzanne took charge of the thrift shop and turned it into a real money-maker for the synagogue. She runs it like a pro. Everything in place, everything organized. She's really made a difference. I respect her and I guess I feel sorry for her,' Libby said.

'You're very kind, Libby,' Judith replied, teased by a sudden insight.

She and Suzanne were very much alike, she realized. Suzanne's life, like her own, had careened out of orbit. The governance of the thrift shop was within her absolute control. Its daily routine, expertly managed, served as a life-preserver, a protection from drowning in a whirlpool of sorrow. In the rush of activity, stale marriages, a difficult son, a dead daughter could be briefly forgotten and dark and dangerous thoughts avoided. As Evelyn had said, routine encouraged avoidance, but Judith was increasingly convinced that avoidance might be all to the good.

That evening, as she and David sat in their living room, holding unread books, cocooned in their separate silences, Mendelssohn's violin concerto playing too softly, she thought of Suzanne and wondered if she lived alone in the elegant house her husband had abandoned. She went to the window and closed the drapes.

David looked across the room and smiled at her, a shy, tentative smile. 'Cold?' he asked.

'Fine,' she said. 'Just fine. I'm just wondering what to do about helping Jeffrey Kahn sort through Sylvia's things. What do you think?'

'It's entirely your decision, Judith,' he replied, his tone even. 'Just consider how much of your time it will take. And, of course, there's the distance.'

He rose to turn the music off. He would not say that he did not want her to spend long hours alone with a grieving widower. He, after all, spent long hours alone with a grieving widow.

He shrugged the thought away. 'Jeffrey is a nice man, a kind man, as I remember him,' he added.

'Yes,' she agreed, her voice vague. 'I'm not even sure he still wants my help.'

But the phone rang the next morning even before she had her coffee. Jeffrey Kahn, his voice hesitant, his greeting apologetic. 'I hope I'm not calling too early,' he said. 'But I wanted to catch you before you left for the thrift shop. I wondered if you'd come to a decision about helping me.'

'No. It's not too early,' she assured him. 'And I must apologize for being so remiss. I had meant to be in touch with you, but it's been a busy time. Things keep piling up.'

The lie came with surprising ease. It was not a busy time and nothing was piling up. She had simply wanted to protect the new and fragile routine of her daily life. That was not an excuse she could offer him.

'But I have thought about your suggestion,' she added.

'It was presumptuous of me to make such a request,' he said too quickly. 'I realize that. Altogether too much to ask. I've heard that there are professionals who do that sort of thing. Consignment shops. But I really don't want to sell Sylvia's things. She wouldn't have wanted that. My daughter told me that charities like Big Brothers or Vietnam Vets will come in and just take everything, cram everything into cartons and trash bags but that seems so . . .' He hesitated, searching for the word.

'Disrespectful,' Judith offered.

'Exactly. Disrespectful.' He spoke the word slowly as though surprised by its aptness.

'I understand,' she said.

She had learned during her time at the thrift shop that the possessions of the dead had to be respected, handled with care, dispensed with wisdom. They were the talismans of vanished lives. Donations were carefully folded by bereaved relatives. Widows brought in garment bags bulging with men's suits, stiff boxes containing newly laundered shirts. A woman, whose elderly mother had died, placed a pile of freshly laundered colorful tea towels on the counter.

An elderly man and his son had carried in a stack of hat boxes. 'She loved her hats, didn't she, Mark?' he had said, and the younger man had nodded.

He had opened one box and removed a soft gray cloche. 'See? Almost new.' He held it tenderly in his large hands. 'You'll be careful with them, won't you?' he had asked.

'Very careful,' Judith had assured him. It was a need she understood.

She remembered how she had carefully fastened each pearl button on Melanie's pink cashmere cardigan. Jeffrey Kahn's wife's possessions were to be handled with care.

'I don't want to impose,' he said.

'It's not an imposition. It's good of you to think of donating to the thrift shop. You know we're always in need of'– she searched for words that would not offend – 'gently used things,' she said at last, choosing Suzanne Brody's often-repeated refrain.

'When would it be convenient for you?' he asked. 'I'd be glad to drive you. We – I – live several miles north.'

'That's all right. I have a GPS. Let's say tomorrow afternoon. I'll be at the thrift shop in the morning but I can be there at about one o'clock.'

'Fine. That's fine,' he agreed. Enunciating very carefully, he gave her his address and added his home phone number. 'Just in case there's a problem,' he said.

She did not remind him that he had scrawled that number on his card which was still in her wallet.

'See you then.'

She hung up and wondered if she should ask Lois or Libby to join her as Suzanne had suggested. It was sure to be an overwhelming project. But she knew, even as the thought occurred to her, that she would go alone.

NINE

That evening, Judith told David that she would be driving to Jeffrey Kahn's home the next day.

'I want to see what's involved,' she said. 'I'm not sure when I'll get home. Perhaps we should plan on going out for dinner tomorrow night.'

He coughed, averted his eyes and spoke with the slight stutter that assailed him at moments of stress. 'I meant to tell you. I'll be home late. I'll grab something in the city. If that's all right?'

She stared at him, waited for him to tell her why he would be home late. A meeting? An urgent project? But he was silent. Subterfuge was not his way. He would not tell a lie, he would not invent an excuse. If she asked, he would answer truthfully, she knew, and she knew that she did not want his truthful answer.

'I suppose it's all right,' she replied coldly. 'By the way, I wonder how Melanie's furniture fit into Nancy's daughter's bedroom?'

He flushed. Her question had taken him by surprise, but he answered calmly. 'Everything looks fine,' he said. 'The bureau, the bookcase. The curtains were an exact fit for her windows.'

He waited, but she did not ask him how he knew. He would have answered honestly, but she left the room before he could speak. The truthful answer he had meant to offer her remained unspoken. He retreated into the living room, to the solace of his music and the softness of the single circlet of lamplight.

Alone in the kitchen, Judith rinsed the wine glasses very slowly and stared into the mirror – Melanie's mirror. She had wanted David to answer her daring question with the same honesty and openness that had belonged to their younger selves. A simple explanation of why he had visited Nancy's apartment would have sufficed, she told herself, even as she acknowledged that she feared just such an explanation.

*　　*　　*

They were exceedingly polite to each other the next morning.

'Drive carefully when you go up to the Kahn house,' he cautioned.

'I will. Of course I will.'

She did not ask him when he would be home that evening.

She drove to the thrift shop, worked for two hours, then collected empty cartons from the storeroom. 'I'm going out to the Kahn house,' she told Suzanne, who helped her carry the cartons out to her car. 'We'll need these, I imagine, for the amount of clothing Jeffrey Kahn described.'

Suzanne nodded. 'You're probably right. And take one of my smocks. Lint and dust settles on black. You probably should have worn jeans.'

'You're right,' Judith said.

She had, in fact, hesitated before selecting the tailored black pant suit she usually wore when she lectured. She had not, she assured herself, dressed for Jeffrey Kahn. She just wanted to look good so that she might feel good. It was a tiny step, she supposed, toward the reclamation of normalcy. Evelyn, who had advocated a new haircut and long walks as leverage against the quicksand of grief, would surely approve.

She tossed the smock that Suzanne held out to her on to the back seat.

The Kahn home was in the less developed northern part of the county. Judith remembered that when Sylvia had told her they were moving all those years ago, she had enthused about having more land and more privacy.

'It's not quite the country,' she had said, 'but almost. No other house even visible from ours.'

It was strange that she remembered Sylvia's words so clearly, Judith thought as she drove northward, passing from one suburb to another. Obedient to the soft voice of her GPS guide, she emerged at last on a country road. She recalled that the Kahns' decision to move had bewildered her then and it perplexed her still. Their home, with its spacious garden, had been directly across the street from her own. Their daughters had been happy in the neighborhood. She had wondered then why they had chosen to uproot themselves and settle in a relatively remote area. The unanswered question lingered.

'You have arrived at your destination,' the GPS informed her, and she turned on to the long gravel driveway.

Jeffrey Kahn emerged from a sprawling red-brick house that overlooked a stretch of greenery that was more meadow than lawn. He waved to her and hurried to open her car door.

'You found it,' he said. 'It's not so easy.'

'The miracle of GPS. But it is a bit out of the way.'

'Yes. Well, that's what we wanted. What Sylvia wanted. Serenity. Security. Very important to her.'

She thought to ask him why but refrained. Her curiosity was unwarranted and perhaps invasive. She was here as an emissary of the thrift shop, offering help to a one-time friend. No need to ask unwelcome questions.

'We should get started,' she said, and as though to prove the seriousness of her intent she shrugged into the smock.

'Of course,' he agreed and carried the cartons up the path.

She followed him into the house, startled by its subdued elegance. Sunlight poured through the wide windows and formed golden circlets on the polished hardwood floors. He led her through the large living room, dominated by a baby grand piano, the walls lined with bookshelves. A deep sofa, upholstered in pale-blue velvet, unmatched easy chairs – the one a dusty pink, the other an apple-green – faced the wild garden. Their feet fell soundlessly on the scattered area rugs – one richly patterned in shades of violet and aqua, another of pure white sheepskin. No decorator had had a hand in the room, Judith knew. It was Sylvia Kahn who had created this interior pastel island of peace and beauty.

Her eyes rested briefly on the photographs in silver frames that stood on the mantelpiece. The Kahn daughters, Amy and Beth, in cap and gown on their graduation days, the faces of both girls bright with happiness. A color portrait of Amy in her bridal gown and then as a young mother, smiling down at a fuzzy-haired infant. There was a candid shot of Sylvia and Jeffrey standing together in their garden. His arm draped her shoulders, her face aglow. The photographer had caught them in mid-laughter.

Staring at the portrait, Judith remembered that Sylvia and
Jeffrey had been one of those couples who looked so alike that
they were often thought to be siblings. Their narrow faces and
sharp features, their gray eyes set too far apart and their high
cheekbones lent them an air of familial aristocracy.

'I remember your daughters when they were much younger,'
she said. 'They are so lovely. You must be very proud of them.'

'Yes. We are.' He paused, remembering that there was no
longer a *we*. 'I,' he corrected himself, 'I am very proud of them.
They're wonderful girls, probably because Sylvia was a
wonderful mother. They were the center of her life. She gave
them strength. When Beth was born, Sylvia gave up her job as
director of a university press and worked at home as a translator
so that she would always be a presence in their lives.'

Judith nodded. She had not given up her job when her own
children were born, although she had taken a semester off to
revel in the miracle of the infant Brian, and with Melanie's
birth she had arranged a curtailed teaching schedule. It was not
a decision she had regretted. At least not *until . . . until Melanie
died.* Bravely, she finished the thought, allowing the silent
admission that she envied Sylvia Kahn who had never missed
a moment of her daughters' lives.

She wandered over to the bookcases, studied the titles.
Classics and poetry. Another shelf devoted to volumes in German
and French. Of course. Sylvia had been a translator. She lifted
a beautifully shaped blue ceramic bowl and set it down.

'It's a beautiful room,' she said.

'Yes,' Jeffrey Kahn replied proudly. And then, as though
anticipating the question she had not asked, added, 'Sylvia did
this all herself. She loved this house. It was very important to
her.'

Judith nodded. Again, she did not ask why, although the
question teased.

'Coffee?' he asked.

She buttoned the smock, aware that he was watching her
closely and oddly pleased at his attention. They went upstairs
and he opened a door at the top of the steps.

'Sylvia's dressing room,' he said. 'Everything is in here.'

They entered and she gasped in surprise. It was the size of

a more than adequate guest room, but the only furniture was a floor-to-ceiling bureau, a full-length mirror, and a vanity table on which small compacts of blush and powder, tubes of mascara and lipstick and two different atomizers half full of pale gold perfumes were neatly arranged. Their fragrance wafted through the dust-filled air. Sylvia's fragrance, Judith knew, and she supposed that Jeffrey Kahn visited the room simply to inhale the scent of his wife's vanished presence.

He walked past her to the far wall and slid open the door of a spacious walk-in cedar closet. Suits and dresses, blouses and slacks, evening gowns and lounging robes all neatly hung on quilted hangers. Judith saw at once that the garments were arranged according to seasons. Woolens to the left for wintry weather, linens and delicate cottons for the summer to the right. Sweaters, all neatly folded, formed even piles on built-in shelves, and below those shelves, crafted of pale ash, there were closed drawers. Lace sachets, filled with lavender, dangled from the walls. The profusion overwhelmed.

'There's so much here,' she said, realizing that it would take weeks to sort through the closet and drawers.

He nodded. 'I know. Sylvia loved her clothes and she took very good care of them. She bought only the best and she rarely discarded anything. I suppose it was because of her past, her childhood.'

He hesitated and Judith waited for him to continue, but he was silent.

'You're sure you want to donate everything to the thrift shop?' she asked as she fingered one garment and then another, the silk of a dressing gown cool to her fingers, the wool of a cashmere jacket soft to her touch. 'Didn't your daughters want anything?'

'They took what they wanted. Mostly scarves and capes. Sylvia loved capes and they each took two or three. They picked out a few things to give to their cousins, my sister's children, and they asked friends if they wanted anything. Very few people did.' He shrugged.

'I know,' Judith said.

There was an unease about wearing the clothing of the dead, a fear perhaps of the contagion of grief and loss. Suzanne had cautioned her never to tell purchasers that the items they selected had been the property of the recently deceased.

'Buyers might think that ghosts hide in the sleeves of sweaters or in the hems of skirts,' she had said.

It was an acute insight that supported Judith's recognition that her initial judgment of Suzanne had been too superficial. Suzanne was skilled at concealing her own sensitivity.

'If they ask, just stress that everything is gently used. No need to offer them a history,' Suzanne had added.

And very few customers did ask about the origin of a garment. The mother who had so eagerly seized upon a snowsuit of fire-engine red for her small son did not want to know that it had belonged to Joshua Greenstein, dead of leukemia two days before his fifth birthday. Mr Jameson, so proud of the suit purchased for his job interview, had not been told that it had belonged to a successful lawyer who had developed early-onset Alzheimer's disease. No need to taint such garments with tales of death and despair.

Jeffrey Kahn glanced at his watch. 'I suppose we'd better get started.'

'Of course.'

They worked steadily for the next two hours, in an easily established routine. He took the garments out of the closet, removed them from the padded hangers and handed them to her. She, in turn, examined the pockets, folded each jacket and dress carefully and placed them in the yawning carton. By tacit agreement, they began with the winter clothing, the heavy suits and the soft wool dresses. Now and again he told a story about one item or another.

He handed her a tartan cape unclaimed by the cape-wearing daughters. They had bought it on a trip to Scotland. It had been their first holiday in Europe, a cruise which Sylvia had resisted because she did not want to cross the Atlantic and she had worried about leaving their daughters.

'But we had a wonderful time,' he said. 'In the end, she was glad that I had persuaded her.'

Judith could understand her reluctance to leave her daughters, but why her resistance to crossing the ocean? Most women would have enthused over the idea of a trans-Atlantic voyage, a European vacation. Another question that remained unasked. She folded the cape and noted that it had been lined with red satin, now faded to a dusty rose.

Each garment had a tale, and she understood that when he shared those discrete histories, he recreated the world that had been lost to him when Sylvia died. The telling, selective as it was, offered him comfort of a kind.

He told her that a cousin, long dead, had fashioned the rainbow-colored stole which he held out to her. A long skirt of navy-blue velvet had been his mother's first gift to his bride. It was faded now but the nap was preserved. Judith folded it carefully, knowing that it would be snatched up by the young women who haunted the thrift shop in search of vintage clothing.

'Sylvia valued everything,' he said and his voice broke.

He held up an orange poncho. 'My sister made this for Sylvia when she was pregnant with Amy.'

'Don't give that away,' Judith advised. 'Your daughters may want it.'

He nodded and set it aside.

She added the velvet skirt to the overflowing carton and suggested that they had done enough for one day, although she knew that they had barely made a dent.

'Coffee?' he suggested.

'Yes,' she agreed gratefully.

She followed him downstairs to the large kitchen, its wooden table scrubbed clean, the windows curtained in red-and-white gingham, copper pots polished to a high gleam dangling above a double oven. A social kitchen, surely, the one-time heart of a household, where a family had gathered and inhaled the scents of simmering stews and slowly rising breads. The bright red linoleum that covered the floor was scarred, the spice containers in the wooden rack above the counter were half empty, the oven mitts were unstained but singed. No Cuisinart, no multi-speed blenders, no Lucite container for takeout menus. Sylvia Kahn had not relied on modern appliances and she had surely never ordered in.

Judith sat in the breakfast nook and looked through the window at a huge oak tree. A bird feeder hung on a low branch, and as she watched, two plump robins flew in and pecked away at the grain, their red breasts swollen with pleasure.

Jeffrey glanced at them. 'The feeder is almost empty. I'll have to refill it,' he murmured.

He placed a bowl of carefully arranged fruit on the table, set small dishes in the shape of strawberries beside it. He passed her a mug of coffee, placed milk, sugar and a plate of anisette cookies on the center of the table and then brought his own mug over and sat opposite her. He was at home in this pleasant room, at ease with its crockery and cutlery. She imagined that he and Sylvia had cooked together, something she and David had never done. Her fault, she knew.

She had always discouraged David's presence in the kitchen. It was a room that she thought of as a bastion against the remembered chaos of her childhood home. She had been fearful that he would disturb her uncluttered counters and orderly drawers and cabinets, her carefully stocked pantry and refrigerator. It occurred to her that, given their new circumstance, it might be good for them to cultivate new habits. She wondered if David would be startled if she suddenly asked him to help chop vegetables or stir a simmering soup. And would she regret losing hegemony in her impeccably organized culinary fortress? Not, she thought, if it presented a new path to intimacy, an intimacy they sorely needed. The idea comforted her.

Jeffrey passed her the plate of cookies.

'I must apologize,' he said softly. 'I didn't know about your daughter's death when I went to the thrift shop. I was told about it later. I want to express my condolences now.'

'Thank you.'

She did not look at him but stared into the cup as though the dark and fragrant brew might contain an anodyne to the too familiar pain that pierced her heart. Melanie had been dead for months. All condolences had been acknowledged and then, blessedly, they had ceased. Jeffrey's words, belated and unanticipated, but expressed with such gentleness, such awkward and hesitant sadness, moved her deeply.

'It hasn't been easy,' she added. 'But I guess you know that.'

He nodded. 'I do. Not easy at all. I didn't think it would be this hard for me to accept Sylvia's death. She was ill for a long time.

Every treatment had been exhausted. I'm a doctor. I knew she was dying. I was prepared. Or so I thought. But no one is ever prepared for the reality of death. I've seen it so many times, but it remains incomprehensible to me, beyond my acceptance, beyond my understanding. Even now, I can't believe that she is gone.'

His head averted, he stared out of the window at the bird feeder where a solitary sparrow pecked away. Perhaps he was weeping, Judith thought, and he did not want her to see his tears. He turned back to her, and she was relieved to see that his eyes were dry, although his chiseled features seemed sharper, as though honed by unremitting pain.

'Melanie's death was very different,' she said quietly. 'Sudden. It came from nowhere. We had no preparation. She wasn't ill. She was a healthy, happy child. She was thirteen years old, alive and laughing in the morning and dead by the afternoon. An aneurysm, they said, an explosion in her heart. We still – David and I – we can't believe that it happened. It is as though our own lives exploded. I can't wrap my head around it. Sometimes I think it was all a dream – her life, a dream. Her death, a nightmare.'

She sat very still, ambushed by her own words. She had never before spoken that way of Melanie's death. She had never twinned David's grief with her own. She marveled at the calm of her tone, the ease with which she had revealed the strange and secret fantasy that her daughter's brief life had been balanced on what Emily Dickinson called 'the ledge of dream'. Strange, she thought, that the economic verses of virginal Emily Dickinson should define her maternal grief.

He nodded. 'That is how I sometimes think of Sylvia. Our life together seems like a dream. And now the dream has ended and I am alone,' he said, each word slowly uttered and laden with sadness.

She lowered her head. His grief collided with her own, but their losses were so very different. They could not be weighed on the same scales. Sylvia had had a life; she had been a wife, a mother, a reader of books, a lover of beauty. Melanie had been granted only a childhood, her future cruelly denied. She could not say as much to Jeffrey Kahn, who leaned forward to refill her cup in this kitchen where he ate all his meals alone.

'It must be a blessing for you to have Brian and David,' he added.

She sighed and hoped that her voice would not break when she answered him. 'Yes. It is, but David escapes into his work and keeps very late hours. Brian no longer lives at home. He was a good brother and he is a good son, but he has his life. He's in law school and engaged to be married. He's building his own future. I don't want him to feel that we – David and I – are dependent on him, that it's his job to soothe our grief,' she said.

Jeffrey nodded. 'I understand. I feel the same way about my daughters. I don't want to burden them with my sadness, my loneliness. That is why I encouraged them to go back to their lives in California. Of course, they worry. They call. They want me to sell the house and move to the west coast but that's not a step I'm ready to take.'

'I've been told that no decisions should be made until at least a year after the death of a' – she hesitated – 'a loved one.'

'It's a relief for me to be able to talk so openly to you. Thank you for listening. How strange that we should meet at such a time after so many years,' he said.

They sat in silence for a few minutes. Her hand rested on the table beside the cup newly filled with coffee which she did not want. He covered it with his own and she sat very still, grateful for the warmth of his touch.

'I should be going,' she said at last.

'Yes, of course.'

He carried the heavy carton out to her car. 'Will you be able to come again?' he asked. 'There is still so much to do.'

'Of course. I imagine that it will take us several weeks to deal with everything, but I think I'll be able to arrange it.'

She took out her diary and they settled on a tentative schedule. Two afternoons a week, perhaps three, depending on his obligations and her own.

'It's very good of you,' he said.

'My pleasure.'

She recoiled against the falsity of her own words. It was not her pleasure. It was her duty. It was her need. It was yet another way to elude the solitude of her grief. Perhaps yet another avoidance. *Damn Evelyn.*

She looked through the rearview mirror as she drove away and watched him walk very slowly into his silent house. She imagined him refilling the bird feeder at an hour when the darkening sky was streaked with the melancholy pastel rays of twilight. His sadness, at that treacherous hour when day drifted into evening, was, she knew, twin to her own.

She turned away and concentrated on the road ahead of her, driving too fast because she was eager, suddenly, to be home, to begin cooking dinner so that the house would be redolent with the scent of a simmering sauce when David turned his key in the door. Perhaps this very night she would ask him to stir the sauce, to hand her a spatula, and they would work together at the stove, their faces bright with the rising heat. And then she remembered that David would not be home for dinner. She would be alone, yet again, staring into Melanie's mirror and chasing the memory of laughter silenced and words unspoken.

TEN

'Helping Jeffrey Kahn sort through Sylvia's things is an enormous job, but I agreed to help him. I'll probably be spending two days a week doing that for a while,' Judith told David the next morning.

He nodded.

'It shouldn't interfere with our schedules,' she added and wondered what schedules she was talking about. There were no social engagements on their calendar. Invitations, kind and hesitant, had been offered after Melanie's death, all politely refused.

'We understand,' their friends said in the soft voices usually reserved for convalescing invalids. Then, after a while, a very short while, there had been fewer solicitous phone calls and, finally, no invitations at all.

'If you're sure it won't be a strain,' he said. 'Actually, I was just assigned a major arbitration, so there'll be a lot of late nights at the office. You won't have to worry about dinners.'

'That's a relief,' she said drily.

So much for the fantasy of kitchen intimacy, David chopping vegetables and stirring stews. The thought was tinged with anger. No, not anger. Disappointment, she acknowledged. Like Jeffrey Kahn, she would be eating many meals alone. She shrugged and did not reply in kind to his desultory wave as he hurried to his car, eager to catch his commuter train.

At the thrift shop, she and Suzanne sorted through the carton of Sylvia Kahn's clothing, Suzanne marveling at the quality of the garments.

'This is only the beginning,' Judith told her. 'There's tons of stuff there. I'll be helping Jeffrey Kahn go through it for the next several weeks. Probably on Tuesday and Thursday afternoons.'

'Fine,' Suzanne said. 'I'll note that on the thrift shop roster.'

She fingered a gray cashmere dress. 'What do you think about sending things of this quality to a consignment shop?'

'Let's see what else I bring in,' Judith said, although she knew that anything Sylvia Kahn had bought would be of similar quality.

She managed her new routine with ease. Each Tuesday and Thursday afternoon, she left the thrift shop and drove to Jeffrey's home. They worked methodically, filling one carton after another, which she delivered to the thrift shop the next day. Suzanne gave Sylvia's clothing pride of place. She dressed a mannequin, plundered from a bankrupt boutique, in the long blue velvet skirt and an elegant white satin shirt. Both items were snapped up by a stylish young woman who frequented the shop in search of vintage clothing.

A sweet-faced young girl, pale and sad-eyed, her shapeless blue cotton dress wrinkled and belted with a fraying rope, bought one of Sylvia's capes. She put it on at once, although the day was warm.

'I'm cold. I'm always cold. It's the medicines. The medicines make me cold. But I have to take them. Otherwise, I'll be sick again. I want to be well. When I'm well, I'll have my own apartment. That will be nice.'

She smiled at Judith, a child's tentative smile in search of support and reassurance.

'Very nice,' Judith agreed and watched her leave, huddled in the cape, its hem trailing in the dust.

'She's from the halfway house up the hill,' Lois confided. 'A lot of them shop here. Mental patients in recovery. Addicts in rehab. Kids, most of them. They need a break.'

Judith told Jeffrey that the cape had been sold. 'To a young girl. A very poor young girl who really needed it.'

He nodded. 'That would have pleased Sylvia,' he said. 'She knew what it was to be in need.'

Again, she refrained from asking questions, although she wondered when and why Sylvia had been in need. She would not ask. There had been no repetition of the intimacies revealed on that first day. She and Jeffrey Kahn were careful to observe boundaries. Their losses were not mentioned. She never spoke of Melanie. His references to Sylvia were infrequent. They worked in companionable silence, their efforts synchronized.

He plucked dresses and jackets from the closet and handed them to her. She shook them loose, went through the pockets, now and again finding coins or loose buttons, supermarket coupons and once, a shopping list, Sylvia's handwriting, small and elegant. *Turmeric. Dill. Squid ink pasta.* It did not surprise her that Sylvia had been a gourmet cook. The long-expired supermarket coupons had been neatly clipped. Sylvia, despite her vast wardrobe, had been a frugal woman.

After two weeks they congratulated themselves on having made significant progress. They celebrated by drinking glasses of wine outside as a flock of Canada geese flew very low.

'Summer visitors, Sylvia called them,' he said.

She nodded, recognizing that his words were a gift of a kind.

One afternoon, she set aside a high-necked dress of sea-green polished cotton, thinking that it would suit Emily, given her dark hair and the apricot-toned sheen of her skin. She felt a great fondness for the very shy, very polite young mother and mentioned her to Jeffrey.

'Asian? Is she Japanese or Korean?' he asked.

She admitted that she did not know, but she was grateful to him for asking, for expressing an interest.

Sharing coffee at the end of the afternoon became a pleasant ritual. Now and again Judith brought pastries purchased at a French patisserie in town. More often Jeffrey set out croissants and wedges of cheese. They sat in the breakfast nook as evening shadows darkened the sky. The bird feeder was deserted, and although the room grew dim, Jeffrey did not turn on the light. They spoke softly, aware of the fragility of their words. When he mentioned Sylvia, his tone was tentative. Their self-set boundaries disappeared and there was a new ease in their exchange.

He offered fragmented memories, crumbs of information. One afternoon they watched a blue jay descend on the bird feeder and he stared at it and turned away.

'Her favorite bird,' he said.

He cut the cheese with an onyx-handled knife.

'Sylvia loved antique cutlery. She bought this at a flea market,

I think. We loved going to flea markets.' His long fingers caressed the smooth stone.

Judith, in turn, offered him carefully selected anecdotes from her own past, telling him one afternoon how she and David had met.

'We were both feeling miserable and lonely, registering for classes at this huge university where we knew no one, and I asked if I could borrow his pen. I never gave it back. I didn't have to. We were together from that moment on. We always marveled at how lucky we were to find each other,' she said.

And they had been lucky, she knew, she and David, so lost and alone, tumbling into love. Luck and love had sustained them as the years rushed past, lost now and again in gossamer webs of disappointment, small clouds of fear, but always returning. As it would again, she assured herself. She listened as Jeffrey spoke in lilting tones of his own first meeting with Sylvia.

She had come to the clinic in a poor section of Baltimore where he volunteered during his first year of practice, concerned that the trachoma she had experienced as a child might have damaged her eyes. He had examined her and reassured her that her eyes were healthy, noting that they were also very beautiful.

'Trachoma?' Judith asked. 'Trachoma in America?'

'Extremely rare,' he agreed. 'But Sylvia wasn't born in America.'

She waited but he said nothing more.

Some days later, going through the pockets of a tweed jacket, Judith found a letter, its faded script in a language she didn't recognize. She handed it to Jeffrey, who glanced at it and nodded.

'It's written in Polish,' he said. 'From a cousin of Sylvia's. Luba. She lives in Israel now. She and Sylvia were close as children. In Reidenberg.'

'Reidenberg?'

He smoothed the letter out and put it in his pocket. Their work for the day was done. She followed him downstairs.

'Yes. Reidenberg,' he repeated as he brewed their coffee, and Judith, familiar now with the kitchen that was not her own, poured milk into the blue ceramic creamer and placed their mugs on the table. He sat opposite her, took the letter from his pocket and placed it on the table.

'It was Camp Reidenberg, actually. A displaced persons camp in Austria where Luba's family and Sylvia's were interned. It was supposed to be a transit camp for Holocaust survivors, but some families, like Sylvia's, stayed there for years.'

'Sylvia was a Holocaust survivor?' Judith asked and immediately regretted the question. She did not want him to retreat into silence.

He did not. He breathed deeply, and when he spoke, it was in a monotone, a slow and reluctant recitation.

'Actually, her parents were survivors. Tzvika and Henia Makover. They had both been slave laborers at Auschwitz. Her father's first wife and his three children were killed there. Her mother's first husband and her small daughter also died there. Of typhus, Sylvia's mother thought, but it could just as well have been pneumonia or malnutrition. Or even gas.' He spat the words out, his fists clenched.

Judith stared at him, her heart pounding, her thoughts tumbling over each other. Three children killed – no, four. They would have been Sylvia's siblings. No, her half-siblings.

She closed her eyes against the invasive image of small, lifeless bodies and felt overwhelmed by questions that she dared not ask. How had Sylvia's mother, Sylvia's father, survived such bereavement? There were days when she marveled that she herself had survived the loss of her Melanie, one cherished child. How courageous, then, that Sylvia's parents, death-haunted as they were, had had the courage to bring another child into the world.

She thought suddenly of the words the very young doctor had spoken in the hospital corridor.

'It was a gentle death,' he had said.

He had intended to comfort them but they had not been comforted. The death of a child, she might have told him, is never gentle.

It is an end to life, an end to hope and dream, frightening in its dark incomprehensible finality. All parents of such vanished children share a mutual bereavement, a mutual identity. Children who lost their parents were orphans, but there was no word in any lexicon for parents who lost their children.

She shivered and looked at Jeffrey, grateful that, absorbed as he was in arranging a plate of pastries, he had not taken note of her distraction and her dark imaginings. He added a wheel of cheese and resumed his narrative as he sliced it.

'Her parents met at Reidenberg where they were placed when the war ended,' he continued. 'They married and Sylvia was born there a year later. There were many such marriages in those camps – widows and widowers clinging to each other in loneliness and desperation. Second families were created, babies born. Births after so many deaths. Sylvia had only one faded snapshot of herself as a child in Reidenberg. Spindly-legged, skeletally thin, her eyes, her beautiful eyes, weakened by incipient trachoma which an American army doctor thankfully cured. Many families left, some after weeks, some after months – they went to Palestine, to America, to England, to Australia – but her parents were inert. They stayed and stayed. The camp was crowded, moldy shacks, huts where small businesses were conducted. Her father called himself a shoemaker and earned a couple of coins repairing the heels and soles of boots that were beyond repair. They lived in a hovel that stank of urine and feces because it was next to a shared bathroom. Sylvia slept on a mattress with her cousin Luba until Luba's family went to Israel. She didn't remember much about Reidenberg, but she never forgot the stench. She said that it was so crowded that when she breathed she was afraid she was stealing someone else's air. They cooked on coal braziers and the sky was always dark with smoke. That too she remembered. Finally some cousins in Baltimore traced them, sent affidavits and tickets. Sylvia was six years old when they came to America. She had never had a new dress. She had never owned a doll. Her parents sometimes called her by the names of their dead children. They were exhausted. They had forgotten how to be parents. They had forgotten how to live. She never had a childhood, my Sylvia. Her parents, she told me, were absent presences in her life, ghosts who barely spoke. She cared for them and fended for herself. Which she did quietly, bravely.'

His voice broke. He mourned his wife's death, he mourned her lost childhood. He was, Judith realized, doubly burdened. She reached across the table and, weeping, she placed her hand over his. He looked at her, encased her hand in his own and lifted it to his lips. His eyes were closed but tears continued to fall. Bonded by sorrow, they sat silently in the gathering darkness. At last he rose and lit the small table lamp so that their faces were bathed in light. Their coffee was tepid and he refilled their cups.

Judith understood now why Sylvia Kahn had hung sachets in her closet, why the atomizers breathed out their fragrance, why the wide windows opened out to a garden planted with a hedge of sweet-smelling roses whose scent surely wafted into the house throughout the spring and summer months. Of course, she had wanted a large house set high on a hilltop where she could see the sky. After a childhood spent in the crowded camp, she craved isolation. It was understandable that the small girl who had never had a new dress became a woman obsessed with the clothing she could now buy with ease. And, of course, she, who had never known a mother's care, would want to be with her own children every hour of every day.

Jeffrey had made everything clear and that stark clarity humbled Judith. She understood Sylvia Kahn who had been determined to nurture and protect her daughters, just as Judith herself had been so fiercely determined to nurture and protect her own children.

She remembered the long nights of Brian's childhood when she and David had stood vigil beside his bed, regulating the nebulizer as he struggled for breath in the throes of an asthma attack. She had wanted to offer him her own breath, her own life, and had wept with relief in David's arms when color at last returned to their son's face and he breathed with ease.

Her sabbatical year had been planned to offer Melanie ballast against the inevitable perils of adolescence. A thwarted determination, a foolish effort. But Sylvia at least had succeeded. She had guided her two daughters into young womanhood, into independence, imbued them with her love. Their faces, in their commencement portraits and in Amy's bridal photo, beamed confidence.

'I'm sorry that I didn't know Sylvia better,' she said, compensatory words but true enough. During the years when they had been neighbors, she had had little time for intimacy.

'She was a very private person.' Jeffrey offered words that were at once apologetic and forgiving.

'I understand.' She glanced at her watch. 'It's getting late,' she said. 'I'll have to hurry.'

Brian and Denise were coming for dinner. She wanted to be home in time to heat up the cassoulet she had prepared that morning.

Jeffrey's solitary meal was already on the kitchen counter. A chicken breast, a small potato, a slice of tomato resting on a bright green lettuce leaf. She wondered if he listened to music as he ate. Was he addicted, as David was, to haunting requiems and mournful sonatas? The vagrant thought suffused her with sadness. They walked to the door together. He heaved the cartons laden with Sylvia's clothing into her car, lifted her hand to his lips.

'Thank you,' he said softly. 'Thank you for everything.'

She did not answer. She dared not confront his gratitude.

ELEVEN

D riving home, her car crowded with the cartons of clothing, it occurred to her that somehow, they had inadvertently violated the privacy that had been so important to Sylvia Kahn. But then the tables of the thrift shop overflowed with similar violations.

Death ended all sequestration. Judith thought of the woman, her eyes still red from days of weeping, her face pale, who had brought in a large white box that contained pastel-colored negligees of the finest batiste, each with a pair of matching satin slippers.

'My mother's,' she had said. 'She never let my sister or me touch them. She wasn't a vain woman, but this was her private treasure.'

That private treasure, of course, was, of necessity, violated. Set out for sale on a trestle table with other sleepwear, the delicate negligees were fingered, a slipper was lost, a pearl button loosened.

But that was as it should be, Judith thought, turning into her own street. The possessions of the deceased were passed on and life went on. The thrift shop offered the comfort of continuity, the affirmation of usefulness. Sylvia Kahn's cape draped the shoulders of a pale, sad-eyed young girl, just as Nancy's daughter now sat at Melanie's desk, placed her own secret treasures in the drawer that had once contained Melanie's diary. Belongings migrated into new homes, new lives, affording usefulness and pleasure.

The thought comforted her. She wondered if it would comfort Jeffrey Kahn, if she would dare offer it to him. But of course she would not. Their intimacy had its dangers. Boundaries, however fragile, had to be observed. She understood that they had, that afternoon, crossed into dangerous territory.

Music and quiet voices greeted her when she entered her home. Brian and Denise had arrived for dinner. Fragments of conversation drifted toward her. Brian and David spoke of meeting for lunch. Denise asked if David had chilled the wine.

Judith hurried into the room and buried herself in her son's embrace, delighted in his wet kiss upon her cheek. Even as a child, Brian's affection had been exuberant. Denise smiled shyly and said that she had set the table and made a salad. David kissed her cheek. His lips were as soft as Jeffrey Kahn's had been when they rested briefly on her hand.

'You look tired,' David said. 'I hope helping Jeffrey Kahn isn't too much for you?'

'I am tired,' she admitted. 'I think I'll leave it for a few days. I'll call Jeffrey and explain that I need time to concentrate on furnishing your office. Which I do.'

'It's beginning to really take shape,' Denise said brightly. 'Brian and I peeked in. The bookshelves are almost finished and they look terrific.'

'Terrific,' Brian agreed. 'It was a good idea to panel the walls.'

'Yes,' Judith said. 'It's working out well.'

She did not tell them that she still hesitated before entering the room, that her heart stopped when she stood in the doorway to consult with the electrician or the carpenter. Always she was stung anew by the swiftness with which Melanie's presence had been erased from their home.

She turned to Denise and asked, too brightly, how her course-work was progressing. She listened attentively to her reply, aware that David had poured another Scotch which he did not lift to his lips but simply swirled as he stared into the glass. She thought of Jeffrey Kahn staring into the darkness from his kitchen window, waiting for nocturnal warblers to peck seeds from his feeder and ease his loneliness. She chided herself for such useless fanciful thoughts and, in mute atonement, she reached out and touched David lightly on the cheek. He stared at her in surprise and smiled that shy smile that had melted her heart the day of their very first meeting and so many years afterward.

TWELVE

She called Jeffrey the next morning. He was not surprised that she wanted a respite. He understood that she was busy. As he was. He had, in fact, been about to call her. He had been invited to a medical conference in California and would be away for a week. He would be in touch when he returned if that was all right.

'Of course,' she said. 'We'll talk then.'

'Yes. We still have a great deal to do.'

'A great deal,' she agreed. 'Have a good journey.'

'Take care,' he said in turn.

Their words were casual, lightly uttered. They were mutually aware of the need for caution. Judith wondered if he would, in fact, call her when he returned. She wondered too if it would matter if he did not and knew with absolute certainty that it would.

She spent the morning at the thrift shop consulting with Suzanne about the prices they could charge for Sylvia Kahn's winter suits and dresses.

'It's all such wonderful quality,' Suzanne said. 'Designer stuff, some of it.'

She fingered the labels. Donna Karan. Ralph Lauren. A Prada jacket.

'We ought to send some of it to a consignment shop. We got a very good price for that gray cashmere dress.'

Judith recoiled at the suggestion. 'But Jeffrey Kahn donated the clothing to us,' she objected.

'The consignment shop will give us a percentage of whatever they sell them for, which is more than we could get here. I'm sure your Doctor Kahn would understand the decision,' Suzanne said impatiently.

Judith flushed hotly. 'He's hardly my Doctor Kahn. But I suppose you're right. The consignment shop does make sense.'

She left the thrift shop earlier than usual, annoyed with Suzanne, annoyed with herself. She drove to the upholstery store to look at swatches for the couch and armchair in David's office. She had settled on a couch which could be pulled open and become a bed, but she was torn between a brown tweed or a nubby gray. She deferred a decision and went home. It was time, she told herself, to return to her own work, to avoid what Evelyn called avoidance. The thought amused her. She opened her computer to the essay she had begun on George Eliot, tentatively entitled 'George Eliot: A Childless Chronicler of Children'. She had, ironically enough, copied out a singular Eliot quote on the day before Melanie's death. It confronted her as she opened the file, underlined and set in a bold font:

Childhood is soothed by no memories of outlived sorrow.

She reread it and wondered if she would ever outlive her own sorrow? Did anyone? Could anyone? Had Sylvia Kahn's parents ever outlived their sorrow for their dead and unburied children? The vagrant thought shamed her. Losses were not all weighed on the same scale.

She thought suddenly of Evelyn's harsh words during a very early session, when Judith, seated opposite her, had said again and again, 'Melanie is dead. My Melanie is dead.' She had used the repetition as a mantra that would force her to accept a grim, ineradicable reality. The wound of loss had been very raw then. No scab of the most reluctant acceptance, as Evelyn called it, had yet formed. No coping mechanisms had been in place.

Evelyn had tapped her notebook impatiently, taken a long sip of water and sighed when Judith repeated the same words yet again. 'Melanie is dead. My Melanie is dead.'

'Yes,' the therapist had finally said with uncharacteristic and perhaps unprofessional directness, 'Melanie is dead but you are alive, Judith. Remember that. You are alive and you must start to live your life.'

She wondered now what Evelyn would say to that simple sentence of George Eliot's. Perhaps she would ask her, but then again perhaps not.

She abandoned the computer and turned instead to her dog-eared copy of *The Mill on the Floss*. It was permissible for her to weep over Maggie Tulliver in the afternoon. Tears for Melanie were reserved for the evening hours.

* * *

She began the new week with a surge of energy, telling herself that Jeffrey Kahn's absence was a relief. David left for the city before she wakened and returned home later than usual.

'That new arbitration,' he said by way of explanation, and she did not press him for details.

With all her afternoons now free, she adhered to a new schedule. Early each morning she dutifully sat at her computer, surrounded by neat piles of her carefully annotated Eliot novels. She had decided on a new theme and opened a file, taking pleasure in the title that had come to mind with a swiftness that surprised her. 'Sorrow and Loss in the Work of George Eliot,' she typed in. Her attention was focused on *Middlemarch* and she read slowly, uncertain as always about what she hoped to find in the narrative. That, she thought, was the mystery and miracle of literature. Numinous worlds sprang into life; all that was hidden was serendipitously revealed. She wrote nothing, yet when she closed the novel and turned her computer off, she had a sense of accomplishment.

She took the long walks that Evelyn had so emphatically recommended and drove very slowly to her therapy appointment to proudly report that she had worked, she had walked, she was coping. A swift lunch and then the thrift shop.

She was relieved that Suzanne rarely asked her to open the shop in the morning. Suzanne's days, it seemed, began earlier and earlier and, accordingly, she opened the shop earlier and earlier.

'It's important to get an early start. There's always so much to do here,' she told Judith, perhaps officiously, perhaps apologetically or perhaps, Judith thought, both.

Judith had simply nodded, but she suspected that Suzanne, like herself, was in retreat from the silence of her home and the aimless hours of a long and lonely morning. The thrift shop offered them entry into an alternate and absorbing world, populated by a roving cast of characters.

Judith recognized repeat shoppers, some who offered her their names in shy bids for familiarity, others who refused to make eye contact. A very tall black man, sad-eyed, his thick hair pewter-colored, came often, sometimes in search of a woman's nightgown, sometimes looking for a robe.

He specified that they had to be blue. 'She loves the color blue,' he said.

The nightgown had to be cotton because she hated the feel of polyester. The robe had to be soft because her skin was very sensitive.

Judith found him a blue belted robe of soft velour and he smiled gratefully.

'I'll bring it to her in the hospital today,' he said. 'She'll be glad of it. She's sick, very sick.'

A week later he returned and placed a shopping bag on the counter. 'I give them back to you,' he said. 'My daughter washed and ironed them. After. You know . . . After . . .'

He hurried out and Judith opened the bag and stared down at the impeccably laundered, neatly folded blue nightgown and robe. She did know. *After.* She recognized the monosyllabic language she herself had so recently abandoned.

A smiling, full-figured woman, olive-skinned, her eyes very large and very dark, arrived regularly on the day hospital workers received their checks. She searched methodically through the children's clothing. Her name was Consuela, she told Judith. She was from Guatemala where life was very hard and she was blessed to be in New York, to have a good job at the hospital. An important job.

'I clean. I make everything nice for the sick people,' she said proudly.

She plucked up rompers for toddlers, sweatshirts with the logos of sports teams for teenaged boys, girls' blouses spangled with sequins.

'For my grandchildren,' she said in her lilting Spanish-accented English. 'The children of my daughter. They say always, "What you bring me, *Abuela Consuela*?" Even my littlest, Rosalita. That *bambina*. She loves dresses the colors of flowers. Pink. Green. Yellow.'

Judith plucked sundresses 'the colors of flowers' and set them aside for tiny Rosalita.

Consuela smiled her gratitude. '*Gracias, Señora Judith*. You are so kind. You make me so happy. You make Rosalita happy.'

Judith treasured her words. It had been a long time since she had made anyone happy.

She knew most of the volunteers, both those who appeared infrequently and those who came regularly. Lois and Libby were the stalwarts, their hours coinciding with her own. She knew about Lois's daughter's allergy, about Libby's twin sons' learning problems and her intrusive mother-in-law. Some of the volunteers spoke incessantly, as they sorted through donations or when they shared tepid coffee during a lull. Others listened, smiled and nodded, all of them aware that their membership of this odd sorority was a combination of altruism and need. Their conviviality was comforting and relaxing, their revelations sometimes trivial – a child had not been invited to a birthday party, an anniversary had been ignored – sometimes heavy with an embarrassing intimacy.

Andrea Weinstein, who came in on Tuesday afternoons, an attractive, dark-haired young woman who spoke with a breathy intensity, confided that she had undergone three IVF treatments in her attempt to become pregnant. 'We're talking about adoption now,' she said.

Opinions were offered as donated garments were folded and priced. An older woman advised against adoption. 'Who knows what the genetic background is?' she asked. 'Do the agencies tell you about hereditary diseases? It's so risky.'

'Having a child at all is risky,' Judith said drily. 'A healthy child with an impeccable genetic history can fall ill. There are no guarantees.'

Her own words, the dispassion of her tone, surprised her. There was an uneasy silence. The volunteers all knew about Melanie. Their kindness did not allow them to reply.

At last a pale young woman spoke very softly. 'Our son and daughter are both adopted. We never thought of it as a risk. We just wanted children, a family. And we're happy to have them.'

Suzanne sat in stony silence and then, too abruptly, left the room.

Libby steered the conversation into a safer precinct.

Occasionally, late in the afternoon, when it was clear that there would be no more shoppers, a pot of fresh coffee was brewed and unmatched mugs from the sale table were stacked on an upturned carton. Cookies were produced from a battered tin and placed on the delicate rose-patterned china dessert plates, which never seemed to sell. Judith handled them carefully. Someone had treasured them. The rose patterns were faded but they were unchipped.

At such impromptu coffee hours, the volunteers sat in a circle on stools and wooden boxes and stirred their coffee with tarnished silver spoons. They knew that their makeshift table was set with the unwanted discards of dining rooms that had once resonated with chatter and laughter. They indulged in occasional bouts of curiosity. Who had owned the charming Delft sugar bowl? Why had that Bennington pottery casserole never been used? They tossed such questions out but did not expect answers.

They traded inconsequential bits of gossip, speculating about a synagogue scandal, a rumored affair between a divorced man and married woman, the startling bankruptcy of a village shop. They talked about congregants who seemed adrift, those who were single or widowed.

'Do you think Jeffrey Kahn will marry again? He's not that old and he's so attractive,' Andrea Weinstein said.

'What do you think, Judith?' Lois asked.

'I have no idea,' she replied, determinedly keeping her tone light.

They drifted into a discussion of how kind it would be to invite people who lived alone to dinner, although no such invitations seemed to be forthcoming.

Judith relaxed and allowed their chatter to float toward her. The luxury of unscheduled time and laconic talk was new to her. She had always been too busy for such an indulgence, lunch hours consumed by errands, her moleskin notebooks crammed with tightly written lists. She had glanced at such an outdated list recently, reading it as though it was written in a foreign language.

Brian's winter coat into storage.
Manuscript to the MLA journal.
Butcher and greengrocer.
Grades to the registrar.
Melanie to ballet class.
Melanie to tennis lesson.
Such lists had lost their relevance. Her world had shrunk,

her obligations were minimal. She was on sabbatical – no grades to be filed, no manuscripts to be mailed. Denise would now see that Brian's winter coat was taken into storage. David was seldom home for dinner. There was no need to rush to the butcher or the supermarket. And, of course, never again would she drive to a tennis lesson or a ballet class. She had wept briefly then and placed the notebook very gently into a seldom-opened drawer.

Late one afternoon a boating accident on the Hudson was discussed. A young girl had been killed. A television reporter had chased after the bereaved mother, thrusting a microphone at her and asking again and again how she had reacted to her daughter's death.

'What a stupid man,' Lois said indignantly. 'How does any parent react to a child's death?'

Another awkward silence. Again all eyes were averted from Judith who stared straight ahead. They dispersed swiftly, their relief evident, when a new group of chattering shoppers entered.

It was pay day at the hospital, and aides and orderlies, still in their uniforms, were happily searching for end-of-the-day bargains.

Judith hurried to offer assistance, to help Consuela find a bathing suit that might fit tiny Rosalita, and a sundress for Rosalita's sister, Juanita. There was no time to speculate about loss and grief, no time to imagine the unimaginable. All thoughts of the drowned girl were banished as piles of blouses and sweaters were tossed about. Wire hangers clattered to the floor. Consuela found a tiny bathing suit in a floral pattern, a pink sundress that had a small tear which she could easily mend.

Judith returned to the cash register and accepted five dollars from a weary, sad-eyed young woman who purchased the carefully folded white tennis dress that Melanie had never worn. The public school was offering tennis lessons. The lessons were free, the rackets lent by the school, but her daughter had craved a tennis dress and she was happy to find one. Judith listened. Agreed that tennis was a wonderful sport and congratulated herself that her eyes remained dry as she wrapped the small garment in tissue paper and placed it in a Walmart bag.

*   *   *

She was tired when she arrived home. There were two messages on the answering machine. David would not be home for dinner. A late meeting. An even later conference call. He sounded neither regretful nor apologetic. The second message was from Jeffrey Kahn. He would be in California for an additional week. He would call her when he returned. He sounded both regretful and apologetic. He hesitated and then added that he hoped she was well. It was, she realized, as close as he dared come to saying anything daring and personal. He had chosen his words carefully. She sighed and counted the days until his return. Seven. Perhaps eight. Not such a long time.

She made herself an omelet and ate it while rereading the last chapter of *Middlemarch*. Sipping her coffee, she marveled at how well George Eliot perceived the intricacies of a long marriage, or perhaps a too-long marriage, and how fluidly she wrote of death.

She snapped the book closed. She wondered how she herself might write about death. It was an exercise that Evelyn had daringly proposed and which she had immediately dismissed. Of course she would not, of course she could not. Her hand trembled and droplets of coffee spattered the table.

The phone rang. It was Brian, his voice buoyant, dishes clattering in the background, Denise singing softly. She imagined her son smiling, happy in his student apartment, happy with his Denise who sang as she washed the dishes. The thought of his happiness soothed and calmed her. How fortunate she and David had been to have untroubled and untroubling Brian as a son. How fortunate Melanie had been to have such a wonderful big brother. How odd that the thought did not sadden her. Was the lack of sadness what Evelyn called 'acceptance'?

'Hey, Mom, is Dad there? I want to ask him something about arbitration law,' Brian said.

'Dad's working late,' she replied.

'You OK, Mom?'

She realized that her voice was muffled, choked off by a confusion of thoughts and that intrusive rejected word. *Acceptance.* How was it recognized?

'Fine,' she assured him. 'Just a little tired.'

Too swiftly, she reminded him to give her love to Denise.

Too swiftly, he told her that Denise sent her own love. Judith assured him that she would leave David a note asking him to call. He assured her that it would not be necessary. He would reach his father at the office the next day.

'Goodnight, Mom.'

'Goodnight, darling.'

She carried her coffee upstairs and paused outside the closed door of the room that had been Melanie's. She did not go in but inhaled the scent of fresh paint and new wood. The furniture she had selected would soon be delivered. A computer table and an office chair. The sleep-sofa and armchair finally upholstered in nubby tweed. Soon it would be known only as David's office. Which, she told herself firmly, was as it should be. That was perhaps 'acceptance'. Was that the second or the third stage of grief? She could not remember, but it was of no importance. She rejected all those clever clinical definitions. She had not denied and she would not accept.

In their bedroom, she lay down on the bed without undressing and fell asleep instantly. David, arriving home very late, gently removed her shoes.

How beautiful she is, he thought.

If she wakened, he would tell her so. He pressed his lips to her cool cheek, but she did not stir. He covered her with a light blanket and placed his hand briefly and gently upon her head.

THIRTEEN

Brian was worried. He had, in fact, been vaguely worried about his parents since Melanie's death. He himself had slowly, very slowly, recovered from his own shock and slowly, very slowly, he had learned to manage his own terrible sorrow, to grasp the stark finality of the loss of his beloved sister. His nights of weeping had ended, the heaviness of his heart had gradually lightened, the shadow of lingering depression had at last lifted, replaced by a transient, manageable sadness. It was only then, during the days of his own recuperation, that he had, reluctantly, recognized what Denise had realized much earlier. His parents were lost to an impenetrable and dangerous despair, each hugging grief unshared, each weighted by separate and solitary sorrow.

Concern for his very self-sufficient mother and father was new to him. Their family life had always been suffused with calm, his mother in control, his father quietly purposeful. Asked to describe his parents' marriage as an exercise in his introductory psychology class, he had said simply, 'Strong, very strong.'

He could remember no anger and very few quarrels during his childhood. Yes, his parents were quiet, sometimes disarmingly quiet. There was a period when he had felt a melancholy in their silence. It was Melanie's birth, he knew, that had released them from that uneasy sadness into a new and happier time suffused with merriment and laughter. He had marveled at their patience and their pleasure as Melanie had tumbled through a charming infancy and an exuberant childhood. How mischievous, how playful she had been, his sister, his little sister.

He had adored her – he and his Denise both. He had been overwhelmed by her death, so painless, so terrible in its suddenness. He understood that her heart had stopped. Inexplicable and uncommon, a doctor friend had explained and went on to speak about the mysterious origins of aneurysms, but Brian had stopped listening. Terrified, he had touched his own heart.

Terrified, he had touched Denise's heart, pressed his ear to her chest and listened to its strong, steady beat as she wept and he wept, their tears melding.

Paralyzed by his own grief during those first bewildering weeks after the ritual of shiva, he was certain that his parents – his strong, self-sufficient mother, his calm father – would sustain each other. They would be all right, he told Denise. They were strong, very strong.

He now knew that he had been mistaken. The emotional seesaw on which Judith and David had been so evenly balanced for so many years no longer steadied them. Melanie's death had catapulted them on to an unforgiving surface of loss and danger. He realized that their mourning was silent and unshared, each hoarding discrete shards of fragmented grief.

He was newly grateful for Denise's exuberant and compassionate love. The daughter of a large and raucous family, she was accustomed to explosions of wild rage and swift reconciliations. She understood his tears and outbursts of grief, and she assuaged his melancholy. She herself had loved Melanie, had thought of her as yet another younger sister, perhaps irritating at times but always adorable. She spoke of her still with sweet tenderness.

Denise contrived to coax him into laughter, even as she allowed him to mourn, recognizing his needs as he, in turn, recognized hers.

Meeting as undergraduates, with the greatest of ease they had become friends; with even greater ease they became lovers. They had studied together, holding hands as they took notes and turned pages. They hiked the Palisades, tall Brian slowing his stride so that Denise, who was so much shorter, could keep up with him. They cooked together in their student apartment, Denise, with her oversized red-framed glasses always sliding down her nose, clusters of rose-gold curls framing her cheerful face, choosing eclectic recipes that required mysterious herbs and spices. Brian obediently and cheerfully dashed out to the supermarket in search of coriander or cumin. He loved her penchant for chaos, her talent for serendipitous adventure, so different from his parents' orderly, organized lives. They became engaged during their senior year. Denise's large, energetic family was delighted. Melanie had danced with excitement. Judith and David had been more restrained.

'You're both so young,' David said.

'You and Mom were just as young,' he countered.

'Different circumstances. Our situation was different.'

David did not elaborate and Brian did not argue. His parents never spoke of their childhoods. He knew only that all four of his grandparents, dead before his birth, were not spoken of with tenderness. He assumed that his mother and father, both, had been in flight from unhappy homes and miraculously had found happiness and love when they found each other.

He had seen the photo album in which Judith had pasted the faded snapshots that recorded their college courtship. There they were, holding hands as they lay beneath a tree. There was Judith, her dark hair caught up in a ponytail, laughing as she looked up at David whose hand rested on her head.

Melanie, of course, bubbled over with enthusiasm. She had loved Denise, had been enchanted by the idea of a wedding, delighted that Denise had asked her to be a junior bridesmaid. She had studied bridal magazines, asked fabric stores for swatches of magenta velvet, magenta silk, magenta satin, all of which she tucked into the crowded cubbies of her desk.

'It will be a wonderful wedding,' she'd told their parents. 'I will wear a magenta gown. I will carry a bouquet of magenta-colored flowers. All my friends are jealous of me.'

Humming the wedding march, she had gripped Denise's hands and danced about the living room with her.

Brian, watching his sister and his bride, saw his mother smile and glance at his father. He was relieved. His parents would not be able to resist Melanie's excitement. It would all work out, he had told himself hopefully.

And then, on a day tinged with the warmth of a hesitant early spring, he had checked his voicemail and heard his father tell him, in a voice so weighted with grief that it was beyond recognition, that his sister was dead.

'Dead.' The word was repeated, followed by an intake of breath and he had understood that his father was crying. 'Dead.' Then a terrible silence. No words would suffice.

That silence had prevailed. It was Denise who observed that, during their frequent visits, David and Judith spoke to each other with a calm civility but without affection. Their coolness angered and bewildered her. 'They should be comforting each other,' she said after one awkward visit.

'I know,' Brian agreed sadly.

He knew that his father now spent more and more evenings in the city, arriving home later and later, or, as it had happened, on very few occasions, not coming home at all. His mother had told him as much, and her seeming indifference to those absences troubled him. Something was wrong, terribly wrong.

And then, one afternoon, rushing across Bryant Park on his way to the library in search of an obscure text, he saw his father and a silver-haired woman having lunch in the outdoor café. He recognized her, having seen her in his father's office and taken note of her distinctive hair. He remembered suddenly that her name was Nancy and recalled that the furniture in Melanie's room had been given to her small daughter. He hurried away, reluctant to approach them. He told himself that it was possible that they had met for lunch to discuss a business problem. Possible but not likely. Glancing back, he saw that their heads were bent close and he wondered if their hands were touching.

The scene haunted him throughout the day and that evening he told Denise about it. 'I don't understand what is happening,' he said worriedly. 'Things are weird between my parents, but I can't imagine my dad being unfaithful.'

'Why don't you have lunch with your father?' Denise suggested. 'It might help him to talk to you. Father-and-son stuff.'

'Don't get carried away by your one three-credit course in family dynamics,' he cautioned her. 'You're not a licensed social worker yet.'

'I'm as much a social worker as you are a lawyer,' she retorted.

They laughed. Laughter came easily to them.

'We have to remember,' he said more seriously, 'that this is a very hard time for my parents. A terrible time. Melanie was the center of their lives. She gave meaning to their marriage.'

'I think it's very sad that they needed Melanie to give meaning to their marriage. If Melanie is dead, does that mean their marriage is dead, that it has no meaning? I think not. I hope not.' She chose her words carefully and held his hand as she spoke. 'They do love each other.'

He thought of those faded snapshots, his mother's face wreathed in tenderness, his father's bright with laughter. 'Of course, they live in different worlds,' he continued. 'They always have. Literature for my mother. Business for my father. And that was all right. They never needed words. But they did need each other. They had what I'd call a quiet happiness. They adored Melanie. They were wonderful parents, caring parents to both of us. And I tried very hard to be a good son.'

He trembled, drew her close, pressed his cheek against the fragrant softness of her wild, thick hair.

'You *are* a good son,' she murmured.

'Yes. I suppose I am. I love them a lot but I sometimes felt that I was an actor in a play and that it was very important that I say my lines correctly so that I wouldn't disturb their calm, so that I wouldn't upset them. I feel it even more now. I don't want to disturb their sorrow. Does that sound crazy to you, Denise?'

She did not answer at once, remembering how her first visits to his home, so different from her own raucous household, had surprised her, even intimidated her. She too had rehearsed her words, orchestrated her actions, careful not to speak too loudly, to weigh her words, certain that David and Judith were quietly judgmental. She had been grateful, then, for Melanie's exuberance, her outbursts of laughter, her gaiety and spontaneity. Denise had been at ease with Melanie who enthused over her small surprise gifts – the magenta scrunchies for her dark hair as irrepressible as Denise's own copper-colored curls, the stationery embossed with her initials, an iTunes gift card.

When Melanie told them that she was doing a school project on the Amish, Denise had suggested that the three of them, Brian, Denise and Melanie, spend a weekend in Lancaster, Pennsylvania. She had brought guide books and she and Melanie had spread them across the dining-room table and read them aloud to each other. They would stay on an Amish farm that doubled as a bed and breakfast. They would ride in an Amish buggy. They might milk a cow. Melanie had giggled. She had never seen a cow.

'Oh, it'll be such fun.' She had clapped her hands and danced around the room, hugging Denise, hugging Brian.

David and Judith had smiled. Denise felt that she had struck a home run. Nothing delighted Brian's parents as much as Melanie's delight. They spoke of joining the excursion to Pennsylvania.

But, of course, they had never visited Amish country. Melanie died the week before they were to leave. Her death incomprehensible. Their sorrow overwhelmed. *It was unfair! So unfair!* They shouted out their anger, wept their way through their rage, then held each other close, seeking comfort in touch, consolation in talk.

Denise, ever resilient, slowly emerged from the miasma of sadness. She struggled to cope with Brian's grief and her own. She would comfort Brian's parents as best she could. She promised herself to tread carefully, but she was resolute.

She infused their dinners with spates of chatter, questions that demanded answers. How had Judith prepared the delicious soup? What did David think of an incipient labor crisis? She nodded at their monosyllabic answers and prattled bravely on, Brian's foot nudging hers beneath the table, Judith and David staring at each other unseeingly.

She asked Judith to meet her for lunch or perhaps for a visit to a museum. Judith always politely declined, but Denise persisted. She congratulated herself on her role in encouraging Judith to volunteer at the thrift shop. She told herself that it was good for Judith to get out of the house, to have a routine. It was good that Judith was helping this Dr Kahn sort through his late wife's clothing. It was yet another step toward coping. Her text for a course on grief counseling claimed that recovery was always a process, never a resolution. Mourners, the author emphasized, had to understand that there was life after a loved one's death. Denise dared not mention that to Judith. She was careful, very careful. Like Brian, she rehearsed her conversations with his parents.

His question did not surprise her. She knew how careful he was not to upset them, especially during the dark days of their unrelieved, unstructured grief. But she thought it important that Brian abandon all care, all constraint, and speak to David with unrehearsed honesty.

'I think your father needs you,' she said firmly. 'I think it would help him to talk to you, to really open up. If he can.'

He nodded. 'All right. I'll try to meet him for lunch, but I'm not sure he'll have the time. His work schedule is overwhelming. There are nights when he doesn't get home for dinner.'

'And that's because he's working late?' she asked drily.

Her question gave voice to his own suspicions. 'I don't know,' he admitted. 'And I'm not sure I want to know. But yes, we'll have lunch. I'll insist.'

They clung to each other then, her head buried in his chest. She was relieved that he had accepted her suggestion and that he had not been angered by the question she had asked and its dark implications.

David, although surprised at Brian's invitation to lunch, agreed without hesitation. Brian suggested an Italian restaurant that he and Denise favored, choosing it because it was in neutral territory, equidistant from his father's office and the university. Neither his father's colleagues nor his classmates would interrupt their conversation.

They both arrived exactly on time and were welcomed by the overweight blonde hostess. She flashed them her brilliant professional smile as she led them to a table.

'So nice to see a father and son having lunch together,' she said and handed them the oversized menus.

It surprised Brian that she had so swiftly recognized their relationship but, looking at their joint reflection in the mirror opposite their table, he realized, for the first time, how like his father he looked. They were both tall and thin, sharp-featured and lantern-jawed, their thick dark hair closely cut. How odd that they should so closely resemble each other and yet be so dissimilar in temperament, something that Denise had noticed at once. He himself was given to easy laughter, a lightness of mood and spirit, whereas David was always serious and sober, a man whose gait was heavy, almost clumsy, and whose words were uttered with great care. Even their tastes in music and literature were different. Brian was addicted to historical fiction while David read only dense biographies and histories. Novels, classics included, did not interest him. Classical music absorbed him while Brian, like his mother, treated music only as background.

He wondered, as he stared across the table at his father, if his parents had ever listened to music together. But of course they had. He remembered now. There had been subscriptions to the Philharmonic and to chamber music concerts, quiet evenings when they sat together in the living room as opera played and David fingered a libretto. Such memories offered him odd comfort, made his dark suspicions seem foolish.

'Good to see you, Dad,' he said.

David nodded. 'This was a good idea, Brian,' he said. 'I'm glad you suggested it.'

The pleasure in his smile filled Brian with guilt. The idea for this meeting had not been his own and he was not glad to see his father.

They studied the menus with great seriousness and discussed their choices, relieved to have something to talk about. Would the pasta be too heavy? Would the fish be really fresh?

They ordered too quickly, pasta for Brian and fish for David, then stared uneasily at each other. Brian filled their water glasses. David coughed and asked Brian about his courses.

'I'm doing all right,' Brian said. 'But not as well as last semester.'

'That's understandable. You've had a distraction.'

Brian cringed. Was Melanie's death a distraction?

David hastily corrected himself. 'It's been a hard time. You'll do better next semester,' he added and recognized that his words were still sadly inadequate, clumsily phrased. Judith would have spoken more sensitively, he knew. But then she lived in a world of words. Grace in both movement and locution came naturally to her. How proud he had always been of that easy grace. Watching her walk toward him had always filled him with wonder – wonder that she had chosen him, that they had chosen each other.

Their food arrived. David discussed a difficult arbitration he was working on.

Brian pretended interest and then set his fork down too heavily. 'I don't want to talk about your work, Dad.'

'I thought it would interest you,' David said evenly, and he continued eating.

'I'm worried about you. About you and Mom.'

He knew he was speaking too directly. Denise would not approve. She had advised caution, a discussion of his own feelings, his own sense of loss. She had suggested he ask questions.

'What sort of questions?' he had asked. He had refrained from reminding her that they had decided he would not rehearse this conversation.

'Like "Is anything bothering you, Dad?"'

He would ignore that suggested question, imagining what the answer might be.

Of course something is bothering me. The same thing that is bothering you. My daughter – your sister – is dead.

Not that those words would be spoken. His father had always guarded his emotional privacy, hoarding all expressions of anger and sorrow. Only Melanie had been able to coax him into demonstrations of gay affection and sudden bursts of laughter.

'Very worried,' he continued.

David nodded, plucked a piece of garlic bread from the basket and shredded it slowly, methodically, building a small hillock of oily white crumbs.

'Of course, you're worried,' he said at last. 'I'm worried myself.'

'What's happening, Dad?' Brian's voice was gentle now, reminiscent of David's own tone during his childhood when he had offered comfort over a boyhood sadness, perhaps rejection from a team, a disappointing grade on an exam. Hugs were foreign to David, but it had been his way to take Brian's hand in his own and stroke it gently, as though the gesture might erase the transient wound. But now their roles were strangely reversed. Brian felt himself to be the comforter and thought that he might reach across the table and take his father's hand in his own and stroke it. Instead, he twirled a piece of pasta on to his fork but did not eat it.

'Since your sister . . .' David paused, breathed hard. 'Since our Melanie died.' His voice trailed off. He lifted his water glass, took a sip and waited for a restoration of courage. He would be careful but he would be honest. He knew that what he had to say could not be easily said. But he would try. He had to try. He owed it to Brian. He owed it to himself. He spoke very slowly but he did not stutter. For that he was grateful. 'Things have been very difficult for us, for your mother and me,' he continued. 'We find it difficult to talk to each other, to share what should be shared. Both of us so deeply loved our Melanie.'

Brian nodded. 'Of course I know that,' he said.

'And I think you also know that her birth came as a surprise to us,' David continued. 'We had thought to have a large family, but the years passed and it seemed then that you would be our only child. You were a wonderful son. We loved you and were so proud of you. Still, we were disappointed and that disappointment became toxic. We feared for our marriage. And then Melanie was born. She pulled us back together. She filled our lives. She became the hub of our lives, the focus of our future. Do you remember the plans your mother made for this year? She did not call it her sabbatical year; she called it Melanie's year – a time we all would share in new vistas of excitement. Everything planned to delight Melanie. And then . . .' Again his voice trailed off. He struggled for control, his eyes cast downward. He took a sip of water, spoke more softly. 'And then she was gone. Our only vista now is one of darkness. Yes. We have you but you have your own life, which is as it should be. We are alone again, your mother and I. Together yet alone. And unprepared.'

'Unprepared?' Brian repeated. 'Unprepared for what?'

'Unprepared for each other, for an empty togetherness. I do not know what to say to her. She does not know what to say to me. We are trapped in a silence of our own making. Do you know that for a long time after Melanie died I could not say her name? It stuck in my throat, it burned my brain. I saw how this wounded your mother. But I had no words. How could I comfort her when I could not comfort myself? I told myself that she would cope, my strong Judith, your wonderful mother. Hadn't she always? And she did. While I choked on my sorrow, she took control of her mourning. She went to a therapist. She took long walks. She developed a routine. Her volunteer hours at the thrift shop, the hours she spends helping Jeffrey Kahn

. . . Such a nice man, Jeffrey, gentle, considerate. I knew him when his family lived on our street. I suppose he and your mother, spending so many hours together, offer each other comfort.'

'Only comfort?' Brian asked and hated himself for the question that had come unbidden.

'Of course. Only comfort.' David's tone was curt, his gaze unflinching. 'We are speaking about your mother, Brian. I have never, in all our years together, had any reason to doubt her. I do not doubt her now. We have always been faithful to each other. I only wish she were happier, that I had the power to make her happy, to puncture her sadness.'

'But you yourself say that she is much better, that she is coping. It will take time, but she'll be herself again,' Brian protested, recognizing the hollowness of his words, knowing that he was struggling to reassure himself as well as his father.

'Yes. That is what I tell myself. Because I love her so much. Because I know she loves me still. But at night, when she thinks I am asleep, she cries. Very quietly. Her grief is her own. She does not invite me to share it.'

David reached again for his water glass, took a long sip, then scattered the small mound of crumbs across the cloth.

'And you. Do you reach out to her? Did you?' Brian asked. He thought of his own nocturnal tears in the days after the funeral and how Denise's hands had been so soft and gentle upon his face, as she wiped the tears away and then entangled her body in his, an embrace of comfort and tenderness. He regretted the harshness of his question, the subdued anger of his tone. He braced himself for his father's resentment, but it was a voice laced with calm and regret that answered him.

'I could not cry with her. Tears did not come to me. And I could not reach out to her. Not then. Not now. My touch is too uneasy, my movements too uncertain. I do not have her gift for words. I feared her rejection, her impatience. I am a clumsy man, a clumsy man married to a graceful woman. Your mother once studied ballet. Did you know that, Brian?' David asked.

'No. Yes. Maybe.'

Yes. He vaguely recalled talk at the dinner table about ballet, Melanie wanting lessons, his mother rising suddenly, uncharacteristically, to laughingly demonstrate a plié. He remembered Melanie proudly showing Denise a newly purchased pair of ballet slippers and a tutu. The ballet slippers had been of white satin, the tutu of a gauzy pink fabric, Melanie's cheeks as bright as polished apples as she put the white slippers on and danced across the room on tiptoe. His heart turned. With each memory of his sister, he mourned her anew.

'But, finally, I too found a place to cry,' David continued. 'Quite by accident. Nancy Cummings, a colleague, with whom I had worked on a couple of projects, was on leave when Melanie died. She only learned about it months later and she came to my office to offer her condolences. Her words, after such a long period of silence, took me by surprise. She took my hand, and when I felt her touch, I began to weep. I couldn't explain it then and I can't explain it now. I sat at my desk and wept. Nancy kept my hand in hers and over lunch the next day she told me that her young husband had been killed in a car crash when she was pregnant with her daughter. A death sudden and unpredictable. She understood what it was to suffer a devastating loss that swept in without warning. We have a common language. She understands and she does not judge. I go to her apartment and I sit on her couch and I cry. And then I help Lauren, her daughter, with her homework. You remember that we gave all Melanie's furniture to Nancy. So I, a man without a daughter, help a little girl without a father, to understand the new math. I do this at Melanie's desk, sitting on that little chair Melanie loved. And sometimes I have dinner with them, and Lauren chatters away just as Melanie used to. And sometimes I am so very tired that I fall asleep on Nancy's couch. Nancy and I work together, which means that we have lunch together. That is when she sometimes weeps. We are – she and I – partners in a grief exchange. I am not having an affair with her. As I told you, I have always been faithful to your mother, as she has been faithful to me. You have no need to worry. Nor does your mother.'

'She doesn't know I'm worried. She doesn't know we're meeting,' Brian said.

He thought to tell his father that he had seen him with Nancy Cummings in Bryant Park, but he said nothing. That incidental sighting, his unfounded painful suspicion, seemed irrelevant now.

'No. I suppose not. I did not mention it to her. Nor have I told her about Nancy. Perhaps I should have. Perhaps I will.' His voice was newly hoarse. He had not meant to say as much. He had not meant to burden Brian with such an outpouring of confidences. It was not fair to his son.

'Of course you should tell her about Nancy,' Brian said, his voice steady although his words were tinged with uncertainty.

David sighed. 'I'm afraid that she would see my reliance on Nancy as a betrayal, an infidelity of a kind. She is, I think, tired of dealing with my needs, my weaknesses. And I, perhaps, am tired of living in an emotional desert.'

The waitress brought their coffee. David laced it with too much sugar and stirred it too vigorously.

'An emotional desert,' he repeated, as though startled by his own use of a metaphor. Metaphors were Judith's domain.

'I think that she has a right to know about Nancy,' Brian said softly. 'I think you owe her that. What she may imagine is probably worse than the truth. I think she will understand.' He wondered if he himself understood, but he respected his father's honesty.

David nodded. 'You may be right. Probably you are right. I will tell her. If she asks. If she cares enough to ask.'

'She cares enough,' Brian said.

He watched his father glance at the bill and calculate the tip. A careful man, a generous man, grief-laden, tenaciously faithful. He was a man who had choked on the name of his dead daughter but had finally found the strength, at last, to say it aloud. It was, Brian knew, Nancy Cummings who had given him that courage, but it was Judith, his wife, Brian's mother, whom he loved. Suffused with relief, he smiled at his father who smiled back.

They stood in the doorway of the restaurant and embraced, the father and son who looked almost like brothers.

*   *   *

Brian held Denise very close that night.

'I don't want us to ever wander away from each other,' he said.

'We won't,' she assured him, her hand resting on his head. 'How could that ever happen?'

It was not a question that required an answer. He kissed her into silence.

FOURTEEN

The chill of early spring drifted into the sweet warmth of approaching summer. Judith, on her morning walk, thought of picnics and light suppers, after-dinner strolls along streets brushed with last pale rays of dying sunlight. It was a season she had always loved. She thought of their student days when she and David had walked at the twilight hour wrapped in a companionable silence. She remembered that when Brian was a toddler they had rented a small house in an unfashionable town on the Jersey shore before the onset of summer. Rates had been affordable. They were on the cusp of a new prosperity, but as always they were careful. Small Brian had jumped fearlessly into the waves and they had hugged each other, their eyes riveted to their courageous son, and decided that it was time to have another child. A girl, a boy? It would not matter, they had assured each other. They had been so young then, so confident that the future was theirs to mold. It had never occurred to them that their plans could be thwarted.

Walking past a bed of daffodils, nursing that memory, she felt a burst of optimism. Perhaps she and David could yet reclaim the closeness that had been theirs during that long-past summer. *Perhaps.* On impulse, before going to the thrift shop, she stopped at a gourmet store and bought a wedge of brie and a focaccia loaf. There was, she recalled, a bottle of white wine in the fridge. They might eat in their garden or even wander down to the river and share a meal at the water's edge. A line from Emily Dickinson sprang into memory. 'There were times when hope had to be helped along,' the poet had written with wry wisdom. That was what she would try to do. Help hope along.

The thrift shop was crowded when she arrived. The new warmth brought a surge of shoppers intent on preparing for the approaching season. Sweaters and woolen clothing, winter jackets and scarves were removed from the trestle tables and

carted to a storage closet and replaced with colorful pyramids
of sleeveless dresses and blouses, T-shirts and shorts. A plastic
bin of bathing suits with a crayoned sign advising that they
could neither be tried on nor returned was placed in a discreet
corner. Suzanne's standards remained high. All items were
impeccably clean and gently used.

Judith took charge of the summer outlay of children's and
infant clothing. She loved the feel of the soft cotton layette
garments and the smoothness of the polished cotton sundresses
and playsuits. She smiled at the logos on discarded T-shirts, the
silk-screened images of Oscar the Grouch, Bert and Ernie, the
Little Mermaid, Princess Elsa and superheroes flying across
cotton surfaces long since faded. It would not be long now, she
thought, before a graduate student wrote a learned thesis on
contemporary history as reflected in T-shirt logos. She had
vetoed less ridiculous proposals.

She set aside a tiny shirt and rompers of sunshine yellow on
which tiny blue birds danced. It had never been worn; the price
tag still dangled. She wanted Emily's dark-haired baby to wear
something that was brand new.

Emily, when she arrived late that afternoon, was delighted
with the outfit. As always, she shopped swiftly and decisively,
a smile wreathing her heart-shaped face as she plucked up a
hooded bath towel for the baby, a sea-green short-sleeved cotton
shirt for her husband. They talked easily as Judith rang up her
purchases. She and Judith had established a casual intimacy
during her frequent visits. Judith now knew that Emily and her
husband, James, had emigrated from Korea. James was a medical
student who worked part-time as a technician at the local
teaching hospital and they lived in a one-room basement
apartment.

'Very small but very clean,' Emily said. 'We are fortunate.'

Fortunate too that he had a scholarship and a small stipend
from the university as well as a very small hourly salary. There
was no complaint in her voice.

Emily was a registered nurse and it had been their plan that
she would work until he qualified, but then she became pregnant
and Jane was born.

'A surprise for us, our baby,' she said, her voice charmingly accented. 'So we are poorer than we had planned, but we manage.'

'A wonderful surprise,' Judith agreed and thought to tell her that she too had had a surprise child, but knew, of course, that she would not, could not, speak of Melanie. She did not want to frighten Emily nor did she want her sympathy.

'Of course you will manage,' she added.

'Things will change,' Emily said. 'James will be a doctor. We will have our own house. Jane will have brand-new clothes. But thank you for finding this.'

She held up the shirt and rompers, the sun-gold hue of the soft fabric almost a match for her sleeping child's delicate skin. She beamed her gratitude at Judith who smiled back at her. As Emily fumbled for her purse, Judith opened her arms and took the baby from her. She pressed her cheek against Jane's satin-smooth hair, inhaled the sweet scent of her tiny body, sniffed her milky breath. The infant, her eyes still closed, her long lashes sweeping her cheek, chortled softly, and Judith imitated the sound. She swayed back and forth, a motion that had always soothed and delighted her own babies, first Brian and then Melanie. The memory pierced her heart.

As she shifted the baby on to her shoulder, the door to the thrift shop opened. She turned. Jeffrey Kahn stood in the entrance, staring at her, a half smile playing at his lips. Flustered and flushed, she surrendered the baby to Emily who, as always, made her farewell with a slight bow. She bowed again as she passed Jeffrey in the doorway, almost brushing against him as she struggled to balance the baby and the plastic carrier bag that held her purchases.

'Judith,' Jeffrey said, smiling, moving toward her, his hand outstretched to grasp her own. 'It's good to see you.'

'And good to see you, Jeffrey,' she said, aware that Suzanne had turned as he entered and that Lois and Libby were staring at him.

'You're looking well, Jeffrey,' she said too loudly. 'California must have agreed with you.'

He did look well. His blue eyes glinted brightly in his newly tanned face. And he had gained weight. His daughters would not have allowed him to dine on a single pale chicken breast.

'It did,' he agreed. 'And how are you, Judith?'

'I'm fine. It's been a good two weeks. I've managed to get some writing done.' The lie fell easily from her lips. It had not been a good two weeks and she had written nothing. 'When did you get back?' she asked.

'Just two days ago. I was in the neighborhood – I had to see a patient in the hospital – and I thought I would drop by and see if you had the time to go on helping me to sort through the rest of her . . . Sylvia's things.' He spoke hesitantly, almost apologetically.

Judith nodded and glanced at Suzanne who was emptying the cash register.

'I am busy but I'll make the time,' she said. 'Of course I will. We've had very good luck with the clothing you donated. Isn't that right, Suzanne?'

Suzanne smiled. 'Very good luck indeed, Jeffrey. You'll recall that I asked your permission to send some of the garments to a consignment shop; as a result, we've received very generous revenue,' she said. 'I'll be sending you a receipt for tax purposes.'

'I'm glad to hear that. It would have pleased my wife,' he replied and turned back to Judith. 'Just let me know when it will be convenient for you to come up to the house,' he said. 'You can reach me at the office or at home.'

'I will. Sometime next week, I think. It's nice to see you again,' she added, and she did not turn to look at Suzanne as he left, closing the door very softly behind him.

She continued to work, sorting through a new carton of donations, remembering the warmth in his voice when he greeted her, his endearing awkwardness when he asked for her help. He was such a nice man, such a good man. And his eyes were of such a deep blue. She smiled. How foolish of her to think of the color of Jeffrey Kahn's eyes.

She left early, driving through streets carpeted with the pink petals of dogwood blossoms. It was a perfect early-spring evening, perfect for an al fresco supper. Their own back garden was ablaze with color. It had been a very long time since she and David had eaten in the garden. Perhaps too long. No. Not too long. They were fine. They would be fine. Love, after all, had propelled them into marriage. Love and need. She had loved David and needed him as he had loved her and needed her. That memory would sustain them, would carry them through the whirlpool of their grief to a safer shore. She thought again of Dickinson's words. An effort had to be made, she told herself. She would try. She had to try.

She hurried into the kitchen, checked the refrigerator and saw that there was arugula and cherry tomatoes, a salad to go with the cheese. Happily, she set everything on the counter and then saw that the light on the answering machine was flickering. She pressed down and heard David telling her he would not be home for dinner. No excuse was offered. No regret expressed.

There would be no twilight picnic, no rekindling of intimacy. She struggled to free herself from the miasma of sadness that descended unbidden. She offered herself words of comfort. There would be other evenings, she told herself. The season of warmth was just beginning.

She thrust the wedge of brie and the loaf of focaccia into the fridge and made herself an omelet which she tossed away half uneaten. The optimism of the morning morphed into the disappointment of the evening. Loneliness overwhelmed her.

She picked up a copy of *Mansfield Park* and thrust it aside. Impossible to read when tears streaked her face, blurred her vision. The book fell to the floor and she made no effort to retrieve it.

She turned to television, surfing impatiently from channel to channel. CNN. MSNBC. CSPAN. The world was in turmoil. Bored reporters commented on chaos, struggled to insert emotion into their over-trained voices. The images of bereaved mothers drifted across the screen in shadowy sequence. Mothers in Syria, mothers in Gaza, mothers in Jerusalem, wizened, sari-clad women in India, weeping African mothers in brilliantly colored gowns clutching emaciated babies to their shriveled breasts. She had stumbled on to a video landscape of maternal misery that dwarfed her own loss. Her grief burst forth, unabated, uncontrolled. Sobbing, her heart pounding, her hands shaking, she switched the set off and lay motionless on her bed, waiting for the spasms of sorrow to subside.

She was awake when David entered, his face ashen with weariness, his voice weak as he apologized for the lateness of the hour.

'That's all right,' she said. She would not ask him why he was so late. She would not burden him with her own inchoate sadness.

'Did you have a good day?'

He was struggling for conversation, she knew. She rewarded him with a reply. 'Jeffrey Kahn stopped by the shop. He's back from California. He wants me to go on helping him deal with his wife's clothing,' she replied.

'If you have the time and if you want to help him, you should do that,' he said.

'You don't mind?' Her question was hesitant, almost flirtatious.

He smiled at her. 'Ah, Judith, should I mind?' he asked and placed his hand lightly on her head.

'Of course not.' She did not add that she was disappointed that he had raised no objection.

That too was a source of wonderment. Had she wanted David to be jealous? *Yes*, she acknowledged, *of course she did.* She was, after all, a student of literary romance and understood that jealousy was a sometime barometer of love.

'I had thought that we might have dinner in the garden tonight,' she said. 'But then I heard your message.'

'Another evening. Yes. Another evening,' he replied, his voice heavy with regret.

FIFTEEN

She called Jeffrey Kahn in the morning and told him that if it was convenient, she would drive out to his house that afternoon.

'Of course it's convenient,' he said.

David's new computer table was delivered that morning and for the first time she entered the reconfigured room, its air heavy with the scent of recently lathed wood and fresh paint. She watched as the driver set the table down against the newly wood-paneled wall where once Melanie's white bookcase had stood.

'Nice room,' the driver said approvingly as she handed him an overly generous tip.

'Yes,' she agreed, and stared down at the beige carpet that had replaced the magenta-colored rug. No hint of Melanie remained. She marveled that she was not moved to tears. Evelyn might call that a step forward, an acceptance of loss. Acceptance, according to Evelyn, was another step in the grieving process. Judith thought to counter that convenient therapeutic wisdom by asserting that there were losses that could never be accepted. They might, however, be assimilated, like wounds that slowly healed, leaving only phantom pain. That was how she had begun to cope with the reality of Melanie's death. She might, or might not, share that thought with Evelyn.

She went to the window, looked out at the apple tree, its tender leaves slowly unfurling. A school bus pulled up to a house across the street, and she turned away and walked too swiftly out of the room that was no longer Melanie's, closing the door very softly behind her.

In the kitchen, she placed the brie, the focaccia bread and the wine in an insulated bag, thought for a moment and added a small jar of olives.

She drove to the thrift shop, worked with Suzanne for an hour, sorting through the contents of a camp trunk overflowing with summer clothing and toys that a harried woman had brought in that morning.

'They're moving – relocating. The father lost his job or something and they had to get rid of a lot of stuff,' Suzanne explained.

Judith nodded. She was not surprised. She had grown used to dealing with the discards of reluctant displacements, sudden stresses.

'I'll need some empty cartons,' she said. 'I'm driving out to the Kahn house this afternoon and I'm sure there'll be loads of stuff to bring back.'

'Of course.'

Suzanne's casual tone matched her own. They had begun to understand each other.

Jeffrey was in the garden when she arrived, kneeling beside a red maple tree. He looked up and waved to her, shading his eyes with his dirt-streaked hand.

'Just planting some herbs,' he said. 'Sylvia's mint is coming up. She always said this was a good spot for parsley and dill. The right amount of shade. The right amount of sun. So I bought flats of parsley and dill. Stupid thing to do, I suppose. When will I use so much parsley and dill? Still, I wanted to do it.'

'Of course,' she murmured.

She nodded. They both knew that the effort of placing the herbs in the soft earth was a tribute to continuity and memory. She bent and plucked a sprig of parsley, drew her finger across a feathery wand of dill.

Sylvia was dead, but still greenery sprouted in her garden. *Life goes on*, Evelyn might say. It was a mantra that was beginning to irritate Judith. She inhaled the scent of the new plantings and thought that it might be time to dispense with Evelyn's expensive and predictable wisdom.

She handed Jeffrey the insulated bag and followed him into the kitchen as he put it in the refrigerator. She noted that he had set a small blue ceramic vase with the first lilacs of the season on the broad wooden table.

Once again they entered the large dressing room and once again they turned their attention to the contents of the wardrobe.

They concentrated on the linens and cottons of Sylvia Kahn's spring and summer clothing, an assortment of long pastel-colored skirts, loose shirts of the softest cotton, sleeveless shifts. A pale-blue chiffon evening gown threaded with silver tumbled from its hanger. Jeffrey held it up and fingered the soft fabric.

'She bought it for the formal dance at my med school's twenty-fifth reunion,' he said. He handed the chiffon gown to her. She folded it and placed it carefully in the carton. 'She looked so beautiful that night,' he added.

His eyes were closed and a single tear glinted on his cheek. Judith turned away, unwilling to encroach upon the privacy of his memory.

'Jeffrey,' she said softly. 'I need to use the bathroom.'

'Right through there,' he said, motioning to the door that led to the bedroom. 'The first door on the right.'

She nodded, and for the first time she entered the bedroom he and Sylvia had shared. It was a large room, the long windows covered with draperies of a sheer material, the floor carpeted in gray, the single silver-framed painting on the ecru papered wall was Picasso's *Woman in White*. A satin coverlet in muted tones of gray and violet was spread across the king-sized bed. One corner was turned down but the other side was undisturbed. Judith marveled that Jeffrey Kahn did not reach across the bed as he slept, in search of his vanished wife. But then perhaps he did and immediately smoothed the linens. That was her own habit on the rare nights when David slept away from home.

Shades of pale lilac covered the bedside lamps and a small mound of medical journals littered his bedside table. There was a single volume on Sylvia's side. Judith opened it with a shock of recognition. Jeffrey's wife had been reading Nellie Sachs as she lay dying.

Vials of perfume and small pots of rouge, tightly closed compacts and tubes of lipstick were neatly arranged on the dressing table. It did not surprise her that Jeffrey had not removed them. Sylvia would forever be absent, but her presence lingered in the room they had shared. Her scent was a comfort he would not easily surrender.

Photographs in matching pewter frames were arranged on

the bureau. Jeffrey and Sylvia on their wedding day, he in a tuxedo, she in white lace, looking at each other in wonder, as though startled by their new-found happiness. Portraits of their daughters in academic cap and gown flanked their wedding photo. Judith had known Beth and Amy Kahn when they were small girls. Amy had been gangly and thin, Beth plump and awkward. It seemed wonderful to her that they had morphed into such fair-haired, confident young women, aglow with achievement and confidence.

In her own bedroom, hers and David's, on their bureau, there was Brian's graduation photo and a portrait of Melanie, each set in matching frames of pale wood. The school photographer had captured Melanie in mid-laughter, her arms outstretched, her nascent breasts straining against the pink cashmere cardigan.

Staring at the portraits of Jeffrey's daughters, Judith felt a surge of sadness. She would never know how maturity would have sculpted Melanie's features. Would they have become as sharply defined as David's, or would her cheekbones, like Judith's, have become more prominent? What would she have looked like at sixteen, at seventeen, at eighteen? Once, watching a television show about abducted children, she had seen computer-generated images that showed how a child gone missing at seven might look at thirteen, how a runaway teenager might look as a young adult. Judith had thought, wildly, absurdly, that perhaps she might send that last photograph of Melanie to the company that did such computer imaging and request a likeness of Melanie at nineteen and perhaps it could be updated with each passing year. The idea had shamed her and she had thrust it away, but it resurfaced as she stared again at the Kahn daughters grown into womanhood.

She turned away from their smiling faces, went into the bathroom where she washed her face with very cold water and then picked up the silver-backed hairbrush that rested on a low table. It was Sylvia's hairbrush. She used it to brush her own dark hair and then examined it and removed a single tendril that clung to the bristles. Back in the bedroom, she opened Sylvia's vial of Madame Rochas and dabbed a drop of the fragrance on her wrist. The door opened and Jeffrey Kahn stared at her.

'I wondered if you needed anything,' he said. 'A towel or something.'

I need my daughter. The words, unspoken, lodged in her throat.

'No. No. I'm fine,' she replied aloud, and then, quite suddenly, she wasn't.

Once again, as on the previous evening, a torrent of sorrow ambushed her. She was racked with sobs; hot tears seared her cheeks and she swayed dangerously from side to side. Swiftly, he caught her, steadied her, held her close and led her to the bed. She lay on the gray and violet satin coverlet and covered her face with her hands.

'I'm sorry,' she said. 'Sometimes it just overwhelms me, the loss, the finality of it all. My daughter. Your wife. The loneliness.'

'Yes. The loneliness.' He echoed the word, his voice strangely resonant. 'The loneliness,' he repeated.

He sat beside her, his hand resting lightly on her forehead and then very gently stroking her hair. She relaxed into the tenderness of his touch and lifted her head. His lips met hers and he stretched out beside her. Slowly, very slowly, they undressed. Their lovemaking was swift and silent, their embraces tender. It was comfort they sought, not passion. They did not speak. He rolled away from her, his hand resting on her arm and then falling to his side. Within minutes they were both asleep.

When she awakened, she was alone in the room. He had covered her naked body with a light sheet and placed a bath towel at the foot of the bed. She glanced at her watch and marveled that only an hour had passed. Swiftly, she showered and dressed. Once again she used Sylvia's brush and stared into the mirror, surprised to see that her cheeks were flushed and her eyes were bright. David had always touched her face lightly after they had made love, rested his fingers upon her eyes.

'So that they won't blind me,' he had murmured more than once.

'David.' She whispered his name. 'Oh, David, what have I done?'

She realized that it was not guilt that she felt but sadness, sadness and love commingled with regret. She yearned to feel

David's hand upon her face, to hear his voice, to claim not his forgiveness but his understanding. She would explain that the moment had overwhelmed her, the need for touch and consolation had been overpowering; they had, she and Jeffrey Kahn, surrendered to the confluence of loneliness and longing. And she knew, turning away from the mirror, that she would explain nothing at all to David. How could she? Why would she?

Jeffrey was in the kitchen, the table set with blue ceramic plates, the brie and the focaccia on a wooden board, oil-soaked obsidian olives in a small bowl, a salad of arugula and red onions on a flat ceramic dish. The chilled wine was uncorked and ready to be poured into rose-colored glasses.

It surprised her that she was ravenously hungry, the very first time she had felt really hungry since Melanie's death. Brian had remarked worriedly on her lack of appetite. David, regarding the uneaten food on her plate, would shake his head wearily. Evelyn had advised her that her appetite for food would return when her appetite for life returned. Perhaps she was right, Judith thought as she placed a large wedge of brie across the crusty bread and took a deep swallow of wine. Certainly she felt more alive at this moment than she had felt during all the months of her mourning.

'You brought a lovers' picnic,' he said.

'But we are not lovers,' she replied gravely. 'I love my husband. David.'

'Of course you do. I know that. I understand that.'

'Do you?' she asked. 'I'm not sure what I understand.'

'We must try not to overthink what happened between us,' he said in the tone she imagined he used in his consulting room. 'We were both tired, both entangled in grief. I was just so in need of togetherness and touch. It was my fault. I did not think. I am sorry. So sorry.'

His voice broke and she feared that he might weep.

'I'm sorry too. But what happened was no one's fault,' she said softly, matching her tone to his. 'Not yours. Not mine.'

Sadly, calmly, they acknowledged the accident of their intimacy. It was solace that they had offered each other, the brief and transient comfort of tenderness and touch. Only that. They could forgive themselves. They could forgive each other. What had happened would not happen again. It was not passion that had moved them, she assured herself, but rather tenderness born of need. The words satisfied her. *Tenderness born of need.*

She reached for the salad, relishing its crispness and color. She told him how she loved wandering through farmers' markets, how she and David would drive miles out of their way in search of ramps or morels. It pleased her to speak of David so softly. It was important that Jeffrey Kahn understand the depth of her affection, the expansiveness of her love.

'You have a good life with him,' he said and immediately steered the conversation into safer precincts.

He spoke of his visit to California, the beauty of the Bay area, his disappointment in the quality of the papers presented at the medical conference, his pleasure at seeing how close his daughters were to each other.

'Yes. That's wonderful,' she agreed and suddenly remembered an evening when Melanie had been nestled between Brian and Denise on the sofa as they planned their trip to the Amish country. Their conversation had turned into a tickle-fest with brother and sister attacking a laughing and defenseless Denise. She and David had smiled at each other, in appreciation of that sweet gaiety, that togetherness.

'Our children, Brian and Melanie, were also close in spite of their age difference. Brian loved being a big brother and Melanie adored him. That made us – David and me – very happy.'

She would have Jeffrey understand that theirs had been a contented family, that her marriage had the steadying ballast of memories shared, of love enduring.

She refilled her wine glass and looked out of the window. A cardinal feasted at the bird feeder and then flew away, his scarlet wings scissoring their way skyward. Within seconds a dun-colored female was beside him and together the winged couple soared beyond her view.

'Do cardinals mate for life? Like swans?' she asked. 'And are they always happy together?'

He smiled. 'I don't think birds worry too much about happiness. Only human beings are blessed – or cursed – with that capacity,' he said. 'Yes, swans do mate for life. I don't know

about cardinals and, sadly, we both know that human beings
do not.'

Judith nodded. 'So many sad stories,' she said and immediately thought of Suzanne Brody who wore a jade ring on the
ring finger of her left hand, which almost obscured the pale
circlet left by her discarded wedding band.

'Too many sad stories,' he agreed. 'There was a time – I
think it was when Amy and Beth were in middle school – when
Sylvia and I thought divorce had become an epidemic. Couples
we knew were suddenly uncoupling. We used to speculate about
who would be next. Which husband would disappear into an
affair, which wife would discover she was a lesbian, who would
abandon their children and slam the door on a newly built split-
level? We made a game of it, perhaps because it bewildered
and frightened us. We ourselves could never imagine a life apart
from each other.'

'It never bewildered me,' Judith countered. 'It was familiar,
perhaps because of my teaching and research. I had read and
written so much about the attitudes of women writers toward
marriage. Even my unmarried writers – or maybe especially
my unmarried writers – had singular opinions. It was Jane
Austen who wrote that happiness in marriage is entirely a game
of chance, a gamble. Perhaps that was why she broke her own
engagement and never married.'

She looked across the table at Jeffrey. She had thought to
amuse him, to introduce an anecdotal lightness into talk that had
become dangerously serious. She realized at once that she had
failed. His avian face was a mask of sadness. His folded hands
cupped his long chin. When he spoke at last, his voice was so
low she strained to hear him.

'If, as your Jane Austen wrote, marriage is a matter of chance
– a gamble – then I think Sylvia and I won the jackpot. We
were so very happy, our life together a miracle. That is why I
am so devastated by her death. I am so lost without her. Lost
and lonely. And that is why I am so grateful to you. For your
help. For what we have shared,' he said.

He reached across the table and took her hand in his own.
'Shall we go on working together?' he asked. 'Can we?' His
fingers, pressing hard upon her palm, were very cold.

'I don't know,' she murmured. 'We would have to be careful. Very careful.'

'I promise that what happened today will not happen again.'

'I need time to think about it,' she whispered. She pulled her hand free of his grasp.

'Of course.' Disappointment dulled his voice.

She glanced at the clock. It was late, much later than she had realized. 'I must go,' she said, turning away. 'I'll get my bag. And there's the carton for the thrift shop.'

'I'll carry it down,' he said, and they mounted the stairs very slowly to the dressing room, now shrouded in the gathering darkness of early evening.

She glanced at the closet. Despite all their efforts, it was still half filled. The fitted drawers overflowed with gently used shirts of the softest cotton, with sweaters carefully encased in plastic bags, handbags whose linings were dusted with amber-tinted face powder.

'You see,' he said sadly, his gaze following her own. 'There's still all this to deal with. You know that I need your help. I cannot manage without you.'

She stood very still, her eyes averted, not daring to meet the plea in his eyes.

'Can we go on? Can we finish?' he asked.

The desperate sadness in his voice melted her resolve. She trembled and leaned against the wall. 'Of course, we must finish,' she said at last.

Driving home, she struggled against uncertainty and regret. She knew herself to be venturing into dangerous territory. What if what had happened that afternoon in that bedroom, so seductively furnished in melancholic shades of gray and violet, should happen yet again? Neither his promise to be careful nor her determination to avoid such a repetition was a sufficient guarantee, she knew. What would that mean to her life with David, their years together, the children who had been born to them, the orderly pattern of their days, their carefully organized home? And their love?

'Love. Our love. David's and mine.' She said the words aloud as she steered the car around a dangerous curve.

How strongly she had felt that love, threaded though it was with regret and sadness, as she had stared at herself in the mirror, clutching Sylvia Kahn's hairbrush.

'Our love. David's and mine.'

She repeated the words more fiercely, as though they could combat her surging unease and banish any confusion. She would not think of those few moments when Jeffrey Kahn's breath had been moist and sweet upon her face, his touch so comforting and tender upon her flesh.

Tenderness, born of need, was what she and Jeffrey Kahn had offered each other. She repeated the reassuring words. There had been no love between them. Love was her life with David. Could she tell him what had happened that afternoon? Could she expect him to understand that what she had shared with Jeffrey had mysteriously, inexplicably, intensified her feelings for him? She did not understand it herself.

Of course she would say nothing to David. He had never recovered from the infidelity that had poisoned his parents' marriage. She would not, could not, reignite his pain. What had happened that afternoon would not happen again. She had Jeffrey's promise. She had her own determination.

Her trembling hands gripped the wheel too tightly and she drove too fast. The car veered dangerously out of lane. She willed herself to calm and she continued on very slowly, her decision made.

She pulled into their driveway, behind David's car. A single light burned on the second floor in the room that had been their daughter's, but even as she stared up at it, the golden window darkened. She spoke his name softly when she entered the house, but she knew that the strains of the last movement of the Brahms *Requiem* obscured her voice. She did not seek him out but went very slowly up to the bedroom, relieved to be alone.

SIXTEEN

D avid wakened early that morning and dressed quickly. Judith was still asleep. He ate a solitary breakfast, went upstairs and kissed her gently on the forehead. She stirred but did not open her eyes. He wanted to apologize for his late arrival the previous evening. He knew she had been disappointed, although she had said only that she had thought that they might have had a picnic supper. He had seen the salad and the brie in readiness for that supper in the refrigerator. He should have explained the urgency of the deadline he was rushing to meet. He sighed. Another mistake but not irremediable. He would make it up to her.

He reached the city, as always, before the cacophony of urban life began and walked toward his office, his face lifted to the soft spring wind. He had always loved the teasing onset of the season of warmth, when the chill of early morning was brushed away by slowly emergent golden sunlight.

A wave of nostalgia washed over him and he walked more slowly, caught up in memories of seasons past, the early spring of their courtship when he and Judith had wandered through the forest that bordered their campus. The shadows of newly unfurled leaves had dappled her bare arms, and her sunlit face had been radiant as they sprinted across the soft yielding earth to a favorite cove beneath the wide-winged oak tree they called their own.

He struggled to recall what they had talked about, lying there in each other's arms. Probably their programmed progress into a beckoning future. Judith had surely spoken, with dreamy confidence, of how she planned to organize their meager budget and manage meals during those whirlwind days when they raced from the university to their part-time jobs. They were aiming high and had no time to waste. And he, as always, had been quiescent, seeking only to please her, knowing that she sought only to please him in those, their halcyon days.

And yes, he remembered with absolute certainty, she had recited poetry. Probably Emily Dickinson, her favorite then. The words were lost to him. He had never really registered them; it was her voice rising and falling in a musical cadence that had soothed him and filled his heart with love. That love meant honesty, revelations.

There were no secrets between them. Their pasts were revealed – her lonely childhood, his parents' marriage embittered by his father's brief and regretted infidelity and his mother's inability to ever forgive it. He had promised that she would never again be lonely. She had said there would never be bitterness between them. They had assured each other of absolute fidelity.

'I will love only you. Always,' she had said, and he had repeated her words.

That mutual promise had been sealed with a gentle kiss. How soft her lips had been, how sweet her breath.

The vividness of that memory surprised him. But, of course, his conversation with Brian had thrust him back in time and forced him to think about Judith, about the nuances of their past and the shadows that darkened their present. Brian was right. He and Judith had to talk openly and honestly, as once they had, as they surely could, and would, again. They could not allow their grief to suffocate their love. Pausing on a corner for a light, he thought about how he could make that happen.

The light changed and he strode toward his office, juggling ideas, approaches, his professional training asserting itself. But he abandoned all such thoughts and reminded himself that he would not be conducting an arbitration; he would be talking to his wife. A conversation too long delayed.

He envisioned sitting opposite Judith in their lamp-lit living room, the windows open to the scent of newly blooming lilacs. That lilac bush had been their first purchase for the house which they had thought to fill with children. *Children.* A seminal item on Judith's dream-bound agenda.

'We'll have a boy. We'll have a girl,' she had said on that long-ago day as they lay side by side in that sunlit cove, planning their future. 'Maybe two boys. Two girls.'

He had not forgotten her words, nor, he supposed, had she.

He would not remind her of them. Of course not. But he might ask her why she had stopped reciting poetry. A question meant to disarm her, although the answer was clear to him. Leisure had been lost to them as they raced through their lives. They rushed to harvest advanced degrees, to enhance resumes that would assure professional success, aiming tenaciously for security. The house in the suburbs, a nest egg in the bank, a future under control. They created a rigid schedule for themselves and they met their own expectations. Brian was born a month after Judith completed her dissertation, a year after David won his first major arbitration.

He remembered how they had juggled their hours after Brian's birth, rushing through their days at work, willing themselves to wakefulness after sleepless nights, dependent on daycare centers and unreliable babysitters, but always delighting in their small son, marveling at his laughter, delighting in his antics. Brian was an easy infant, a happy toddler, and they were at ease with him. Poetry was abandoned. Nursery rhymes and improvised stories prevailed. Judith told old favorites and created new tales. She was a queen, David was a king, Brian their enchanted princeling. They wore crowns fashioned from the rims of pizza boxes and spoke in sonorous royal accents. Brian laughed and plucked off their crowns, saving them to wear to nursery school on dress-up day.

They were happy. Life was good. She was on a tenure track. He was in line for a partnership. They bought a home with four bedrooms and a playroom. It was time, they agreed, for a second child, and then, perhaps, a third. Only children both, survivors of solitary childhoods, they longed for a large family. For Brian's sake and for their own.

But Judith did not become pregnant. Anxiety robbed their intimacy of passion. Indifferent doctors who spoke of body temperature and ovulation suctioned all pleasure out of what had been their sweetest moments. Lying beside each other, conditioned to disappointment, they dared not speak. Silence offered them refuge.

That corrosive silence had been wonderfully shattered by Melanie's birth. They relaxed into joy, reveled in delight as she tumbled through childhood. They soared on dreams of the happy future that awaited her, awaited them. With her death, the dream morphed into nightmare and they plummeted into a quicksand of grief.

'A quicksand of grief.' He said the words aloud, startled that they had occurred to him, startled that he found what Judith might call 'a useful metaphor'. He waited for the traffic light to change, possessed of a new determination. They would emerge from that quicksand, he and his Judith. They would pull each other out. That was what they had to do. That was what they would do. The light turned green and he hurried across the street, newly invigorated, newly hopeful.

He reached his office and thrust all emotional pondering aside. There was work to be done. A new project for an important client demanded extensive research. Nancy had already ferreted out relevant information and they worked together throughout the day, organizing a PowerPoint presentation.

He marveled at Nancy's quiet competence and watched as her slender fingers flashed across the keyboard, her head bent so that sheaths of her silver hair swept across her cheeks. He concentrated on writing his analysis, consulting her notes, breaking off now and again to dial Judith's cell phone. Each call went at once to voicemail but he left no messages. She had mentioned resuming her work with Jeffrey Kahn, but had she planned to do it so soon? He could not remember. It was of no importance. He went back to work, finishing just as Nancy placed the folder with the completed printouts on his desk.

'Thanks,' he said. 'I never thought we'd finish today. I owe you.'

She smiled. 'I might just call in that IOU,' she said, and he heard the hesitation in her voice. She did not easily ask for favors.

'What's up?'

'Lauren. She's in a panic about a math test tomorrow. She asked if you could help her tonight and I told her I didn't want to impose – you've been so generous with your time.'

'You're not imposing.'

He glanced at his watch, dialed Judith's phone again and this time he left a message.

'I'll be home late. Probably very late. Something came up. Tried to reach you earlier. Sorry.'

'She won't mind?' Nancy asked. 'Your wife?' She rarely mentioned Judith by name, creating her own boundary to their intimacy.

'I don't think so,' he replied, and she hurried to her office to gather up her things.

He waited, the certainty that Judith would mind nagging at him. He realized, with a surge of guilt, that he wanted her to mind. He wanted her to miss him, to express regret, to glow with happiness when he arrived, forgiving his lateness in her relief at his presence. He would promise her an al fresco dinner and then, seated at a candlelit table, he would follow Brian's advice and, at last, tell her about Nancy, about the innocence of their friendship and the relief it offered him. Judith would understand. Of course she would.

'I'm ready,' Nancy said, and, abandoning all thoughts of Judith, he followed her to the elevator.

Lauren was waiting for them when they arrived at the apartment. Her sweet impish face was puckered with anxiety, her fair hair neatly braided, each plait carefully tied with a pale-green ribbon that matched her sweater, the colors chosen perhaps to match her large eyes. David thought her very pretty and imagined that one day she would be beautiful.

She smiled as they entered and stood on tiptoe to kiss her mother, then held her hand out to David with grave solemnity. She was an affectionate child, a polite child, conditioned to loneliness, eager to please and be pleased.

'Thank you for coming to help me,' she said demurely.

'I'm glad to do it,' he replied and followed her into her bedroom.

Her math book was open on the little white desk that had been Melanie's, her index cards were neatly arranged on the uncluttered surface, her notebook open to neatly copied problems, the numbers marching down the page in careful columns. While Melanie's bedroom had always been a scene of cheerful chaos, Lauren's room was tidy, the floor clear, everything in its place.

Lauren – quiet, fatherless Lauren – was a latchkey child, who came home each day to an empty apartment. It occurred to David that she craved order and imposed it on her own small space, creating a fortress against dangerous carelessness. It had, after all, been carelessness that had killed the father she had never known.

'So what's the problem?' he asked, faking a casualness he did not feel.

He sat down beside her and she showed him the worksheet, the index card on which she had tried to tackle the problem, and pointed to the text which he decided actually complicated a very simple procedure. Quietly, patiently, he explained it to her and watched as she licked her pencil and began to work, making an error, recognizing it, beginning again and then turning to him, her face wreathed in a triumphant smile. He set her another problem. She grinned and solved it.

'I see. I see,' she exclaimed.

Her delight delighted him. They exchanged hugs and he remembered Melanie's hugs, her special way of scrunching up her face to make him laugh as he held her close. He banished the memory and looked down at Lauren. Her expression was grave with gratitude.

Hand in hand, her fingers pressed tightly against his own, they went into the kitchen where Nancy had set the table for three. Her hair was coiled into a loose chignon and her cheeks reddened with the heat of the oven as she pulled out a casserole. They ate with quiet pleasure, a pseudo family, safe in their pretend world.

'This is so nice,' Lauren said. 'I love it when you come here.'

He nodded. 'I like coming here.'

'Then you should come always. Tomorrow and the next day and the day after that.'

'I can't do that, Lauren. I have a wife. I have a home.'

'But I think you like it better here,' she said daringly. She smiled and leaned closer to him. 'You like us, don't you? You like me. You like my mother.'

Her words, her sudden movement, startled him. She was, he realized, playing the nymphet, seducing him on her mother's behalf.

He was silent. He knew that whatever he said would be wrong. She was just a child, a fatherless child, spinning out a dangerous fantasy.

'Lauren, that's quite enough,' Nancy said reprovingly and flashed David an apologetic glance. 'Time for you to go to bed.'

Obediently, she gave her mother a goodnight kiss and held her hand out to David. 'Thank you,' she said, once again the submissive and grateful child.

David and Nancy carried their coffee into the living room and sat in uneasy silence.

'She doesn't understand,' Nancy said at last. 'She didn't know what she was doing.'

'But you and I both know what she was doing,' he replied quietly.

'She's just a child. And you're not seducible.' She hesitated. 'Are you?'

He looked at her, her silver hair tumbled loose and caping her shoulders, the color rising in her angular face. She was flushed with the temerity of her own question. He thought to tell her how very beautiful she was at that moment, both her strength and vulnerability revealed in the steadiness of her gaze, in the sadness of her eyes.

'No. I am not seducible. Nor, I think, are you,' he said at last and took her hand in his own. Her fingers were very cold. 'But I am fond of Lauren. It would be nice to take her out somewhere, perhaps to a show or a museum. To show her that what we have – you and I – is a very special friendship.'

'Yes,' she agreed. 'A friendship.'

'We must not endanger it,' he cautioned.

They needed no words to explicate what that danger might be.

'I know.' She spoke in a whisper and wrested her hand free.

He rose to leave and she walked him to the door. They stood on the threshold for a minute in the dim light of the hallway and then, too swiftly, he hurried away, not daring to look back, knowing that she stood there still, wreathed in longing and loneliness.

He was relieved to catch a late train and relieved, when he arrived home, to see that Judith was asleep. He touched her shoulder. A smile played at her lips, but she did not awaken. This was not an hour for explanations. He lay down beside her and inhaled the scent of the newly blooming lilac bush as it wafted through their open bedroom window. A new season meant a new beginning.

SEVENTEEN

He slept surprisingly well and awakened as dawn broke. Judith did not stir. He did not disturb her. They would talk that night. He dressed quickly, moving quietly through the wide-windowed room bathed in the milky half-light of a day not yet begun. He had purposefully gifted himself an extra two hours before he had to catch his train to the city. It had become his habit to do that at cautious intervals, always triggered by the impulse to visit Melanie's grave. And this morning, with the thoughts of the previous night still fresh in mind and memory, brought that impulse.

Closing the front door very softly, he went outside and paused beneath the lilac bush, heavy with blossoms. He broke off a slender branch and placed it on the seat of his car.

He drove through the empty streets of the sleep-bound suburb, reveling in the quiet and the gathering brightness as the sun rose high in the cloudless sky. He reached the highway, took the familiar exit and within minutes arrived at the imposing iron gates of the small cemetery. The gates were still padlocked, but as he approached, a sleepy-eyed groundskeeper arrived, keys in hand.

He was an old man, a long-time synagogue employee and familiar to David who had seen him at too many burials. On such occasions the caretaker wore a suit, shabby but well pressed, a white shirt and a tie, but on this morning he was dressed in jeans and a blue cambric work shirt.

'Morning, sir,' he said.

'Good morning,' David replied in turn. 'I wasn't sure you'd be around this early.'

'Lots of folks come early in the morning,' he said. 'I guess because it's quiet. Because it's private.'

'Yes. Quiet. Private,' David repeated. That was what he was in search of. Quiet. Privacy.

He parked his car and, holding the sprig of lilac, he walked along the gravel path to a new section of the cemetery. He paused at the small pink marble gravestone that Judith had chosen with such care. Emergent rays of pale sunlight played across his daughter's name, so deeply engraved, and the Hebrew acronym inscribed beneath it. The rabbi had explained that the letters meant *Love is Stronger than Death*, a quotation from Psalms. He had accepted the inscription, although he had thought the psalmist wrong. It was a mistake to underestimate the power of death.

He saw that there were tightly furled buds on the dwarf rose bush that Judith had planted and he wondered when they would burst into full blossom. He placed his hand on the gravestone. Its surface was cold to his fingers despite the gathering brightness of the morning sun. Gently, he placed the lilacs upon it.

At a neighboring grave, a black-coated man swayed in prayer but David offered no prayers.

'I'm here, sweetheart,' he said softly. 'I'm here because it's a beautiful morning. I miss you. We miss you. Your mother and I. Both of us. Together. We love you. We miss you.'

Suffused with a new calm, he turned and walked back to his car, pausing at the entryway to place a ten-dollar bill in the charity box that stood on a stone bench. Glancing at his watch, he saw that he could easily catch the next train. The sun was high now, the cloudless sky ablaze. He was ready for the new day, eager for the advent of evening.

Judith too was energized by the advent of a new warmth. She willed the brightness of the passing days to banish the darkness of her mood. She would not think about what had happened with Jeffrey Kahn, yet the thought recurred. Again and again, she assured herself that their coming together had been transitory, based only on the need of the moment, the overwhelming mutuality of their mourning. They had, each of them, acknowledged as much. It had happened, it was over, it would not happen again.

Driving down suburban streets, she saw children dancing through the rainbow-rimmed sprays of sprinklers that rained down on newly green, sweet-smelling lawns. Women in summer dresses and men with their jackets slung over their shoulders walked slowly, their faces lifted to the gold-streaked sky. She forced herself to smile. Struggling toward normalcy, she returned the wave of a crossing guard, sounded her horn lightly at a small boy who darted into the road. She relaxed and reminded herself of how much she loved the season of sunlight.

Fans whirled in the thrift shop, piercing the shafts of brightness that shot through the unshaded windows, spangling the counters and sending motes of dust across the overladen racks.

Each day of the new season brought a new cast of volunteers. Empty nesters arrived, middle-aged women who sought to dispel the summer lassitude with self-righteous forays into volunteerism. Feeling useful and virtuous, they reorganized the shelves and decorated the dangling price tags with smiley faces and small hearts. They trained false smiles on the customers who wandered in.

Judith arrived later each morning and left earlier. She automatically folded and refolded garments that had been cast carelessly aside, hurried from one bin to another in search of a wanted item, manned the cash register, counting bills, wrapping coins for deposit. The orderly chores countered the uneasiness that still assaulted her when she thought of Jeffrey Kahn, when she thought of David, when memories of Melanie surfaced unbidden.

On this morning, a pale woman wearing the uniform of a hospital aide joyously claimed a brand-new royal-blue bathing suit, the Bloomingdale price tag still attached. Judith wondered when she would find time to swim and how she would crowd her fleshy body into the flimsy Lycra suit. But the suit was not for herself, the woman explained. She was buying it for her daughter, to cheer her up because her husband had recently left her. He was a drunk. It was just as well. Her daughter deserved better.

Judith nodded, marveling at the confidences that were imparted with such ease in this cluttered room. But then all secrets were safe here, all revelations secure. They all lived in different worlds and, like itinerant airline passengers, would never see each other again. She herself could safely tell this poor pale woman that she had allowed a man who was not her husband to make love to her. A barely contained hysteria suffused her at the absurdity of the thought.

The proud man who had so scrupulously reclaimed his IOU purchased three neatly pressed short-sleeved shirts. It was very hot in the mail-room where he worked, he told Judith.

'But I'm not complaining,' he added.

He would not complain. He had a job. He had the money to pay for the shirts which Judith assured him were in excellent condition. He made a great show of counting out the bills.

'Two dollars. Three dollars. Four dollars,' he intoned in his deep baritone voice. Judith returned the favor by echoing his count.

An elderly jeweler, his bald head shiny with perspiration, nattily dressed in a dark three-piece suit, a starched white shirt, sat at a low table, a loupe held to his eye, with which he examined small pieces of jewelry that he held in his trembling hand.

'He comes every summer,' Suzanne told Judith. 'His shop is high-end and his regular customers travel in the summer so he has time to scrounge. He's found some good pieces here and he always gives us a very fair price. Last summer he paid us well for a beautiful lapis necklace that was entangled in a mess of junk jewelry. People just don't know what they're giving away.'

'I suppose,' Judith agreed.

An hour later the jeweler counted out crisp ten-dollar bills in payment for Sylvia Kahn's amber necklace and earrings. Suzanne flashed Judith a conspiratorial smile and Judith smiled back.

She acknowledged that she was beginning to respect Suzanne, even to like her. They occasionally ate their hasty lunches together in the cluttered rear room and spoke of going together to a new salad place that had opened nearby. Judith suggested a possible date and both of them consulted their pocket calendars, each aware of the danger of empty hours.

The morning drifted into afternoon, her routine untroubled, her life unaltered.

She was grateful that her days were so carefully orchestrated, mornings and afternoons divided into discrete assignments. Nothing had changed.

She continued to spend the requisite afternoons at the Kahn house, she and Jeffrey extremely polite, extremely cautious.

Her essay on literary approaches to grief had expanded beyond Eliot and Austen, and perhaps beyond an essay. She found herself rereading Edith Wharton, yet another childless woman writer with a deep understanding of loss. Wharton had lost family and friends, endured an unhappy affair and, finally, opted for divorce from the husband she had never loved.

Judith took careful notes, not working at her computer but inking her ideas into the lined notebook she had scavenged from Melanie's room. The smallest notation filled her with a sense of accomplishment. The vaguest insight comforted her. She made note of a moving letter from Wharton about the dissolution of her marriage.

I am tired out, the author wrote to unfaithful, unreliable Teddy Wharton. *I have done all I can . . . I now think it best . . . that we should live apart.*

They had been married for twenty-eight years. An odd coincidence, Judith thought. She and David had also been married for twenty-eight years. But she, of course, had not done all she could nor did she think that they should live apart. She could not imagine her life without David, who had been all things to her, friend and lover, husband, sharer of joy, silent hoarder of unshared sorrow. In recent days, David had spoken of wanting to talk, talk seriously, he had said, but she had resisted, now pleading a headache, now claiming she had to work on her research. She was not ready for a serious talk. She feared what he might say, what she might say. She sensed that David was relieved by the delay. He did not insist. There was no urgency, she told herself. They needed time, she and David; they needed patience.

She said as much to Evelyn and the therapist nodded approvingly. She did not, however, tell Evelyn about that much-regretted hour in Jeffrey Kahn's bedroom. It was an odd omission, she knew. Therapists were supposed to be secure recipients of such confidences. She did not speak of it, she knew, because such a revelation to Evelyn, who would surely want to explore it in depth, might vest it with an importance she struggled to deny. She repeated her mantra. *It had happened. It was over. It would not happen again.*

Still, when Denise was searching for literary references to

problematic marriage for her summer workshop on couples counseling, Judith showed her Wharton's letter. Denise read it carefully.

'Sad,' she said, handing the book back to Judith. 'The death of any marriage is very sad. My professor keeps insisting that marriages should not be taken for granted. She claims that couples have to work at them if they are to survive.'

'There are some marriages that should not survive,' Judith said. 'Certainly, Wharton's marriage to Teddy was doomed from the start. It probably lasted longer than it should have. Some marriages do.'

'I'm not sure.' Denise's reply was tentative. She knew herself to be on dangerous territory. She feared that Judith might speak of her own marriage but dismissed that thought at once. Brian had often spoken of his mother's penchant for privacy.

'She lives inside her own head,' he had said.

Denise, who spoke to her mother and sisters daily, who giggled and wept through long lunches with a cadre of friends, who certainly did not live within their own heads, had nodded and shrugged. 'Different strokes for different folks,' she said playfully. 'Still, your mom seems a lot more energized, less mired in misery. The best she's been since Melanie's death.'

'Having a routine is good for her,' Brian agreed.

Judith herself acknowledged the importance of the routine she had established. She congratulated herself on her growing pile of index cards, on the new method of storage she had introduced at the thrift shop.

At the Kahn house, the huge double closet in the dressing room approached emptiness, although the drawers and shelves were still full. Their contents too were arranged in seasons. There were Sylvia's winter sweaters of fine cashmere and heavy wool, the cotton cardigans for spring and early autumn, and the loose sleeveless shirts she had worn during the summer. Judith carefully printed the name of each season with a black sharpie on separate cartons. *Summer, Winter, Spring, Fall.* She wondered if Sylvia had been aware of the passing seasons as she died her long and lingering death. It was not a thought she shared with Jeffrey.

The rhythm they had established was scrupulously choreographed.

The air of the dressing room was saturated with the scent of pastel-colored satin sachets filled with lavender which Sylvia had scattered in the drawers, her initials embroidered across each small fragrant sack.

Sometimes they worked in companionable silence. Sometimes they talked quietly. It was, she assured herself repeatedly, as though nothing had happened.

He spoke with gentle concern of his patients, with quiet pride of his daughters. She related small incidents from the thrift shop, told him of her affection for Emily, the pleasure she felt when she held Emily's baby. He kept his radio tuned to the classical music station of the local university. One afternoon a Straus waltz played and he stood and invited her into his arms. They danced with great solemnity across the floor of the dressing room, gracefully avoiding the open cartons and the piles of clothing yet to be sorted. They glided away from the bedroom even though the door was closed. They would take no chances. She curtsied and he bowed when the music ended, and they both laughed.

Late each afternoon, before she left, they sat in the kitchen. Always there was a pitcher of iced tea with sprigs of mint from Sylvia's herb garden floating in the golden liquid. Always there was a bowl of summer fruit. Occasionally, Judith brought cheese or croissants. They ate with pleasure, pleased by their own restraint, their ability to have restored a sense of ease. And yet, she acknowledged, those afternoons were tinged with a dangerous, even a pleasurable, excitement. Often, as she drove home, she pulled the car over to the side of the road and sat quietly, allowing the rose and mauve shadows of early sunset to soothe her.

It was an hour she and David had always loved. Often, during their courtship and the early years of their marriage, they had met at day's end and walked hand in hand through the gathering darkness. She would suggest to David that they resume those twilight walks. The idea calmed her and erased all thoughts of Jeffrey.

It pleased her that the work on David's home office was almost completed. His books were arranged on the newly planed shelves, his diplomas hung on the paneled walls. The sand-colored area rug was stretched across the polished hardwood floor. The furniture she had chosen – the beige recliner and the convertible sofa that opened into a comfortable bed – was in place.

Brian had set up his father's computer and Denise had contributed a mouse pad with a picture of herself and Brian. A wooden file cabinet had been donated to the thrift shop and Judith had purchased it and stocked it with file folders that remained empty. David had thanked her for her efforts.

'You did well, Judith,' he had said. 'You thought of everything. But then you always do.'

'You'll be able to spend more time working from home,' she had replied.

'Yes. Of course. It will make life easier.'

But he did not spend more time working at home. Two or three times a week he told her that he would not be home for dinner. A pressing deadline, a very late conference call, a very early meeting. Twice that month he did not come home at all. He was regretful. She was understanding. They needed time. That was something they both silently agreed on. His determination to be honest with her had not changed, but he wanted the time to be right, the press of work abated. That, at least, was what he told himself.

David was not at home one evening when Brian and Denise arrived for dinner. Judith explained that he was working late. 'You'll have to forgive him,' she told the young couple. 'Things seem to be crazy at the office.'

'Well, if you forgive him, we'll have to do the same,' Denise said lightly, but Judith saw that her son's eyes were dark with worry.

Denise called the next day. She had been given tickets to an exhibit at a small gallery.

'Women painters. Mary Cassatt. Vanessa Bell. Frieda Kahlo. Judy Chicago. An esoteric collection. But I thought it might interest you. We could have lunch. There's a great salad place, a café with a view of the avenue that just opened. I know Monday is your writing day, but why not take a break?'

Why not indeed? Judith thought.

It was a nice gesture on Denise's part and the exhibit that seemed to span so many generations did interest her. It occurred to her that she might include women artists who had also confronted grief and loss in her essay. The idea intrigued her. She agreed. More than agreed. She looked forward to it.

EIGHTEEN

They met at the café, choosing a window table that faced the street. Judith relaxed. She studied her reflection in the glass and was pleased with herself. She wore her apple-green linen dress and carried the bag she had ordered to match it. She felt contentedly stylish. It was pleasant to sit in a room flooded with sunshine and cooled by a gently purring air conditioner. Denise was full of goodwill and eager to please, her auburn hair in an unruly cascade about her shoulders, her green eyes bright behind her red-framed glasses. Disorganized as always, books and paper bulging out of her faded brown book bag, a button missing on her rumpled white blouse, her wildly floral-patterned skirt too long, she discussed the menu choices.

Judith had heard it said that men chose to marry women who resembled their mothers. It seemed to her that Brian had done the exact opposite. Still, she was beginning to like this very disorganized girl who would be her daughter-in-law.

'Wine,' she said suddenly, unexpectedly. 'Let's have a carafe of white wine.'

The sweet-faced waitress nodded and swiftly returned with the wine. They lifted their glasses in silent toast and looked out of the window at the passing cast of pedestrians. Denise shared Judith's penchant for people watching, for speculating about the strangers they would never see again, who were so briefly in their field of vision. An older man walking with a small boy was a divorced father, Denise volunteered.

'Married a woman too young for him and now she's left him and is living in a commune in Oregon.'

'Maybe just a grandfather and grandson,' Judith protested.

Two well-dressed women walked by, one speaking angrily, the other looking miserable.

'Sisters,' Judith volunteered. 'Arguing about who will take care of their sick mother.'

'Colleagues at an ad agency accusing each other of professional treachery.'

They laughed. The game was fun. Their imaginations soared. Neither had expected the other to be an active player in the whimsical game. Judith shared the Virginia Woolf story of a woman on a bus speculating about another passenger, convinced that she was a lonely spinster, only to discover how very wrong she was when the woman descended at her stop to be greeted by a swarm of affectionate children.

'It must be wonderful to have so many literary references to draw from,' Denise said. 'I have only case histories.'

'Fiction can offer only so much comfort. Poetry is actually more helpful,' Judith said carefully.

The very young rabbi who had tried to comfort her when he paid a shiva visit had suggested that she read Psalms, but she had turned instead to Dylan Thomas. Over and over she had read, *Do not go gentle into that good night. Rage, rage against the dying of the light.*

Judith did not quote the Thomas poem to Denise. Instead, she suggested that she read Emily Dickinson.

They continued to look out of the window as their salads arrived. And they were still staring, their forks raised, arugula dangling in a verdant string, when a man in a light summer suit and a woman wearing a pale-blue dress and broad-brimmed straw hat passed by, each holding the hand of a small girl who walked between them. The trio paused as the woman removed her hat. Her silver hair floated loose and she brushed it back from her face. Her companion turned to her and smiled. They walked on as Denise's fork clattered to the table. Judith sat motionless, her own fork frozen in her lifted hand.

'David. It was David, wasn't it?' she asked, her voice faint, her face blanched of all color.

'Yes. Yes, it was,' Denise agreed miserably.

Their game was over. All pleasantness abandoned.

'And he was with Nancy. Nancy, who works in his office. We gave her Melanie's furniture. That was Nancy with him. It was her, wasn't it?'

'I don't know,' Denise replied. 'I've never met her.'

'No. Of course you haven't.'

Judith drained her wine glass and turned her attention to her salad. They ate too quickly and went to the exhibit. The paintings were interesting, the curator's notes insightful. They paused dutifully before each picture. Judith clutched her moleskin notebook but she did not open it. They left the gallery and stood in awkward silence on the corner.

'I'm sorry,' Denise said.

'There is nothing for you to be sorry about,' Judith replied. 'Maybe it was for the best. We will have to talk now. David and I. Yes, we will have to talk.'

A cab pulled up and she bent and kissed Denise on the cheek. An unusual gesture for Judith, Denise knew.

'It was good of you to invite me,' she said. 'I appreciate it.'

'Thank you for coming,' Denise said in return.

The cab pulled away. Denise took out her cell phone. She thought to call Brian but changed her mind. There was time enough for him to deal with the dilemma of his parents' marriage, time enough for both of them to assimilate the lessons they might learn from it.

Judith was in the living room when David arrived home that evening. Although it was still daylight, she had drawn the drapes so that the large room was dimly lit. Still wearing her apple-green linen dress, she sat in a circlet of light cast by a single lamp. He stood in the doorway, briefcase in hand, and stared at her in surprise.

'Judith, are you all right?' he asked.

'Why wouldn't I be?' she asked.

He put his briefcase down and sank into the chair opposite her. 'You look tired,' he said. 'Do you want to go out for dinner?'

'I had lunch in the city with Denise. I'm not really hungry. And I don't imagine you are. You had lunch out as well, didn't you?'

'I did, as a matter of fact. But how did you know?' He spoke with the slightest of stutters, that childhood disability, long conquered, recurring in moments of stress.

'I saw you. You and Nancy. And Nancy's daughter. Lauren. Denise and I had a window table at a café near the museum and we saw the three of you walk by. You made an appealing picture. A pretend charming, happy family, taking a leisurely walk on a lovely day.'

She bit her lip. She had not meant to descend into sarcasm. She had not wanted her words to spill out laced with bitterness. She was newly suffused with anger, anger at herself, anger at David, but she would trade that anger for honesty. She wanted him to be honest about his relationship with Nancy Cummings. She would offer him honesty in return. Yes, she would dare to tell him about Jeffrey Kahn. It would be a mutual exchange, their confessional slate wiped clean, their self-inflicted silences at an end.

She waited.

He stared at her. 'We were not pretending to be a happy family, as you put it,' he said, his stutter gone, his courage ignited. 'We are colleagues, Nancy and I. We are also friends, and we were taking her daughter to the children's wing of the Met for an art class. An innocent enough outing. I would have mentioned it to you if I thought you cared. I come home late. I don't come home at all. You ask no questions. Not about my work. Not about where I've been. You have been so remote from me since Melanie died.'

He sank into the chair opposite her and leaned forward, his head in his hands.

Her anger melted, warmed by relief. He had, at last, spoken their daughter's name, spoken it full-voiced, in a sentence completed, to her. They were no longer stranded on their separate islets of grief, no longer restricted to the cryptic language of the bereaved.

She understood, with sudden clarity, that they had been mutually paralyzed by their grief, choking on words they could not utter. They feared to speak to each other of the enormity of their loss. They had no blueprint for comfort. Closeness eluded, fatigue overwhelmed. Entangled in a web of sorrowful anger, furious and frightened, they had retreated into silence and solitude. But now, seated together in this lamp-lit room, staring out at the shadows of encroaching evening, Judith knew they had to speak, to share, to exchange revelations, however damning and painful they might be. And, watching David, as he dropped his hands and stared at her, his eyes soft, she saw that he understood.

'I'm asking now,' she said quietly. 'I'm asking you to tell me what you were doing when you claimed to be working late. I want to know who you were with and where you slept on the nights you didn't even come home. You owe me that much, don't you?'

The question had at last been asked. Her cheeks burned and her heart beat too fast.

He sighed, loosened his tie and went into the kitchen. He returned carrying a glass of white wine for her and bourbon for himself. He took a small sip before sitting down.

'I was with Nancy Cummings,' he said softly. 'With Nancy and her daughter, whenever I was late coming home. When I stayed at her apartment, it was because I was so exhausted that I fell asleep on her couch. I did not sleep with her. There is nothing sexual between us. Nothing romantic. You remember my promise, your promise, that we would always and forever be faithful to each other. I have never broken that promise.'

She remembered. Of course she remembered. A naïve promise made by the very young, very naïve lovers they had been on a sun-swept day. They had pledged that, unlike his parents' bitter coupling, they would always be true to each other. And then, hand in hand, they had walked to a nearby stream and, giggling with delight, for no reason at all they had washed each other's faces. She remembered still the feel of his hands as he touched her cheeks. He had such very large hands. She stared at them now, took a sip of her wine, struggled to regain her composure.

'Nothing sexual, nothing romantic,' she repeated and marveled that her voice remained calm even as she gripped the arms of her chair for support against the sudden dizziness that threatened to overwhelm her.

'I've never lied to you, Judith. You know that. I won't lie now. I will tell you the truth, as I told it to Brian.'

'Brian? You spoke to Brian?' she asked. Her hand trembled.

David drained his drink, stared at the empty glass as though pondering a refill and then set it down. She held her own glass tightly but she did not drink. She wanted no buffer to the pain she was certain his words would cause her.

'Yes. Brian called me some weeks ago. He and Denise were

concerned about what they saw as difficulties between us. And so I told him how I was coping. I explained that I was trying to spare you my grief, that I was afraid you would see it as weakness.'

'Why?' she asked. 'Why were you afraid of that?'

'Because you are so strong. You were strong enough to weep, to say Melanie's name aloud, to acknowledge her death, to find help where you could. My tears were frozen. I felt powerless. I loved you too much to impose my misery on you. I felt more alone than I had ever felt. And then one morning Nancy Cummings came into my office.'

He paused. She sat motionless, her hands clenched. He continued, speaking very slowly, all traces of that incipient stutter vanished as he described his initial meeting with Nancy, her instinctive understanding, her own story and how, mutually and similarly bereft, they had comforted each other. He spoke of Lauren, how he tutored her as once he had tutored Melanie, and then, with a surge of courage, he told her how he had wept in Nancy's comforting presence and then, exhausted by his tears, had fallen asleep on her sofa.

'On her sofa,' he said emphatically. 'Not in her bed.'

'Did you want to sleep in her bed? Did you want to make love to her?' she asked harshly and was immediately shamed by her punishing questions. She had no right to ask them. His guilt would not mitigate her own.

David's story, she reflected, was not unlike her own experience with Jeffrey Kahn. Jeffrey too had offered her a gentle expression of sympathy and understanding at a time when all condolences had ended. Even as Nancy and David had found common comfort in the mutuality of sudden loss, so she and Jeffrey had entered into a mutuality of grief. Nausea overcame her as she acknowledged that it was there that all similarity ended. She had, in fact, collapsed on to Jeffrey Kahn's bed. She had allowed him to make love to her. David had only felt the touch of Nancy Cummings' hand upon his own; he had slept on her sofa and taken comfort from her understanding of his grief. But, in the end, he too had been unfaithful. His infidelity had been emotional and unregretted.

She drained her wine glass, newly calm. The scales then were oddly and unevenly balanced. They were both guilty of betrayal. His answer to her question was irrelevant.

He stared at her as though trying to understand what she had asked but when he replied his voice was firm, unwavering. 'No,' he said. 'I did not want to sleep with her. It never occurred to me. You are my wife, you are my love. I could not, would not, ever betray all we have been to each other. What I want from Nancy is her understanding, her compassion. Her friendship. I want to continue helping Lauren because she is a lonely, father-less child. But I want to come home to this house, to you, to our life together.'

She stared down at her hands. They were no longer trembling, no longer clenched. His words had steadied her, had imbued her with courage. It was a time for honesty. She braced herself.

'I too have something to tell you. Jeffrey Kahn . . . Jeffrey Kahn and I . . .' Her voice broke.

She paused, and he put his hand to her lips.

'Don't say anything else,' he cautioned. 'I don't want to know.'

But she understood that he did know. Her voice, when she uttered Jeffrey's name, had betrayed the truth and it was a truth he could neither bear nor accept.

He was very pale. He drained his glass and rose from his seat, swaying unsteadily. She feared that he might fall.

'David,' she said, her voice broken, and held her hands out to him. 'Let me explain.'

'No. I don't need your explanation. I d–don't want your explanation.' The stutter had returned and would not be subdued.

She lowered her head. She did not know, after all, what explanation she could offer him.

They stared at each other.

'Are you hungry?' she asked.

He nodded. 'Ridiculously enough, I am.'

Hand in hand, like wounded children, they walked into their well-lit, cheerful kitchen.

She opened a can of mushroom soup, made a simple omelet. They ate in the dining room, politely passing each other salt and pepper shakers, she offering him the sliced sourdough bread he favored, he filling their water glasses and adding slices of lemon, the habits and gestures of their long marriage in place.

Washing up, she stared at her reflection in the small mirror that stood on the windowsill. Melanie's mirror. Was it really herself she was looking at? she wondered bitterly. Was she that sad-eyed woman, her face blanched by sorrow, vagrant strands of silver ribboning the cap of her smooth dark hair, who stared back at her from that mist-covered looking glass? Angrily, she wrapped the mirror in a tea towel and thrust it into a drawer.

It was David who went upstairs first. She heard him enter the room that had been Melanie's, that was now the office she had furnished so carefully. She heard him pull the sofa bed open. Swiftly then, she climbed the stairs and stood beside him.

'I need time,' he said. 'I think we both need time. Time alone. Apart.'

'Yes,' she agreed and did not recognize the sound of her own voice.

She went to the linen closet, pulled out sheets, a pillow, a blanket. Together, wordlessly, they made the bed, pulling the sheets tight, spreading the blanket wide. They had, after all, made up so many beds during their long years together. The domestic mechanisms of their marriage remained in place. He plugged in the hallway night light. She filled a glass of water and placed it where he could reach it easily in the night. Their movements were rote, their needs immediately apparent to each other.

She held out his pajamas, newly laundered, carefully folded. He took them from her and placed his hand very gently on her head. She nodded, as though the tender gesture required a response of a kind, and then left him to go into the bedroom. They would sleep apart for the first time since they had moved into this wide-windowed house.

NINETEEN

Their lives had changed but their routines remained strangely unaltered. Each morning David closed the sofa bed and stowed the linens and pajamas neatly in the closet. Judith brewed the coffee and set the table for breakfast. Sometimes they ate together, sometimes not. Most evenings he returned home for dinner, always calling to tell her which train he was taking. Judith's small, clever meals were dutifully prepared. They sat opposite each other at the carefully set table and spoke in the cadence of polite strangers – about the gardener's carelessness, a rooftop leak that had to be repaired, an electric bill that had gone astray. When he knew he would be late, he left messages on the answering machine and she never asked for a reason.

Immediately after dinner, when she had cleared the table, she retreated into the bedroom where she surrounded herself with the books she did not open and stared at the telephone that did not ring. He, as always, listened to his music, turned the pages of the newspaper and then went upstairs in his stockinged feet and very softly closed the door. The refurbished room had become his nocturnal fortress of solitude and sadness.

One morning, as they sipped their coffee, Judith shattered the quiet by telling him that Brian and Denise planned to spend two weeks at the end of August with Denise's family at their New Hampshire home. Denise's mother had called Judith and generously invited them as well.

'Not a good idea,' David said and she nodded her agreement.

They had always vacationed at the end of August but in this, the summer of their discontent, they had made no plans. It occurred to Judith that they were, in fact, on vacation from each other, their days apart, their evenings alone.

Determinedly, she adhered to her routine. Much to her own surprise, she wrote a précis for her long-delayed monograph, changing the topic and even choosing a tentative title: *An Approach to Grief and Loss in the Work of Women Writers*. Too expansive, she thought, but she could change it later. In the interim it offered her focus. Self-monitoring, she worked on it only during the set hours reserved for writing and research. She did not even think about it during her mornings at the thrift shop nor during the afternoons spent sorting through the rapidly diminishing clothing and personal effects that had belonged to Sylvia Kahn.

David, she knew, was faithful to his own routine. She did not know if Nancy Cummings continued to assist him. Their conversations were brief, civil and impersonal. One morning he told her that he was having lunch with Brian. She did not tell him that she was spending the afternoon at the Kahn house. She imagined her son and her husband seated opposite each other as she followed Jeffrey Kahn up to the dressing room. They stood on the threshold and stared at the nearly empty racks.

'Soon we will be finished,' she said.

'Still a great deal to do,' he countered, and she understood that he did not want their shared effort to come to an end.

The shelves were emptied and they turned their attention to the more personal items tucked into pale-blue quilted containers. There were delicate summer nightgowns and sturdier flannel ones, a profusion of undergarments, slips and bras, camisoles and a frothy collection of panties. The pastel-colored lingerie was beyond Jeffrey's scope. He abandoned them to Judith's discretion and busied himself instead with outdoor wear stored in a basement cedar closet, assembling coats and jackets in piles for her consideration.

She recalled her own frenetic swiftness as she dealt with Melanie's undergarments, the barely worn training bras, the flimsy panties embroidered with flowers or stamped with the days of the week, the cunning nightgown imprinted with magenta butterflies. She had brought them all to Goodwill.

Emptying those quilted containers of the dead woman's intimate clothing, she thought that Sylvia's daughters should have undertaken that task. Daughters were supposed to do that. She had done as much for her own mother and then for David's

mother, those dutiful but unloving women, both of them bred
to frugality. They were women who had mended the elastic
waistbands of their worn white cotton underpants and replaced
the straps of brassieres worn thin. Judith acknowledged that she
had seethed with resentment as she had stuffed those sad
remnants of vanished lives into shopping bags and thrust them
into the gaping maws of supermarket charity bins. But she,
unlike Jeffrey's daughters, had done her duty.

She sighed. She knew her annoyance at the Kahn sisters
living their lives to be entirely irrational. Annoyed with herself,
she worked swiftly, pausing to set aside two silk peignoirs, one
apricot and the other a pale violet, as well as a cotton robe of
sunshine yellow.

'Your daughters may want these,' she told Jeffrey, showing
him the peignoirs. 'When Beth marries, she may even want a
trousseau, if brides still have trousseaus. But I'd like to give
the robe to Emily, my little Korean protégé.'

'Yes. Of course,' he agreed, not even glancing at the garments.

He turned to her, his gaze concerned. 'Judith, is everything
OK? You've seemed so sad, so preoccupied these last few days.'

'I'm fine. It's just a difficult time for us. For David. For
myself.'

'Not because?' She heard the fear in his voice.

'No. Nothing to do with you.'

She spoke the lie with casual certitude and placed the
peignoirs in a newly emptied drawer, pressing a lavender-filled
sachet between them. At the very least, Sylvia's daughter would
carry her mother's scent to her marriage bed. She folded the
robe and placed it in an empty shopping bag. She would not
allow Emily to buy it. She would put money in the thrift shop
till and give it to her as a gift.

'You're fond of this young Korean girl?' Jeffrey asked, a new
topic, a safe topic.

'Very. I've sort of adopted her. A symbiotic relationship,
although she's unaware of it. She needs a mother and I need a
daughter.'

There was a familiar ring to the words she had not articulated
before. Of course. David had said as much when he spoke of
Nancy's child. Lauren needed a father and he needed a daughter,

he had said. She and David, bereaved mother and bereaved father, had each claimed a surrogate child. She smiled at the strange parallel. And Jeffrey, relieved by her smile, pulled her to her feet.

'I've bought croissants,' he said. 'And blueberry jam. The first of the season, they told me at the farmers' market.'

They sat opposite each other at the wooden kitchen table and sipped their iced tea on which sprigs of Sylvia's mint floated, smearing the deep blue jam on the golden pastry, talking softly, easily. She told him about Emily, about her brave little family, her beautiful baby and her hardworking medical student husband.

'I may be able to help them,' Jeffrey said. 'If he has any interest in ophthalmology, I just received a grant which covers a research assistant. Not a lot of money but more, I imagine, than he is making as a hospital aide.'

'That would be terrific,' she said.

He reached for his wallet, fumbled for his card which he handed to her. 'Give this to his wife and tell her he should call me. It would be my pleasure to help him.'

Driving home, she thought of Jeffrey's instinctive kindness, his need to make things better for others. Perhaps that was what had attracted him to Sylvia, whose life had been shadowed by the ghosts of the half-siblings she had never known. No. It had been more than that. Jeffrey had loved her. He had demonstrated that love in the serenity that he had offered her, their gracious home furnished with the softest of fabrics in the softest of colors at a sylvan remove from any urban or suburban intrusion. Garden fragrance drifted in through the wide windows in spring and summer, crisp clean air in fall and winter.

It was sad that Sylvia's death had been too early, too painful, but how good her life with Jeffrey had been. The depth of his grief reflected the depth of his love.

Tears came unbidden. Blinded and trembling, shamed by the envy she felt for a dead woman, she pulled over to the side of the road. She struggled, as the last rays of the dying sun danced in rhomboids of light across her windshield, to free herself from the weight of that sudden sadness.

*   *   *

'Your mother and I talked,' David told Brian.

They sat opposite each other at the same table in the same restaurant where they had last met. It was David who had initiated this meeting and Brian who had accepted with reluctance.

'Yes. I suppose you had to. Denise told me that she was having lunch with Mom and they saw you with Nancy and her daughter,' he said drily.

It angered him that he and Denise were enmeshed in this painful interplay between his parents, inadvertent actors in an unanticipated and frightening scenario. They felt strangely vulnerable, assailed by a threatening uncertainty.

Tales of familial dysfunction were not new to them. They were of a generation who exchanged the names of therapists and traded tales of childhood traumas. They read Facebook posts that abounded with unhappy confidences, revelations of despair, irrational promises of hope.

Things will get better. Hang in there.

Such reassurances were repeated with disturbing frequency.

Their close friends, Jennifer and Marc, both of them children of divorce, had separated only a year after their wedding. Brian had sat with Marc in a coffee shop and watched tears stream down his friend's face.

Frannie, Denise's college roommate, drifted from one lover to another. Her mother had been twice married. Her father lived with a girl as young as Frannie herself.

Brian and Denise had considered themselves to be exempt from such sad scenarios, protected as they were by the stability of their own families, their parents' long and intact marriages, their happy childhoods. Their past rendered their future secure, their horizons serene. They would marry and, like their parents, live happily ever after.

But that 'happily ever after' had vanished. Brian's family was shadowed by loss; his parents were no longer an indomitable couple.

Denise, sitting with Judith in the café, had seen the pain that flashed across her face as she watched David walk by, holding the hand of another woman's child. That pain, she thought, was but a symptom of a darker contagion to come. She feared its impact on Brian, on herself.

'We should move up our wedding date,' she told Brian. 'Why should we wait?'

'You're right,' he agreed.

They would preempt all danger and outrun the storm that threatened his parents and hovered darkly over their own future.

Brian watched his father butter a roll and set it aside. Only a short while ago, seated at this same table, he had listened patiently to David's explanation of his relationship with Nancy. Listened and pretended to understand. He listened to David now, but his patience was exhausted, his understanding strained by resentment. Why had his father delayed that promised conversation with his mother until she saw him strolling down Fifth Avenue with Nancy Cummings and her daughter? That silence had poisoned his mother's perception, ignited her suspicions. He could not blame her.

David passed him the buttered roll which Brian set aside.

'It was your mother, of course, who had the strength to speak about it, to ask me directly about my relationship with Nancy,' David said as the waiter placed platters of steaming ravioli in front of them.

He poked at the pasta he did not want, aware of Brian's annoyance and aware, too, that it was justified. Judith should not have been the one to initiate that painful conversation. He should have had the courage to talk to her before she saw him with Nancy and Lauren and jumped to dangerous assumptions.

'And you told her the truth?' Brian asked.

'Of course I told her the truth. I have nothing to hide.'

'And? What will happen now?'

Brian dared not speculate about his mother's reaction, dared not phrase the questions that haunted his dark imaginings. How angry had she been? How hurt? *Would they separate? Would they divorce?* The very words caused his stomach to clench, his heart to grow heavy. He had lost his sister; he did not want to lose his parents as well.

David smiled bitterly. 'The sky did not fall. We are, for all intents and purposes, as we were. Alone and together.'

'But at least now there is more honesty between you.' Brian spoke slowly, awkwardly. These were not words a son should offer his father.

'Yes. I was honest. Your mother keeps her own counsel.'

Judith's secret would remain her own. A mother did not burden her son with such a revelation. She would never speak of Jeffrey Kahn to Brian. Nor would he, of course. He called, too loudly, for a glass of wine, looked questioningly at Brian who shook his head. He did not want wine. He did not know what his father meant. He did not want to know.

'So you will go on as before?' he asked.

'For now, yes.' He did not tell Brian that he and Judith slept in separate rooms. His son would discern as much when he and Denise visited. Or perhaps not. Everything was in flux even as everything seemingly remained the same. Decisions were in abeyance. For now they were going on as before, living together, sleeping alone.

Brian felt a rush of relief. He wanted the home of his childhood to be undisturbed, his parents' marriage, however damaged, to endure.

'And Nancy?' he asked. 'You and Nancy?'

'She will continue to be part of my life. Judith – your mother – understands that.'

'Understands and accepts it?' Brian's tone was sharp with anger and disbelief.

'For now, yes,' David repeated.

For now. Clearly, for his father and his mother both, *now* was not forever. There was a *before.* There would be an *after.*

'All right,' Brian said. But it was not all right.

They finished their meal in silence. David drained his glass of wine and asked for another. They did not order coffee.

'My love to Denise,' David said as they parted, and Brian nodded.

What would he tell Denise? he wondered as he turned the corner. The truth, he decided. The honesty that had eluded his parents would be the cornerstone of their marriage. There was, and would be, nothing that he could not or would not share with Denise.

TWENTY

A burst of heavy heat, as summer drifted to its inevitable end, tented the thrift shop in lassitude. The fans revolved too slowly and the room was dimly lit to prevent the bright unshielded ceiling bulbs from adding to the oppressive sultriness. The pitcher of cold water on the front counter, available to thirsty customers and staff alike, grew warm within a half hour and had to be replenished. Even on pay days and on the bi-weekly arrival of welfare checks, there were few customers. The factory and hospital workers were on vacation or haunting air-conditioned cafeterias and coffee shops. Only a few regulars drifted in to sort their way through the clothing on the long tables or to finger the lonely garments that hung limply from twisted wire hangers.

'I don't know why we're bothering to open,' Suzanne complained to Judith.

'I know,' Judith agreed, but she was relieved that the shop did open, that she had a place to go, that the routine that was holding her life in place had not been disturbed.

Emily entered late one afternoon, the baby fully awake and sheltered in the cloth sling that rested between her mother's breasts. Seeing Judith, whom she now recognized, Jane's tiny rosebud mouth blossomed into a smile, but she made no sound. Emily wore a pale-blue cotton shift, a once-shapeless thrift shop purchase that she had tapered so that it fell in graceful folds around her slender body. It was loosely belted with a sash of crimson silk that matched the ribbon that tied back her silken smooth black hair.

'I am here to find some undershirts for my husband,' she told Judith in a very soft voice, as though the request for such intimate garments was an embarrassment.

Judith led her to a table across the room. The previous afternoon, a white-haired woman, recently widowed, had carried in two shopping bags bulging with her late husband's underwear.

A separate Bloomingdales bag had contained pristine packets of singlets, still in their cellophane wrappers.

'We thought he was getting better. I bought these undershirts because we thought he was getting better. And he was such a particular man. So clean. He never wore anything that was stained. So I wanted to have everything new and ready for him when he came home from the hospital. Only he didn't come home,' she had told Judith, her lined cheeks very pink, her eyes bright with unshed tears.

Judith had struggled to find comforting words. In the end, she had only murmured her thanks for the contribution. 'Someone will put them to good use,' she had assured the woman who had shrugged and shuffled out of the shop.

And they would be put to good use. Emily was delighted that they were brand new. 'Some things, you want them to be new,' she said in her stilted English. 'Things so close to the body. My husband, James, he is very clean, very particular.'

Judith smiled to hear the young Korean wife echo the words of the elderly Jewish woman.

She took the few bills Emily counted out, thrust them into the register then led the young woman into the back room and gave her the cotton robe that had belonged to Sylvia Kahn.

'It's beautiful,' Emily said, fingering the soft apricot-colored fabric, holding it against her body. 'But I can't afford it. I can't spend money on something like this.' She blushed, ashamed of her poverty, or, perhaps, of her craving.

'It is a gift,' Judith assured her gently. 'My gift to you.'

'But why?' Emily asked.

Judith hesitated. She could not tell Emily how important their brief encounters were to her, how seeing the baby offered her moments of sweet pleasure. 'It pleases me to give it to you,' she said at last. That at least was true. 'Allow me to do that.'

Emily bowed her head in appreciative acquiescence.

'And there is something else.' She handed Emily Jeffrey Kahn's card.

'Doctor Kahn? Who is this Doctor Kahn?' Emily asked.

'Doctor Kahn is my friend,' she murmured and hesitated at the word. Was that what Jeffrey Kahn was to her? *Friend.* The very word seemed inaccurate but she could think of no other. *Lover?* No, of course not.

She and Jeffrey were not, and never had been, and never would be lovers. They were friends, companions in grief, thrust together into an accidental intimacy, a dangerous coupling that was never repeated, that never would be repeated. She had tried to persuade herself that it could be easily dismissed, easily forgotten, but that, of course, had been a fragile fantasy. David's reaction when she had tried to speak of it, to explain it, had taught her as much. 'Jeffrey Kahn and I,' she had managed to murmur before David recoiled. She did not blame him, but she was tired of blaming herself.

She smiled wearily at Emily. 'A friend,' she repeated. 'A doctor. An ophthalmologist. He has a grant and he wants to hire a medical student to assist him in his research. I told him about your husband. If James is interested, he can call Doctor Kahn.'

Emily stared at her, stared at the card, then placed it carefully in her purse. 'You are so kind. I cannot believe how kind you are. You are like a miracle in my life.' She grasped Judith's two hands in her own and lifted them to her lips. Judith, in turn, touched her cheek and then rested her fingers on the baby's brow. Sunlight, streaming in through the only window in the small room, brushed their faces with a fleeting radiance.

Emily left, purchases in hand, the belt of Sylvia Kahn's apricot robe dangling from a plastic bag. She glided through the thrift shop, smiling at Suzanne who was busily sorting through a carton of newly donated china ornaments.

Judith joined her and, working together in perfect agreement, they decided to discard a chipped china pug dog but clapped their hands when they discovered an intact Lladro flautist.

'A thrift shop reward,' Suzanne said.

'Among others,' Judith agreed. She thought she might buy the Lladro, perhaps start a new collection, but she did not.

They ordered ice cream sodas and sipped them together, as they discussed a new public television series they were both watching. She and Suzanne had, Judith realized, as she drove home, drifted into friendship.

* * *

The heat-heavy days passed slowly. Customers were few, but antique dealers in search of treasure and an occasional jeweler ferreted through the jewelry that Suzanne kept in a small safe. The Lladro flautist sold within a day for a very good price to a woman who collected ceramic sculptures.

On a particularly hot afternoon, a pink-haired woman who owned an upscale jewelry shop in town shrieked loudly over her discovery of amber earrings and a necklace to match. Judith knew that she would place them in a velvet-lined leather box and price it high. She was angered when the woman haggled over the very modest amount Suzanne asked.

'We do this for charity, you know,' Suzanne said coldly.

'I am in business. I am not here for charity,' the woman retorted.

Suzanne remained firm, her price was accepted, and Judith flashed her an approving smile. Suzanne smiled back. They were increasingly in sync.

A trio of girls, students at the nearby extension unit of the community college, wandered in and headed to the racks on which vintage clothing hung. Mini-skirts hugged their bodies and exposed their sun-reddened thighs. Their bare arms were sleek with sweat, their T-shirts were too tight. Their trebling laughter shattered the summer silence. They tried on evening gowns of yesteryear, argued amiably over a wildly colorful wrap dress, draped stoles of gossamer fabrics over their shoulders. One by one they disappeared into the corner concealed by the plastic shower curtain, the improvised dressing room, and emerged in improbable and ridiculous finds which they proudly modeled. They giggled, tossed out derisive comments and hugged each other in foolish delight. There was laughter and applause for a very short, pale girl who had swathed herself in folds of pink tulle, a discarded bridesmaid's dress.

Judith watched them, overwhelmed by an unexpected melancholy, a flare of too familiar resentment. She knew its source. Her daughter would never idle away a summer afternoon with a group of laughing, carefree teenaged friends. She stared at the girls who pirouetted in front of the sun-streaked mirror in their ridiculous costumes.

Why should they be alive when Melanie was dead?

The viciousness, the irrationality of the thought shocked her. She averted her gaze from the happy trio, seized by a new determination. She had to stop wallowing in her own untamed grief and envy, she told herself firmly, reprovingly. It was wrong. She would have to wait for time to pass, for time to ease her pain, mitigate her anger. Time was what she needed. David's words echoed in memory. 'We need time,' he had said and belatedly she agreed. She willed herself to patience, to reluctant acceptance and amused admiration for these vibrant, giggling girls. She smiled at them and told them how pretty they looked.

The pink bridesmaid gown was purchased as well as the colorful wrap dress, and Suzanne, on impulse, tossed two of the stoles into another bag for the girl who was empty-handed.

'Come again,' she told them. 'We have some wonderful gently used clothing.'

They warbled their thanks and left, hurrying back to stifling classrooms and courses taught by very bored perspiring teachers.

'We never would have sold those stoles anyway,' Suzanne told Judith apologetically.

'Of course not,' Judith agreed.

That afternoon, as she prepared to leave, she suggested that she and Suzanne should confirm a date for lunch at the new salad place.

'Tomorrow?' Suzanne said at once.

Judith was surprised at the alacrity with which her suggestion was received. She had half expected to be refused.

TWENTY-ONE

The next day they drove together to the pleasant new restaurant, its walls papered with whimsical dancing flowers, its glass-topped tables and spindly white-legged chairs not unlike garden furniture. It was very distinctly a woman's refuge, flooded with light, the soft-voiced servers in long gauzy skirts, gliding gracefully across the room, balancing trays laden with brightly colored salads and fruit smoothies in tall glasses. Asked if they wanted a window seat, Judith, too swiftly, refused. Suzanne looked at her quizzically.

'I'm taking a vacation from people watching,' Judith explained. 'You never know whom you might see.' She laughed at the absurdity of her own words. There was no danger of seeing David on a weekday afternoon in this suburban village.

Suzanne nodded and studied the menu. They ordered and smiled at each other. Although they were at last comfortable with each other in the thrift shop, they felt a tentative unease in such neutral surroundings. Judith struggled to find an opening, but it was Suzanne who began their conversation.

'I'm glad we're doing this,' she said. 'Although it's taken us long enough. How long have you been working in the thrift shop?'

Judith thought for a moment. 'Since early spring. Late March maybe. The beginning of April? I really can't remember.'

She reflected now that the months had swept by with a swiftness she had not anticipated, each day punctuated by incidents and relationships she could not have imagined. She thought of Jeffrey Kahn. She thought of Emily. She thought of the confidences offered by weary customers, Consuela's pride in her grandchildren, the exchanges with the younger volunteers, their impromptu tea parties at which they drank from abandoned mugs and stirred their drinks with tarnished spoons.

'That's about right,' Suzanne agreed. 'I must admit that when you first came, I never thought you would last past a week. A lot of our volunteers drop out pretty quickly, you know.'

'I've noticed,' Judith said. 'Altruism has a very brief life.'

Their iced tea arrived and Suzanne trailed a finger across the frigid edge of the glass. Her nail polish was a dull bronze, and Judith thought it an attractive shade even as she realized that months ago she would have scorned it as she had scorned everything about Suzanne. Why had she been so intolerant, so swift to judgment?

'I myself wasn't sure I would stay on,' she continued. 'It was Denise, my son's fiancée, who sort of bullied me into it. With the best of intentions, of course. She thought I was too much alone, that volunteering would be good for me. I said I would give it a try because I knew that she and my son had worried about me since my daughter's death. And, to be honest, I was worried about myself. So I agreed to give the thrift shop a try, although I didn't think it would work out. I thought that I would be uncomfortable with the volunteers who were so much younger than me and even with . . .' Her voice trailed off.

'Even with me, I suppose.' Suzanne smiled as she completed the sentence. 'I understand. I myself didn't feel very comfortable with you when you first began volunteering.'

'Why?' It surprised her that she had caused any uneasiness in Suzanne, who had seemed to her so cool and controlled, so confident of her decisions.

'I'll be honest. A kind of envy. I saw you as someone of my generation, who had done all the things I had not done, who had everything that I myself wanted. A career, a husband, a son whose life was on track.'

'And a daughter who died,' Judith added drily.

It was, she knew, an unfair weapon, but it was safer than telling Suzanne that her envy was misplaced, that Judith's marriage was endangered, her son's life peripheral to her own, and that her career now seemed distant and stagnant to her. Within months her sabbatical year would end with little to show for it. Her marriage was bounded by uncertainty, her present and her future shadowed by grim and compounded losses.

Surprisingly, Suzanne reached across the table and lightly touched Judith's wrist.

'I know. Nothing can compare with the death of a child,' she said very softly. 'But your daughter's death was a medical tragedy. It was not a loss for which you feel responsible. My own loss fills me with guilt.' She spoke slowly. Her voice, always modulated and always commanding in that very modulation, drifted into a whisper.

Their salads arrived. Judith forked a rose-shaped radish, a plump asparagus spear and dipped them into a golden dressing.

'*Your* loss?' she asked tersely, rigid with resentment.

Was Suzanne equating her divorce, the loss of her marriage, with the death of a child, with Melanie's death? The very idea was ludicrous. But then she remembered hearing that Suzanne's son had serious problems. She struggled to remember his name. It surfaced. Eric. Yes, Eric. He had been Brian's high school classmate but not his friend. Tall and good-looking, the subject of dark rumors to which Judith had paid little attention and could not now recall. Was Suzanne thinking of Eric when she spoke of a loss?

Puzzled, she spoke again, softening her tone. 'I'm sorry. I don't know what you mean by your loss,' she said.

Suzanne, her color high, her eyes too bright, responded, her voice even more subdued. 'Yes. *My* loss. The loss of my son, Eric. He and your son were in the same class all through elementary school and high school.'

'I think I remember him,' Judith said carefully. 'But I'm not sure.'

'Probably because he and Brian were not friends. They moved in a different crowd. I assume that Brian didn't do drugs and didn't stumble into your house drunk or stoned when he was only a high school sophomore, that he wasn't off and on probation.'

She averted her gaze as she continued speaking, her every word etched in pain. 'And that's only the short list. What psychologists call the markers. It's a term that I know now. But I didn't know it then or probably I just didn't want to know it. His father and I tried not to think about them. Markers. A clinical word that we were sure did not apply to our son. We were both furious with the psychiatrist who first used it. We preferred to rationalize, Stan and I. We were in denial even as we sought help, even as we knew we needed it, he needed it. We didn't like the psychiatrists who offered darker and probably more realistic scenarios. We fed ourselves excuses and we liked the experts who agreed with our mantra. "All adolescents have problems." "Eric will mature." "Most kids go through a rough patch." "Things will get better." But of course things didn't get better. They got worse. Bit by bit, Eric was lost to us. And I watched it happen. Whatever I did, whatever I said, was the wrong thing to do, the wrong thing to say. I was the mother of a child playing in traffic and I didn't dart out into the road to save him. I couldn't. I was paralyzed. We both were. Stan and me, bewildered parents of a bewildering son. I blame myself for that paralysis. For not knowing what to do, what to say. For watching my beautiful boy become a stranger, who lied and stole and didn't give a damn about anyone or anything.'

Judith stared at her and struggled for annealing words. 'I'm sure you and Stan tried to be good parents, that you loved your son,' she said at last. 'You can't blame yourself. We've had workshops at the university to discuss kids like Eric. All sorts of dynamics and dimensions are at work. Peer pressure, brain chemistry, a culture of uncertainty.'

She spoke too quickly. She recognized the foolishness of her formulaic assurances. She knew nothing of Suzanne's family, but she did know how too many parents obsessed about the impact of their actions and attitudes on their children. The pages of glossy magazines exploded with useless advice, conflicting opinions. Tough love competed with demonstrative affection. Permissiveness and stern discipline vied with each other. Guilt had become the parental mantle, one which she herself had assumed.

Absurdly, briefly, in the days immediately after shiva, when the house was eerily empty, she had become obsessed with the thought that she might have prevented Melanie's death. She accused herself of missing vital signs, perhaps a headache too lightly dismissed, a sudden mood change that might have been a warning signal. She had confided her fears to her own internist, shared them with physician friends, all of whom had been adamant that she could have done nothing different. The aneurysm had been an undetected ticking bomb that could not have been defused. There had been no recourse, neither medical nor maternal. Its detonation had been inevitable.

In therapy sessions, Evelyn had patiently, and then impatiently, struggled to disabuse her of such absurd and unwarranted guilt. Angrily, unprofessionally, she had at last shouted a direct command. 'Stop that nonsense, Judith. No more stupidity!'

To Evelyn's admitted surprise, her outburst succeeded. Reason was restored. Judith accepted the doctors' assertions. Melanie's death was, as Suzanne had put it, a 'medical tragedy'. It could not have been prevented. Just as it was very possible that nothing Suzanne and her husband could have done would have prevented Eric's self-destructive behavior. His sad history could be called a psychological tragedy, an emotional tragedy.

'You're not being fair to yourself,' Judith told Suzanne, who shrugged.

'Maybe. Maybe not. We had always known that Eric had difficulties. He was what the nursery school teachers called an "acting out" toddler. Temper tantrums. Wild behavior. Grade school was no better. Pediatricians, psychologists assured us he would outgrow it. They talked about emotional delays. There was some therapy. They fed us theories about neurological development. ADHD. Chemical imbalance. Medication. Nothing made a difference. But Eric would mature, the experts said, and we decided to believe them because that was the easiest thing to do. And so we waited. We escaped into our own lives, Stan and I – he into his practice, conventions, seminars, investment clubs, while I sat on boards, organized galas for charities, haunted trunk sales, joined a bridge club, a book club – although I hate bridge and couldn't concentrate on reading. By high school it was clear that Eric was not maturing, that his problems were only getting worse. Everything accelerated. There was truancy, suspensions, meetings with guidance counselors, therapists, more medication. We tried everything. Psychologists. Psychopharmacologists. New medications. Ritalin, Adderall, specially designed compounds. Nothing worked. We tried a boarding school where Eric lasted three weeks before running away. He began experimenting with drugs and we countered it with packing him off to rehab. An exercise in futility.'

She paused and Judith saw that her eyes were bright with unshed tears. She reached across the table and took Suzanne's hand in her own. They sat quietly for a moment, their fingers intertwined, two women draped in separate sadnesses, offering each other the comfort of touch.

'But you tried,' Judith said at last. 'Give yourself credit for that.'

But even as she spoke, she knew that her words offered no comfort.

Suzanne sighed, nodded. 'Yes. We tried. Of course we tried. He was – he is – our son, our only child, and we loved him even as we began to despair of helping him. And we didn't give up. We rode the merry-go-round of advisors who had no real advice to dispense, no gold ring to catch. Some said tough love. Others talked intensive therapy, or maybe mindfulness, or maybe meditation. We went to therapists with Eric, without Eric, together, alone. Nothing worked. Nothing helped. And then we began to blame each other. I accused Stan of being an absent father, too busy with his practice, too intent on making money. And he accused me of spending too much time away from home, too many committees, too many bridge games, too many dinner parties. We were both right and we were both wrong.'

Judith nodded. She and David too, throughout these months of unshared grief, had been both right and wrong. She would not, could not, of course, say as much to Suzanne who continued to unleash a torrent of confidences as though the flow of words might lighten the heaviness of her heart.

'And then the police began coming.' Suzanne's voice was muffled. 'Eric was stopped for driving under the influence. Maybe alcohol, maybe drugs. We took away the keys to the car, threatened to stop his allowance. Two weeks later another arrest. A baggie of cocaine was found in the glove compartment of the stolen car he was driving. We called in a favor from a lawyer friend and posted bail. Then there was a call from a Manhattan hospital. Eric in a knife fight, his cheek slashed. We rushed down and Stan stitched him up himself. He's a good plastic surgeon. There's a scar, but it could have been a lot worse. Eric was actually proud of it. We bought and bribed our way out over one thing after another, shouting at him, shouting at each other, but we knew we had to do something drastic. There was a rehab center in Utah; they call it a residential therapeutic community – clever of them to find such a promising name. We were told it had a fabulous success rate, especially with kids like Eric. We had no choice – or at least we thought we had no choice – and we managed to get him there. He hated us for that. We flew there again and again for sessions that did nothing. Sometimes he refused to see us and the psychiatrists were vague about his progress. We argued with them, with Eric and with each other. We were exhausted, our marriage was drained. In the end, Stan left. It was inevitable, I suppose. He packed a suitcase, and I was alone in our home, which was really no home at all. Just a big, very expensively decorated house where three people who hardly talked to each other had lived for too many years.'

'You didn't try to talk to each other, to go for marriage counseling?' Judith asked, seized with a terror that had little to do with Suzanne's story.

'I told you. We had been to therapists. Not helpful. As for talking to each other – we had forgotten how. Silence becomes a habit.'

'Yes. Yes, it does,' Judith murmured. She knew that.

'And so we were divorced. I keep the writ of divorce in the top drawer of my bureau. It's the death certificate of my marriage, the certification of my bereavement, my loss. Strange, isn't it, that when a marriage dies there is no ritual to mark it. No burial, no shiva. No comforting visitors. But there is sorrow. And regret. And shame. And guilt.'

She fell silent and leaned back as though exhausted, her fingers circling the tall glass that had contained her iced tea and was now empty.

'And Eric?' Judith asked. 'Is he all right now?'

'We don't know. We may never know. He's gone. Ran away from that high-priced rehab. Disappeared from our lives. Both our lives. It's been three years since we heard from him. He may be alive, he may be dead. My heart stops every time the phone rings, whenever I receive a letter written in an unfamiliar hand. Sometimes I wish him dead so at least I would know. Isn't that a terrible thing for a mother to say, for a mother to think? And then there are days when I'm sure that he'll call, that he'll come home. I live in limbo, balanced between fear and hope. Without my son. That's *my* loss, Judith, *my* terrible loss.'

'I'm sorry,' Judith murmured and felt the inadequacy of the words.

'I apologize for throwing all this at you. I didn't mean to. It's really not my style,' Suzanne murmured. 'But please, don't feel sorry for me,' she added too quickly. 'Things are getting better. I'm taking hold of my life. I sold my house and bought myself a condo. And the thrift shop has been a lifesaver. It gave me focus, a meaningful project, and it showed me what I was capable of accomplishing. I'm thinking about registering for a graduate program in marketing which may be a good fit. I'm sleeping better and crying a lot less.'

'Me, too,' Judith said. 'I'm sleeping better and crying a lot less.'

She was suddenly suffused with admiration for Suzanne who managed to live day after day with such horrific uncertainty, never knowing whether her son was alive or dead, ill or healthy, homeless or sheltered. She, herself, was fortunate, she thought bitterly. Melanie was safe in death, mourned and remembered.

A single line of a poem, read and reread the previous evening, danced through her mind. She would share it with Suzanne who had on this sunlit day shared so much with her.

'Adrienne Rich has a line of poetry that speaks to me,' she said quietly. 'It's a small necklace of words that sort of sums up what I've been trying to do since my daughter's death and it's what you're actually doing, Suzanne. It reads, "Piece by piece I seem to re-enter the world." Piece by piece, Suzanne, you and I are both re-entering the world. The thrift shop and, I suppose, my involvement with Jeffrey Kahn, those are pieces that help with my re-entry.'

She was briefly surprised that she had included Jeffrey in the mosaic she was building, but she understood why she had done so. It was Jeffrey's compassionate caress, his body against her own, that had guided her back into a world where touch and tenderness soothed and comforted. It was Jeffrey, she realized with a clarity that resisted explanation, who had enabled her to respond to David's touch, David's tenderness.

The insight startled. Certainty gave way to doubt. David might never accept her relationship with Jeffrey, but perhaps he might come to understand it as she was slowly reaching an understanding of the compassion he accepted from Nancy. They were, Jeffrey and Nancy, herself and David, an unlikely quartet, temporarily entangled in a ballet of uncertain choreography.

'Jeffrey Kahn,' Suzanne said, picking up the thread of the conversation and smiling in wistful apology. 'I didn't mean to imply anything when I called him your Doctor Kahn. He's a nice man, isn't he?'

'He's a very nice man and Sylvia, his wife, was a very nice woman,' Judith agreed, relieved to be jerked away from thoughts she could not share. 'The Kahns were our neighbors years ago, before they became exurbanites. David and I liked them both.'

She knew that she mentioned David to dispel any lingering suspicions about her relationship with Jeffrey Kahn that Suzanne might harbor. Their nascent friendship, despite the confidences they had shared, had clear parameters.

Piece by piece, Adrienne Rich had said, and Judith understood that each such piece was fragile and had to be handled with care.

Suzanne nodded. 'Yes. The Kahns were a lovely couple,' she agreed. 'Sylvia was an interesting woman. He must miss her terribly.'

'He does. Of course he does,' Judith agreed.

Newly relaxed, newly in sync, they agreed to share a dessert. The honesty of their exchange, however limited, however painful, had been cathartic, and they spoke with ease, trading trivia, exchanging bits of gossip as they dipped their spoons into a chocolate mousse. They paid the bill, and Judith suggested that they go together one evening to see the new French film playing at the local arts theater.

'David won't mind?' Suzanne asked.

'No. He often works very late,' she replied. 'Let me know when you have a free evening.'

Such an arrangement, an evening out with a friend, was new to her, but she recognized its thrust. *Piece by piece* she was re-entering her world, however new and unpredictable that world might be.

Driving home that evening, she thought of what Suzanne's life must be like. She supposed that her condo would be tastefully furnished. Probably she had a cohort of friends and accepted casual invitations. Judith imagined her going home each night to that tastefully furnished condo, entering a darkened and silent room, and staring at a silent telephone, haunted by fear, teased by hope. Eric's disappearance was surely an agony, riddled as it was with dark possibilities and even darker probabilities.

They had been spared such suffering, she and David. Melanie had not vanished. She had died. Death, however bitter and grievous, was vested with certainty. It granted no latitude to dangerous speculations, grim imaginings. She understood why Suzanne had confessed to now and again wishing her son dead. Then, at least, all doubt could be put to rest. She too could plant a rose bush beside her child's grave.

Judith drove ever more slowly, suffused with pity for Suzanne for her solitude and her uncertainty, the life that she lived alone.

How would she herself cope with life alone if she and David were to divorce, Judith wondered. *Divorce.* A death of a kind, Suzanne had called it. 'Divorce. Death.' She said the words aloud. The repetition dizzied. A refluxion rose in her throat and she tasted vomit on her tongue.

Gasping for breath, she willed herself to calm and drove on through the gathering dusk. She turned the corner on to her own street and saw the glow of lamplight in the living room window. Reassured, breathing more easily, she parked and called his name as she turned her key in the door.

'David.'

He called to her in turn. 'Judith.'

Their voices melded. They met in the doorway and smiled tentatively at each other.

They ate dinner, their conversation, as always, careful, their voices calm. He told her that he had had lunch with Brian. She did not ask what they had talked about. She said that she had had lunch with Suzanne. He, in turn, did not press her for details of their conversation. She described the restaurant, the clever salads they served, the floral theme of the décor.

'Do they serve dinner?' he asked.

'I don't know. Why?' She wondered if he might suggest that they try it one evening and then she remembered that they were no longer a couple who went out for casual dinners. They were together but alone. But that might yet change. They were playing for time, both of them. She refilled his coffee cup and smiled at him hopefully.

'No reason,' he replied, and she recoiled in disappointment.

As always, he retreated into the living room, and as always she methodically cleared the table and washed up, leaving the counter in organized readiness for the next day's breakfast, his mug, her mug, plates and cutlery neatly arranged. She folded the napkins and stared at the arrangement, overwhelmed by a wild desire to sweep everything away, to leave shards of ceramic on the floor and to slam the door on the disarray. Instead, she opened the drawer in which she had placed Melanie's mirror, unwrapped it and stared at her own reflection. She wondered if her features had always been so finely sculpted or whether they had been honed to a new sharpness by her uncontained sorrow. She noted that a new arrow of silver shot through her dark hair. She sighed, rewrapped the mirror, watered the African violets on the windowsill and centered the pot more carefully. She arranged David's vitamin pills neatly in the tiny ceramic saucer crafted by Brian at a summer camp whose name she could no longer remember. Such small efforts soothed her. She recognized that she was striving for normalcy, for a return to the days when she and David had anticipated each other's needs, performing small acts of kindness and consideration.

Sighing, she dimmed the kitchen light and secured the garden door.

'Goodnight, David,' she called but she knew that the strains of the Berlioz *Requiem* obscured her voice.

In the room they no longer shared, she curled up in their large double bed where she now slept alone and surrounded herself with a small protective literary fortress – George Eliot's essays, a new biography of Jane Austen, the final collection of Virginia Woolf's letters, the slender volume of Adrienne Rich's poetry. She touched each book in turn but did not lift a single volume. Surrendering to a sudden and crushing fatigue, she fell into an uneasy sleep.

For the very first time she dreamed about Melanie. It began happily. They walked together, she and her daughter, through a beautiful garden, lined with beds of golden rosebuds and

long-stalked purple irises. Their hands were linked. Melanie
bent to pluck a blossom. The golden rose turned blood-red in
her hand. Suddenly, she sprinted forward and ran wildly down
a path. Judith called her name and chased after her, her breath
coming in painful gasps, but Melanie did not turn. Instead, she
ran faster and faster, leaving a trail of crimson petals that turned
into small pools of viscous liquid. At the end of the garden
path, an abyss of damp earth yawned open before her. She
shrieked as she stumbled into it and shrieked again as the dark
quicksand enveloped her, as she sank, slowly, inch by inch, into
that oozing grave while Judith wept and shouted her name.

'Melanie! Melanie!'

The sound of her own voice wakened her. Her throat was raw;
her white nightgown was drenched with sweat. Her heart pounded
in an unfamiliar tympanic beat. Trembling, she struggled to
contain her fear.

'Melanie! Melanie!'

She was fully awake now, but she could not stop calling her
daughter's name, each syllable resonant with the terror she could
not control.

It was David who restored her to calm.

He sat beside her, held her close and comforted her, his hands
gently stroking her quivering body. 'A dream. Only a dream,'
he said softly. 'Everything will be all right, Judith.'

His words, his tone, were familiar. Always, during the early
years of their marriage, when she had been haunted by infrequent nightmares, he had known instinctively how to soothe
her, how to reassure her. The habit of decades had been neither
negated nor forgotten. The comfort he offered, as always,
filled her with gratitude.

He stood, looking strangely boyish in his striped pajamas,
his feet bare, crusty bits of sleep interrupted rimming his eyes.
She had wakened him, she knew.

'David, thank you.' Her voice was a whisper.

'It was just a nightmare,' he murmured. 'It's over. You're
fine.'

'Yes,' she said. 'I am.'

She pulled the covers back, thrust the books that littered his
side of the bed to the floor, straightened his pillow, each gesture

a silent plea. She wanted him to lie down beside her. She wanted to feel herself safe in his arms.

He hesitated, smiled and shook his head. 'Not now. Not yet.'

When?

The question. unasked froze in her throat. Wounded, her eyes closed, she leaned back and hoped that she would not weep.

Leaving the door ajar, he padded down the darkened hallway to the room where he lay alone and awake through the long night.

TWENTY-TWO

David left the house earlier than usual the next morning, the lone passenger on the very first commuter train. He ate breakfast at a McDonalds near Grand Central, something he had never done before, the routine of years violated. It had long been Judith's habit to set the table in their breakfast nook each evening, and every morning the scent of coffee, brewed on a percolator timed to the morning hour, drifted through the room. In that she unknowingly emulated his mother who had doggedly imposed order on his boyhood home, everything in its place, never a cup in the sink or a dirty plate on a counter. It had been, he supposed, her compensation for the emotional chaos she had endured when his father confessed his brief and much-regretted infidelity.

David had long nursed the fantasy that if his father had remained silent, their lives would have been different. Unsaid words could not be regretted. It was that fantasy, he thought bitterly, that had prevented him from telling Judith about Nancy and imposed silence when she, in turn, spoke Jeffrey Kahn's name.

'Jeffrey Kahn and I,' she had begun, and he had not allowed her to finish the sentence.

He had feared that the words she might add would forever alter the increasingly uneasy balance of their shared life. He had opted for the safety of silence, the pretense of ignorance, a withdrawal from intimacy. A foolish and dangerous option.

He drank his watered-down orange juice and realized how foolish he had been, how futile his effort to pretend not to know what, of course, he knew. His marriage, his and Judith's, was not a replica of his parents' tortuous coupling. It was of their own making. Its future, its survival would be determined by their own choices. Her misstep and his own would not cancel out the years they had shared, the love that had sustained them, the terrible loss they had endured. That he had realized during the long hours of a sleepless night, haunted as he was by the memory of her ghostly pallor in the aftermath of the nightmare. He had held her close as she trembled and shrieked their daughter's name.

Lying awake, isolated images had floated through his mind in a disorderly jumble of memories and half dreams. Drifting images. He saw Nancy, so quiet, so consoling, burdened with a grief that matched his own, unafraid of his tears. Melanie. And Judith. His Melanie. His Judith. How clearly they appeared to him in reverie. Melanie whirled into Judith's outstretched arms. They danced together, his wife and his daughter, and he smiled at their grace even as he himself clumsily spilled a glass of wine. Had that ever happened, he wondered, or was it a waking dream wrested from the depths of his imagination?

Judith. Yes. His Judith. He knew that he should not have left her when she so clearly wanted him to stay, when she needed him so badly. He did not understand why he had done that. Yes, he did know. He had left their bedroom, although he had, in fact, yearned to lie down beside her, to enfold her in his arms. But even at that moment he had feared the conversation that would surely follow such closeness and he had not known what he would say, what he wanted to say.

He had turned back before he closed the door and had glimpsed the tears that silvered her cheeks. Her outstretched arms, within the wide white wings of her sleeves, were atremble, and yet he had not returned to her bed, to *their* bed. He had failed her again, as he had failed her through all the long nights of their sadly separate mourning.

He lay in a tangle of sweat-drenched sheets, and in the miasma of a half sleep he saw her, graceful, so graceful, gliding through her grief, hand in hand with Jeffrey Kahn, a man bereft, a man in need. As she was. As he himself was. As Nancy was. All of them thrust together by losses grievous and incalculable. He slept briefly and jerked into wakefulness at dawn, the invasive images of those dark imaginings intact. He fled his home, fled the neatly set breakfast table in search of a neutral landscape.

Seated at the formica table, he stirred his coffee, newly

determined to concentrate, organize his thoughts, sort through memories, weigh realities. He and Judith could not continue to live in limbo. It was time to assess their marriage, its strengths, its fragilities. It was time for them to come to a decision, which should not be difficult.

Decisions, he thought wryly, were his stock in trade. He was trained in a discipline that required the careful weighing of alternatives, the balancing of conflicting arguments, conflicting views. He envisioned a balance sheet, similar to those so useful in his work. There would be two headings: *Judith, David.* Or perhaps *Marriage, Divorce.* He would list assets and deficits, the choices and settlements available to each of them, the pros and cons of alternate decisions. He found a pen in his briefcase, plucked up a paper napkin and outlined a ledger page, drawing two wavering lines, writing too swiftly. Two columns. *Marriage. Divorce.*

He stared at the word, saw that he had misspelled it and crossed it out. The word itself, in its dark and hopeless enormity, filled him with despair. He crumbled the napkin and tossed it on to a tray already littered with trash. All rational thought was abandoned. He knew himself to be incapable of making a decision. Not yet. No, not yet. There was Nancy to consider.

It was Nancy, after all, who had rescued him from his solitary sorrow. It pleased him that her daughter slept in the bed that had belonged to Melanie. It comforted him to watch the child pad barefoot across the red carpet, her tiny toes, like Melanie's, plump and pink. He recognized that he was indulging in a fantasy, but it did not impact on fidelity to Judith.

He would not, could not, be unfaithful to her. He loved her; he had pledged himself to her. He had been foolish not to tell her about Nancy from the outset, but he knew it to be a foolishness born of fear, fear that she would not understand, fear that she would think him weak, fear that in turning to Nancy he had rejected her. And, he acknowledged, he had perhaps done just that. Unwittingly, unwillingly.

'Jeffrey Kahn and I,' she had begun.

It was a sentence that he would not allow her to complete, its ending clear despite words unsaid. With that silence, the balance of their marriage was altered; weights were redistributed on trembling scales that listed now one way, now another.

They needed more time, he had thought then, a suspension of intimacy, the clarity of nocturnal solitude. They were at a crossroads and there were decisions to be made.

He remembered that Judith, years ago, had spoken of marriage, all marriages, as novels with many chapters. They were in a new chapter then, their roles reversed, their narrative undefined, their separate needs elusive. *How would it end?*

'How?'

He spoke the single word aloud, indifferent to the startled stares of the two women at the next table. They shrugged and continued their conversation. He stared down at the Egg McMuffin he could not bear to eat and sipped the bitter coffee now grown tepid. He felt the cold shadow of fear and knew, at last, how he wanted the next chapter of his marriage to read.

A homeless man sank into the seat opposite him, his eyes rheumy, a rank odor emanating from his unwashed clothes. He pointed to David's untouched food.

'You gonna eat that, buddy?' he asked.

'No,' David said and shoved it toward him.

He glanced at his watch. He would call Judith and suggest that they have dinner out. He imagined talking to her very softly across a table set with a white cloth on which a small lamp glowed. The thought comforted him. They would dispel their silence, talk their way into a future. Alone? Together? He dared not speculate. Walking very slowly, he headed up Madison Avenue toward his office.

He waited until early afternoon to call Judith. She did not answer her cell phone. He tried the thrift shop and spoke to Suzanne Brody. Judith had been in earlier but she had left for the Kahn house and would not be back that day.

'Yes, of course,' David said. 'I should have remembered.'

He could not remember what he had never known. He sat quietly at his desk, his eyes closed, and willed himself to calm. Rationalizations tumbled over each other. Of course she was at the Kahn house. Why wouldn't she be? She had told him that there was still much to be dealt with there. She was responsible. She would not leave a project unfinished.

All right, then, he told himself. *She will be home before dinner. I'll call her then and ask her to choose a restaurant.*

He thought again of the lamp-lit table covered with a white cloth and was comforted.

TWENTY-THREE

Unlike David, Judith wakened from her fitful sleep later than usual. Dizzied after her dream-haunted night, she stood in the kitchen and saw that David's breakfast setting was untouched. The fragrance of brewed coffee, the special blend he favored, wafted through the room but the carafe was full. She took it as a sign, akin to his retreat from their bedroom the previous evening. The routine of their marriage was dangerously altered. She poured the coffee into the sink, dressed quickly, stopped at a Starbucks for a latte and a croissant, and drove too rapidly to the thrift shop. Glancing in her car mirror, she was startled by her own pallor and too swiftly rouged her cheeks.

She stood behind the counter, drinking her coffee, and watched as a middle-aged couple, both of them overweight and dough-faced, argued fiercely over whether or not to purchase a small coffee table. They gesticulated angrily and stormed out, the table abandoned, hatred in their eyes. They were frequent customers, timewasters who wandered in now and again, and inevitably disagreed fiercely over the smallest purchases. She wanted to buy a ceramic napkin holder. He refused. He wanted a bedside lamp. She snatched it from his hand. They were skilled at hurling anger at each other. Judith thought it probable that their uncontained fury gave focus, however negative, to their marriage.

What was it that gave focus to her own marriage, she wondered but dared not follow the thought further. She did not want to recall the previous evening; she closed her mind to the memory of David leaving their bedroom in silence, her plea rejected, the tears that streaked her cheeks ignored. She, in turn, had not called after him, compounding his rejection with her own. They had each opted for a muteness that was neither comforting nor cathartic.

'Hi, Mrs Mandell, do you think you can help me?'

Audrey, a sweet-faced girl, a frequent and favorite customer, smiled shyly at her.

'Of course. No problem. I'll be glad to help you.'

The distraction from her own dark thoughts was welcome and she listened with great attentiveness as Audrey explained that she wanted curtains for the kitchen of her newly assigned apartment in a halfway house. Judith knew that Audrey was a recovering addict who had recently completed a county-sponsored program. She knew, too, that Suzanne always went out of her way to help her, but Suzanne, standing nearby, was busy with another customer.

'Everything is so great.' Audrey spoke in a burst of manic enthusiasm. 'I love the apartment. I have a boyfriend. He lives a floor below me. I registered for classes at the community college. Phlebotomy. You know – taking blood. I even have a job interview.'

'Wonderful,' Judith said, and she and Suzanne locked eyes.

They did not believe Audrey but they envied her ability to reinvent herself, to take delight in small, uncertain pleasures – a course that she might fail, an interview for a job she might not get. They themselves were incapable of self-deception. The losses that limned their lives, their vanished children, their marriages, the one ended, the other endangered, were ever present in mind and heart.

They smiled at Audrey, cautioned her to get enough sleep, to eat nourishing meals. Suzanne found a set of almost new red-and-white checked curtains and Judith charged her only half the price scrawled on the tag.

Their own kindness pleased them and they turned to greet the next arrivals, two dark-haired women, their faces ashen, their eyes reddened with weeping. They entered very quietly, both of them moving with matching grace and swiftness, their faces and their expressions so similar that they had to be sisters. One of them thrust a wedding dress, sheathed in a clear plastic garment bag, across the counter. The other placed a bag that contained long white gloves and white high-heeled strapless slippers next to it. As swiftly as they had entered, they hurried out, before questions could be asked or a donation receipt filled out. Suzanne and Judith, Libby, Lois and the other volunteers stared after them, saddened and intrigued.

The pristine dress was held up and admired. The sheer sleeves and the bouffant skirt met with approval. Almost at once, there were speculations about its history and alternate stories were suggested. Clearly a wedding had been canceled, but which of the sisters had been the bride? Lois thought that the young women were twins. An older woman, who was a very occasional volunteer, recognized the sisters as the daughters of a quiet couple who lived on her street. The girls had always been inseparable, had often dressed alike, although they were not, in fact, twins. She could not remember their names, but she had heard that one of them was to be married, at summer's end.

A discussion ensued about what might have led to a broken engagement at such a late date. Perhaps the groom had opted out. Lois knew of a marriage canceled because the girl's fiancé had confessed to being gay. They toyed with the possibility and dismissed it. Libby thought it was probably the bride who had decided against the marriage. It might have meant moving to a distant city and leaving her sister.

The volley of creative scenarios gathered momentum even as they smiled absently at customers and sorted through piles of new donations. They traded hypothetical situations and frivolous imaginings woven of suspicion and supposition. Such flights of fancy, such harmless fictional invasions of other people's lives, were a thrift shop perk.

'What do you think, Judith?' Libby asked.

Judith could often be counted on for creative scenarios, but oppressed by her own dark mood, she remained silent. She had registered the misery on the sisters' faces. She could not, would not, mock its source, close as she was to her own nocturnal sadness. She did not want to think about weddings and marriages.

She carried the bridal gown, staggering beneath its weight, to a rack already crowded with formal finery. It dangled there, a ghostly presence, amid discarded gem-colored prom dresses and pastel bouffant bridesmaid gowns.

Briefly, she stared at herself in the mirror, noting that she had lost weight. Her favorite black shirt and her black cotton slacks hung too loosely on her narrow frame.

Why had she chosen to dress like a widow this morning? She was still a wife, albeit a wife who had slept alone and wakened to an empty house, an absent husband, an undisturbed breakfast table.

Dispirited, she wandered back to the counter, relieved that the chattering volunteers had dispersed for lunch, where, of course, additional fantasies about the mysterious wedding gown would be created.

Suzanne glanced at her. 'Are you all right, Judith?' she asked. 'You look very pale.'

'Fine,' she replied.

But she was not fine. She moved slowly, struggling not to sink into a quicksand of sadness, the lingering residue of her fearsome dream and her anxious wakefulness. She realized that she was hungry, but the thought of food repelled her. Always, at times of stress, she had found herself unable to eat. In that, she and David were strangely similar.

Helping Suzanne wrap coins in paper cocoons, she recalled a distant summer when Brian, still a small boy, experienced an asthma attack that could not be controlled by either inhaler or nebulizer. He had been rushed to the hospital and she and David had sat at his bedside in anxious vigil, willing each other to hope, willing Brian to recover. She remembered still the light touch of David's hand upon her head, the softness of his lips when Brian's breath finally came with ease and the color returned to his face.

Satisfied that he had recovered, they had gone out for breakfast, an enormous diner breakfast – pancakes and eggs, croissants slathered with jam and butter. They had eaten voraciously, emptying carafes of coffee and ordering pie, ravenous because neither of them had been able to eat or drink during the long hours of anxious waiting.

It occurred to her that David had ignored the carefully set breakfast table that morning because, beset by anxiety, he could not eat. The thought offered no relief but incurred a lingering sadness, a longing for the vanished days when she and David had held each other close in the aftermath of losses or disappointments. They had comforted each other over the betrayal of friends, professional and personal hopes inexplicably dashed, the deaths of their parents, all the cascading events of a long marriage. What was important to the one had been important to the other. She wondered if that mutuality of caring and sharing would be reclaimed. She wondered if she wanted that reclamation. The question haunted. No answer presented itself.

She listened to the thrift shop chatter without interest as she moved robotically, silently, busying herself with small chores, moving a bin from one counter to another, folding scattered garments. Scraps of conversation floated toward her. Suzanne wondered what she might charge for the wedding gown. She knew of a consignment shop that handled only wedding gowns. Libby thought they should wait. The bride might yet reconsider. A customer asked if they had any maternity dresses. A child cried and would not be comforted.

Judith went to the rack where the bridal gown hung. She zipped open the clear plastic garment bag and released the heavy long white dress, cradling it in her outstretched arms. It was of fine ivory silk. Golden butterflies embroidered in satin thread floated across the bouffant skirt. It was those sun-colored butterflies that sent hot tears streaming down her cheeks and ignited wild and irrational regret.

She should have raced after the sad-eyed sisters and pleaded with the newly reluctant bride to reclaim the dress, to proceed with the wedding. She should have offered her Jane Austen's insistence that a happy marriage was entirely a matter of chance. A chance should be seized. Never mind that one sister would be left behind. In time she would opt for a similar gamble and sail into uneasy, unpredictable marriage in that same butterfly-spangled dress. There were, after all, no guarantees, not in life, not in marriage.

Austen, that spinster chronicler of likely and unlikely romances, had understood that every coupling was a unique novel, divided into chapters. Final chapters, both happy and unhappy, hung in the balance. That was, after all, what kept pages turning and hearts beating as sense and sensibility converged. She remembered discussing that with David, all those years ago, and she wondered if he had any memory of that conversation.

She wiped her eyes and smiled wryly at the absurdity of her own thoughts. How could she have urged that almost-bride and her sad-eyed sister to seize upon Austen's advice when she herself did not know how the final chapter of her own marriage would read? Or, indeed, how she wanted it to read. Should the final line be *Judith and David lived happily ever after*? Or *They parted with great sadness*?

The ridiculous irrationality of her thoughts staunched any remaining tears. She returned the wedding dress to its plastic shroud. She was tired, she realized, so very tired.

The thrift shop phone rang and Suzanne answered it. 'Judith,' she called. 'It's for you.'

She hurried to take the call, hoping that it would be David. But it was Evelyn, apologetically canceling an appointment that Judith had meant to cancel herself.

David would not call. She decided that she was not even sure that she wanted him to.

She knew with sudden certainty that she did not want to remain in the thrift shop nor did she want to return home. She realized, with surprising clarity, exactly where she wanted to go. She turned to Suzanne. 'I'm going to drive out to the Kahn house. There's still a lot to do there,' she said. 'I'll grab a yogurt on the way.' She was, she realized without surprise, ready to eat.

She picked up her bag and left, managing a casual wave.

In the car, driving northward, she tried to remember if she had told Jeffrey she would come that afternoon, but it did not matter. If he was not at home, she would sit on the stone bench in his garden and watch the birds of summer congregate in the feeder that hung from the lowest branch of his flowering cherry tree. It was, she told herself, sylvan solitude that she sought.

She parked in his circular driveway and saw at once that his car was gone and the front door was closed. He was not home. His absence did not disappoint her. She went into the garden where amber rays of sunlight danced through the thick-leafed branches of fruit trees and shone brightly on the garden that a dead woman had planned and planted with such care. Vegetables and flowers were interspersed. Tall irises, in all their purple splendor, towered over dwarf tomato plants heavy with ruby-red fruit. Pale green cucumbers dangled from delicate vines. Wands of dill waved in the slight breeze and bright green sprigs of parsley gleamed in the dark, well-watered earth. Jeffrey weeded diligently and harvested carefully. He was, she knew, in all things, diligent and careful, a devoted custodian of his wife's bright and fragrant legacy.

Judith realized that she was hungry, very hungry. She had

not, after all, stopped for yogurt. She plucked one tomato and then another, and ate them swiftly, allowing juice and seeds to run down her chin. She crunched a cucumber, chewed on sprays of dill and parsley, then turned on the garden spigot, cupped her hands and filled them with clear cold water. She drank deeply. Satisfied, newly calm, she was overwhelmed by a haunting fatigue. Of course she was tired. She had barely slept the previous night. She stretched out on the stone bench. Indifferent to the hard surface and blanketed by sunlight, she fell into a deep and dreamless sleep.

She awakened to his touch on her face. Jeffrey very gently wiped away the tomato stains on her chin. Flustered, she sat up and laughed nervously. 'I'm sorry. I fell asleep waiting for you. What time is it?'

He glanced at his watch. 'Three o'clock.'

She gasped. She had been asleep for two hours.

'I must have been really tired,' she said. 'And I'm afraid I looted your garden.'

'I hope you enjoyed whatever you ate. The tomatoes are especially good this year,' he said soberly, but his lips twitched in a barely perceptible smile of amusement.

'They are. They were,' she agreed. 'I wasn't sure whether we were supposed to meet today but I took a chance and drove out.'

'No. I think we had agreed on tomorrow, but I'm glad you're here. It's a relief not to come home to an empty house.'

She said nothing. She did not want to tell him that she herself had wakened that morning to an empty house.

'We still have enough time to get something done,' he said. 'You mentioned going through Sylvia's handbags next.'

'Yes. Let's start on them today.'

She knew that sorting through that large accumulation would not be an easy task. Women were addicted to their handbags. They were donated in great profusion to the thrift shop where Suzanne stored them in overflowing cartons in the back room, periodically selecting a few to be offered for sale. Only the previous week Judith had helped a wizened elderly woman rummage through an overflowing bin until she finally selected a small black leather bag,

'Just big enough for what I need,' she had said happily.

Standing at the counter, she had transferred the contents of her larger battered bag into her new purchase.

Two days later she returned and handed Judith two crisp hundred-dollar bills. She had found them, wrapped in Kleenex, in the zippered compartment of the bag. She had refused any reward.

'I do not keep money that is not mine,' she had said self-righteously.

Suzanne had included the bills in that day's receipts and returned the purchase price of the bag to the elderly customer.

Judith was certain that there would be no hidden cache of bills in any of Sylvia Kahn's purses. Sylvia had been too familiar with poverty to ever be careless with money.

'I warn you, there's a lot to deal with. Sylvia had a passion for handbags,' Jeffrey said.

She followed him up the stairs to the dressing room where he flung open the door of a multi-shelved cabinet. She gasped at the enormity of its contents. He lifted one bag and then another, handing each to her.

'I don't know why she bought so many,' he said apologetically. 'She would bring one home and apologize for buying it and tell me that she knew she did not need it but she couldn't resist. She would return it if I thought she should. But I always told her it was fine, that of course she should keep it, and so she continued to accumulate them, year after year. She took wonderful care of them. She wiped the leather ones with a chamois cloth, massaged them with a special oil. I would sometimes stand in the doorway and watch her as she sorted through them. She sat on the floor, right here, examining one and then another, sometimes trying to decide which one to use that day, sometimes transferring the contents of one bag to another, occasionally simply rearranging them. I teased her, told her that she was like a child surrounded by toys, trying to decide which one she should play with. Stupid of me to say that to my Sylvia who had never had a childhood, had never owned a toy.' His voice drifted from sadness into silence.

'A lot of women have a handbag obsession,' she said, careful to keep her tone light. 'I can relate to that. I have too many myself. We carry around all sorts of stuff we'll probably never need. Insurance of a kind, I suppose.'

She glanced at her own bag, an oversized sack of soft brown leather, its contents so heavy it often caused her shoulder to ache. She chastised herself for carrying so many items yet discarded nothing. She took a mental inventory. There was a small leather folio of tattered photographs: David and herself on their wedding day, snapshots taken on vacations, studio portraits of Brian as a small boy and then in cap and gown at his college graduation, one of Melanie wearing her precious pink cardigan and smiling impishly, a frayed and fading Polaroid shot of her parents whose faces she could barely remember. A small leather address book, its thin pages crowded with the names of friends and acquaintances, relatives and colleagues, some crossed out, others underlined, was thrust in a separate compartment with the keys to all the way stations of her life – the house, the car, her office at the university. A red ribbon was looped around the key to the thrift shop.

Her pigskin wallet bulged with credit cards and loyalty cards, cards for the local library and the university library, as well as a discreet amount of cash. Her insurance cards and driver's license were in a thin case of red Moroccan leather that matched the pouch containing her makeup, gifts from Denise, ever anxious to please. And, of course, a pocket volume of Emily Dickinson's poems, her 'emergency' reading. She read Dickinson in doctors' offices, in supermarket lines and now and again while waiting for a very long light to change. She acknowledged that it was because she was too often unwilling to be alone with her thoughts.

Once, hefting the bag, David had commented on its weight. 'What do you have in there?' he had asked.

'My life,' she had replied.

It had not been a casual answer. She had thought then and thought now that the lives of most women might be revealed by the contents of their handbags. Surely that had been especially true of Sylvia, whose early life had conditioned her to be especially careful with those portable amulets of her existence. Jeffrey Kahn was wrong. She had not thought of her handbags and their contents as toys. The importance of official documents, her driver's license and insurance card guaranteed Sylvia's identity. Her house keys meant that she, who had lived in a fetid shack, had a home. Her handbags, obsessively purchased and carefully organized, their contents transferred with such care, offered reassuring proof of her late-gained security.

Judith sighed and they began to work, faithful to their established routine. Like all of Sylvia's possessions, the bags were carefully arranged and stored according to the season of their use. They began with those designed for winter. They were of different sizes and of different-colored fine leather, black and brown, deep maroon and dark blue, a cheerful red and a sober forest-green, some zippered, some buckled.

Jeffrey handed them to her, one by one, and Judith opened each and stroked the faded linings on some of which the scent of face powder lingered. Satisfied that they were empty, she placed each one carefully in the yawning carton.

They tackled those purses clearly meant for spring and summer, some crafted of fabric in pastel colors, others woven of straw, two envelope purses, one white, the other a bright yellow. In one she found a penny, in the other the dried petals of pink primrose. She left both the penny and the petals in place, snapped them shut and passed them to Jeffrey. But when she found a carefully folded handkerchief embroidered with the initials *S.K.* in a crocheted purse she handed the white linen square to him. He lifted it to his cheek. His tears dampened the delicate fabric and his shoulders quivered.

'I'm sorry,' he said. 'It overwhelms me sometimes.'

It. The word that substituted for death, for irrevocable loss, for grief uncontained. Words the bereaved avoided, words they feared. *It* was a substitute, however inadequate.

'I understand.'

She understood. Of course she understood. She went into the bathroom where she ran a wash cloth beneath cold water. He remained seated on the floor, a grief-stricken mourner frozen into rigidity, still clutching the handkerchief. She passed the cloth across his brow, then his cheeks, bringing it up to rest beneath his eyes. He moaned softly. His body uncoiled. He swiveled toward her, gripped her wrist and drew her toward him. Almost at once he released her.

'I'm sorry,' he said. 'It's just that I needed – need – to touch someone, someone who cares. Someone' – he stumbled over the words but spoke them at last – 'who understands.'

'I know,' she murmured.

She remembered how grateful she had been for David's reassuring touch the previous night. The gentle stroke of his hands across her quivering body had banished the terror of her dream and, for that brief moment, restored him to her. Why, then, had he left their room and why had she not called after him? She supposed it was because they were mutually frightened, fearful of rejection which, at such a moment, might mean the death of hope. Jeffrey Kahn had no such fear. All he wanted from her was the transitory comfort of closeness.

She took his hand and lay down beside him. Fingers clasped, they fell asleep and awakened to the gathering shadows of early evening.

'It's late,' he said. 'Shouldn't you be getting home?'

She glanced at her cell phone. David had called more than once but he had left no messages. She called her home. There was no answer. Her heart sank. Where was he at this twilight hour? She feared the answer and did not call his cell phone.

'I can stay for a bit,' she said. 'Coffee would be great.'

He smiled. 'I can do a little better than that,' he said.

She followed him into the kitchen where, with the swiftness of the solitary dweller, he prepared a salad, a platter of cheese and opened a bottle of wine. They sat opposite each other at the well-scrubbed table and talked easily. He told her that his younger daughter was in a new and what she described as a 'serious' relationship. She had not said much more.

'And, of course, I do not ask too many questions. My daughters are adults. Their lives are their own. I understand that. But still I worry about them. Not constantly. Only every other hour.' He smiled ruefully.

She, in turn, told him that Brian and Denise had decided to marry sooner rather than later. They saw no reason to wait until Brian finished law school.

'And you approve?' he asked.

'I think so. I've grown to like Denise and I think they're right for each other. But my approval is hardly important. David and I recognize that.'

'Of course not. We are only parents.'

There was no bitterness in his voice, only the recognition that their children, grown and independent as they were, would forever inhabit the orbit of their concern.

She nodded and remembered the Yiddish aphorism that when children are little they sit on a parent's lap, and when they are older, they sit upon the heart. It was true. Both her children sat heavily upon her heart, Brian in life and Melanie in death. She hugged the thought to herself.

He told her that he had met with Emily's husband. 'An impressive young man. His med school record is excellent.'

'Did you offer him the fellowship?'

'I did. And he accepted it. He told me how grateful he was to you for befriending his wife.'

'It's a friendship that requires very little effort,' she said.

'You have a talent for making even difficult things seem effortless.'

He reached across the table and touched her hand. She stared at him and too swiftly pushed her chair back and sprang to her feet.

'I really must go,' she said.

'Of course.'

His acquiescence was immediate, commingling regret and easement. They had approached a dangerous border and were mutually relieved to have passed safely across it.

'I'll call you about when I'll be available next week,' she promised.

'All right.'

As always he carried the cartons out to her car. As always he reminded her to put her lights on and drive carefully. He stood in the driveway as she drove away. Through her rear-view mirror she saw him stare after her, his shoulders hunched, his hands stuffed into his pockets, lonely and solitary. She knew he would soon return to his silent house and worry about his daughters who lived across the continent.

She drove very slowly, the car window open, a soft breeze

brushing her face. The radio was tuned to a station that played golden oldies and she smiled when the DJ selected 'Greenfields', a song she and David had loved in their student days.

> *Oh to be young then and close to the earth*
> *To stand by your wife at the moment of birth . . .*

She sang along, surprised that she remembered the words but, of course, it was a song to which they had laid claim. 'Our song', they had called it. They had slow-danced to the lilting voices of The Brothers Four in the tiny living room of their graduate school apartment, her chin on his shoulder, her natural grace compensating for his awkwardness. They had moved as one, on those quiet evenings, each step a gentle glide into tender togetherness.

She drove on, humming now, and trying to remember when they had stopped dancing, why they had stopped dancing. The song ended. She switched the radio off. A wave of sadness washed over her. She pulled over to the side of the road and waited for it to subside.

When she reached her home, she remained in the car for a few moments and then stepped into the shaft of silver moonlight that stretched across the pathway. The house was dark but there was an amber aureole of lamplight in the room where David now slept. She saw his silhouette at the window, saw him move away.

She fumbled for her key, but before she could find it, David opened the door and she stepped into his outstretched arms.

'I was worried about you,' he said.

'I was worried about myself,' she replied.

They walked up the stairs hand in hand, and paused, looked at each other, smiled, then turned and went into their separate rooms. In that quiet parting they willed themselves to patience, acknowledging, with sadness and optimism commingled, that the time for a decision had not yet come.

TWENTY-FOUR

Judith arrived at the thrift shop the next morning a full hour before it was due to open. Juggling her coffee and biscotti, she disentangled the key from the long red ribbon and entered the empty room. Heat hung heavy on the air and she turned on the fans, training them on the gently used garments that dangled on wire hangers and formed colorful pyramids on the trestle tables.

She walked past the small table on which small household items were cleverly arranged, the displays whimsically altered from day to day. She took note of rainbow-colored glass tulips, a souvenir of someone's long-past Venice vacation, placed next to a snow globe that held the Eiffel tower in its cloudy interior. Bird-shaped bookends carved of heavy dark wood stood sentinel over a heavy gold ash tray of depression glass. It was a sad assortment, she thought, those rejected legacies of homes once furnished with care and pride. Decorators and antique dealers occasionally visited the thrift shop in search of small treasures. Judith had packaged a menagerie of crystal animals for a shrewd interior designer who had returned within a week to pluck up a family of marble-carved polar bears. Collections were markers of a marriage, of shared passion and delight. One couple she knew collected turtles, another focused on penguins. Wood carved, of kiln-fired ceramic, stone sculpted, her friends recounted the history of each acquisition, one bought on honeymoon, another discovered during a vacation.

It was copper that she and David had collected from the earliest days of their marriage. Candlesticks and graceful bowls, planters and pots, all regularly polished to a burnished gleam that emitted brightness and warmth. Their very first find, back in their student days, had been a coffee pot, blackened by age and discarded on a curbside. David had hammered out the dents and she had rubbed its surface until it glowed. They had set it on a sagging shelf in their sparsely furnished apartment and smiled at each other, proud of the graceful *finjan* made bright and beautiful by their joint effort.

As the years passed, and their circumstances changed, they had accumulated other copious treasures, each a reminder of happy vacation discoveries. The proud bird that perched above their fireplace had been found at a yard sale in rural Vermont. The string of bells was from a Paris flea market. Brian, during his rambunctious boyhood, had raced happily through the house jangling them. A set of hammered copper cups purchased in a Montreal antique shop had been used by Melanie for the tea parties at which she had served her dolls an imaginary brew.

Judith, moving slowly through the empty shop, was assaulted by memories, interrupted by a thought that came unbidden. If she and David were to part, if their possessions were to be divided, she decided that she would not lay claim to any of their copper pieces. In a new life she might begin to collect pewter instead, a cold and wintry metal that would hold no memories.

She trembled, a dangerous biliousness filling her throat at the invasive imagining of such a terrifying impasse. She had never before considered the dissolution of her marriage, the dismantling of her home, of her life. Gasping for air, she willed herself to calm, dismissed the noxious thought. A separation, and what might follow, was not a reality, only a dark and tenuous possibility. It would not, could not happen. The wounds of their marriage could be healed, their grief assimilated.

She offered herself assurances, repeated them as a mental mantra, and was suffused with relief when Suzanne arrived and bustled about, turning on the lights, filling the cash register. Normalcy was restored.

Suzanne asked Judith's opinion about pricing a newly donated designer gown and she considered it carefully, grateful that it elided the haunted fantasies that had obsessed her earlier. The familiar routine rescued her from wild irrationality.

Mid-morning brought a spurt of activity and during a brief surcease a harried woman entered, pushing a shopping cart loaded with household items, atop which a long mirror was unsteadily balanced.

Judith rushed to help her. 'That's a lot for you to manage,' she said.

The woman sighed. 'It is. But I'm emptying my daughter's room. She's moving to California. You can't imagine what a job that is.'

Judith nodded. She did not tell the woman that she knew exactly what a job that was. She helped the woman unload the cart, expressing admiration for the soon-to-be-gone daughter's collection of movie posters and ceramic cats.

'You'd think she'd want them,' the woman said sadly.

'Well, she's starting a new life,' Judith offered.

'Thanks so much for helping me. You've been very kind.'

'I'm glad I was able to,' Judith replied and realized that she spoke the truth.

Kindness now came more easily to her; it softened her heart, eased her thoughts. She carried the long mirror to the corner concealed by a shower curtain, their improvised dressing room, and hurried back to the register.

It was pay day at the hospital and Suzanne anticipated an onslaught of customers. She was not wrong. Shoppers swarmed in, intent on scavenging bargain buys for late-August vacations. Bathing suits and bath towels were snapped up as plans for day trips to neighboring beaches were happily discussed. A portly grandmother, a clerk in the county government office, plundered the shelves in her search for sun hats for her grandchildren. She was treating them to a weekend at the Jersey shore, she confided proudly. Three young women, hospital aides, favored by the volunteers for their easy laughter and exuberant conversations in Spanish, seized newly donated gem-colored terry-cloth robes. They had chipped in to rent a cabana in New Rochelle.

Consuela, the Guatemalan grandmother, plucked up two pastel-colored sundresses. 'One for Juanita. The other for my *bambina*, my beautiful little Rosalita,' she said happily.

Judith, caught up in the excitement, rushed from one table to another. She carried cartons from the stock room to replenish the rapidly depleted shelves.

That frenetic activity continued throughout the week as the race to exploit the last precious days of summer continued unabated.

*   *   *

She did not call Jeffrey Kahn. She was too busy, she told herself and then wondered fretfully why he had not called her. She drove to the university and took refuge in the library, dutifully filling one index card after another. She told herself that she was making progress on her essay, which, Evelyn assured her, was a certain sign of recovery. But recovery from what? *Death? Grief? Fear?* She refrained from dredging for an answer.

David went to a two-day conference in Boston and called her each night.

'Are you all right?' they asked each other.

Are we all right? she thought to add but instead complained about the heat. 'I miss you,' she added, but he had already hung up.

Did she miss Jeffrey Kahn? she wondered. Did he miss her? The idle thought filled her with guilt. Why would she miss him? Why would he miss her? She was only teasing herself, flirting with danger.

She went to lunch with Suzanne, who pecked nervously at her salad and glanced repeatedly at her cell phone.

'Is something wrong, Suzanne?' Judith asked.

'I'm not sure. I've been getting a lot of calls on my landline. Hang-ups. Sometimes late at night. Sometimes early in the morning. The same thing on my cell phone.'

'What about caller ID?'

'The numbers are always different and can't be recalled. Probably throwaway cell phones. Maybe pay phones. I think it's Eric calling.' Her voice broke.

'Why?'

'Instinct, maybe. Hope, maybe. Fear, maybe. Or all of the above, maybe.' She spoke in a monotone. Her fork clattered against the plate as it dropped from her trembling fingers.

'What about Stan? Eric's father. Has he been getting such calls?'

Judith would not call Stan her ex-husband. *Ex* was Latin for *out of*, but surely even after divorce husbands and wives were not out of each other's lives. Not when there was a child. A child alive, a child dead, a child whereabouts unknown – all heavy presences on parental hearts.

'I spoke to Stan,' Suzanne said. 'His home number is unlisted.

Eric wouldn't have it. He has a new cell phone number, which Eric also would not have. Eric might call the practice, of course, but he hasn't done that. At least not yet, as far as Stan knows.'

'What can you do?'

'Not much. Eric doesn't know where I live now. I added the thrift shop phone number and address to both my voicemail messages saying that I can be reached there. It will give Eric a place to go if he wants to find me. A public place.'

'You're afraid of him?'

'No. I'm afraid of myself.'

'I understand,' Judith said.

She too was afraid of herself, paralyzed by a fearful uncertainty that prevented her from calling Jeffrey Kahn, from talking openly and honestly with David. She knew that a decision had to be made, that she had to go forward, but she did not know how or when.

'You will know what to do, what to say, when the moment presents itself,' Evelyn had said unhelpfully, and Judith had bolted angrily from the therapist's consulting room and then regretted her anger. Evelyn, who knew nothing about her afternoons with Jeffrey Kahn, could hardly offer helpful advice.

It startled her to repeat Evelyn's words to Suzanne. 'You will know what to say to Eric when the moment comes,' she said.

'I hope so,' Suzanne murmured.

Neither of them finished their salads.

The very next day, as they prepared to close the shop, a young woman rushed in. Her auburn hair was pulled back in a ponytail, her freckled face reddened by the pitiless August sun, the bodice of her yellow halter dress sweat-stained. She was familiar to the volunteers who knew and liked her. A student at the local community college who waitressed and babysat, she usually ferreted out T-shirts and jeans. Judith had noticed her wandering through the shop over the last several days, lingering in the rear where evening gowns swayed forlornly and leaving without a single purchase. But on this visit she walked purposefully to the rack where the wedding dress, still encased in its clear plastic shroud, hung. She plucked it up and disappeared behind the shower curtain into the improvised dressing room.

All movement in the shop paused. The volunteers and customers who had watched her waited in frozen expectation. They smiled as she emerged and stood before the full-length mirror, her bright hair floating about her shoulders, the ivory silk hugging her slender body, emphasizing the narrowness of her waist, the fullness of her breasts. The long skirt, across which the golden embroidered butterflies flew, fell from her hips in graceful folds. She was aglow, a princess bride, proud and graceful. As she studied herself in the mirror, turning from side to side, now bending low, now pirouetting, the watching women applauded. She whirled about and bent her head in gratitude for their admiration.

'It's a miracle,' she said. 'I'm getting married next month and I never thought I'd be able to afford a wedding gown. Not one like this.'

'We all hope you'll be very happy,' Suzanne said.

She spoke for all those assembled in that cluttered room, where fans did battle with unremitting heat and rhomboids of light danced across the scarred linoleum floor. She spoke for the watching wives, contented in their marriages, and for those who struggled against unhappiness, for the single women who lived in hope, for those like Suzanne herself who had married in good faith and divorced in sadness. And, Judith thought, she spoke for wives like herself, who trembled in the limbo of a life that was newly uncertain, who waited too long to say 'I miss you' to absent husbands and fantasized about men to whom they owed no attachment.

'We'll be happy,' she promised and disappeared behind the shower curtain.

She reappeared minutes later, wearing her flimsy sundress, her hair pulled back, cradling the wedding gown, her freckled face still aglow. She went to the cash register and handed Judith four five-dollar bills, a ten and a handful of quarters.

'Coffee-shop tips and babysitting money,' she said apologetically. 'I had to wait until I had enough and I was so scared someone else would grab the dress.'

'You could have asked us to put it aside for you,' Judith said. 'We do that.'

'I didn't know.'

'And now you do. Live and learn. And the best of luck.'

'Red-headed gals look great in white,' Suzanne said as she placed the bills in the register and counted out the change.

'Denise, Brian's fiancée, is a redhead,' Judith murmured.

She thought of the young woman who would marry her son: exuberant, generous Denise. Denise, when she told Judith that she and Brian would marry sooner than they had planned, had said, shyly, that she hoped Judith thought of her not as a daughter-in-law but as a daughter.

I had a daughter, I do not need another . . . Judith had thought to say, but she had remained silent and turned away. Denise, after all, had meant well. She had been, in all their interchanges, kind and considerate. It was unfair to drain her wedding plans of joy.

She had smiled apologetically at Brian's bride and promised herself that she would not turn Melanie's absence at that wedding into a spectral presence; that, yes, she would, in fact, try to think of Denise as a daughter.

'She seems really nice, Brian's gal,' Suzanne offered. She had met Denise once or twice on her fleeting visits to the shop.

'She is nice. More than nice,' Judith agreed.

Her cell phone rang then. It was David, speaking with the stutter that indicated unease. She braced herself for disappointment but was instead surprised.

'I'm taking an early train,' he said. 'Do you want to eat in or go out?'

'It doesn't matter. We'll decide when you get home.'

She felt a thrill of hope. She glanced at her watch. If she hurried, there would be time enough to wash and blow-dry her hair, to change into the white summer dress David had always favored.

'Do you mind if I dash out?' she asked Suzanne who was staring down at her own silent cell phone.

'No. Fine.' Suzanne waved but did not look up as Judith left.

David had wanted to take Judith out for dinner since his return from Boston, but the press of work had been overwhelming. Nancy had stayed late when she could and more than once they had worked at her apartment because she did not want Lauren to be alone. They had talked vaguely about working on a new project that evening, but Brian had called that afternoon.

'How are you doing, Dad?' his son had asked hesitantly. 'How's Mom doing?'

'Fine. We're both fine. We may go out to dinner tonight.'

The lie that he had told with such ease morphed into truth. He realized that he did in fact want to have dinner with Judith. Uneasily, he had called her. With the greatest of ease, she had agreed.

He went to Nancy's office and told her that he had decided to leave early that day. They would discuss the new project the next morning. He placed a copy of *Pippi Longstocking* that he had bought that morning on her desk.

'For Lauren,' he said. 'It was one of Melanie's favorites.'

'That was thoughtful of you, but I'm not sure it would be wise to give it to her.' She spoke very softly, her head bent low, her hair falling in silver sheaths about her narrow face. He pulled a chair up, the better to hear her, the better to see her.

'Why not?' he asked.

'She's confused about you. About us. She's still nursing the fantasy that you could be her new father. She asked me about it again last night.'

'And what did you say?' His voice was gentle; his heart was heavy. He could not tell her that he had, more than once, entertained the fantasy of Lauren as his surrogate daughter, although Nancy herself had never been part of such fleeting illusions.

'I told her that you were a colleague, a friend, and you wanted to be helpful to us. And she and I are helpful to you because you are very sad, because your daughter died.'

'A good answer.'

'But not adequate. She did not believe me.'

'I see. Then what must we do, Nancy?'

He did not know what he wanted her to say. Did he want her to tell him that their strange liaison was at an end, that they would each have to cope with their separate sorrows alone? Or perhaps she might suggest that their relationship become more intimate, that her daughter's fantasy be treated as a possible reality.

It occurred to him that even as Lauren fantasized about a

father, Nancy herself might have fantasized about becoming his lover, his wife? How foolish he had been not to have thought of that earlier. She had been widowed for ten years. She was not a nun. She must have had lovers or, at least, loving relationships, given her gentle manner, her quiet beauty. Surely, over that decade of her aloneness, other men had come to her apartment and sat beside her on the soft gray couch. Did she think of him as different from those men? His marriage had never been part of their odd intimacy. It was possible, even probable, that she did not think of him as Judith's husband.

'I don't know what I want us to do, David. You are important to me. And to Lauren. But our relationship is confusing to her and, to be honest, it is sometimes confusing to me. I suppose we need time, time to figure out our options and to understand them.'

'Options?' he repeated, as though the word was foreign to him.

'You must know what I mean,' she replied, and he nodded, although the truth was that he did not know.

She reached for the book. 'I'll give it to her. Of course I will.'

'I hope she enjoys it,' he said. He thought his words foolish but did not know what else he might say.

'I'm going away for a few days. I have to think. You understand?'

'I do.'

She smiled. He smiled back. He felt her eyes upon him as he left her office.

He went to an empty conference room where he sat alone at the long table of polished dark wood. His elbows resting on the gleaming surface, his head in his hands, he tried to organize his thoughts. *Options*, Nancy had said and he understood, with startling clarity, what she had meant.

He should have spoken to her of Judith. She had, he supposed, not unreasonably, assumed that his marriage was unhappy, that the solace that he found with her had a dimension that went beyond their shared grief and extended into the possibility of a shared future.

He had to speak to her immediately, to apologize, to explain and offer what comfort he could for the false hope he had generated. He raced down the hall to her office but she was gone. The room was dark, her computer screen blank, her air conditioner stilled. The overhead light was on. He pressed the switch and welcomed the new darkness. His sense of urgency dissipated. There would be time enough to talk when she returned.

He walked swiftly to Grand Central, stopped at a flower kiosk and bought Judith a bouquet of yellow roses. It was the first time he had carried flowers home since Melanie's death.

Judith accepted them with a rueful smile. 'The last roses of summer,' she said.

She arranged them in a tall vase on the dining-room table, already set for dinner. They were eating in then and he was glad of it. He smiled as the scent of garlic and basil sauce wafted in from the kitchen. She had cooked his favorite meal. He thought she looked very beautiful in the sleeveless white cotton dress he had always liked. She wore only the lightest of lipsticks and the dark helmet of her hair was smooth and shining. He knew that if he pressed his face against it, he would inhale the familiar fragrance of her lilac-scented shampoo.

He went to the window and stared out at the brilliant late summer sunset that blazed across the sky. 'August,' he said.

'Yes. Brian and Denise will be leaving for New Hampshire soon. Next week, I think.'

'I remember.'

'We owe ourselves a vacation,' she suggested daringly.

'An idea.'

They stared down at their plates, both aware that it was, in fact, a strange idea for a couple who still slept in separate rooms, but an idea that neither of them was willing to dismiss, that, in fact, engaged them both.

They spoke quietly over dinner. She told him about the young girl who had claimed the bridal gown. He asked for a second helping of the pasta and told her of an interesting case he had arbitrated – a quarrel between two brothers over the brand name of a pizza bar. They laughed, pleased at the ease of their exchange, aware that, however tentatively, they were moving toward each other.

Over dessert she talked again about the possibility of a vacation. 'We have to make plans quickly. My sabbatical is almost over. I begin teaching again in mid-September.'

'Of course,' he agreed. 'When do you think? And where?'

'Very soon. I thought perhaps the Shakespeare Festival in Canada. Stratford. It ends next week.'

It was a calculated suggestion. They both loved Shakespeare. They both loved Stratford. They had, more than once, stayed in an inn where the room they favored had a large many-pillowed double bed that overlooked the lake. They had delighted in lying there together as dawn broke, watching the light of early morning glide across the quiet waters.

'Next week. Not possible. There are things I must settle,' he said.

Nancy would be away for much of that week. He could not, would not, leave without talking to her, clarifying their relationship, offering a release to her, to himself. It was incumbent upon him to wait for her to return. It was – he struggled to find the right word – honorable. Such an old-fashioned word, *honorable*, and yet it seemed right to him.

Judith stared at him. 'Surely someone else at the office can step in and take care of any business that has to be settled.'

'No. This is personal.'

'Nancy,' she said flatly.

'Yes. I have to talk to her. Let me explain . . .'

But he did not finish the sentence. Judith disappeared into the kitchen. He heard the clatter of pots and pans signaling an end to what they might have said to each other. He did not trail after her. Words of the explanation he had meant to offer deserted him.

The phone rang. Brian calling to say goodbye. He and Denise were leaving for New Hampshire early the next morning.

'Have a great time,' David said. 'And drive carefully.'

It was unsettling that Brian would be driving an ancient Volvo borrowed from Denise's father. He had resisted David's offer of a new car. They didn't need it. They didn't want it. Parking in Manhattan was always a hassle. The Volvo was fine.

'We're both good drivers,' Brian said, his tone edged with annoyance. 'The car was just serviced.'

Judith interrupted. 'Our love to Denise's family,' she said.
'I'll tell them.'

'You will be careful?'

'Mom!'

'Sorry,' she apologized.

She knew their warnings – hers and David's both – to be
gratuitous. They understood that monitory warnings had little impact
on the capriciousness of life. Unforeseen dangers were inevitable,
unpredictable. Pedestrians were hit by speeding cars, sudden rip
tides claimed the lives of experienced swimmers, a lurking aneurysm
stopped the heart of a healthy child. It was an understanding painfully earned and jointly held, a burden they would not impose on
their son.

'Have a wonderful vacation,' she added in appeasement. 'Take
good care of your Denise.'

'I will. I do.' Joy returned to his voice.

She hung up and she and David looked at each other.

'They'll be fine,' she said.

'Of course they'll be fine.'

She pleaded fatigue and went upstairs. He went into the dimly
lit living room and listened to the first movement of the Berlioz
Requiem.

Alone in the bedroom, Judith turned the dog-eared pages of
The Collected Poems of Emily Dickinson, searching for a half-
remembered line. She raced from one poem to another and at
last found the words she sought. *You cannot make Remembrance
grow . . .* She closed the book. She would not have remembrance grow; she could not bear the pain.

TWENTY-FIVE

B rian called from New Hampshire to assure them that all was well, that they were having a great time. 'Great,' he repeated.

The need to tell his parents that all was well was a new self-imposed protocol that he both observed and resented.

'I don't want to have to constantly check in,' he complained to Denise.

'Why not? It's just a phone call and it relieves their anxiety,' she countered.

She was right, he knew, and he made the calls, often catching Judith on her cell phone as she drove to the thrift shop.

'I'll tell Dad,' she said after one such call, and he felt a surge of optimism at her casual reference to his father. 'New Hampshire must be beautiful at this time of the year,' she added.

'Yes. Yes, it is,' he agreed and hung up, grateful to Denise for her sensible advice, grateful to Denise for simply being Denise.

Judith was right. New Hampshire, during the waning days of summer, was beautiful, with its golden dawns and cool, moonlit evenings. Brian and Denise walked down woodland trails, paddled a canoe through the serene waters of a tree-shaded lake and planned their wedding, deciding at last on Thanksgiving.

Their decision to move up the date of their marriage puzzled Denise's family, but they offered her parents no explanation. They had, after all, come to their decision without offering an explanation to each other. Brian had suggested it after his somber lunch with his father and Denise had agreed. Their silent apprehension was shared.

They knew that David and Judith slept in separate rooms and spoke to each other with the exaggerated politeness of casual strangers, adrift as they were on dangerous currents. Brian and Denise were determined to marry before they were thrust against the threatening shoals of his parents' encroaching estrangement.

It had occurred to Brian that his marriage might help his mother and father to heal the rift in their lives, that it would offer them a window on a future in which mutual happiness could be celebrated. He imagined them dancing together on his wedding day, united by his happiness, perhaps anticipating new vistas. Denise – his wonderful, generous Denise – would be a daughter to them. A family of four would be reconstituted. Magical thinking, he knew, but it comforted him.

The lazy days of late summer passed and they discussed their plans with Denise's approving family. The wedding would be smaller and more intimate than the celebration they had originally planned. Denise wondered what had happened to the magenta fabric swatches Melanie had collected so carefully. Not important, of course. There would be no junior bridesmaid. Only her own two sisters would be in the wedding party and they would not wear magenta. It was decided that her family's rabbi would officiate. Judith and David would not want their own rabbi who had eulogized Melanie. Their wedding would not be death-haunted.

'I want both my parents to walk me to the wedding canopy,' Brian whispered to Denise as they held each other close.

'Of course you do. And of course they will. Not to worry. This is just a really bad time for them. It will pass over,' she assured him. 'They will be fine.'

'Will it?' he asked doubtfully. 'Will it pass over? Will they be fine?'

She did not answer him. Instead, she spoke of leaving earlier than anticipated if the heat continued to intensify. Brian agreed. He did not want to risk a recurrence of the asthma that had haunted his childhood and occasionally became threatening when the temperature peaked dramatically.

Denise called Judith and told her that they had decided on a Thanksgiving Day wedding. 'I hope that works for you both,' she said. 'For you and David.' The coupling of their names was reassuring.

'Fine,' Judith agreed.

Clutching the phone, she looked through her kitchen window at her garden bathed in the dappled sunlight of late summer. Her asters were already in full blossom. September loomed, ushering in melancholy autumn with its pale sunsets and falling leaves. Very soon the branches of the apple tree would be bare. The season of vacation was ending; her sabbatical drifted toward its unsatisfactory, unsatisfying conclusion. She shivered. 'I'm sure it will be fine for David as well,' she added, and wondered why her voice was so faint and why she gripped the phone so tightly.

'Hey, Mom, are you all right?' Brian, who had been listening on the extension, asked, his question laced with concern. 'Is Dad home?'

'No. He had an early-morning meeting. An important new case. And I'm fine.' She managed a lilt, a dismissive laugh. 'Of course I'm fine. Why wouldn't I be?'

'Just asking.'

'Is it very hot up there?' she asked.

'Hot enough. If it gets much worse, we'll probably leave. Mom, are you sure you're all right?' he asked again.

'Of course. I'm fine. Really.'

She hung up, suffused with an inexplicable sadness. She had not lied. She was all right. Not fine perhaps, but all right.

She was ready to leave for the thrift shop when David called. He would not be home for dinner. A late meeting. An important project.

'I understand,' she said and wondered what it was she understood. That he was lying? That his absence was a relief of a kind? She shrugged, hung up without saying goodbye and glanced at her watch. Suzanne, who had a doctor's appointment, had asked her to open the shop that morning and she did not want to be late.

The phone was ringing even as she turned the shop key in the door. She hurried to answer it but heard only a soughing release of breath and then the sharp click of a hang-up.

Certainty gripped her. She was certain that the ghost caller was Eric. Suzanne had left the thrift shop number on her answering machine so that her son would have it. She decided that if the phone rang again, she would say his name, softly, unthreateningly.

And the phone rang again.

'Eric?' His name emerged as a question.

'Eric? Who is Eric?' Jeffrey Kahn's voice was tinged with amusement.

'A long story,' she replied. 'How are you, Jeffrey? It's been a while.'

Ten days actually. She knew because she had been counting them even as she had refrained from calling him. They had not spoken since the evening they had sat opposite each other at his kitchen table, speaking so very softly about their children, careful to avoid any mention of the tenderness they had so dangerously offered each other earlier in the day.

'I was away. A medical conference in Philadelphia.'

'I see.' She thought to say, *You might have told me*, but remained silent. He was under no obligation to tell her anything at all.

'I wondered if you had any time to help me this week. There are some odds and ends I need your advice on. Also, my basement is full of furniture – most of it my daughters' discards – and I thought you might have some ideas about where I might donate it.'

'Well, I'll try to arrange something, although this week is a little tight. Someone I work with may need my help, and David and I were talking about taking a vacation of some sort. Let me call you. I do want to help you.'

'Thank you. There's no need to rush. I'll wait for your call.'

She heard the relief in his voice and knew that his ambivalence matched her own. It was true that Suzanne might need her support, but it was also true that she delayed returning to his home because the thought of being alone with him unnerved her. Her mention of David and their mythical vacation had been a protective lie. But what, then, was she protecting? Her vulnerable marriage, her fidelity?

She sighed as Libby and Lois entered together, tanned and carefree, laden with shopping bags overflowing with their children's outgrown summer clothing and chattering about carpool schedules and the unreliability of babysitters. She envied them the innocence of their concerns. Libby held the door for a tall, unkempt young man, a zigzag scar ribbing his pale cheek.

Judith glanced at him and noted that although he was painfully thin, his shoulders hunched, his eyes red-rimmed, he was oddly handsome. Probably another young recovering addict from the nearby drug rehab center in search of T-shirts or jeans stored in a giveaway bin.

He approached her. She looked up and smiled.

'Do you have stuff for guys? Like maybe a leather jacket? Denim maybe?' he asked hesitantly.

She pointed him toward the sagging rack hung with men's clothing and turned back to sorting through a bag of new donations.

'All summer stuff,' she murmured to Libby. 'We'll have to store it until next spring. We'll get to it in late March.'

Her own words cast a spell of sadness. *Next spring. Late March.* The anniversary of Melanie's death. Where would the memorial candle flicker? Would it be reflected in the burnished copper tray in their living room or would its fragile flame keep vigil in a barren apartment, awaiting the furnishings of a life yet to begin? Her life alone.

Trembling, she banished the question, angry at herself for wallowing, however briefly, in such bitter, self-imposed misery, for creating a dark and improbable scenario. She was overreacting, she told herself. Not everything was a portent of approaching danger. Inhaling, exhaling, she calmed herself, carried the summer clothing into the storeroom and shoved it into a storage bin.

'To be dealt with *next spring.*' Defiantly, she said the words aloud.

It was a busy morning. A manufacturer gifted the shop with his overstock of new backpacks and news of their availability spread. Alert mothers of schoolchildren rushed in to snap them up, paying in crumpled bills. By noon Judith had counted two hundred dollars and banded them together. The owner of an antique jewelry store, a heavily made-up woman swathed in a profusion of scarves, arrived and collected several necklaces she had reserved. She paid with three crisp hundred-dollar bills. By noon there was over six hundred dollars in the register, an unusually large amount for the shop, but no one could be spared for a sprint to the bank to deposit the cash. They would have to wait for Suzanne.

Judith smiled at an older woman who placed a man's Harris tweed jacket on the counter.

'My husband's,' she said. 'Almost brand new. He wore it twice, maybe three times. I hope you can sell it.'

'I'm sure we can,' Judith assured her.

She carried the suit to the rack of men's jackets. To her

surprise, the youth who had entered earlier in search of a leather jacket was still there, fingering the cuffs of one garment, the collar of another.

He stared at her nervously. 'I'm still looking,' he said.

'That's fine. No problem,' she replied calmly.

It was not unusual for itinerant shoppers or browsers to linger. The shop was a refuge for the unemployed, for those with too little money and too much time, for young people seeking sanctuary from a world that had no place for them. She smiled at him and found a hanger for the tweed jacket.

An hour later, Suzanne arrived. Judith followed her into the storeroom.

'Anything unusual happen?' she asked, her voice edged with anxiety.

'Everything's fine,' Judith assured her.

She decided against telling Suzanne about the early voiceless phone call. It could have been anyone. A prankster. A wrong number. A telemarketer.

'But we have too much cash. Over six hundred dollars and we were too busy to send anyone to the bank,' she added.

'I'll go,' Suzanne offered. 'You've been keeping an eye on the register?'

'Yes. Lois is covering it now.'

They went into the shop but Lois was not at the register. She waved to them from the corner where she was helping two laughing young women examine a pile of vintage evening dresses. They left without buying anything just as Suzanne opened the register. With a cheerful ring, the drawer slid open.

They gasped. The metal compartments were empty. Loose coins clattered and two lonely dollar bills were in the rear tray. The neatly banded wads of larger bills were gone.

'Lois!' Suzanne called angrily.

Lois rushed over and stared down at the emptied drawer. 'I've only been away from the counter for a second. Two seconds. I thought it was all right. There was only this one guy still in the rear. He'd been here for a while. I didn't think I had to worry about him. He left maybe a minute after you came in, Suzanne.'

'I remember him,' Judith said. 'He came in very early. Very thin. Almost handsome, actually, except for a scar on his cheek.'

'A scar? A zigzag scar?' Suzanne's voice was faint. 'On his cheek? His right cheek?'

'Yes. I think so. No, I'm sure. His right cheek.'

'Eric,' Suzanne whispered. 'Eric.' The whisper became a shout.

She rushed to the door and stared out into the entry way. 'Eric! Eric!' She screamed the name, her face raddled with tears, her shoulders quivering. 'Eric!' The scream became a shriek interrupted by the rush of footsteps.

Frightened, Judith moved toward her but paused when she heard the sound of a muffled voice, an awkward muttering of barely audible words.

'Mom. Mom. Please don't cry. Please don't be angry. I'm sorry. Here's the money. All of it.'

Judith watched as he waved the clutch of bills, as his arms, his very thin arms, opened wide and Suzanne collapsed into them. Moving as one, each supporting the other, they limped into the shop and disappeared into the storeroom. The door remained ajar. Judith turned to Lois.

'I think it's best if you leave.'

Lois nodded. 'I'm so sorry,' she murmured.

'It wasn't your fault. It wasn't anyone's fault,' Judith said.

She smiled reassuringly. She wanted to tell the younger woman that no one was to blame, that sad, inexplicable things happened without fault or reason. A son might go astray. A daughter might die. She thought to repeat the Yiddish proverb that lingered so stubbornly in memory. *When children are little, they sit on your lap. When children are grown, they sit on your heart.* Instead, she hugged Lois, who hurried out.

Judith hung the 'Closed' sign on the shop window and sat on the high stool behind the register. Suzanne would want her to stay, she knew. The partially opened door was an invitation to bear witness, perhaps to offer intervention.

She heard their voices. Eric's soft and broken. Suzanne's soft and comforting, at once disappointed and forgiving, latent anger muted by hesitant hope. Eric was weeping, weeping and talking, his every utterance thickened with shame and grief.

'I wanted to come home. I wanted to see you. To see Dad. I was so tired of my life, so tired of being me. I wanted to stop running. I wanted to stop using. I tried detox once and then again. Finally, I went cold turkey, did it on my own. And it worked. It was so terrible that I knew I would never touch drugs again; I never wanted to feel what I felt, holed up in a crummy SRO in LA, shaking and vomiting and wanting to die. That was two years ago. I've been clean ever since, Mom. I swear.'

'I believe you.'

Judith marveled at Suzanne's calm.

'I wanted to come home right after that but I got sick. Pneumonia. They said at the clinic I went to that a lot of ex-addicts come down with it. I didn't want you to see me looking the way I looked then. So I waited. I worked some lousy jobs. Custodial stuff, burger flipping, but I made enough money for a bus ticket home, enough to get some decent clothes, get a haircut.'

'You should have called us. We would have helped. Your father and I. Surely you knew that.'

'I couldn't. Not after what I put you through. I was too ashamed. I wanted to show you that I'd changed, that I got cleaned up on my own. But I fell asleep on the bus to New York, and when I woke up, my wallet and my backpack were gone. I had just enough cash in my pocket to get up here. I crashed at a shelter one town over, where they let me use the phone. I called you, just to hear your voice and then I hung up. Once. Twice. I don't know how many times. When you added the thrift shop number and address to your voicemail message, I guessed you had figured out that it was me calling. I got up the guts to come to the shop, but you weren't here. I waited. But the longer I waited, the more scared and ashamed I got. I thought if I had some money, I could get myself cleaned up, get something to eat so I'd stop shaking, get a haircut and then maybe you wouldn't be so shocked. So, bum that I am – bum that I was – I took the money from the register.' His voice broke.

Judith shivered. Poor boy. Poor Suzanne.

'But you didn't run. You waited. And when you heard me call your name, you came to me. You didn't spend the money. I don't think you could have. Because you're not a thief. You're not a bum. You're my boy. My son.' Suzanne spoke slowly, each word heavy with relief and pain.

Silence, broken by the whispering murmur of sobs – whether his or hers, Judith could not tell. She slid off the high stool. Through the half-opened door, she saw Eric kneeling before Suzanne who embraced his trembling body, her head bent so that her cheek rested on his tousled hair. Judith closed the door. Against all odds, Suzanne's son was restored to her. She needed neither witness nor protector.

Breathing deeply, she left the thrift shop and was startled to see Emily at the door, staring in puzzlement at the 'Closed' sign. She turned to Judith, still rocking the stroller in which Jane slept, her silken black lashes brushing her golden cheeks.

'Did I make a mistake?' she asked. 'Did you change the hours? I thought the shop would be open.'

'We had a special situation so we closed early,' Judith explained. 'Did you want something in particular, Emily?'

'No. I actually came to see you, to thank you. James is so happy to be working for your friend, Doctor Kahn.'

'I'm glad I was able to help.'

'He is such a nice man, my husband says. Your Doctor Kahn. There is an apartment at his hospital, a small apartment for doctors' assistants. He said he would try to arrange for us to live there. Oh, how kind and nice he is.'

'Yes. He is very nice, very kind. My friend, Doctor Kahn.'

She felt a pang of guilt. He was indeed her friend and she had promised to call him. She would – of course she would. But not yet. She was not ready. Not after David's rejection. She was too vulnerable to his kindness, his niceness.

She glanced at her watch. With the closing of the shop, the empty afternoon stretched out before her.

'I go to the park now,' Emily said shyly.

'I have some time. I'll walk with you.'

'How nice. How good of you.'

They smiled at each other. Walking together, their pace unhurried, they crossed one street, then another, until they reached a small park. Judith pointed to a bench shaded by a red maple tree. They sat side by side.

'I used to come here when my daughter was a baby,' Judith said.

'Your daughter?' Emily asked.

'Yes. I had a daughter. Melanie. She was called Melanie.'

She looked skyward, surprised that she had spoken those words with such ease, that her voice had not broken when she uttered them.

'She died,' she said softly. 'A few months ago.'

Emily turned to her, her dark eyes lucent. She took Judith's hand and stroked it gently. Her understanding was implicit in her touch, her sympathy eloquent in its silence. They sat hand in hand as a soft wind rustled the branches of the tree that shaded them. A star-shaped leaf fluttered on to the baby's cheek. Jane's rosebud lips parted in a smile and her dark eyes opened. Emily lifted her daughter out of the stroller and placed her in Judith's arms. Gently, gratefully, Judith cradled her. She bent her head close and inhaled the baby-sweet scent, pressed a finger lightly against the smooth rose-gold cheek.

That delicate aroma triggered a memory of a long-ago twilight hour, when she and David had bathed the infant Melanie together, smiling in wonderment at the softness of her skin. She recalled how their fingers had met to form a tender crown upon the child's head. David had lifted Judith's hand, wet and soapy as it was, and pressed it to his lips and then held it for the briefest of moments. She smiled and placed the baby in Emily's outstretched arms.

'I must go,' she said. 'But this was so nice. Come to the shop soon. I've put aside some nice autumn outfits for Jane.'

'Thank you. I will.'

Judith hurried away, anxious suddenly to drive home, to turn to the book she had left open on her desk. She had refrained from reading Dickinson's poem, with its monitory warnings, in its entirely. *You cannot make Remembrance grow . . . nor can you cut Remembrance down*, the poet had warned.

But Judith did not fear to read it now. On this day, at this moment, she no longer feared remembrance. She had seen Suzanne set aside all memory of years of pain and reclaim her son. She had remembered the touch of her husband's lips upon her hand. She was newly ambushed by hope, hope nurtured by remembrance, remembrance ever fragile, ever enduring, remembrance that, as the poet assured her, cannot be cut down.

TWENTY-SIX

D uring the last days of an ending summer a heatwave swept over them. Exhausted and enervated, David and Judith agreed that they could not recall an August when the temperatures had rocketed to such a dangerous high. They hoped that it was cooler in New Hampshire. Judith recalled that Denise's parents' summer home was not air-conditioned.

'Brian has a low tolerance for heat,' she said worriedly. 'His asthma. Those attacks were always during the summer.'

'He knows he has to be careful. And it's been a long time since he's had an asthma attack,' David replied reassuringly.

'We all have to be careful,' she said wearily.

He nodded in silent agreement. They were careful. They kept their conversations in check, refraining from trespassing into dangerous emotional territory. There would be no further discussion of a vacation. They remained in limbo, both of them adhering to frenetic schedules, despite the sweltering heat.

David's office was understaffed. Nancy had not returned – had, in fact, called to tell him that she was extending her time away. Did he mind? He did not. He was, in fact, relieved, despite the demands of the new and complex arbitrations he was negotiating. The conversation that they had to have would be difficult, he knew, and he was glad to postpone it. Determined to cope, he arrived at the office earlier and stayed later. Judith said nothing about his absences. It occurred to him that she might, in fact, welcome them. He dismissed the thought. She herself was extremely busy.

Suzanne curtailed her hours at the thrift shop and, apologetically, asked Judith to fill in for her.

'So many arrangements to be made for Eric,' she confided over a hasty lunch as she explained the logistics of the thrift shop operation, which Judith would assume. Funds to be transferred to the synagogue account, bills to be paid, donations to be recorded, stock to be sorted and organized. 'It seems complicated at first, but you won't have to do it for long. Just until I get things organized for Eric, for myself.'

'How is Eric doing?' Judith asked cautiously.

'Some days are better than others. He's come a long way, but there's been a lot of damage. There's a great deal to be arranged. I've been researching support groups, talking to therapists. He does want to go back to school. There's a course that would qualify him to work as a substance abuse counselor, but I don't know if they'll accept him. He's twenty-four years old and he doesn't even have a high school diploma. It won't be easy, but I think it's doable. He's motivated. Most days at least.'

'And how is it for you, most days?' Judith asked.

Suzanne sighed. 'Some days are harder than others. But everything is easier for me than it was. At least I know he's alive. At least I know where he's sleeping, what he's eating. My heart doesn't stop every time the phone rings. I'm coping. With difficulty, but I'm coping. Look at this.'

She showed Judith her pocket calendar, every hour of every day crammed with the demands of motherhood resumed. Appointments with counselors, with therapists, with tutors.

'What about Eric's father?' Judith asked.

Suzanne shrugged. 'Stan is supportive. He's helpful, generous. We're in close touch and he's doing what he can, but there's not going to be a fairytale ending for us. We're not going to be a united family, living happily ever after. He has his new life and I have mine. We have Eric but we don't have each other. We don't want each other. Maybe we never did. I read somewhere that the unexamined life is not worth living. I would say the same thing about the unexamined marriage. Not worth saving.'

'Aristotle,' Judith said. 'Aristotle wrote that. About life. He didn't mention unexamined marriages.'

She twirled a piece of lettuce about on her fork and wondered whether her own marriage, after careful examination, would be worth saving. Would remembrance be enough to guarantee its endurance? How odd that she had come to rely on Dickinson, that white-gowned vestal virgin of Amherst. A strange source of comfort.

She turned her attention back to Suzanne who was fumbling

in her bag for a sheaf of deposit forms and earnestly explaining
how the bank balance of the thrift shop could be reconciled. 'I
want to thank you for taking all this on, Judith,' she said.

'Actually, I'm glad to do it,' Judith assured her.

Her answer was honest. The additional work granted her a
reprieve of a kind. Amorphous concerns about her undefined
future were buried beneath the demands of the present. Decisions
she was not yet ready to make could be deferred. She managed
the thrift shop and scavenged time for her research.

As she transcribed her notes, she wondered when she would
be able to weave them into a coherent essay. Emails from the
chair of her department and her editor arrived regularly and
with increasing urgency. She offered evasive excuses. She could
not, after all, explain why she prioritized sorting through gently
used clothing over writing a learned paper on the essays of
George Eliot or the poems of Emily Dickinson. She could not
explain it to herself.

On a heat-heavy night, she walked down the hall to the room
where David slept. She willed him to awaken, but he was lost
in a dream. His lips moved soundlessly and she returned to her
own bed. She wondered what she might have said to him if he
had awakened. She did not know. She lay awake, juggling
competing fantasies, and wondered which of them she might
allow to fall.

She called Jeffrey Kahn the next morning and explained that,
given Suzanne's absence, she was spending more time at the
thrift shop. She had not forgotten her promise and she would
call him soon, very soon.

'I understand,' he said.

She wondered what it was that he understood even as she
acknowledged that the muted disappointment in his voice gave
her a frisson of pleasure.

Jeffrey had not hung up. She heard papers rustling. She heard
the intake of his breath.

'Are you still there?' he asked, and she imagined a wisp of
hope in the question.

She remembered that David was working late that night and
it occurred to her that she might ask Jeffrey if he wanted to

meet for dinner. She immediately rejected the idea. That was a line that could not be crossed. Not yet. Probably not ever.

'I will call soon,' she said again and hung up.

The day she spent without interruption at the shop seemed endless and she was grateful when the closing hour arrived. She switched off the fans that did little to mitigate the oppressive heat and straightened stacks of sweaters. They had set out fall clothing too soon, never anticipating the blistering spell of heat. She slammed the windows shut. They had not admitted the slightest breeze.

She dashed to her car, gratefully switching on the air conditioning and then, unwilling to return to her empty house, she went to a diner where she flipped open her laptop and read yet another email from the department secretary, asking about the syllabus for her fall semester course.

'Working on it,' she wrote back and wondered when she would work on it – whether, in fact, she even wanted to plan her courses. It occurred to her that more than her marriage required urgent examination.

She sipped her latte and munched the sandwich she could not remember ordering.

David worked late that night. He called Judith from Grand Central but she was not at home and he did not leave a message. He refrained from calling her cell phone, from asking where she was, what she was doing. He feared her honesty. On the train, settled into his seat, he tried to remember why, in fact, he had tried to call her. Perhaps he had been repeating the long-abandoned habit of his graduate school days when he would leave the silent library after long and solitary hours, and call her, just to hear the sound of her voice. They had, he recalled, developed a formula for such purposeless calls.

'You're there?' he would ask.

'Of course I'm here. I'll always be here.'

That loving reassurance invigorated him, sent him back to his research newly energized. He could use a new bout of energy now, he thought, as he leaned back in his seat and dozed off. She was asleep when he arrived home and he did not wake her.

TWENTY-SEVEN

The heatwave swept through New Hampshire, subsiding briefly during the evening hours. Brian and Denise took a nocturnal walk through the copse of slender birch trees that bordered her parents' property. The sultriness of the long day had vanished, but the air was weighted with a lingering torridity. They moved slowly, hand in hand, but Denise was suddenly aware that Brian's breath came in labored gasps.

'What's wrong?' she asked.

'Asthma,' he said. 'I had it as a kid and sometimes it acts up again when it's very hot. I should have told you.'

'Do you need an inhaler?' Her voice was heavy with concern.

'No. It's not that bad. I used to carry one but I never needed it so I tossed it. I'm OK, except sometimes in the summer.'

'It didn't happen last summer.'

'But last summer wasn't this hot.'

'Wasn't it?'

She did not remind him that there had, in fact, been a heatwave the previous year, but everything had been different then. Melanie had been alive, Judith and David contented and loving, she and Brian moving happily through untroubled days. She understood that it was fear and loss that clogged Brian's lungs, not the heat-heavy air. She gripped his hand, her own chest tight with an unfamiliar rage. She was furious with Melanie for dying. She was furious with David and Judith for their inability to cope, for inflicting their unshared grief on Brian. *Damn them! Damn them!*

Her anger blazed. It seared, it cleansed and then, mysteriously and gratefully, it subsided. She stared up at the star-spangled sky, suffused with a new calm, a new determination.

They walked on, Brian breathing more easily, leaves and twigs crunching beneath their sandaled feet, the brilliant half-moon silvering the tree tops. A gentle wind cooled their faces.

'If it stays this hot, we should leave,' she said. 'Go back to

New York. Spend a few days with your parents. I could do with air conditioning.'

'Would you mind?' he asked, and she knew that it was what he longed to do.

'I don't mind anything as long as we're together,' she said.

Her answer filled him with gratitude. He knew how important her large and laughing family was to her, how much she looked forward to their annual shared vacation in their shabby rambling summer home. He too loved being there, loved the mindless gaiety of her siblings, their foolish and swiftly resolved quarrels, the excitement of welcoming bands of relatives and friends who descended upon them with or without warning. Both his parents had been only children. There had been no extended family of aunts and uncles, boisterous cousins. He had been an only child for most of his childhood and now, since his sister's death, he was an only child again. Again and forever. Living in the heart of Denise's large and affectionate family was an experience that had amazed and delighted him, a vacation that he looked forward to each year.

But this year had been different, pursued as he was by a lingering melancholy. He lay awake worrying about his parents, about what might have occurred between them in his absence. The heat was oppressive, their bedroom airless. At night he struggled to breathe, fell briefly asleep and then, soaked in sweat, was thrust into wakefulness by a rush of anxiety, amorphous worries, amorphous memories.

Somewhere in the house a visiting child laughed in her sleep and he thought of Melanie. The soft voices of a man and a woman drifted through the darkness and he thought of his parents who had forgotten how to talk to each other. He fell asleep again and dreamed of his father sitting beneath an umbrella in an outdoor café with a silver-haired woman.

He labored to conceal his sadness. He wanted to be fair to Denise. He knew that she suggested leaving New Hampshire and going to his parents' home only because she understood his unarticulated anxiety, his desperate need to be with his mother and father, to know what was happening between them. Her generosity filled him with gratitude.

They paused beneath a towering oak. He tilted her chin and

kissed her very gently on the lips. Her heart beat against his and he wondered if his parents had ever stood together in the moonlight and felt the wind upon their faces.

'No. We'll stay. Unless it gets much hotter. I'm fine.'

'You're sure?'

'Sure. Would I lie to you?'

She laughed. Breaking free from his embrace, she sprinted toward the house and he, his breath coming freely now, raced after her, his laughter matching her own. They were fine. They would be fine. They were immune to the contagion of his parents' unhappiness.

TWENTY-EIGHT

T he days passed but the heat did not abate. The temperature soared and Judith bought yet another fan for the shop and placed a pitcher of cold water and a pyramid of paper cups on the counter. Weary customers smiled at her gratefully, sweat glistening on their faces as they took delicate sips and counted out damp crumbled bills. Sunlight streamed through the grimy windows and formed pools of brightness on the scuffed linoleum. The volunteers arrived later and left earlier. Exhausted mothers fingered the almost depleted stacks of summer clothing while their half-naked toddlers crouched beneath the fans, small hands raised to catch the slightest breeze from the whirring blades.

Judith and David ate hasty breakfasts. They discussed Brian who now called each of them every day, Judith in the morning, David in the afternoon. The frequency of his calls disturbed them. It was, they knew, symptomatic of his anxiety about what was happening between them, but they had no soothing words to offer. Not to him. Not to each other. Not yet. In the interim they shared their concerns. They had each heard a hoarseness in his voice and they worried that his asthma had recurred.

'Denise's parents should air-condition that house,' David said irritably.

'And the synagogue should air-condition the thrift shop. Or change its name from "Gently Used" to "Beastly Hot",' Judith rejoined.

'Is it getting too much for you?' he asked.

She shook her head. His concern pleased her. 'No. I can manage. But I think you're working too hard, David.'

She stared at him worriedly. He had lost weight and his shoulders slumped, as though surrendering to the burden of the stress he was enduring. She knew that he was juggling more than one complex arbitration, and because of vacation schedules, there was meager support staff. David's personal assistant,

Amanda, always pleased to share office gossip, answered a rare phone call from Judith and complained that David was at a meeting, and his desk was piled high with urgent memos. It was irresponsible for junior executives to absent themselves from the office at such a busy time, she added. Did Judith know that even Nancy Cummings had tacked extra days on to her vacation? Her question was sly, her tone righteously indignant.

'Yes. I know,' Judith lied. 'She probably had a good reason. I'm sure David is managing without her.'

She had not known but she was at once relieved and annoyed to learn that Nancy was away. It explained David's continued reticence. She speculated that he was waiting for her return and that was why he could not commit to their own vacation plan. It was a calming thought, but he might have told her. He should have told her. She thought to mention Nancy's absence as they stood together in the kitchen, mutually concerned about their son, mutually concerned about each other, but she opted for the safety of silence.

She drove too slowly to the thrift shop, reluctant to spend another sweltering day in its stifling confines. Alternatives occurred to her. She thought of the cool stillness of her carrel in the university library and smiled bitterly. She did not want to be there either. Nor did she want to spend the day at home.

Where do I really want to be? she asked herself.

The question teased. She thought of the redwood bench shaded by the maple tree in Jeffrey Kahn's garden, cooled by the soothing scented breeze that wafted over the neat beds of herbs. Yes, she wanted to be there, but she knew that to be a vagrant fantasy. She had an obligation to the thrift shop and that pleasant garden was not her garden.

She struggled with the heat-swelled shop door but finally thrust it open and hurried to turn on the fans and fill the water pitcher. She washed her face in the claustrophobic bathroom but did not dry it, unwilling to relinquish the brief relief of the moisture on her parched skin. She drenched her pocket comb and passed it over her dark hair, dampening it into a sleek dark cap that briefly cooled. She flashed herself a rueful smile in the sliver of a mirror and went into the shop.

Customers were already drifting in. Judith smiled at familiar faces, helped a flustered young mother, whose two small daughters clung to her skirt, find a maternity dress.

'Just what I need, another kid,' the young woman said bitterly.

Judith did not answer her. She smiled gratefully at Lois and Libby who had arrived earlier than usual.

'*Señora Judith. Buenos dias, Señora Judith.*'

She turned and was pleased to see Consuela. The Guatemalan grandmother who visited the thrift shop frequently in search of clothing for her many grandchildren was a favorite customer. She always smiled happily as she placed each carefully chosen item on the counter and proudly spoke of their antics and successes.

Judith loved hearing her stories. She knew now that mischievous Jesús played tricks on the other children in the daycare center. Juanita, Consuela's oldest granddaughter, had won a prize for her summer school science project. Héctor was the star of his computer camp.

Consuela glowed at their small successes. She crossed herself vigorously. How blessed they were to live in America.

'In Guatemala would they have had such chances?' she repeatedly asked Judith.

She was grateful when Judith found a floral-patterned sundress for Rosalita, the baby of the family. 'Oh, my beautiful Rosalita. She will look like a princess. You are so good to find such a pretty dress for my *bambina*, *Señora Judith.*'

Judith was always happy to help Consuela. Her words of appreciation, her beaming smile, validated the role of the thrift shop in the larger community. But on this hot morning Consuela was not smiling. Her narrow face was veiled in sadness. A silver tear drifted down her cheek and settled in the corner of her mouth. She did not wipe it away.

'Consuela, what's wrong?' Judith asked anxiously.

'I need a dress. A black dress. For a funeral. We have a death. Our family has a death.'

Her words released the tears which fell freely, bathing her face in grief.

'I'm so sorry,' Judith said and held out a tissue which Consuela pressed to her face. She struggled to remember the names of the grandchildren. She prayed that it was not one of them. 'Who?' she asked hesitantly. 'Who has died?'

'Rosalita. My Carmen's Rosalita. My *bambina. Nina.* So beautiful. So little. Not yet three years old.' Her shoulders quivered. She held up three fingers. 'Not even three,' she repeated. 'A fever. She had a fever. So high. She was on fire in my arms. The ambulance came. Then the hospital. The same ward where I clean. The doctor there, he knows me. A good man. He tried. That I know. One hour. Two hours. Nurses flew in. Other doctors came. We waited. We prayed. But he came out of the room, the doctor. He was crying. The doctor, he was crying. "Consuela, I'm sorry," he said. It was the fever *rheumatica.* It took her to God. She was dead, our beautiful *bambina.* God wanted her to be His angel. So we have a funeral for our Rosalita. A wake. Then a funeral.'

Judith thought that she too would cry. The nervous young doctor who told them that Melanie was dead had not wept. He had not said he was sorry.

She put her arms around Consuela. Libby filled a paper cup with water and handed it to her.

'*Gracias.*' Consuela drank. She accepted another tissue and wiped her eyes. 'I should not cry. The priest came. He told me that Rosalita is happy now. She is with the angels. She is in a better place, so I must not cry.' But her tears came again.

'I will find you a dress, Consuela,' Judith said.

She took her hand and together they walked to a rack of women's clothing. Judith went at once to the simple black dress that came from Sylvia Kahn's closet. It was almost new. Jeffrey had told her that Sylvia had worn it only once or twice because black depressed her. Judith handed it to Consuela, who carried it into the makeshift dressing room behind the shower curtain. She emerged minutes later and nodded. It fit her perfectly.

'I buy this,' she said. 'I wear it now. I go to help with the wake. I must dress my Rosalita.'

She did not look in the mirror. The floral-patterned house dress she had worn hung over her arm. Judith took it and put it in a plastic shopping bag, added a black headscarf and a packet that contained a pair of black stockings. Consuela fumbled in her purse for her wallet.

'Please. Just take everything. Our gift to you,' Judith protested.

She tried to remember what she had worn to Melanie's funeral and recalled that it had been Denise who had selected a black suit and rummaged through her closet for the right shoes and a scarf which, in the end, Judith had not worn.

'No, I must pay,' Consuela insisted. 'How much?'

'Five dollars will be fine,' Judith said hopelessly. 'I am so sorry for your loss, Consuela.'

'No. Do not be sorry. The priest is right. She is in heaven, our Rosalita.' She crossed herself, looked upward and forced a smile, although her face was frozen into the mask of incomprehension peculiar to the newly bereaved.

She left, closing the door softly behind her. The shadow of her grief lingered in the heavy air, spangled now with tear-shaped sunbeams that forced their way through the grimy window panes and wept their way across the scuffed linoleum.

'So sad,' Libby said.

'Awful,' Lois agreed.

A customer who worked with Consuela at the hospital told them that Consuela had occasionally brought Rosalita with her on days when Carmen, her mother, could not find a babysitter.

'She was such a good *bambina*, that pretty Rosalita. She played quietly while her *abuela* worked. She had a doll. A doll with blonde hair. She played with that doll. A lot of hours she played with that doll. Poor Carmen. Poor Consuela. A terrible thing to bury a child,' she said.

'Yes,' Judith said. 'A terrible thing.'

But the woman was no longer listening. She had moved to the rear of the store and did not see the tears that glistened in Judith's eyes.

Judith worked steadily for the rest of the day, willing herself not to think of Consuela, but now and again a wave of sadness washed over her. It occurred to her that she might have asked about attending the wake and realized at once how foolish and inappropriate that would have been. She was neither friend nor family. She could not invade their mourning. She would not impose her loss upon their own.

She was relieved to see David's car in the driveway when

she arrived home. This was not an evening when she wanted to be alone. He was in the garden watering the lawn that had once filled them with pride and pleasure. She realized, with a flash of shame, that she now scarcely glanced at it, that she had ignored the gardener's warning about a dying rose bush and overgrown back hedges.

'I'm home,' she called, struggling to keep her voice light.

He was not deceived. Wheeling about to look at her as she stood in the doorway, his eyes darkened with concern. She was pale, her head lowered, her hands tightly clasped. 'Are you all right, Judith?' he asked, allowing the hose to puddle water at his feet.

'Yes. Fine. It's the heat. That's all. I'll make a salad, a gazpacho.'

'Great. A gazpacho.'

'You're home early.'

'I'm waiting for some documents to be overnighted. Tomorrow's going to be a marathon. Double deadlines. I don't know whether I'll be able to meet them.'

She saw the worry lines that creased his brow, the slope of his shoulders as though they were weighted by the unfinished work he had left on his desk. She knew how important it had always been to him to fulfill his obligations on schedule. She understood why it was especially important now. It offered him control over at least one part of his life.

'Don't worry,' she said. 'You'll do fine.'

She placed her hands on his shoulders, moved them to his neck and gently massaged it, waiting until she felt him relax before she turned away. He stared after her as she disappeared into the kitchen and then lifted the hose again.

She worked quickly, assembling the ingredients, arranging the vegetables in a neat row on the counter, soothed by the orderly process that briefly dispelled the chaotic grief that had haunted her throughout the day. Who was it, she wondered, who had written that women loved their kitchens because there they exercised absolute control? Shirley Jackson, she thought, but perhaps not. Christina Stead? Possibly. She smiled at the vagary of the question, and as her mood lifted, she took pleasure in plunging neatly sliced tomatoes, slivers of cucumber, wands of scallions into the blender. Their emulsion canceled the last shreds of her melancholy and she submitted to a new determination. She would not think of Rosalita, three-year-old Rosalita, dressed in white, lying in lifeless innocence in a small coffin lined with pink satin. She was grateful that Jews did not have wakes, that her memories of Melanie were imbued with life. Pulling apart a clump of parsley, she began to weep, the tears flowing freely, her shoulders heaving in a paroxysm of grief.

'Judith!' David's arms were about her, his body supporting hers as he led her into the living room and sat beside her on the sofa. Gently, he loosened the parsley from her grasp and then, oddly, popped it into his own mouth. 'What is it?' he asked. 'Why were you crying?'

'Later. I'll tell you later.'

She slipped free and returned to the kitchen where she added garlic to the gazpacho and thrust a baguette into the oven. They ate in silence and it was only after she prepared a pitcher of iced coffee and filled their glasses that she told him about Rosalita's death.

'A little girl. Three years old. A three-year-old girl should not die,' she said and her voice broke.

'No child should die.' His words echoed hers. His sadness twinned her own.

She felt the heat of his tears upon her fingers and knew that her cheeks were wet. As one, they mourned Rosalita, a child they had never met, and, at last, bonded as they were in sorrow, they grieved together.

They slept in the same bed that night, although they did not speak, nor did they touch, only listened to the rhythmic rise and fall of each other's breath until the break of dawn when he placed his hand gently upon her head.

TWENTY-NINE

David left the house before Judith awakened the next morning. He thought to leave a note of explanation for her but then decided that he would call her from the city.

The deadline on both of his projects had to be met by the end of that day. The amount of work that remained overwhelmed him. He hoped against hope that Nancy would return to the office in time to help him, but there had been no word from her. He worked throughout his commute and sprinted to his office from Grand Central. He switched on his computer and cursed at the number of emails that would have to be answered. His fax machine was spitting out documents and he glanced at them briefly as he harvested them. He would manage, he told himself grimly as he shoved them into a file folder which immediately slipped from his hand.

'Goddamn it,' he said, angered by his own clumsiness.

He was on his knees, gathering them, when his office door opened and Nancy Cummings entered, stooped and collected the fallen pages, her silver hair curtaining her face. Relieved, grateful, he smiled and opened his arms wide. She stepped into them.

'Am I in time?' she asked.

'Just in time. I'll have my messages transferred to your extension,' he said. 'Amanda is taking the morning off. A dental appointment, a doctor's appointment. She always arranges them on a deadline day.'

'We'll manage without her.'

Their laughter mingled and, still laughing, they carried files and laptops into the conference room and braced themselves for the long day ahead.

Judith was not surprised that David had left so early. She knew that he had more than one deadline imminent and she understood how concerned he was about meeting them. She was briefly irritated that he had not left her a note, but then he had probably raced out to catch an early train. It was not important. He would call later in the day, she thought with new and comforting certainty.

Sipping her coffee, she remembered she had promised Suzanne that she would open the shop that morning. She felt a nagging reluctance. A lazy day without obligations would have been nice, but that was not an option. And where, after all, did she want to go on such a heat-heavy morning? What did she want to do? Shrugging, she dressed swiftly and drove to the shop, where she hurried through the ritual of turning on the fans, opening the windows and filling the water pitcher. Customers drifted in. Lois and Libby arrived and immediately suggested an early closing.

'So damn hot,' Lois said, and Libby shook her head vigorously.

'Let's wait and see,' Judith said.

They did not have to wait. The phone rang. The executive director of the synagogue advised her that the entire building had to be closed. A structural problem. There would be no electricity, no water.

'The damn heat. Everything is on overload according to Con Ed. But it's just as well. They're predicting a major storm, so it's safer for everyone to get home in advance of it,' he said.

'Of course,' Judith agreed.

The few customers completed their purchases and left quickly. Lois and Libby saw the closure as a gift of time. They spoke happily of a dash to a new café, iced cappuccinos, cold salads.

'Come on, Judith. You deserve a break,' Lois said.

She hesitated but shook her head. 'Thanks, but I have a million things to do.'

They hurried out and she locked up, then stood outside, jangling her car keys. Church bells sounded and she remembered the wake for Rosalita. No, she would not attend. The family would want privacy. She certainly understood that.

The empty hours stretched before her. She thought of her unfinished essay, of the syllabus yet to be organized, of calls she should make. Her dishwasher needed a small repair. There was a leak in the downstairs bathroom. She shook her head. She did not want to sit at her computer. She did not want to deal with plumbers.

The question she had asked herself earlier recurred. *Where did she want to be? What did she want to do?* She knew. She pulled out her cell phone and dialed David's office. She would suggest an early dinner in the city. A simple enough plan. Spontaneity reclaimed. She thought of the restaurants they had once favored, wondered if she could squeeze in a facial. Her spirits lifted as his phone rang, rang again and went to voicemail.

'You have reached the office of David Mandell. If your message is urgent, I can be reached on extension two-four-two, Nancy Cummings' line. Otherwise leave a message at the beep.'

Judith's brief exuberance faded. Her heart sank. She did not leave a message. She did not dial extension 242. Nancy was back then, but David had said nothing about her return. A strange omission. Or perhaps not so strange. Her optimism had been premature.

She went to her car, turned on the ignition and the air conditioning, and sat quietly for a few minutes. Then she flipped her phone open and made another call.

Jeffrey Kahn answered on the very first ring. Yes, he was at home. Yes, it would be wonderful if she drove up that afternoon. It was so good of her to call. He would be happy, really happy to see her.

Yet again she felt that guilty frisson of pleasure. A man was waiting for her. A man who would be happy to see her. She smiled ruefully at the adolescent frivolity of the thought and drove to the small gourmet shop which stocked the brie Jeffrey favored. It was the courteous thing to do, she told herself. She was simply being thoughtful. Her cell phone rang. Brian. An unlikely hour for him to call.

'What's wrong?' she asked. The question was reflexive and immediately regretted.

'Nothing's wrong. Why should anything be wrong?'

She heard the too familiar annoyance in his voice. 'Sorry,' she apologized.

'I just wanted you to know that Denise and I are on our way to New York. It got too hot for us in New Hampshire and our apartment will probably be no better. Is it OK if we crash with you and Dad until this damn heatwave is over?'

'Of course it's OK. You know that,' she said.

'Don't wait up for us. We're going to stop en route and they're predicting a storm. We probably won't get there until pretty late.'

'Fine,' she said. 'Give your father a call and let him know.'

He hesitated. 'I'll do that.'

She heard the annoyance in his voice and she knew he was wondering why she herself did not tell David. She wondered that herself. It would have been easy enough to call him on Nancy Cummings' extension. What an odd game they were playing, she and David, the rules undefined, absences and silences unexplained, sleeping together, sleeping alone, missed calls and half-truths darting across the chessboard of their marriage. Ridiculous.

'Drive carefully,' she cautioned and was relieved when it was Denise who took the phone to reply.

'Can't wait to see you,' Denise said, as always ready to tamp down any tension.

'Yes. It will be great to see you both,' Judith replied.

She wondered whether she should cancel her visit to Jeffrey but decided that there was no need. Brian and Denise would not arrive until well after dinner. Their room was made up. She would stock up on small treats for them at the gourmet shop, the dates stuffed with walnuts that Brian loved and the miniature quiches that Denise liked.

Entering the shop, she was surprised and pleased to see Suzanne at the counter. During their last conversation, Suzanne had been despondent. Things were not going well, she had confided. Maybe her fault. Maybe Eric's fault.

'I guess I've lived alone for so long that I'm finding it hard to share my space. Not that I'm not relieved, grateful, so grateful, to have him back in my life, to know that he's all right, making progress. But things are tricky. I feel as though we're balanced on a tightrope. One false step and we plummet. I watch every word I say. I'm afraid if I ask him to hang up his bath towel or put his laundry away, he'll explode and be off. Still, I'm trying, and so is he,' she had said.

'It will get better,' Judith had assured her. 'Everything gets better. Peace comes.'

The lie had fallen easily from her lips. She knew that things did not always get better, that, in fact, they often got worse, much worse. Peace had not come to her marriage. Not yet. Hope curdled into sadness. Too many words remained unsaid, too many feelings remained unshared. She was a woman buying cheese to be eaten in odd intimacy with a widower beset by loss and loneliness.

But today it seemed Suzanne's situation had indeed improved. Smartly dressed in a white skirt and a rose-colored shirt, she waved cheerfully to Judith who noted that the straps of her sandals were braids of rose and white leather. Suzanne must be feeling a great deal better to pay attention to such a fashion detail, Judith thought maliciously.

Suzanne was not surprised to hear about the synagogue closing. 'It's just as well. There are alerts about a storm heading south through New England, but they've been saying that for a week. They want us to think that this damn heat is coming to an end. In any case, we have to see about air conditioning the shop. We don't want next summer to be like this one.'

'You're absolutely right,' Judith agreed. She would not tell Suzanne that she could not think of the summer to come any more than she could plan for the next week or even the next day. 'How are things going with Eric?' she asked.

'Better. Much better. He's seeing a wonderful therapist, never missing an appointment. And he's moving out of my condo. Stan found a program at a community college up county, got him a conditional acceptance and wangled a dorm room for him for the fall semester. Eric's apprehensive but excited. And I'm apprehensive but excited. You know how it is.'

Judith nodded, although she did not know how it was, did not want to know. She shook her head when Suzanne suggested that they have lunch at the salad place. 'Sorry, I can't,' she said. 'I have to get things ready for Brian and Denise and I want to complete some research.'

'OK. I'll be back at the shop next week. We'll do it then.'

Suzanne shoved her credit card across the counter, thrust her purchases into her canvas tote and left. Judith added a jar of olives to her order and wondered why she had not simply said that she was driving up to Jeffrey Kahn's. A stupid evasion. She had nothing to hide, nor did she have anything to reveal.

She paid, left the store and was immediately overwhelmed by the heat that seemed to have intensified and assumed an almost corporeal force. She felt that she was pushing against a fiery wall as she rushed to her car, sweat dampening her clothes and streaking her face. Struggling for breath, she fumbled for her sunglasses and shielded her eyes against the glaring bright-ness of the noonday sun. Driving faster than usual, she headed north with the air conditioning on high and the radio tuned to the station that played the ballads of her younger days. Once again 'Greenfields' came on and she switched to a news station.

Now and again, newly relaxed, she glanced out of the window. As on her previous trips, she enjoyed the changing scene of the northern road as the suburban towns disappeared and were replaced by large expanses of well-manicured but as yet undeveloped acreage. The grassy verges were neatly mowed, the trees pollarded, the hedges trimmed. Now and again, at a comfortable distance from the road, houses could be glimpsed, quiet exurban retreats nestled in the sylvan landscape. Here, Judith thought, was the serenity, the refuge, that Sylvia Kahn had sought, that Jeffrey had granted her. She thought of how Jeffrey spoke of his daughters, concerned about Amy who worked too hard, about Beth who was single and might be lonely. His voice lifted when he confided that she was in a new and promising relationship.

He, like all parents, was riding on a merry-go-round that never stopped. She thought of Suzanne so brave in her white skirt and rose-colored top, her news of Eric optimistic, but her tone wary. Suzanne, Judith thought sadly, would spend the rest of her life poised for disaster, hope and dread uneasily balanced.

That, at least, Judith thought, she and David had been spared. Brian, stable and self-sufficient, loved by Denise, loving Denise, was fine and would always be fine. And Melanie was safely dead.

The absurdity of her own thought shocked her. She bit her

lips in self-inflicted fury and struggled to negate it, summoning up memories of Melanie, their Melanie, alive before death had snatched her from them.

'Our Melanie.' She said the words aloud, remembered David whispering them to her as they sat side by side at a school play in which Melanie played a princess.

'Look at our Melanie,' he had said, his face bright with pride and pleasure.

She remembered how he had taught her to ride a bicycle, how he had run beside her and called to Judith, 'Look at our Melanie. She's a natural, our Melanie.'

The memories converged, continued. She parked the car and allowed them to sweep over her. She forgave herself for the thought that had come unbidden. Those memories were chapters, she realized, chapters in both her daughter's brief life and in the longer chronicle of her marriage.

How odd it was, she reflected, that she who had been trained in the art of the narrative, who taught others to understand the impact of sequence and the significance of metaphor, had never thought to apply that skill to her own life. Yes, she remembered speaking to David of marriage, all marriages as sequential chapters in a novel. But she had not told him that the endings of novels had always both eluded and intrigued her. She had never wanted a story to end. That had been the joy of critical reading. *Would Emma Bovary die? Would Jo March find love?* For her, from childhood on, every book had been an excursion into mystery, every conclusion an unexpected revelation. It should not surprise her now that the next chapter of her marriage eluded her even as she hurtled toward it.

She sighed and, in search of a distraction, switched the radio on and found a news station. International news, national news, local news, all uniformly bad, followed by the somber voice of a meteorologist warning that a dangerous storm threatened.

She opened her window and peered out. The sun still blazed and the air remained heavy. But the ominous warning droned on.

'High winds and torrential rains are anticipated. Listeners are urged to take precautions.'

Briefly, she thought of turning around and driving home. She could call Jeffrey and tell him that, in view of the weather, she would not be coming. But she knew she would not do that. She drove on. She was, after all, almost there. Within minutes, she drove up the gravel driveway and was startled to see a U-Haul van parked in front of Jeffrey's garage.

Puzzled, she looked over at the herb garden and saw that beyond its marigold-fringed border, in the shaded area, a picnic table had been placed and chairs arranged. Four chairs. The number was unsettling. Jeffrey had set the table for guests. Another couple, obviously. It was a presumption that angered her. She took the bag that contained the wheel of brie from the car and stared coldly at Jeffrey who approached her, smiling happily.

'A surprise,' he said.

Emily, cradling her baby, came forward, holding hands with a slender, fine-featured young man who was surely her husband, James. The young couple bent their heads in shy greeting.

'Are you pleased?' Jeffrey asked. 'I was going to tell you that they would be here when you phoned, but then I thought it would be a nice surprise for you.'

'I am surprised,' Judith said. 'And pleased. But I'm not sure I understand.'

'It's simple enough. An apartment for a research assistant became available and I offered it to young James here. He was delighted, of course, but worried about furnishing it. They've been living in student housing, one room with just the basics – their bed, a crib for the baby, a table and two chairs. So I told him my basement was crammed with all the furniture from my daughters' college rooms and their bachelorette apartments. Couches, beds, chairs, tables, lamps. All sorts of kitchen equipment. I asked him to bring his Emily here so they could choose what might suit. We settled on today because the lab is closed. And then you called and I thought we could all have lunch. A picnic party.'

He smiled the happy, satisfied smile of a man delighting in his own kindness and generosity. He had, Judith realized, on this sun-bright day, emerged from the long shadow of mourning. He was hosting a picnic, welcoming young people into his home, into his life. A new chapter of his life was beginning. *Chapters. Every life a novel.*

'What a good idea,' she said and handed him the cheese.

Emily held her hand out. 'Mrs Judith, this is my husband, James,' she said, and the young man bowed from the waist.

'It is my honor to meet you,' he said. 'My wife has told me of your great kindness. How good it was of you to introduce me to Doctor Kahn.'

'I'm glad I was able to help,' Judith said as Emily held the baby out to her.

With Jane in her arms, she walked to the picnic table and took her seat in the welcoming circlet of shade. She surrendered to a contentment she had not known for months. Not since – she lifted the baby's tiny fingers to her lips – not since Melanie died. The words came to her without the familiar stab of pain.

Jeffrey had prepared a simple lunch of salad, fruit and store-bought sushi. Judith added the cheese and they ate with pleasure. Judith asked Emily about the apartment.

'It is wonderful. Small but wonderful,' Emily said excitedly. 'It has windows. Many windows. Now I can look out and see the light. I will make curtains for the windows.'

'Someone just donated some very pretty curtains to the thrift shop, but if you don't like them, we have some nice bolts of fabric you could choose,' Judith suggested.

'Ah, the thrift shop. I think it has saved my life.'

And perhaps mine too, Judith thought.

She cut a strawberry into small pieces and held a juicy segment to the baby's mouth, delighting in the sweet touch of the tiny tongue against her finger.

The meal over, they paraded down to the basement. The discarded furniture of the Kahn sisters' younger years was shrouded in heavy cloths and dust-encrusted plastic sheeting, but when Jeffrey removed the coverings, they saw that every-thing was in excellent condition.

Gaily patterned futons and a bright orange couch encircled a low coffee table, its particle-wood surface scarred by circlets left by carelessly placed glasses and cigarette burns. Judith saw it as a stage set in readiness for a performance with the Kahn sisters and their friends of yesteryear, crouched on the futons, their drinks set casually on the table, laughing and talking, lovely girls and handsome young men, inching their way into adult life. How fortunate they had been. How fortunate they were.

She wandered over to a sturdy table, its wooden surface polished to a high gleam, flanked by chairs painted sunshine yellow.

'Sylvia polished that table,' Jeffrey said. 'She refinished it and she polished it.' He stroked it as though he might capture the touch of his wife's hand.

'It looks wonderful. Everything does.'

Suzanne would approve, she thought. Each piece of furniture had been gently used and gently preserved. Emily and James moved through the basement, murmuring their pleasure, their gratitude, discussing what they might take and where they would place the couch, the futon. Judith, holding the baby, trailed after them, but when Jeffrey began to open the cartons of kitchenware, she smiled apologetically and said she would take the baby into the garden.

She sat in the shade, Jane asleep in her arms. The heat had not abated, but scuttling clouds chased the sunlight and disappeared, leaving shreds of shadow adrift across the waning brightness. Perhaps the predictions had been right. Perhaps a storm was on the way. If so, Judith realized, she should leave. The winding northern roadway was badly lit and said to be perilous in inclement weather. But she remained motionless, Jane's rhythmic breath warm against her neck.

She watched as James and Jeffrey emerged from the basement, struggling beneath the weight of the table, Emily following them, holding a lamp, all of which, with some effort, they loaded into the U-Haul.

'Are you all right?' Emily called to Judith.

'I'm fine,' she replied.

She did not add that she was more than fine. The sleeping infant's sweet scent and the lightness of her little body suffused her with a remembered pleasure. Just so she had held first Brian and then Melanie in her arms, happily surrendering to the delight of sitting quite still and staring down at their precious faces relaxed in untroubled sleep. She reclaimed that lost delight as she brushed her lips lightly across Jane's sun-bright cheek.

Jeffrey and James hurried now, hoisting the futons while

Emily carried up one chair and then another. Finally, Jeffrey sank down on the grass beside Judith.

'I think we're done for today,' he said. 'They'll have to come back with a strong young friend for the heavier stuff – the coffee table, the couch. And anything else they want.'

'You're very generous.' Judith spoke very softly, fearful of waking the baby who shifted in her arms, gripped a tendril of her hair between her tiny fingers and released it.

'I'm glad to give the furniture away and know that it's all going to be used.'

'That's how we feel at the thrift shop. We're constantly congratulating ourselves on turning the dross of some into the gold of others.'

'I'm not congratulating myself.'

'Of course not. I know that.'

The edginess of his tone frightened her and she realized how little she knew of his reactions and sensitivities. His emotional makeup, the landscape of his moods, was a mystery to her.

'They are such nice young people, Emily and James,' he added, as though to apologize for his transient irritability.

'Yes. Yes, they are.'

The door to the U-Haul slammed shut and the young couple hurried over. With great gentleness, Emily took Jane from Judith's arms, and James, with balletic grace, bowed from the waist and smiled at them.

'How can we thank you?' he asked.

'No thanks necessary. It's my pleasure,' Jeffrey replied.

'Just be happy,' Judith added. 'That is all Doctor Kahn and I would want of you.'

How effortlessly she had coupled the words. *Doctor Kahn and I.* Not 'Jeffrey and I'.

They all smiled and James, with his arm around Emily's waist, her head inclined toward the infant still asleep in her arms, helped her into the cab of the U-Haul. They waved as James slowly negotiated the long driveway and then accelerated. He was, Judith realized, hurrying toward a new beginning, a pleasanter life in a modest apartment blessed with the miracle of windows for which his wife would fashion curtains. He and Emily would sit on chairs the color of sunlight, at the wooden kitchen table which Sylvia Kahn had so lovingly sanded and polished.

Judith smiled at the extravagance of her own imagined scenario but she hugged it close, grateful for the unexpected clarity it offered. *Yes and yes again.* Lives changed but life went on. Chapters ended and chapters began. Continuity was not violated.

'They're a sweet little family,' Jeffrey said, startling her out of her reverie.

'Yes. They are,' she agreed.

'I miss my family. I miss my daughters.' Sadness weighted his voice.

'Of course you do. My son and his fiancée are away on just a short vacation and I miss them.'

He had not said that he missed his wife. She would not say that she missed her daughter. He knew, as she did, that the dead are missed in one way and the living in another. The dead, she now knew, were missed with grave finality, recognition of their loss accompanied by wavelets of sorrow and memories that ebbed and flowed in an unpredictable tide.

The absent living, however, are missed with wistful longing, soothed by the anticipation of togetherness to come. Jeffrey missed his daughters, but he understood that one day they would run toward him through the California sunlight. They would visit and their laughter would once again trill through their childhood home. He would hear their voices on the phone and plan visits and vacations.

He missed his wife, with the full knowledge that she was gone forever, present only in his remembered love and in the vagrant memories and fragmented images that brought him both pain and comfort. He would see her hands in the polished wood of the table she had restored, inhale her scent in the room they had shared. He would miss her and remember her all the days of his life.

Judith missed Brian and Denise, but they would soon return. Quiet evenings and long leisurely weekends would be shared. There would be a wedding, and she and David would dance together in celebration of their son's happiness. The yearning she felt in Brian's absence would be assuaged the moment he burst into their home and encircled her in his strong arms, offering her love and laughter.

But she would miss Melanie always and forever, sustained only by remembrance of days past. Her daughter's laughter would resonate in memory, her smiling face would linger in the kitchen mirror. Looking at the apple tree, Judith would hear that trilling voice call out, *A leaf, a blossom.* Melanie was gone but she was not lost. She was missed and mourned but never would she be lost. Not to her and not to David.

David. Her heart broke with tenderness for him, for herself.

Jeffrey looked up at the slowly darkening sky and she followed his gaze. 'It will rain soon,' he said.

'Yes. Of course it will. We'd better get everything inside.'

They hurried to bring the chairs in, to gather up the remnants of their picnic. They set the food down on the kitchen table and, standing side by side in the dimly lit room, they stared at each other. He put his hands on her shoulders, a light and tentative touch. She moved away, a gentle retreat. His arms fell to his sides.

'Why did you come here today, Judith?' he asked.

'I don't know. Impulse. An impulse I didn't understand. Perhaps it was because one season is ending and another beginning and I was in search of both – an ending and a new beginning. I think it was because I wanted calm and I always found that with you. That was important for me, as it was, I think, for you, during those weeks we worked together. It was good for both of us to share all that we shared, but I realized today that now . . .' Her voice drifted off. She could not find the words she needed to complete the sentence.

He completed it for her, sadness and acceptance commingled in his voice. 'And now that time has ended,' he said. 'And we are each in need of a new beginning.'

She nodded, weak with gratitude. Their parting would be as gentle as their time together had been, as calm as the compassionate understanding they had offered each other. 'I should leave before the storm breaks. David will be worried,' she said.

'Yes,' he agreed. 'Of course he'll be worried.'

He walked her to her car, waited while she opened the door, then held her face in his hands and kissed her on the cheek. 'Thank you,' he said. 'Thank you for everything.'

She nodded and drove too swiftly away, looking back only

when she reached the bottom of the long driveway. He was gone, and she imagined that he was sitting in his living room, phone in hand, talking quietly to one much-missed daughter or another. He was sad, she knew, but not regretful, as she was sad but not regretful. They had used each other with great gentleness.

She drove more slowly as the rain began, the fat drops weeping their way across her windshield. She hoped that David would be home when she arrived. She hoped that they could watch the storm together, as they often had in the early days of their togetherness.

THIRTY

D avid and Nancy had worked without respite throughout the day, racing against the looming deadlines. The dark wood table in the conference room was covered with their spreadsheets and the files they reached for blindly as they struggled through the final stages of the complicated arbitrations. Glaring sunlight poured in through the long windows, sending rhomboids of light dancing across their computer screen. The air conditioner hummed, losing power, gaining power. David prayed that it would not die until they were finished. Nancy called maintenance and arranged for fans to be set up.

'Just in case,' she murmured.

'Yes. Just in case. Good thinking,' he agreed, without looking up. 'I don't know how I would have managed without you. I might have missed the deadline,' he added.

'There was no need to worry. I had the date marked on my calendar.'

'Of course. I should have known.'

He realized that he had, over the past several months, come to rely on Nancy both professionally and emotionally, a replication of his reliance on Judith. The thought troubled him. It was time for him to rely on himself. He shrugged and concentrated on the figures that had to be integrated into his report. Time enough for emotional archeology when the projects that had consumed him for so many weeks were over and done with.

The day wore on. They worked through lunch, ordering sandwiches which were only half eaten and allowing empty paper coffee cups to accumulate until Nancy swept them into a wastepaper basket. He tried to reach Judith, but cell phone reception in the conference room was notoriously unreliable. His messages were being routed to Nancy's extension and he would be told of any urgent call. Judith would understand. He had told her how difficult his day would be.

At four o'clock Amanda entered to report that the office was closing early because of the heat and the impending storm. She plunked down a pitcher of iced water and smiled benignly at them, assuming the pose of a den mother pleased with her diligent boy scouts.

'Everyone's leaving,' she reported. 'Your phone messages are on your desk, David. I fielded most of them. Nothing urgent. Oh, yes. Brian called and said to tell you that he and Denise would be driving down from New Hampshire and he'd be in touch later. There are a couple of letters that need your signature. Do you need anything else?'

He shook his head and thought to ask her if Judith had called, but he was all but certain she had not.

'No. We're OK. Actually, we're almost finished. We need maybe another hour. Everything will be sent on time, thanks to Nancy.'

'You got back just in time,' Amanda said, turning to Nancy, who nodded without looking away from her computer screen. 'The AC is supposed to be OK for another hour so you should be all right.'

'We'll be fine,' Nancy said dismissively.

Amanda frowned. She did not like Nancy. She waved and hurried out, leaving the door slightly ajar. Her very high heels clattered down the corridor, her laughter echoing as she joined her waiting friends. David thought he heard her mention Nancy's name. But whatever she had said, whatever she conjectured, was of no importance. He was immune to office gossip and there was, after all, nothing to gossip about.

He closed the door and turned to Nancy. She was pale and beads of sweat pearled her neck. She sat very erect as she stared at her screen, checking the pixelated numbers of their final entry. She made one correction and then another. Leaning back, she twisted her long silver hair into a loose bun, dipped a tissue into the water pitcher and moistened her face. Droplets fell on to the bodice of her dress.

'You're tired,' he said.

'I am.'

'Please. You don't have to stay.'

'But I want to. We can finish this in an hour. I don't have to rush home. Lauren is still away. Let's wrap this up.'

'If you're sure.'

'I'm sure.'

He smiled gratefully and concentrated on his notes, composing his recommendations as she passed relevant data to him. The room grew darker. He went to the window. The invasive sunlight had vanished and gray clouds canopied the street below. Pedestrians looked up and quickened their steps, racing against the threatening storm. Automobiles and buses moved slowly, their headlights casting narrow ribbons of light across the darkening avenue. The air conditioner ceased its hum and Nancy switched on the standing fan. He returned to his computer, smiled his gratitude, made one last entry, snapped his fingers and grinned.

'That's it,' he said. 'Print this out, press "send" and let's get out of here.'

She set the printer, snapped up the pages as they were spat out and sorted them into folders. 'Done,' she called out. 'We did it.'

She clapped her hands and they smiled at each other, pleased with their achievement, pleased with their mutual effort and their joint triumph over the completion of the two complex projects.

'We're a good team. Thanks, Nancy. Thanks a million.'

She turned away, a blush rouging her cheeks. As she gathered up the spreadsheets, he went to his office and tried to reach Judith on both their home phone and her cell. On both, he heard her recorded message. He left none of his own and returned to the conference room to help Nancy sort the spreadsheets into file boxes. That done, he watched her print out labels, smiling at how meticulously she completed the smallest task. Together, they carried the bulky file boxes to his office. He tried to think of a way to express his gratitude to her for the long hours she had devoted to his project, for the meticulousness of her effort.

'Let's celebrate,' he said. 'A drink. Dinner. We owe it to ourselves. At least, I owe it to you.'

She stared at him. 'You don't owe me anything, David,' she said very quietly.

'But I think I do. And I'm starved. You're not hungry?'

'Starving,' she admitted. 'But Judith – your wife—'

'I can't reach her. I'll leave her a message. There's no way I can put off eating until I get home. So you'll have to join me. I hate to eat alone.'

Still she hesitated. 'I just don't feel up to a restaurant. All I want to do is take a shower, cool off and relax. How about if you come home with me? We'll order in. Indian. How's that for a compromise?'

Her suggestion surprised him. In Lauren's absence, they had pointedly avoided her apartment, an unspoken acknowledgment of their mutual fear.

'Do you really want to do that?' he asked.

'Yes. Why not?'

It was not a question he wanted to answer. Instead, he dialed Judith's cell phone yet again and left a murmured message telling her he would have dinner in the city, offering neither excuse nor explanation.

'All right. Your apartment, then.'

He cursed his hesitancy. He cursed his acquiescence. But it was something he had to do, he told himself. This would not only be a 'thank you' dinner. It was an opportunity to abandon all artificial caution, to clarify their awkward intimacy and establish new parameters.

She went to the ladies' room and he stared at his phone messages, lifted the receiver to return a call but instead dialed the thrift shop. It was closed. *Due to inclement weather.* Judith had recorded the message. Again he dialed his home and again the answering machine picked up. *Where was she in this inclement weather?*

He slammed the phone down and decided, with irrational certainty, that he knew exactly where she was. He imagined her with Jeffrey Kahn in the garden of his isolated home, staring up at the storm-swept sky. Sadness and anger commingled. Anger triumphed over sadness. He picked up his attaché case, dimmed his office light and left.

Nancy waited for him at the elevator. She had loosened her hair. It floated to her shoulders, the color of ice. He thought that if he lifted a single silver tendril it would be cold to his touch.

They did not speak in the cab that carried them to her

apartment. They were silent as she opened the door, as he followed her in. The small rooms were blanketed in heat and she hurried to open the windows and allow the rain-cooled breeze to sweep in.

'I'd forgotten how good rain could feel,' she said and leaned forward. She held her hands out to the rapidly falling droplets, and because she laughed, so did he. The downfall was steady and thunder rumbled in the distance.

'At last,' she murmured and moistened her face with the drops that glittered on her fingers.

'At last,' he agreed.

She lifted one hand to her cheek and lightly touched his chin with the other. Instinctively, he gripped her wrist and at once released it, reminding himself that the rules of the strange games they had been playing for so many weeks had not changed.

She stepped back. 'I'll take a quick shower,' she said. 'The takeout menus for Bombay House are on the table. You order.'

'Yes. OK,' he said.

He studied the choices, struggling with a decision. Samosas? Mulligatawny soup? Always it was Judith who decided what to order, knowing his preferences as she knew his preferences in all things. The intrusion of the thought unsettled him. He opted for the more familiar foods, placed the order with the restaurant and wandered into the living room, glancing at the books on Nancy's shelves, the pictures on her walls. There were the framed museum reproductions and battered copies of Modern Library editions. College leftovers, Judith would call them. Her words, when she made such comments, were judgmental but not meant to be unkind. She was rarely unkind but she had been trained to analyze and assess. In literature, as in life, furnishings gave clues to the nature of characters. She had written papers analyzing the domestic realms of Emma Bovary and Anna Karenina, the unhappy suburban households of Cheever and Updike. The placement of a couch, chairs set at a distance from each other, a canopied bed or a sagging cot offered clues about the quality of a marriage.

Visiting his parents' home for the first time, Judith had immediately discerned that his father's small den had only one chair, that his mother slept in an alcove on a bed that was narrow and unwelcoming, evidence of the separate lives they had lived.

'Such a waste. Things could have been so different. For you. For them,' she had murmured. 'She could have forgiven him.'

He had agreed then, and yet he himself had withheld forgiveness and retreated into an unshared room, an unshared bed.

'Jeffrey Kahn and I . . .' Judith had said, and too swiftly he had silenced her.

He had feared what else she might say. He had feared his own response. He had feared that their marriage, so dangerously wounded by loss, could not sustain yet another fissure. He had been wrong. So very wrong.

He thought to call her cell phone again, but the bathroom door opened and he glimpsed Nancy disappearing into her bedroom, closing the door softly behind her.

He walked down the hallway to Lauren's bedroom. Her treasures, a family of china rabbits, brightly jacketed books, a collection of sea shells, neatly arranged on the bookcase and bureau that had belonged to his daughter. The familiar candy-striped comforter covered the bed and a faded Raggedy Anne rested on the pillow, a replacement for the tattered teddy bear that had been Melanie's nocturnal companion from earliest childhood. That bear, he knew, was in a carton that contained her baby blanket, her favorite books and a photograph album, which Judith had thrust into a corner of her closet.

He moved across the room. The magenta rug was soft beneath his feet. He went to the window that overlooked a narrow urban alley. The curtains that matched the cheerful comforter hung straight. In Melanie's room they had been tied back with sashes so that they would not obscure her view of the apple tree just below her window. She delighted in shouting out its progress.

'There are leaves,' she had called to them. 'Come see. Leaves.'

'There are flowers. White flowers.'

One morning he had sprinted up to a low-hanging branch and plucked a cluster of blossoms which he had placed on her pillow as she slept. The tender memory tugged at his heart and he turned away.

The doorbell rang and he went to answer it. A smiling Indian youth handed him two insulated bags and his smile grew even broader as David pressed a large bill into his hand, declining the offer of change. He placed the fragrant containers of food on the kitchen table and turned to see Nancy in the doorway holding out two glasses of wine.

Her hair was damp, her face rosy from the shower. She wore a long-sleeved white belted robe, sheer enough to reveal the fullness of her breasts, the narrowness of her waist, the slight plumpness of her thighs. She smiled shyly, uncertainly.

He took the glass from her and answered the question he read in her eyes. 'You're beautiful,' he said. 'So beautiful.'

He marveled at her daring, at her courage, even as he castigated himself for the false encouragement he might have offered her. How wrong he had been to open his arms and welcome her into his embrace when she entered his office that morning. Regret had haunted him throughout the day. He understood that it was possible – no, probable – that she had misunderstood his intent. His spontaneous gesture of relief and gratitude might have been perceived by her as an acknowledgment of a new commitment between them.

He moved toward her, steeling himself against a possible surge of desire, but all he felt was the weight of sadness, a pathos he could neither ignore nor deny. He was a man in late middle age, staring at the luminous body of a vulnerable young woman. It shamed him that he had, inadvertently, yet reprehensibly, encouraged her in a false hope, a dangerous fantasy. It was, he knew, a triple betrayal. He had betrayed himself, betrayed Judith, betrayed the lovely and lonely young widow who stood before him.

'I'm sorry,' he said softly. 'So sorry. You have been a wonderful friend to me. I care deeply for you. As a friend. You understand what I am saying?'

'Yes.' Her response was a barely audible whisper. 'I thought . . . I was wrong.'

She turned and left the room. He sat on the soft gray couch and waited. Minutes later, she stood before him, dressed in jeans and a T-shirt, her hair tied back. Her eyes were dangerously bright and he hoped that she would not weep. She did not.

'I should go,' he said.

'But the food . . .' She pointed to the kitchen and they both smiled wistfully.

'No longer hungry,' he said truthfully. 'Freeze what you don't eat. You and Lauren will have a feast.'

'Yes. We will. Thank you.'

He took her hand and raised it to his lips. 'I'm grateful,' he said. 'For everything.'

She nodded. 'As I am.'

They smiled at each other in a mutuality of relief and regret.

He knew that she would weep when he left. He himself felt close to tears, yet weak with relief. He had been honest. She had been brave. There had been neither drama nor recrimination, only acceptance. *Acceptance.* The word teased. Of course. He remembered Judith telling him that Evelyn, her therapist, claimed that acceptance was the final stage of grief. Perhaps he and Nancy, together, through their long weeks of sharing, had reached the final stage.

He kissed her on the cheek. She touched his hand lightly and he left, closing the door softly behind him. He waited in the hallway until he heard the click of her deadbolt. He wanted her to be safe.

Standing in the shelter of her building's canopy, listening to the drumbeat of the falling rain, he scoured the street for a cab. His cell phone rang. *Judith*, he thought hopefully. Judith, worried because he was so late arriving home, because it was raining, because she cared. About him. Only about him.

He flipped his phone open. A peal of thunder obscured the voice he had difficulty recognizing until she said her name.

'Denise. David, it's Denise.'

Another bolt of thunder and then her muffled words. 'Brian,' she said. 'Accident. Parkland Hospital. Come. Please come.'

His heart pounded. His hand trembled. He clutched the phone tighter, but deafened as he was by terror, he could barely hear her.

The thunder was still. Lightning flashed, illuminating his phone pad.

'Alive? Brian. Is he alive?' His words dropped like stones into the sudden quiet.

'Alive. Yes, thank God. He's alive.' She spoke more clearly

now, her words tumbling over each other as he struggled to process them. 'Serious,' she said. Had she prefaced it with 'not'? Yes. 'Not serious.' 'Alive.' Another roll of thunder sounded but it did not obscure her plea.

'David. Just come. We need you. You and Judith.'

The urgency in her voice propelled him into action. 'Yes. Yes, of course. I – We . . . We'll be there as soon as possible.'

He darted into the street, indifferent to the sheets of pouring rain. Miraculously, a cab appeared. Miraculously, the driver knew where Parkland Hospital was. David sank back and dialed Judith's cell phone.

Pick up, he commanded her mentally as his cab raced through the silent rain-swept streets, with her phone ringing again and again.

Judith, always a careful driver, did not shift her eyes from the road before her as the storm intensified. Her phone rested on the seat beside her, easily available, a precaution repeatedly stressed by David, ever worried, ever vigilant. Thunder rumbled and a flash of lightning splintered the new darkness. She leaned tensely forward and decelerated into the slow lane. Her phone rang just as she switched her turn signal off. She thought to ignore it but, glancing down, she saw that the caller was David. She pulled on to the shoulder, trembling with gladness. His call, his worry about her, was a sign of his caring. How foolish she had been to believe otherwise.

'David, I'm on my way home. Traffic is OK. The road is fine. No flooding. I'm driving carefully.'

Breathlessly, she offered him words of reassurance, words to assert their new normalcy, to affirm that they were joined in togetherness, their concern for each other a durable bond.

His answer came slowly, his voice barely audible, his words hampered by the stutter of his boyhood. 'Judith, l–listen to me. Listen. There's been an . . . an a–accident. Accident. Denise called. Brian. Brian is hurt. He's in Parkland Hospital. I'm on my way. Meet me there. Parkland Hospital.'

She struggled to hear him over an explosion of thunder, a flash of lightning, the tympanic beat of the pummeling rain. She captured discrete words. *Brian*. And yes, *accident*. Then

Parkland Hospital. She shivered and tried desperately to string them together, to understand what he was telling her.

'What?' she screamed into the phone. 'What are you saying?'

But the connection was lost. The phone was silent, inactive. Her battery was dead.

'Brian,' she repeated, her voice clogged by terror. 'Accident. Parkland Hospital.'

'No!' she screamed as the words came together, as she understood what their junction meant. Cars sped past her, their headlights flashing across the dark ribbon of the unlit road.

'No! No!' she shouted into the darkness. This was not happening. It could not be happening. Tragedy had already infected them. It should have immunized them from any repetition.

She bit her lip, tasted blood upon her tongue as reason overcame denial. Control asserted itself. She activated her GPS, pumped in Parkland Hospital and, with robotic obedience, followed the disembodied navigating voice, careful to drive slowly as the rain wept its way across her windshield, willing herself to remain dry-eyed.

'You have arrived at your destination,' the omniscient navigator advised her. She stared at the illuminated sign that read *PARKLAND HOSPITAL* and, with her heart sinking, she parked and raced into the building.

THIRTY-ONE

David waited for her in the reception area, his face pale, his shoulders slumped, a posture so ominous that she paused and swayed from side to side, paralyzed by fear. He sprinted toward her, steadying her, his arms enfolding her quivering, rain-soaked body. He spoke. Judith saw his lips moving, but she did not listen. She would not listen. Unheard words had no power, no validity. She should not have listened when that very young doctor, with awkward temerity, had told them that Melanie was dead. She had willed him to silence and thought to block his mouth with her clenched fist. His words denied would be death denied. She had, of course, recognized the absurdity of such a fantasy. Dead was dead. It could not be negated. Magical thinking did not trump reality.

Yet it was the luxury of fantasy she invoked again in this unfamiliar hospital's glass-enclosed reception area, decorated with flowering plants that did little to mask the mingled odors of disinfectant and anxiety. She leaned against David, her hands pressed to her ears, so that she might block the sound of his voice, the import of his words. She felt his breath against her face, the pressure of his touch as he pried her hands loose. She heard his voice, newly firm, newly clear, the stutter vanquished.

'He's all right, Judith. Our Brian is all right. Just a minor injury. Nothing serious. Nothing dangerous.'

She collapsed in his arms, so weak with relief that she could not stand. He led her to a seat on a narrow couch and sat beside her, using his white handkerchief to wipe away the commingled tears and raindrops that streaked her face. He held her close until she stopped trembling, his hand resting on her head.

'I was so frightened,' she gasped.

'I know. So was I. Scared to death.'

Relieved survivors of anticipated grief, they recognized the commonality of their mutual terror. They were partners in memory, the paths of their separate pain, so long divided, now merged. Her sobs came in rhythmic release. Cradled in his embrace, all control abandoned, she allowed her tears to flow freely. Calmed, she rested her head on his shoulder, laying claim to his comfort, his reassurance. She smiled. He smiled. On this stormy night, fortune had smiled on them. They had not lost their son. They had not lost each other.

'A minor injury?' she asked, repeating his words.

'A cut on his forehead. They're stitching it up now. There was a lot of blood and that was what freaked Denise out. She's with him now.'

'An accident. You said an accident. What happened?' she asked because now he could safely answer.

His words came slowly and Judith listened intently, soothed by the familiar gentle cadence of his voice. 'They were driving back from New Hampshire, Denise at the wheel, when the storm intensified. Sheets of rain and a wild wind strong enough to shake the car, she told me. They were on that winding stretch of highway, the one that we try to avoid because it's always treacherous, always badly lit. She was concentrating on the road when Brian began to wheeze and she saw that he was deathly pale. He was gasping for breath. She didn't know what to do. There was no place to pull over so she accelerated, hoping for an exit. Looking at Brian, her eyes off the road for a split second, she didn't see that a huge branch had come down right in their path. She drove into it, crashed against it.'

Judith trembled. 'They could have been killed. Both of them.'

'They were lucky. They were thrown forward. Brian's head hit the windshield but they were wearing their seat belts. Otherwise . . .' His voice trailed off. He could not complete the sentence. 'Otherwise' would have to suffice.

'Yes. Lucky,' she agreed. She would not dwell on the 'otherwise'.

'Very lucky, because the car behind them stopped and the driver was a doctor. He saw that Brian was having difficulty breathing and knew he was having an asthma attack. He had medication and an inhaler in his bag and administered it right there. It saved Brian's life. Crazy how the accident turned out to be a blessing.'

'Crazy,' Judith agreed.

David sat back, exhausted, and Judith took up his white handkerchief, replicating the lightness of his touch as she, in turn, wiped his eyes. They sat in silence, hand in hand, draped in their own fatigue, their posture that of weary travelers recovering from a long and arduous journey.

'Judith! David!'

Denise rushed toward them, her voice resonant with relief. Her red-framed glasses were askew and her wild bright hair framed her face. The thin white cardigan she wore over an unevenly buttoned plaid sundress was inside out. Judith thought her beautiful in all her disarray.

'Brian wanted to make sure you were all right. We were so worried about you driving through the rain, Judith.'

Her words tumbled over each other as her eyes darted from Judith to David.

'I'm fine. We're both fine,' Judith said.

She stood, opened her arms wide and, for the first time, she embraced the wonderful, disheveled girl whom her son loved. Their faces pressed close, they smiled. They were family to each other, mother and daughter, bonded in happy embrace. The suffix *in-law* was disowned. *Law* did not bind. Love did. Judith and Denise were bonded by their love for Brian, their recognition and understanding of each other.

David stood apart from them, reluctant to intrude on their new intimacy. He stared at his slender wife, strands of silver threading her dark hair, and the vibrant young woman who would marry their son. He was suffused with calm. The recent past, laden as it was with sadnesses and silences, was a closed chapter. There would be no explanations, no revelations, no trading of reprisals and recriminations. No forgiveness was necessary. All was understood. The dark time had ended. They stood at the precipice of a new season, a new chapter.

He took Judith's hand. Her arm encircled Denise's waist. Walking slowly, three abreast, they entered the small white-walled room where tall Brian, an oversized bandage across his high brow, his breath effortless, his smile broad, waited for them.

EPILOGUE

The air was lightly brushed with the first chill of autumn. Determined mothers had plundered the thrift shop's supply of donated backpacks. Yellow school buses lumbered down the street, and Judith, watching from the window as Melanie's laughing and chattering schoolmates clambered aboard, remained dry-eyed. As the bus disappeared, she thrust her lecture notes into her briefcase and drove to the university where she taught three days a week. She spent the other two days at the thrift shop, an arrangement David had encouraged.

'It's time for us to get on with it,' he had said, and she had understood that he wanted their life to be restored to an orderly pattern, their days predictable, the dissonance of their wild grief quieted. They came together each evening, calmed by the familiar rhythm of their hours apart, earned fatigue acknowledged, their marriage newly threaded with resilience.

One evening, she complained of not having enough shelf space for a series of new books on Victorian women writers that had just been shipped to her.

'There's an empty shelf in my office. Use that,' he suggested.

'Yes. Of course. Your office.'

Neither of them, by design and intent, spoke of it as Melanie's room. They had settled into a new reality.

Their arms laden with the new books, they went upstairs. It was weeks since she had entered the room. David had begun to work more frequently from home and she refrained from invading his privacy. He had made some changes, she knew, and she glanced around with a critical eye, relieved that the contractor had reconfigured it so that a storage closet had been constructed where the bed had been. David's computer and printer fit neatly in the space where the bureau had stood. He had hung the Daumier prints, her gift to him on a distant anniversary, over his desk. The copper pipe stand they had bought in a dusty Vermont antique store rested on its leather surface.

He had made the room his own, but Melanie had a presence. Dried flowers were arranged in an endearingly clumsy blue ceramic vase she had crafted in an arts and crafts class. In a silver-framed photograph, placed on a shelf above his computer, she smiled down, her eyes shining, her hair floating about her shoulders.

Judith took it down and tried to remember when it had been taken. Not long ago, she realized, because Melanie was wearing her prized pink cashmere cardigan. She traced the contours of her daughter's heart-shaped face and pressed her lips against the cold glass before replacing it. Then, carefully, methodically, she arranged her own books next to it and joined David who was standing at the window.

In silence, they looked out at the apple tree, its leaves laced with russet. Oddly, a single apple, silvered by early moonlight, dangled from a slender branch.

She took David's hand and pointed to the fruit, now swaying gracefully in the gentle evening wind.

'Beautiful,' he said. 'Melanie would have loved it.'

They stood very still, remembering their daughter's high sweet voice as she called to them to report the tree's progress, season by season, announcing that new green leaves had unfurled, that white blossoms had appeared.

'The flowers are like stars,' Judith remembered her saying. 'They look like sweet-smelling stars.'

'Melanie might have told us that the apple was dancing in the wind,' she suggested.

'Yes. Melanie might have said that.'

He pulled her close and she marveled that they could imagine their daughter's words, that they could say her name with ease, although pain and tenderness mingled in its utterance.

They looked at each other, exchanged sad smiles and then, hand in hand, they left the room.

Judith went to the thrift shop the next morning, arriving early because she and Suzanne had agreed to go through the cartons in which warmer clothing was stored. They dealt swiftly with the cartons of snowsuits and those crammed with winter jackets for men and sweaters for boys, placing them in bins which they carried to the trestle tables. They spoke softly as they worked, exchanging scraps of information about their lives. Judith asked about Eric.

'He's managing,' Suzanne told her. 'Some days are better than others. The occasional midnight phone call. The occasional early-morning apology. Things are not wonderful, but I'm coping.'

'Coping is good,' Judith said. 'Day by day is good. Remember the words of poor Adrienne Rich. "Piece by piece I seem to re-enter the world."'

As she herself was doing. Each piece found its place in the jagged puzzle of acceptance, some with pain, some with ease. But she was moving forward. No. *They* were moving forward. She and David together.

'I remember,' Suzanne said and smiled in silent acknowledgment that, piece by piece, throughout the seasons of warmth, both she and Judith, however tentatively, had re-entered their worlds.

Suzanne asked how the plans for Denise and Brian's wedding were progressing and thanked Judith for her invitation.

'I'm glad you'll be there,' Judith said. 'And I'm glad we finally got the guest list sorted out.'

The small wedding that Denise and Brian wanted had inevitably expanded to include Denise's large extended family, the young couple's friends, and friends of both sets of parents. Laboring over their own guest list, Judith had asked David if he wanted to invite Nancy Cummings.

He had thanked her for the generosity of her suggestion and told her that Nancy had relocated to the Boston office. A promotion that she had welcomed. He did not tell Judith that he had taken her out for a very expensive and very awkward lunch and gifted her with a membership to the Boston Museum of Fine Arts. There was no need to speak of it. It was over and done with.

'Weddings,' Suzanne said as she carried out another carton. 'I try not to think of mine. More trouble than it was worth. Oh, I forgot to tell you. Jeffrey Kahn came in the other day with a load of his wife's scarves to contribute.'

'Too bad I missed him,' Judith said, carefully turning away

so that Suzanne would not see her color rise. She remembered those scarves, swathes of rainbow-colored silk, squares of soft wool in the rustic shades of autumn, all lightly scented and carefully folded.

She and Jeffrey had spoken about going through them and had even scheduled two appointments. He had canceled the first because of a patient's emergency. She had canceled the second because David had surprised her with tickets for a concert. They spoke of rescheduling, but no effort had been made. He was busy, she knew, and, of course, so was she. And probably, she acknowledged, neither of them wanted to find the time.

'He asked about you,' Suzanne continued. 'He wanted me to tell you that he was going to California for a while. One daughter getting married, the other about to give birth. I'm sorry I didn't mention it sooner. It slipped my mind.'

'No problem,' Judith said. 'I'm glad for him. Glad that his daughters are doing so well.'

She was glad. Glad and relieved. She wanted him to have his share of happiness. She hoped he would remember to give his daughter the cape Sylvia had worn during her own pregnancy. Of course he would. He was a careful man. She was pleased that he too was re-entering his life 'piece by piece'.

Suzanne slit open the carton across which she had scrawled *Girls' Sweaters* and placed a large pile on the counter, loosing the scents of mothballs and Wool Lite.

'Let's separate out the cardigans,' Judith suggested. 'That's mostly what the mothers look for.'

'Good idea.'

They worked swiftly, cuffing the sleeves and buttoning each one.

Judith held up an ivory cable knit. 'This one's lovely,' she said. 'Practically new.'

It was new. A price tag fluttered from the sleeve when she cuffed it.

'Now that's what I call gently used,' Suzanne said, her voice tinged with sarcasm. 'And here's another beauty. Double-ply cashmere. And look at the pearl buttons. Why would anyone give this away?'

She held it up and Judith stared at Melanie's pink cardigan, purchased with much hesitation and given away with much regret and sorrow.

She took it from Suzanne and stroked the soft wool, traced the smoothness of each nacreous button and pressed it against her cheek. She folded it carefully and placed it on top of the pile which she carried out to a trestle table.

There was a spurt of buyers when the hospital morning shift ended. Judith, counting out bills at the register, looked up to see Consuela.

'*Señora Judith*, it is good to see you,' the Guatemalan woman said shyly, and Judith reached across the counter and took her calloused hand in her own.

'I am so glad to see you, Consuela,' she said. 'I've missed you. Have you been well?'

It was a neutral question. She could not ask if Consuela had adjusted to her grief, if her sorrow had been diminished, if she still mourned her youngest granddaughter, her Rosalita who had loved party dresses the color of flowers.

'I am well. It is good that I am working so that I can help my family. I go to mass and I burn candles and make novenas for my Rosalita. She is in heaven, the priest tells me, and she is happy in heaven. But I am in this world and I must take care of those who are in this world with me. My children. My grandchildren,' Consuela replied, her voice very low.

'Yes. Your grandchildren. I remember that you told me that your Juanita won a prize,' Judith said, happy that she remembered the child's name, recalling how proud Consuela had been of the girl's achievement.

'Ah, my Juanita.' Consuela's face brightened. 'I come today to look for a present for my Juanita. She is so smart. She goes now to a special school for children who study well, and she says that all the girls in her class wear such nice things. I want to buy something pretty for her, a dress, a sweater. What do you think, *Señora Judith*?'

'I think a cardigan,' Judith said, and she led Consuela to the table on which the sweaters were piled. Without hesitating, she pulled out Melanie's pink cashmere cardigan and handed it to her.

Consuela held it tenderly, fingering the wool, touching the

buttons. 'So soft it is,' she said. 'So wonderful the color. We have flowers of just such a color in my country. And the little buttons. See how they shine. Like stars.'

'Like stars,' Judith repeated. *And like apple blossoms. Sweet-smelling stars*, she thought. Melanie's words were a tender memory.

'She will feel so pretty in this sweater, my Juanita.'

'I know.'

They smiled at each other in silent acknowledgment of shared, hard-earned insight.

Happily, Consuela followed Judith to the register. Happily, she placed a crumpled five-dollar bill on the counter as Judith found a box for the sweater, folded it carefully and shrouded it in tissue paper.

'Be well, Consuela,' she said as she handed the purchase to her.

'*Vaya con dios, Señora Judith*,' Consuela replied and took Judith's hand in her own.

Judith and Suzanne left the shop as folds of smoky dusk shadowed the fading pastel hues of a melancholy sunset. Judith looked up just as the amber-colored crescent moon broke free of an obscuring cloud, hovered briefly in the still starless sky and drifted from view.

'Dinner?' Suzanne asked hesitantly.

'Actually, David is picking me up,' Judith said. 'Another night?'

'Yes. Another night,' Suzanne agreed.

They touched each other's hands lightly and parted.

'Judith, over here.' David, his arms outstretched, stood in a circlet of light cast by a street lamp. She walked toward him, making her way slowly through the chill of the encroaching darkness into the warmth of his embrace.

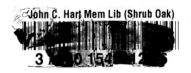